Sleight Of Hand

A Novel by Nick Alexander

Nick Alexander

Nick Alexander was born in 1964 in the U.K. He has travelled widely and has lived and worked both in the U.K. the U.S.A. and France where he currently resides.

The other four novels in this series - *50 Reasons to Say "Goodbye"*, *Sottopassaggio, Good Thing, Bad Thing,* and *Better Than Easy,* are also available from BIGfib Books, as are his standalone novels – *13:55 Eastern Standard Time* and the bestselling, *The Case Of The Missing Boyfriend.*

For more information or to order copies please visit his website: www.nick-alexander.com.

Acknowledgements

Thanks to Fay Weldon for encouraging me when it most counted.
Thanks to Rosemary, Jerôme and Giovanni for their help with the final manuscript. Thanks to Apple computer for making such wonderful reliable work tools, and to BIGfib Books for making this physical book a reality.

Legal Notice

For Stewart, Craig and anyone else
who ever had to fight to stick around.

Paradise Lost

It was the incident with the dog that did it. We were sitting having a drink at Max's – a scruffy wooden bar at the edge of the national park. It had become a ritual of ours, a Friday night mojito, sometimes two – our attempt at marking the beginning of the weekend – at marking the passage of time. Neither Ricardo's random callouts as a doctor, nor my occasional translation work, nor the weird, season-less weather of Colombia provided much clue as to where you might be in the week, the year, in life. Our stay here so far felt, somehow, out-of-time – as if contained within brackets.

Max's was a perfect beach-bar and (in season) a sometimes-restaurant: a wooden shack built on stilts with the dense forest of the national park to the west, the occasionally raging Caribbean to the north, and a dusty/muddy car park everywhere else.

It was a twenty minute walk along the coast from our house and often, outside the tourist season, we, along with the effervescent, whistling Max, were the only people there. Occasionally there would be a couple of gamekeepers playing draughts in a corner, and of course for those few months of the year when Europeans and Americans take their brief holidays, the place would look more like Club Med than a lost corner of the Caribbean. But generally the only noise was the endless salsa drifting from Max's thankfully weedy transistor radio, and, depending on the direction of the wind, the sound of the waves.

Before the *corronchos* arrived it had all felt pretty perfect. The late afternoon sun was warm, the mojitos were cool enough for condensation to be trickling down the outside of the glass, and Max's radio had, rather superbly, run out of batteries. Not only had I finally finished and emailed my fifty-thousand word drudgery on EEC agricultural policy, but Ricardo's so often absent colleague was, for once, on-call: a whole weekend to ourselves.

Ricardo drew a circle in the dew on the side of his glass, looked up and smiled at me. "You know, Chupa Chups, there are moments when this place really is pa..." he said, and then paused, distracted by the sound of a car.

Like all nick-names *Chupa Chups* came about by accident. I had asked him what the lollypop brand name meant, and Ricardo had translated it as, *"Sucky Suck."* For weeks, I had been unable to see or hear those words without cracking up laughing, and the name had stuck. It still made me grin, even though I was mortified when from time to time, he accidentally used it in public.

We both turned to watch as a Porsche Cayenne appeared from the forest track. It stopped at the edge of the car park in a cloud of dust, and four young men in Miami-Vice suits got out – one of the guys actually had his jacket sleeves pushed up.

Ricardo sighed and looked back out to sea, and I copied him and did likewise, for there are men that you don't watch in Colombia – men, often enough, with Porsche Cayennes.

The four men lingered by the car talking energetically or maybe arguing. With the distance and their accents, and over the salsa music drifting from the car, I couldn't understand a word. Their over-loud voices sounded, though, like a challenge. The main thing they seemed to be saying, was, *"Look at us. Look over here. Aren't we something?"* And that was when the dog appeared.

It was irritating, it's true – a mangy, skinny half-breed sniffing around the edges of the terrace, pissing in a corner, pushing under tables and around chairs in its hunt for crumbs, and then around our feet, and finally out into the car park, and over towards the Porsche.

It snuffled its way around the rear of the car, and then fatally, and I mean, *fatally,* pissed on one of the tyres. One of the Porsche boys – the fat one with pocked skin, gave it an ineffectual kick and it yelped before starting somewhat lazily, to bark.

I became aware that my stress levels were rising. My skin was prickling and my throat felt suddenly dry, and I wondered briefly if I was being paranoid, or if I was channeling some future catastrophe, or if Ricardo, so calmly looking out to sea, was, as often, radiating his own specifically Colombian understanding of the situation.

One of the guys shouted over and asked, "¿Es éste tu perro?" – *is it your dog?* and Ricardo glanced over and simply shook his head in reply. To me, as an aside, he murmured, "No contestes." – *don't reply.* From the fact that he had chosen to speak in Spanish I knew I wasn't imagining *anything:* the only reason Ricardo ever used Spanish with me, was to avoid drawing attention to my status as a non-Colombian. I held my breath, and we both turned and looked back out to sea.

Nothing happened for a minute or so and despite the tension provoked by *not*-looking, I managed to start to breath again.

And then I heard the boot open and one of the guys laughed, and another cheered, and as cover, I raised my glass for a sip and glanced over just in time to see the fat guy pull an AK47 from the boot of the car and raise it to his hip. I opened my mouth to warn Ricardo but he kicked me hard, so I turned back out to sea and remained, like he, stoic, merely imagining the dog's dancing body as the rounds of gunfire let rip and hoping that there, that day, the dog would be the only one to die.

In the year since we had been living here, there had been other events of course: the disappearance of the Swedish girl last summer, the stabbing at a party we attended, the minicab murders... And even if Ricardo found reassurance variously in the fact that the Swedish girl had been found (with apparent amnesia) and the stab victim had survived (with a scar), and the minicab murders had all happened more than two-hundred kilometres away, for me these were all straws on a camel's back, drops of water in a proverbial French vase.

But the tipping point, the moment I specifically thought, *"No, I don't want to live here. I want to go home,"* was when they shot that dog. Because that's when I realised that these guys in suits in Porsche Cayennes have machine guns stored next to the wheel-jack. And that's when I saw that Ricardo sighed. As my own body jerked at each fired round, Ricardo *sighed* – he had become used to this. And I didn't *want* to get used to it.

I had assumed that the guys would now come to the bar, but once no more amusement was to be found in filling the dog with bullets, the gun was put back in the trunk, and the four guys simply climbed back into their 4x4 and accelerated off in a cloud of dust and fading salsa rhythms.

With a *whachagonnado* shrug and a raised eyebrow Max descended leisurely to the car park, and scooped the corpse of the dog into a bin-bag. When he had done this, his hands still bloodied, he leant against the fence and rolled himself a cigarette.

I said automatically, "I want to go home," and Ricardo, assuming that I meant to Federico's beach-house, downed the last of his drink and, with a nod and a weak smile, stood up. I chose, for the time being, not to explain further.

Ricardo took the coastal path back to the house and I didn't argue. The route through the forest was shorter but felt, if you were in a particular kind of mood, more menacing.

The path was pretty narrow, so I followed him – a little numb from the adrenalin aftershock – watching his buttocks move up and down, his shirt slowly sticking to his back, and then glancing left at the brochure-perfect beaches and right into the long shadows of the forest, and back again at the perfect beach. I thought about the contrasts of Colombia, so beautiful, so friendly. And yet...

Ricardo only turned once to speak to me during the walk. "I'm sorry about that," he said, as if it had somehow been his fault. But I knew what he meant. It was his country. He had brought me here. I knew how he took such things personally.

As we walked, I wondered if this feeling – that I had had it with Colombia – was a new permanent state of being or simply a momentary reaction to danger, and I decided that I needed a trip back to Europe to find out. I hadn't been back since we moved here over a year ago. It was time.

But if I told him how I felt, would it damage our relationship? That would be the last thing I would want.

Faithful, good natured, straightforward Ricardo – the man I thought I would never meet.

A part of him, the Colombian part, will always remain alien to me. It's hard to explain what the essence of that difference is... Perhaps a coldness that enables him to sigh as someone machine-guns a dog to smithereens is what best sums it up. Maybe a lightness of being that means that these things don't get to him the way they do to me – an optimism that is entirely unaffected by murder, rape or natural disaster. I know that all sounds contradictory, and really that's the whole point. The fact that I can't decide whether to describe it as solid and unshakable, or courageously optimistic, or cold and unfeeling, says it all: alien. Simply.

But other than this undefinable otherness, we are the most perfect fit I have ever found.

Back at the house, Ricardo said, "You just relax Chupy and watch the sunset and I'll make dinner," and I knew that the business of the machine gun and the dog – the most violent thing I had ever witnessed – was now over for him. For Ricardo it required no further discussion.

I checked my email to make sure my translation had reached its destination (it had), and was just about to shut down the computer for the evening when a rare email from Jenny popped up. Her mother had died, she said. She felt incredibly sad and alone, she said.

And my first thought, my very first shameful thought, was that *here* was the perfect excuse for a trip home. And then, I thought, *"And you reckon Ricardo is the cold one?"*

The Stranger

So here I am, staring at the booking screen.

"Tu ne l'as pas encore réservé ?" Ricardo asks me. – *Haven't you reserved that yet?* He leans in and nuzzles my neck.

We converse in either French or English, apparently randomly. In French because France was where we met, and in English because Ricardo needs the practice. Despite the fact that *I* need the practice most of all, we *never* speak Spanish together. Ricardo's reaction to the slightest mis-pronunciation on my part is a shouted correction. It's something that's just too irritating for our relationship to repeatedly survive, so we avoid it by speaking any other language.

"I can't decide how long to go for," I tell him, peering at the booking screen. "Plus I can't work out whether to do just England or whether to go back to Nice as well." Part of the reason I can't decide how long to stay is that I'm not sure how Jenny will react to my presence. Being her oldest friend *and* the man who stole her boyfriend complicates things somewhat.

"I suppose leaving the booking open costs too much," Ricardo says. "Have you looked?"

"A fortune," I say. "Nearly two-thousand extra."

"Book for two weeks then," he says. "Or three. And then if you get bored buy a flight, with... you know... the one you use before."

"Easyjet?"

"Yeah, if you get bored in London you can still book a return to Nice."

"I suppose," I say.

"You could check my flat for me, check they haven't wreck the place. If you need to put it on my card..."

"No," I say. "Thanks, but it's fine."

Ricardo straightens and rubs the base of his back, and then saying, "Well, only you can decide," he heads back through to the bedroom.

I flick back and forth between two itineraries and chew the inside of my mouth and wonder if it's OK to bring up Jenny's potential reaction with Ricardo. For obvious reasons, she isn't a subject we tend to discuss.

The phone chirrups so I swipe it from the cradle. "Aló?" I say.

Ricardo's nephew Juan is on the line. He sounds unusually grave.

"Ricardo, c'est Juan," I shout.

"Je le rappelle," he answers. – *I'll call him back.*

"I think you'd better take this one," I tell him.

Ricardo reappears in the doorway. He has the five ironed shirts that Maria left over one arm. He frowns at me and reaches out for the phone with his free hand.

"Juan?" he says. "Sí ... Sí ..." And then he takes two steps backwards, glances behind to check his position and sinks onto the edge of the bed. *"Sí,"* he says again, more definitively.

I look at his rounded shoulders and his glazed expression and at the darkening sea behind the window, and I shiver and wonder who has died.

When he hangs up, Ricardo says, "You should book that flight."

I nod. "What's happened?"

"Maman est morte," he says. Then he snorts and smiles and says again, "Aujourd'hui, maman est morte," – it's the opening line from Camus *L'Etranger*.

"Oh babe," I say. I think how strange it is that both Jenny and Ricardo's mothers should die on the same day, and then discount the thought as too banal to be vocalised. "Oh God, I'm sorry."

Ricardo shrugs, which is unexpected.

"How?" I ask. "How did she..." It seems to me to be something one might ask at such a moment, but then as I say it, it seems cold and unnecessary.

"In her sleep," he says. "Lena found her."

"The maid?"

"Yeah. You *know* who Lena is," Ricardo says.

And it's true. I'm not really sure why I asked, except perhaps, to buy time. "Are you OK?" I ask – another stupid question.

Ricardo shrugs again. He looks strange: kind of blotchy and pale at the same time. "I think so," he says quietly. "I'm not sure. It was hardly unexpected." And then he stands and vanishes from view.

I listen to the sound of him slowly hanging the shirts in the closet and then stand and follow him to the bedroom. He caresses the sleeve of the final shirt and then slumps back onto the bed. "I have no parents now," he says. "That's strange, huh?"

"I suppose it is," I say, tears welling up on his behalf. I take a seat beside him and slip an arm around his shoulders. I think he will either shrug it off or start to cry too, but ever-unpredictable, he turns and kisses me.

A little surprised, I remain impassive as his tongue darts in and out of my mouth, and then I think, *"It's his mother... whatever he needs,"* and kiss him tenderly back.

But tender isn't what Ricardo has in mind. He grabs my t-shirt and lifts it over my head. "Take your jeans off," he says. "I want to fuck you," and so I do. And he does.

Under the circumstances, which are bizarre to say the least, I don't particularly enjoy it... He's rough and direct. He pushes in before I'm ready and without enough lube – it hurts. It's like being shagged by a stranger, apparently more to do with a need for release, a yearning for closeness than anything else, but I shut up and fake it: I shut up and take it.

The death-fuck is quickly over, and as I dry my chest with a hand towel, I expect Ricardo to say something about his mother.

He reaches for his box and starts to roll one of his occasional joints and with a nod towards the door says, "You should go and finish booking that flight."

"Surely, I should stay... I mean... don't you need me to stay, babe?"

"Pourquoi ?" he asks, sealing the joint, and then, picking the flakes of grass from his chest and putting them back in the box he adds, in English, "I have to go Bogotá tomorrow. There's no point you stay here."

"But don't you... I mean, shouldn't I come with you?"

"What for?" he asks, lighting the joint, and taking a deep hit. I'm not sure if he's on the verge of tears or if it's the smoke that is making his eyes glisten.

"Well to help with... stuff." With my pitiful Spanish, I'm not sure what I could help with, but all the same.

Ricardo shakes his head. "No need," he says. "And you can't come to the... *l'enterrement...*"

"The *funeral,*" I tell him.

"Sure. You can't come to that. You know this."

"I know you don't want... I mean... I know you *didn't* want her to know. But surely *now?*" I can feel my anger rising.

"It's a family thing," Ricardo says. "A latin thing. Trust me."

"I'm not family?"

"You know what I mean," he says, offering me the joint. "It's for cousin and nephew and..."

"Husbands and wives," I say.

"Well yes."

"But not boyfriends."

Ricardo shrugs.

"Juan knows I'm here," I say. "He must have spoken to me at least twenty times. Federico does too."

"But they don't know who you *are*," Ricardo says.

"Well, who do you think they *think* I am?" I say. "The cleaner? The *gardener?*"

Ricardo shrugs. "I don't know. It's up to them. That's the point. You have to leave people the space to understand what they want to understand. It's the latin way."

"The Catholic way," I say. "The closeted way."

"If you want," Ricardo says. "Look. We've already..." He turns to look out of the window and sighs.

I blow out a column of smoke. If I go any further this will now turn into an argument – an argument we have indeed had repeatedly. And I think that this really isn't the right moment.

Ricardo takes the joint from me and says, "And you don't really want to win this anyway. You want to go see Jenny."

I shrug.

"You need to decide, Chupy, if you want to win this argument or be happy," he says.

I take a few seconds to think about this and then decide that he's undeniably right. "Sure," I say. "Whatever. If that's what you need. Really. It's fine."

He winks at me and then pushes me gently towards the end of the bed. "Go book the flight," he says. "And book one for me for tomorrow as well. Use my card. We can take the same."

"As far as Bogotá?"

"Yes, to Bogotá"

"Return?"

"One way. I don't know how long."

"Sure," I say standing. "Are you sure you're OK?"

Ricardo shrugs again. "I told you. I don't know," he says, flatly. "But I have to go to Bogotá tomorrow – this I know. So do the booking for me."

"Right," I say. "Sure. Oh, and the cat?" I ask. "What do we do about her? Where is she anyway?"

"Under here," he says, pointing down at the bed. "I'll call Maria. She can spring-clean and feed Paloma."

"Autumn-clean."

"OK, Autumn-clean..." Ricardo repeats, then, with an almost quizzical expression, he says again, "So I have no parents now."

"I'm sorry," I say.

He shrugs. "I suppose it is better than visiting them in an old person home."

A Trip with Lolita

At first sight, I decide that my neighbour for the flight to Madrid is a transexual. She's taller than me (even without her platform soles) and has Pete Burns cheekbones, Angelina Jolie lips, and "surprised" eyebrows. She looks like the subject of a documentary on cosmetic surgery catastrophes.

I squash my legs against the bulkhead as she slides into the middle seat beside me and think about just how much longer the flight is going to seem with so little legroom. I wish that the four-foot-not-many-inches guy now sitting down on her right was my neighbour instead.

She glances at him, then smiles at me but says nothing. As she rolls towards me in an effort at extracting the seatbelt from beneath her buttocks I get a retch-inducing whiff of perfume.

I turn to look out at the Bogotá rain and think about Ricardo heading off to his mother's house. He seemed fine of course. He was positive and effervescent during the drive to Santa Marta, and then warm and smiley for the flight to Bogotá. When the fifteen-seater went through a white-knuckle patch of turbulence, he even quipped, *"He died on the way to his mother's funeral."* But I remember only too well from when Tom's father died, how quickly "fine" can turn to "breakdown." But if he doesn't want me there – and he clearly doesn't – then there isn't much I can do.

Lolita Jackson, as I nickname my six-foot beauty, doesn't speak to me until the Iberian trolley dollies arrive with our first meal. Given the choice of chicken or fish, I half expect her to reply, "Neither – I'm a tranny actually," but she plumps for *"pollo,"* and hearing her voice, I think, *"God, she's a woman."* I can't help but wonder if "tranny" was the look she was aiming for when she embarked on the surgery path all those years ago.

On hearing me request my vegetarian meal, she breaks her silence and asks me in near-perfect English where I'm from.

"England," I say. "Near London."

"So you're on holiday?" she asks.

"No, I'm kind of living here," I say. "Well, living *there.*"

"So you like Colombia?"

"Of course," I say, reaching past her for my tray which has now arrived. "Everyone loves Colombia." If there's one thing I have learnt it's that the only opinion you should ever express about their homeland is one of pure positivity.

"A miserable country of third-world under-achievers," she says.

"Really? I like it," I say, unflummoxed by the remark. It's very fashionable in Colombia to slag the place off. I know it's all bravado. "So you're not Colombian?"

"Sure I am, but I live in Valencia these days. It shows, doesn't it?"

"Sure," I say. I restrain myself from adding, *"You have that euro-tranny look down to a tee."*

"I prefer Spain," she says.

"Well, Spain is great too."

"So you *like* Colombia," she asks again, incredulously.

"I do," I say. "It's amazingly beautiful. Don't you think so? "

"I suppose. And the people?"

"Oh, they're incredibly friendly," I answer. "The happiest people I ever met." And it's all true. Colombia *is* stunningly beautiful. It's like a dramatised version of France, only with rain-forests and a few Caribbean beaches thrown in for good measure. And the people *are* the most welcoming, smiling, contented people I have ever come across.

"Yes in Europe people love you or hate you, or they just don't care."

"Right," I say.

"In Colombia we love you or we kill you. Sometimes both at the same time."

I laugh. "Yes, well, there is that."

"And that doesn't worry you?"

I shrug. "Nowhere is perfect," I say.

"It's got much better since Uribe got in," she says.

"Yes, everyone says so."

"Though it's probably time for him to go now. But you didn't used to be able to go out at night," she says. "It's not scary anymore."

"No, well, I'm sure... I mean, if you were used to it before. It must feel very different."

"You never came before?" she asks. "In the eighties and the nineties when they had the... what do you call it when you can't go out at night?"

"Curfew?"

"Yeah, the curfew."

"No," I say. "No, thank God. Even now, it's about as scary as *I* can cope with."

She twitches her nose, and then peels the aluminium foil from her dish with her vast fluorescent fingernails. "It's pathetic," she says.

"Airline food?" I ask.

"The way you people look down your noses at everyone."

"I'm sorry?"

"You would think that nothing bad ever happens in Europe," she says.

"Oh," I say, realising that I have broken the golden rule of untainted adulation. "I didn't actually say *that*."

"There are murders and gangs and drugs in Europe, you know. Where do you think all the cocaine goes? Who do you think they grow it for?"

"No, you're right," I say, frowning. "You're totally right."

She forks a lump of non-specific vegetable matter from her dish and makes a "Humph," sound, and then pops her headphones into her ears. And that's the end of our conversation.

As I eat my meal, I think about the differing nature of violence in England, France and Colombia, because of course, as Lolita says, shit does happen back home. If the media are to be believed, then it happens more and more.

But it is somehow *different* shit. It's drunken shit, and racist shit, and sometimes homophobic shit. But it's shit that I understand, and for the most part, shit that I know how to avoid. I can sense when a bar brawl is about to happen and leave. When faced with a group of a certain kind of men after a certain hour in a certain part of town I can cross the road. It's the way Colombian violence springs from a glassy lake that unnerves me. It's the way it vanishes back into it leaving barely a ripple. It's the way it bursts from smiling happy people who, often without even dropping that smile, pull a knife or a gun. There's no aggro, no negotiation, no tension. It's often not even about obtaining anything. It's just about stopping some dog, or some*one*, doing some*thing* that is found to be irritating. It cracks like thunder, and then vanishes leaving the bystanders to roll a cigarette and sweep up the storm damage. In the end what makes it so unnerving is that lack of understanding... it's that I don't get the context.

There is a specific Colombian attitude to life as well. It's as if, living amidst so much mayhem, they have learned to enjoy every moment. And they have looked death in the eye and accepted its inevitability as well. So, no matter what you discuss, you will hear how Colombian thinking has been forged between a rock and a hard place. On money: *better spend it today. You might be dead tomorrow.* On suicide: *Well, if you don't like the film, I can't see why you should have to stay to the end.* On paedophilia: *What's the point of all that? A trial and a judge, and years of prison. Such a waste of money. Far better to deal with it the Colombian way. Click. Done. Over.* On cigarettes: *I'd rather die of cancer at fifty than sit in my own piss till a hundred.*

And when you hear these viewpoints often enough, your own relationship with death starts to shift too. Life starts to seem like it *is* an episode of Desperate Housewives, where the *obvious* answer to a whole clutch of problems is murder. It's catching yourself thinking the Colombian way, that's the most unnerving of all.

The Best Laid Plans

Sixteen hours after takeoff, I walk out into the arrivals hall at Heathrow. I'm feeling stoned and confused. I'm not sure if the issue is one of time or space. Maybe it's the weather (raining in Bogotá, raining in Madrid, sunny in London). Maybe it's the joint I shared with Ricardo yesterday... Was that *really* just yesterday? But it's probably all of the above. I left Bogotá in the early evening, snoozed in a plane for ten hours and found myself having lunch in Madrid. I then dozed for another three hours and woke up here in London. Nothing in our genetic makeup was ever programmed to deal with this. Our bodies will probably take another million years to catch up.

I head straight for the train station. I'm travelling with hand-luggage only, quite proud of the fact that my days of lugging suitcases around and flying home with unworn clothes are now over.

The train journey to Camberley takes another hour and a half – an hour and a half I spend trying to coax my iPhone to connect to a network, any network. But despite Comcel's assurances that my Colombian sim card would work here, it clearly doesn't. And now of course I can't call Comcel to get it fixed, or Jenny to see if she's home, or even check my email to see if she knows I'm coming.

Between these increasingly hopeless checks to see that my phone still doesn't work, I look around the carriage and play spot the difference. When you return home from a long period overseas, something new is always revealed about your countrymen. Today I'm noticing how varied everyone's clothes are. There are guys in sober suits, and a lad in a pink hoodie, and a woman with bumblebee stockings. The guy opposite me is a goth, with pink hair and zips on his clothes and an assortment of scrap metal protruding from his head. Who would have thought that goths still existed? In Colombia, as in most of the world, the majority of men still haven't strayed from white shirt and pleated trousers.

21

I'm noticing how at home I feel too. Even though these people have nothing more to do with me than the average Colombian, I understand who they are. I have no worries about how they might behave.

And whereas when I lived in France, I always used to notice how often the Brits smile at each other – how often they laugh – today I'm noticing how subdued everyone seems. I wonder what the French must think when they arrive in Bogotá. The effusive carnival of Colombian society must be quite a shock for them.

The sun is setting by the time the taxi pulls up in the anonymous close containing Jenny's mother's house. Stupidly I don't ask the driver to wait, so by the time I realise that no one is in, he is disappearing from view.

"Shit," I say tiredly. The best laid plans of mice and men. Or in my case, I would have to admit, the *worst* laid plans. No working phone, no-one in, no taxi, nowhere to stay.

"You twat," I mutter, heading for the neighbour's house.

On the doorstep, are two red-cheeked gnomes. They are something I never really believe that people actually own. I stand, staring at them in a tired daze until I hear someone unlatch the lock.

"There's no-one there," the woman, who looks uncannily like June Whitfield, says as she opens the door.

"Hello. Yes, I know," I say. "Do you have any idea where she is, or when she might be back?"

The woman thins her lips and stares me in the eye. I realise that this thin-lipped pulling in of the mouth is where the thousands of tiny wrinkles around it have come from.

"I'm sorry," she says, looking not-very-sorry-at-all. "I can't help you."

A wave of fever sweeps over me. I feel so overcome with exhaustion I might just faint, or cry. "When did you last see her?" I try.

"You'll have to ask her daughter if you want to know more," she says.

I frown. "Sarah?"

The woman tuts warming very slightly from "glacial" to merely "icy."

"Look, who are you looking for?" she asks.

"Jenny," I say. "Jenny Holmes."

"Right," she says. "Sorry, I thought you were looking for Marge."

"Well, no. She's dead isn't she?" I ask, wincing at the realisation that I should probably have used, "passed away," or some such euphemism.

"Yes. I didn't know if you knew, you see."

I nod and force a smile. "Sure. I understand. No, I'm here for the funeral."

"I see."

"So can you help me? Do you know where Jenny and Sarah are?"

"I'm afraid I don't. They left the day... well, the day it happened."

"Do you have a number for her? Because I only have the house number and her email address, and she doesn't seem to be answering email. Well, she wasn't answering when I left."

"I'm sorry," she says, crossing her arms now. "I can't help you."

"Do you know when they will be back?"

"Well on Friday I would imagine," she says.

"Friday?"

"For the funeral."

"Right," I say. "And do you know where that is?"

The woman sucks her bottom lip and then says, "Look love, I'm sorry. I don't know you from Adam. I have to go. My tea's getting cold."

I watch the door close and think, *"So much for the friendly Brits."*

The neighbour on the other side isn't in, and the man in the house beyond that, who is fixing the wing mirror on his Freelander, tells me that he's sorry, but that he *"Didn't have much to do with her."*

But as I turn despondently away, he adds, "I think the funeral's at Saint Paul's if that's any help."

I pause and look back. "Saint *Paul's?*"

He laughs. "Yeah, just the local one." He nods beyond me towards the main road. "It's just over there. I think that's where the missus said they're having it."

Saint Paul's is less than a hundred yards from the entrance to the close, but it's locked and bolted (I for some reason assumed that churches, like petrol stations were open 24/7) so I add the phone number to my non-functioning iBrick and start to walk back towards the town centre wondering what to do next.

I take a bus back to the station, and for want of a better idea, take another train to Waterloo. If the funeral isn't until the day after tomorrow then I might as well head for London. Two nights in Camberley on my own *isn't* what the doctor ordered.

Unsure if I need breakfast, lunch or dinner, I eat a reliably bland cheddar sandwich from the trolley and then at Waterloo I take the tube to South Kensington.

I once stayed in an Easyhotel at South Ken' and I remember it being cheap and I remember the street being stuffed with other low-cost hotels. But more than anything, in my exhausted, despondent state, I'm feeling the need for some kind of familiarity, no matter how corporate, no matter how orange.

I check into a windowless, not-quite-as-cheap-as-I-remember room which is stunningly tiny. Indeed, the single-piece moulded bathroom is so small that when I bend over in the shower to pick up the soap I have dropped, I actually hit my head on the edge of the toilet bowl.

I briefly wonder if I shouldn't have checked some of the other places in the street first – but I don't wonder for long. Within seconds I sink into a groggy, jet-lag, or perhaps concussion-induced slumber.

Pathetic or Rather Beautiful

The eggs are grey and taste like an eraser. The hash browns are greasy and lukewarm. In fact, eating breakfast at McDonald's ignores just about every aspect of aesthetics, taste or ethics I can think of. But they do have *free wifi*, and with free wifi I can use Skype to call Ricardo. Waking up alone for the first time in fifteen months has left me desperate to hear his voice.

The second I switch my phone on though, the unadjusted clock informs me that it is now one a.m. in Bogotá – the call will have to wait.

I check my email, hopeful that Jenny will have replied but find an email from Ricardo instead.

Hello Chupa Chups.

So it is done. Maman est morte. And buried. And Ricardo is drunk.
I hope you have not arrive too late for the mother of Jenny. I can't really believe what you say that they keep the body for a week. I probably shouldn't ask, but doesn't it smell? In Colombia we prefer not to hung around. Death is a well-oiled machine here, but then you know that.
Everything here is fine. It was lovely to see all family, but I drink too much, first at the wake with mother, then after at the goodbye dinner. Yes, too much drinking. But I miss you Chupa Chups. I realise that you are my family now. And the bed is empty without you.

Love Ricardo.

Slightly watery eyed, I reply, telling him that I miss him too, that my phone isn't working and that I'll send him a new number as soon as I have organised a UK sim card. And then I Skype Jenny's home number but of course, she's still not there. Hearing the ghostly voice of her mother on the answer-phone is unsettling.

I phone Saint Paul's church too, and the vicar confirms that the funeral is tomorrow at 2pm. And then I look down at my breakfast and think, *"Twenty four hours in London. What do I want to do?"*

I raise another mouthful of "egg" towards my mouth and then let it drop back onto the tray. One thing I don't want to do, it seems, is eat grey, rubbery, McDonald's egg.

I spend a nice enough day in London. The good weather holds and the place feels familiar and pleasant as I head for Oxford Street to buy a sim card for my phone, as I browse the books in Prowler Soho, as I head out to the Tate Modern to spend a few hours wandering, wondering, *"But is it art?"*

But ultimately the main thing I notice about London is that Ricardo isn't here. Everything I see that impresses me, I want to show to Ricardo. Everything that shocks or amuses me, I want to discuss with Ricardo. Amazingly, after little more than a year together, I'm realising that, without him, I feel like half a person.

In the evening, I head, for familiarity's sake, back to Soho. There's a great atmosphere in Compton's – the place is buzzing with the after-work crowd. I even get chatted up by a cute beary red-head who tells me that he's, "in media."

But even Compton's feels flat without Ricardo: the only reason I ever used to hang around in gay bars was because they held the possibility of finding love. And now I don't need the product I once hoped they would provide, they seem about as much use to me as a plumbing supplies store. Further, without that all-consuming hunt for love to occupy me, I'm at a loss to know how to spend even a single evening in London.

After two pints and a lonely veggie buffet down the road, I head for an Internet café. In the end, the only thing I can think of that I really want this evening is a full-sized keyboard so that I can send Ricardo a proper email telling him how much I miss him. I can't decide whether this is pathetic or rather beautiful.

Ricardo: Not Selfish

Oh my beloved Chupa Chups. What would you say if you knew? I think you would leave me in an instant. I think that our time together and our time to come would be in the trash can before I could finish the first sentence.

Because the truth, pumpkin, is that I thought about cheating on you the moment that you booked that flight. Actually, *thought*, is probably overstating it, I didn't *think* about it, and I honestly didn't begin to scheme how I might make it happen, but my horizons definitely broadened to include the possibility at that moment.

If I had thought about it – which, again, I promise, I didn't – I don't suppose I would have bet on a suitable opportunity presenting itself anyway, but when she smiled at me at the graveside, when she squeezed under my umbrella for protection from the Bogotá rain, I became aware of what might now happen.

Her name was Cristina, and she was the kind of dark, curvaceous beauty I have always gone for. She smelt of shampoo and Angel, a chocolatey aroma that instantly whisked me back to my first flat in La Candelaria, to a long lost summer of youth with the hysterical Esperanza – poor Esperanza, she killed herself, you know. Ironically, Esperanza had no hope, you see.

So it was like being offered time-travel, and I thought, *Now how would that be?* Because though I had occasionally cheated on my girlfriends with guys, I had never done it the other way around. I had never cheated on you Chupy – where would I have found the time? But with you now so far away, it was hardly going to hurt you, now was it?

After the funeral we sat side by side at the meal, she the only single woman, and I the only single guy, and then Cristina asked me where I was staying, and I said that I was going back to my mother's place, and she leant into my ear and asked, *Are you sure you want to be alone this evening?*

I said that I wasn't – I wasn't sure at all. That's all I did, that's all it took. Would you hate me for such a small thing? Probably.

In the end we went back to hers instead, which I realised was a relief because, despite my bravado, I hadn't been looking forward to a night alone at my mother's flat.

When I saw all the guy-stuff in her apartment, when I realised that she didn't usually live alone, it all felt safer. I thought it would be all the more containable, because after all, we were both cheats now. Her husband was away on business and she was lonely and sad from the funeral and she needed a good screw. It suited her fine.

She was soft and warm and she wanted to baby the little boy who had lost his mama, and what can I say? That suited me fine too. I know that you would rather I had denied myself the pleasure; I know you would rather I had chosen to remain sad and alone, and she horny as hell on the other side of town, but that's not the way I'm made, babe and I think deep down you always knew that.

I wasn't feeling devastated, I can't hold that up as an excuse, but I wasn't feeling on top of the world either. You were on the other side of the Atlantic, and I couldn't even phone you. I was missing you, and being held, being reassured that I was sexy, being reminded that I was still a good lay, seeing that I still had what it takes to send rivulets of sweat running down her sleek, smooth back – it was life affirming. Isn't everyone's reaction to death a desire for sex?

Whatever... As you would say, it was just what the doctor had ordered. Of course you wouldn't say that at all, you would call me selfish. At best.

But I have always known what you need better than you know it yourself. I had seen from your time with Tom how toxic honesty can be and I had seen from the beginning that you needed a perfect monogamous relationship. Or failing that, the *illusion* of one.

And I had decided from the moment we got together that if I couldn't give you the first, I would give you the second, because I love you Chupy. I really do.

And one way or another I decided to make sure that we would both get exactly what we wanted out of our life together. And if at times our needs weren't compatible, if from time to time, a little sleight-of-hand was required, then so be it.

I determined, by whatever means, to make sure that we were both happier than we had ever been before. Which despite what you would think, never struck me as selfish at all.

A Chink in Destiny

I get to Saint Paul's fifteen minutes before the service.

It's a warm September day, and the stress of facing Jenny and perhaps Tom, plus the black roll-neck jumper I am wearing – it's all combining to make me sweat. I spot them even before I have passed through the gate to the grounds, standing with their backs to me, both smoking, which is a surprise, because the last time I looked they had both quit.

I walk slowly along the path hoping that they will turn around, and then, when they don't, I pause a few feet from their backs. I swallow hard. I lick my lips and cough. "Hello," I say, simply.

They both turn to face me, Tom quickly, Jenny more slowly. Tom's eyes widen, and Jenny's expression remains entirely blank as if I am a foreign language film that she doesn't quite understand.

Her hair has grown much longer since we last met, and they both look thinner than I remember, but that's perhaps the effect of all the black. Or maybe the cigarettes. Tom, who always did look good in a suit, looks stunning. But angry.

"What the f..." he says. "Sorry, but what are you doing here?" Then to Jenny, he adds softly, "You didn't tell me *he* was coming. How could you not tell me?"

Jenny drags on her cigarette and then whilst blankly staring me in the eye, she says, flatly, "I didn't know."

I step forward to shake Tom's hand but he moves away making it impossible.

"OK," I say. "Fair enough. Look, I'm sorry Tom, but do you think I could have a quick word with Jenny?"

I reach out and touch her arm. She doesn't flinch. "Would that be OK?" I ask her.

Jenny glances at Tom and shrugs one shoulder, then starts to move towards the side of the church.

"Tell him," Tom says as we move away. "Just tell him to go, Jenny."

Once we are out of earshot, I say, "Look, Jenny, I wanted to come today, maybe I was wrong. If you, you know, you do want me to go..."

Jenny nods slowly.

"I would understand," I say.

She continues to nod and sighs deeply. "Well, good," she says.

"You wrote and told me," I say. "You sent me that email and I thought that might mean that you wanted me here... but it doesn't matter."

"You should have warned me," she says. "I haven't had time to think."

"I'm sorry," I say. "I wrote, email... and I phoned your... I phoned the house. And I went there too. But you weren't there."

"We've been in a hotel," she says. "The house has death in it."

I nod. "I see," I say. "Look I'm so sorry Jenny."

She nods. "About?"

"Your mum."

She nods again. "Right."

"About everything," I say. "Of course I am."

She nods. "Everything," she says, and I mentally add it all up and realise the enormity of everything I have been hoping she might cope with today. Her mother is dead and here's her ex-best-friend Mark who cheated on her other best friend Tom before running off to Colombia with the first boyfriend she had had in years.

"I'm sorry. This was stupid," I say.

Tom appears at the corner of the church. "Jenny, the service is about to begin," he says.

Jenny nods at him, then says to me, "I'm sorry. I don't know what to say... It's... It's all so hard anyway," she says. "Without you and Tom and... It wrecked so much. But you know that. I'm not sure if now is the time. I don't want to be... But I'm not sure if there will *ever* be a time."

I nod. "I know. I'm sorry. I'll just go. Really, it's fine. This was a stupid idea." I feel a sudden need to vomit, and have to swallow actual bile rising in my throat.

Jenny nods. "I'm sorry," she says, touching my arm very lightly, and then starting towards Tom.

I remain immobile and nod slowly as I think, "*Wow, what now?*"

After two steps though, Jenny hesitates and looks back. "Did you come for this?" she asks me quietly.

"I'm sorry?"

"Did you come all the way for this? For the funeral. Or were you already here?"

I shrug. "No, I... I really just came to see you."

She nods robotically. "I see," she says.

"Anyway, bye," I say, nodding towards Tom. "You should go."

"Come to the house," she says.

"The house?"

"Yes. Tom can't stay long anyway. So come to the house afterwards. Have something to eat. Say hello to Sarah. *Then* go."

A chink in destiny. Sometimes that's all you need. I blink back tears. "Are you sure?"

She pulls a face. "Honestly? No. But come anyway."

As they vanish into the church, I head for a sunny bench on the far side of the grounds. *In memory of Fred Rawlins who was loved by one and all.*

I'm feeling a bit shaky, and am grateful to Fred for his sunny bench. I check my phone, newly resuscitated by an O2 sim card. There's a text from Ricardo in response to mine. "*OK NEW NUMBER TELL ME WHEN TO CALL,*" it says.

I answer, "Now?" and it rings almost immediately.

"Chupa Chups!" he shouts, hurting my ear.

"Hello. God it's good to hear your voice."

"And yours. Where are you?"

"In Camberley. Outside the church."

"The church?"

"Jenny and Tom and the others are inside. They're having the service for Jenny's mum. Right now."

"I can call back later."

"No, it's fine. It was a bit difficult, with Jenny and Tom. So I stayed outside."

"Difficult?"

"Yes."

"Why?"

"Why? What do you mean, *why?"*

"OK. Sorry. Stupid... Are you OK?"

"Yes. I miss you."

"But you're not sad you go to England?"

"No. I don't know yet really. I only saw Jenny for a few seconds. We'll see how it goes afterwards."

"And London? Did you have fun?"

"I told you, I missed you so much, I couldn't enjoy it much."

"But you must. I miss you too, but you have to enjoy your trip."

"Are *you* OK?"

"Yes. I'm good."

"You still in Bogotá?"

"Yes. Tomorrow I'll go back."

"How are you feeling?"

"Fine."

"But you must be feeling sad?"

"It feels strange. That she's gone."

"I'm sure."

"But we knew, didn't we? She was old. And ill. It's kind of relief too."

"Right."

"Maybe I shouldn't think this, or say it... How is Jenny?"

"She didn't look brilliant. She's lost loads of weight."

"Well, that's maybe a good thing."

"She's looking a bit skinny actually. And tired. She's smoking again."

"Well, you can look after her a bit now."

"I'm not sure she wants me to."

"No, of course. Well, be extra nice to Sarah."

"Of course."

"It will help."

"Help?"

"It's psychology, Chupy. If you're nice to her kid, it will make things easier. It's the way women work."

"Sure. Well, I *was* going to kick her and spit on her, but now you mention it, I think I'll buy her an ice cream instead."

"It's probably better. Is it ice-cream weather over there?"

"Yes. It's lovely actually. I'm sitting on a bench in the church garden in the sun."

"It's raining here."

"It's *always* raining there. Do you miss me a bit?"

"I miss you so much pumpkin, you have no idea. The worse is sleeping alone. The bed so cold. But I know you'll be back soon."

"Two weeks seems like too long now."

"Yes. But it'll be fine. You'll see."

"This call must be costing a fortune."

"Yes. It's a mobile, so a fortune. Where are you staying tonight?"

"I don't know yet. I have my stuff with me, so probably at a hotel nearby."

A sparrow lands on the furthest arm of the bench and looks at me quizzically. I wish I could show Ricardo.

"If you have a normal phone, text me the number and I can call you," Ricardo says.

"OK. And if I have wifi I can Skype you. Are you at your mum's place?"

"No Chupy. I'm staying with friends. I didn't want to stay in the flat on my own."

"Oh good. I'm glad you're not on your own."

"Just text me the number and I'll call you."

"OK. Love you."

"You too, mi amor. You too. Good luck with Jenny and Tom."

"Thanks. I'll need it."

"Ciao."

"Ciao."

"Bye."

"Bye."

"I'm hanging now."

"OK. It's hanging *up* though."

"Sorry?"

"You have to say, *hanging up*. Hanging is something different."

"OK. Bye."

"Bye."

"Are you still there Chupy?"

"Yes."

"OK, here goes. I'm really hanging *up* now."

"Bye."

I sigh and smile at the phone and slip it back in my pocket.

"He's gone now," I say to the sparrow. "Now, what do *you* want?"

Being spoken to apparently is not what the sparrow wants. It hops and flutters away.

And then, feeling a hundred times happier than before the call, I head off in search of a cup of coffee and a sandwich.

One At a Time

Wakes are always strange affairs. Sometimes everyone is shell-shocked and miserable – people who really just want to be alone with their grief. But just as often everyone ends up drunk and full of inappropriate laughter.

Jenny's mother's sendoff is in a class of its own though. It feels like a subdued, unpopular village fête. Three old ladies are serving cucumber sandwiches and pouring tea, mainly, it would seem, for themselves.

The single man, a dapper, grey haired chap, is smoking his pipe, respectfully blowing his fumes through a cracked window. At the bottom of the garden, beneath an apple tree, I can see Tom and Jenny sitting on a floral swing-chair. They are holding glistening tumblers with slices of lemon and ice cubes. I see that Tom alone spots me peering out at them. And I see that he pretends not to notice.

I tuck my bag in a cupboard under the stairs and, refusing a cup of tea, head for the kitchen. If I have to face Tom again, I need a drink first.

I find a bottle of Bombay Sapphire in the fridge, and pour myself a stiff gin and tonic.

"There's vodka in the freezer if you prefer," a voice says behind me. I turn to see the man with the pipe, now extinguished, winking at me. "That's what the other youngsters are drinking," he explains, nodding towards the garden.

"More of a gin man, myself," I say, realising as I say it that I have for some reason copied his clipped major's accent.

"Mother's ruin," he says.

"So they say. Can I serve you one?"

"No, strictly tea here I'm afraid," he says. "Driving and all."

I hold out a hand and we shake. "Mark," I say.

"Mark also," he says. "A friend of Jenny's, is it?"

The *"is it,"* amuses me, because, with his accent he sounds like Armstrong and Miller.

I resist the urge to reply, *"Isn't it, though?"*

"Yes," I say, "a friend." I wonder if that's a lie.

"I knew Marge way back when she used to come to dos at the Rotary club. Didn't know her well, of course. Not a great socialite, our Marge. And she stopped coming when Frank died, but I heard the turnout was low, so..."

"That's sweet of you," I say.

"The ladies are from the church."

"Right," I say. "Was Marge religious?"

He shakes his head. "Not really. Too pragmatic for that I should think. C of E. You know, weddings and funerals."

"Right."

"Anyway, you go talk to Jenny," he says, opening the back door for me. "I'm sure that's why you're here."

I force a smile, take a deep breath, and step into the back garden. "See you in a bit," I say as the door swings shut behind me.

The sun is moving behind a neighbour's bush and the temperature is dropping fast. Tom is already striding towards me, his jacket flapping as he walks.

"Tom!" Jenny protests behind him, and then she sighs and simply looks the other way.

"I can't believe you're here," he says.

"I can't believe your stress levels," I retort.

"Funny guy. Can't you just leave us alone?"

"Can't you just chill, Tom?"

"Chill? Jesus, you've got a nerve. Do you think Jenny wants to see you? Do you think I do?" His eyes are flaming. A vein on his forehead is pulsing like a beacon, and I can't help but notice that there is something rather magnificent about him when angry.

"Today isn't really about you, Tom," I say in a tone as warm as I can muster. "It's about Jenny."

"And you think that what Jenny needs today is to see you?" Tom says. "You really think that the one thing Jenny needs right now is *your* sorry arse turning up?"

"Tom, I get that you hate my guts," I say. "And I understand that. And I'm sorry about that. Really. But..." I see that Jenny is now standing and crossing the lawn towards us.

"This isn't about me," Tom says. "And I don't hate your guts. I don't give a fuck about you. But really. Her *mother* has just died. And the last thing she needs right now..."

"I invited him, Tom," Jenny says, resting a hand lightly on his shoulder.

"But he's a cunt," Tom says.

"Maybe, but I *invited* him," Jenny says again.

I would have preferred it had Jenny disagreed, but such is life. If you don't want people to describe you as a cunt, you have to avoid acting like one, and as I have discovered, that isn't always easy. Karma.

Tom works his mouth, his cheeks are turning blotchy. He glances at me, and then turns away to face Jenny. "I'm sorry Jen but... I really don't think I can do this," he says. He pushes past me into the house and slams the kitchen door behind him.

"I'm sorry," I tell her. "I had no idea that it would be so difficult."

Jenny thinks about this for a while, and then, unexpectedly she laughs – a genuine, honest, cackle of a laugh. "You didn't?" she asks, tears in her eyes.

I frown at her.

"Oh Mark," she says, her mirth fading to bitterness as she speaks. "You've really no idea, have you?" She hands me her glass and heads back towards the swing chair. "Get me a refill. Vodka and tonic, ice, lemon. I need to get *spectacularly* drunk."

When I re-enter the kitchen, Tom continues our game of musical chairs by immediately returning outside. "Glad to see we're being grown-up about this," I mutter as I fish the vodka from the freezer.

I wait a little while before returning outside. I watch Tom, his back to me, his arms flapping, as he protests to Jenny. It strikes me that he looks a bit like a penguin.

I think, "*Of course, this is* exactly *what Jenny needs.*"

Jenny sighs and rolls her eyes, and looks away, and then finally shrugs and says what looks like, *"Well what do you want me to do?"* at which Tom stomps off to the front of the house. I take this as my cue and push back outside.

When I hand Jenny her drink, she says, "He's still angry, that's the thing."

I nod and raise an eyebrow. "Yes, I kind of picked up on that," I say.

"I'm not exactly... whatever the opposite of angry is... myself," she says, sipping at her drink.

"I'm sorry," I say. "I really am. But there's not much more I can say."

"No," Jenny says, avoiding eye contact. "Well... just keep saying it then. Maybe if you say it enough. Maybe it's like anti-wrinkle cream."

"Anti wrinkle cream?"

"The more you use it, the better it works."

"Right. Where's Sarah?" I ask, thinking that a subject change might do us good here.

"At nursery," Jenny says. "I decided she's too young for funerals."

"Sure," I say. "Will I see her?"

"In a bit," Jenny says. "I have to go and get her at five. Actually what time is it?"

"Fourish," I say. I check my phone. "Ten to actually."

"Look... I'm sorry, but..." Jenny glances to the side of the house and then pulls a face.

"Yes?"

"Tom is leaving at half four. He has a taxi booked. Would it be too much to ask for you to... you know... go for a wander say. Just till half four?"

I smile sadly and shake my head. "Of course not. Do you need anything? Any shopping or anything?"

"No. Only vodka."

"There's a bottle and a half in the freezer. And masses of tonic too."

Jenny shrugs. "Then no... nothing."

"OK, I'll see you in a bit."

"Thanks," she says.

At the front of the house, Tom is sitting on the wall. "I'm off, Tom," I tell him. "She's all yours."

"She told you where to go then," he says.

I nod calmly at him and head off across the close. I feel a desire, of all things, to hug him – to walk over and hold him until he weeps. In his current state, of course, he would probably punch me first.

As I walk to the main road, as I retrace my steps to the greasy cafe, I think about all the years Tom and I spent together. All the places we have been. All the adventures we had. And it just breaks my heart that it has all come to this.

If he could see inside my head, he would understand of course. He would realise that none of it was meant, that I never did anything with malicious intent. But of course he can't see inside my head. He has decided, instead, to lock me out. And like an autistic child in therapy, I want more than anything else to sit and hold him until he breaks.

It's nearly five when I get back to the house and a lone church-lady is finishing the dishes in the now-spotless kitchen.

"Hello. I'm Penny," she says. "You were here before, weren't you? Jenny's outside. I think she's had a bit too much to drink."

"Yes," I say.

"Are you hanging around for a bit? Because I didn't want to leave her on her own."

"I'm not sure," I say. "Probably. Hopefully."

She purses her lips at me.

"It's complicated," I say.

"The course of true love never did run true," she says. "You go talk to her. She needs her friends right now and there don't seem to be many of you around."

I peer out at Jenny swinging alone on the love seat, and then return to the hallway for a coat before crossing the garden to join her. "Put this on," I tell her. "You'll catch your death of cold."

Jenny looks up at me and wobbles her head in a drunken gesture of acquiescence. I drape the coat over her shoulders.

"What happened to your finger?" I ask, noting a fresh, bloody plaster.

"Shlicing frozen lemons," she says. "With the ham slicer." She sounds plastered.

I pull a face as I imagine the scene.

"I'm sorry about Tom," she says. "He's just a baby really."

I nod and take a seat next to her. "Yes, I know."

"You broke his heart though," she says.

"Yeah. Well... he didn't do much for mine," I reply.

Jenny raises an eyebrow and stares me in the eye for the first time today. "Don't go there," she says. "Really. Not with me. Don't dare."

"No," I say. "Sorry."

"That was an awful thing you... Really."

"I'm sorry. It wasn't meant, if that makes any difference."

"What does that mean?" she asks. "It wasn't *meant?*"

I shrug. "Sorry, even I don't know."

"No," she says, thoughtfully. "It *is* cold," she says, standing, and then reaching out to steady herself on the arm of the chair. "I didn't notice really."

"How many of those have you had?"

"Three. Four, maybe. This tastes disgusting though," she says, emptying the drink on the grass. "What did you put in it?"

"Nothing. Vodka. Tonic. Have you eaten anything?"

"Yes, I..." she says, then freezes. She remains totally immobile, staring at me, and then her eyes slip out of focus until she's looking *through* me. I notice that her left arm is trembling slightly.

"God you *are* cold," I say. "Come inside."

And then a freaky thing happens. Her eyes roll upwards until I can no longer see the pupils.

"Jenny?!"

Her hand slips from the arm of the chair, and I lurch to catch her as she crumples to the ground.

Jenny: Catch Me When I Fall

I couldn't decide whether to hit Mark or hug him. That was my main dilemma. I was feeling raw and emotional, and yet numb and dreamy all at once. My mother was dead and Tom was rabbiting on about some guy he had just met and how he *lived* at the gym which was reassuring I suppose in a *life-goes-on* kind of way. I was part-listening to Tom but mainly I was lost in my own thoughts about whether I should have brought Sarah along to her gran's funeral. She seemed too young to face death to me – I had wanted to protect her. But I was thinking now that I had only put off the inevitable. She would be back at the house soon enough, and I would have to start explaining where her gran was. Or lying.

We both turned around. I don't remember why, but Tom and I both turned around at the same moment, and there he was looking tanned and scared. And my reflex was to bitch-slap him so hard that he would have fallen over. Or to reach out and hug him. I just couldn't decide which.

Tom's presence, his crackling anger, didn't seem to leave the space required for me to work it out. So I did nothing. I just gaped, I think.

My mum was my last family member to go. I once had a brother, Frederic, Freddy, Fred, his name got shorter as the years went by until it vanished all together. He had a motorbike accident when he was eighteen. I was eleven. He died, as they say, instantly.

Dad died a couple of years afterwards. Mum always says... she always *said* he died of sorrow, but he didn't – he died of kidney failure.

And now Mum. She wasn't supposed to go yet. There had been no hint of it. She was one of those super-grannies you see whizzing around, shopping, gardening, walking... Most of the time, she had more energy than me. I honestly thought she would go on forever.

One day she went to Waitrose and when she got back, at the moment she carried the bag of shopping over the doorstep, her heart conked out. Just like that. Like a motor that had run out of petrol. I didn't know heart attacks could happen like that, without warning. A neighbour found her lying amongst her groceries and phoned the ambulance, and she phoned me as well, but by the time I got back she was gone. The groceries had been picked up too. They were all stacked neatly in the fridge. Even the tins and the toilet roll were stacked in the fridge.

I have never felt so alone in my life. If I hadn't had Sarah to look after, I'm not sure what I might have done.

Of course I had faced loss before. Freddy, and then Dad... my divorce from Nick, then losing my boyfriend and best friend both at once because the one ran off with the other... But I still had Mum. And Mum wouldn't leave me, no matter who she met, no matter what I did. The advantage of family. Well, that's what I thought.

With Mum gone that only really left Tom. I don't really know how I ended up with so few friends. Moving around, maybe. Nick drove a few away, as alcoholics do. Of course, I *knew* other people, but they were my daughter's playmates' parents really, my links with them as fragile as my daughter's own friendships – which at four-and-a-half were *very* fragile.

And Tom, well, he never really stepped that far into my life, not the way Mark did. Tom had always been too wrapped up in himself to really get in there and make a difference, for good or for bad. But he was there for me when I left Nick. And he was there when Mum died, and he was the only person who was. I'll give him that.

It's a terrible thing to admit, but once Mark arrived, all I really wanted was for Tom to leave. I wanted to work out how I felt about Mark, and with Tom buzzing around like an angry wasp it was impossible to even think straight.

I had been in the back garden all day. I couldn't bear to be inside the house because it had death in it. That will sound irrational I'm sure, but I could sense it, hanging like a damp mist in every corner of the house. Everywhere I looked I could see a shadow of that missing person, missing from her kitchen sink, missing at the door to her bedroom, missing from the hall floor where she had, they said, collapsed.

Sarah thought the hotel was a great adventure, and seemed to assume that it was normal for Mummy to behave this way in the new environment. We lay on crisp white sheets with their memories of men on business trips and young couples and secret affairs, but not death. At least they didn't smell of death.

We zapped through a thousand channels of rubbish TV and shared chocolate from the mini bar. And I felt like a passer through. I felt like everyone else. I felt like *anyone* else. And that was a huge relief. If we could have stayed there forever, I think I might have done so.

I thought the house would be OK after the funeral though. Well, I didn't really, but I *hoped* it would.

It was a hellish day of course. I hadn't seen Mum die, so the vanishing coffin was my moment. It happened during prayer, but I opened my eyes and peeped through tears as it vanished from view, and I thought, *"Who will catch me now? Who will catch me if I fall?"* and then wondered if that wasn't a song lyric. It sounded corny enough. But true.

When we got back, the house didn't feel better, in fact, I couldn't even step inside the hall. Her shadow lay there strewn across the tiles like a police outline and I simply couldn't step over it so I went around the back and sat in the garden instead. I decided that getting really drunk would probably make stepping inside an achievable goal.

The air still crackled with Tom's irritation and then later, once he was gone, with Mark's simpering need for forgiveness and I still couldn't tune in to how I felt because I was busy thinking about my mum being dead, and someone somewhere burning her coffin, and Sarah coming home, and stepping inside the house, and having to overcome my own fear for her sake, and I just didn't seem to be able to find any spare brain capacity to decide whether to hit Mark or hug him. I think I slipped into my bitchy-and-aloof routine instead.

When Mark stood to lead me inside, I couldn't find the words to tell him how afraid I was of the shadows in the house. My drink tasted of Fairy Liquid – it suddenly reeked of the stuff – and my skin prickled with the cold. The garden looked, for some reason, fluorescent and blue tinged and it sounded, as if I had taken acid, like it was speaking to me – a deep incomprehensible voice coming frighteningly from the lawn. I wondered if someone had drugged my drink, and then wondered *who* had drugged my drink.

And then I felt Mark's arms around me and wondered if and when I had taken the decision to hug him.

Top Of The World

Penny comes running from the house, drying her hands on her pinny as she runs. "What's happened?" she asks.

As if *I* know. I am crouched beside Jenny; her head on my lap. The left side of her body, just the left side, is twitching. Her eyes are open, but her pupils have rolled out of view.

"Some kind of fit," I say. My voice sounds calm, which surprises me. "Call an ambulance."

"Perhaps she's fainted," Penny says. "She's had a hard day. I haven't seen her eat..."

"She *hasn't* fainted," I interrupt. "Call a bloody ambulance."

Penny stands, hesitates, and then runs back inside, leaving me cradling Jenny in my arms.

I watch as she starts to foam at the mouth, a mixture of vomit and saliva. I tilt her head sideways so that it runs from her mouth onto my trousers. I wonder if I should slap her. People always seem to slap people who have fainted in films. Would that be the thing to do?

"Jenny? Jenny? God, I don't know what to do Jen," I tell her, casting around in case anyone else is present, in case someone *else* knows what to do here. But we're all alone at the bottom of the garden.

A lump forms in my throat at the realisation that Jenny might actually be dying here – dying in my arms because I simply don't know what is wrong, or what to do.

Our lives have been so intertwined, almost obscenely so. Twenty years ago, Jenny was my last ever attempt at dating a woman; her daughter was conceived on the day Steve and I had the car crash – the day Steve died. And Tom and I saved her from her violent ex and gave her a new life in France, for a while. I took that life away by running away with Ricardo. It almost seems logical, unsurprising even that she might die now with her head on my knees.

"Please don't go, Jenny," I say, stroking her hair, tears sliding down my cheek. "Please hang around. I need to make it up to you."

Penny returns, the cordless phone in one hand. "She's twitching," she says into the handset. "Yes. Like electric shocks. She's being sick too. Vomiting, yes. Drugs? I don't think so. Has she taken any drugs?"

I wipe my eyes with my free hand. "No, just alcohol," I say.

"Just al... yes. Yes, quite a lot. Is she diabetic?"

I shake my head. "No, I don't think so. No, definitely not."

"Or epileptic?"

"She's not anything. What we need is a fucking ambulance."

"He says she isn't anything and that we need... yes."

"It's on its way already," she tells me. "OK. Yes. Yes. Hang on." She crouches beside me and touches my shoulder. "He says to roll her on her side so she doesn't choke. Like they do on television. The recovering position."

I move from beneath her and lower Jenny's head to the ground and do as I'm told. With her right arm bent upwards and her legs splayed, she looks like one of those crime scene outlines. And then I sit and push on her back to keep her in the recovery position despite the violent twitching of her entire left side.

For ten minutes, nothing else happens. It's the longest ten minutes of my life.

Jenny continues to jerk and vomit and I sit and hold her.

"Nothing bad can happen to her like that," Penny says. "That's what the man said."

And then suddenly, the twitching stops and Jenny starts to snore as loudly as I have ever heard anyone snore.

I frown for a moment, and then look up at Penny. "I think that's better, yeah? That's got to be better."

Penny nods at me wide eyed, and then after a moment's thought, she says, "She probably *needs* a kip after all that twitching," and we both laugh stupid, nervous laughs.

As the sirens near, Penny runs to the front of the house to welcome them. Two guys in uniforms jog impressively around the side of the house looking like something from a TV documentary.

A forty-something neighbour in shirtsleeves appears over the fence. "Is she all-right?" he asks me.

I don't bother to answer, so when Penny arrives, he asks again. "Is she all-right?"

"We don't know love," she says.

"She had a fit I think," I tell the ambulance men. "She was twitching. All down her left side. And vomiting."

"She's had a little accident as well," Penny says, nodding at Jenny's stained dress.

"Is she on any prescription drugs?" one of the guys asks as the other checks her pulse.

"Not that I know of, but I wouldn't really know."

"Recreational drugs?"

"No."

"She had a bit to drink," Penny tells them. "And a lot of stress. Her mother died."

"Is she diabetic, do you know?" he asks.

"No, I don't think so. Almost definitely not," I answer.

"Epileptic?"

"No, no. I don't think so."

The older of the ambulance men lifts her head and pushes open her eyelids. "She's out. A seizure."

"So we're taking her in?" his mate asks.

"Yep." He lowers her back to the ground and then unrolls a stretcher beside her.

"What does that mean?" I ask. "Is she OK?"

"She's top of the world," the older guy says.

"No, I mean..."

"She's had a seizure mate. But she's breathing," he says. "Which is always a good start."

They lift her onto the stretcher and then march off towards the front of the house. I start to follow them, but then pause. "I don't know where Sarah is," I tell Penny.

"I'll stay. In case she comes home," she says. "You go with her. Call me when you get there. Call me here at the house when you know something."

"Thanks," I say.

I squeeze her shoulder, and then, in a blur, I'm jogging to the front of the house and I'm sitting in an ambulance and I'm watching Camberley spin by and I'm thinking, *"Life! Jesus! You just never know what it's going to chuck at you next."*

Sugary Tea

Jenny comes to precisely as the ambulance pulls into the hospital. She opens her eyes, looks around and says, "I... Um. Mum? *Mark?*"

"Hello sweetie," I say, stroking her hand. "We're just arriving at the hospital."

"Hospital?" she repeats.

"You had some kind of fit."

"You're going to be fine," the ambulance man says, bursting the rear doors open and jumping down.

In the emergency ward, they check her blood pressure and ask strange questions designed to test whether Jenny can still move and think: can you touch your nose with your left hand? Who is the prime minister of England at the moment?

Jenny's sassy, "Prime Minister of the United Kingdom, surely?" seemingly convinces them that her brain is still functioning. She is moved to a wheelchair and driven to a curtained enclosure.

I sit next to her for ten minutes holding her hand until she remembers who I am and pulls it away. That pulling away breaks my heart: I am the only person here for her today, and that gesture says, *even if you were the last person on the planet...*

Twice, she says, out of the blue, "But, I don't understand," and I do my best to reassure her.

"You had a fit, and I'm sure the doctors will tell us more in a bit," I say.

After about half an hour, she falls asleep. I step beyond the curtain to ask one of the nurses if it's OK for her to do so.

"I expect so," the nurse replies unconvincingly. "You'll have to ask the doctor when he arrives."

Another half an hour goes by. Jenny drifts in and out of sleep.

I cross the ward to the front desk. "Excuse me," I say. "But shouldn't something be happening by now? It feels like we've been parked and forgotten."

The nurse shrugs. "If you want fast, go to McDonald's," she says.

I glance at her name tag. I have every intention of reporting her, but she sees the direction of my gaze and apologises.

"Sorry," she says. "It's been a really long day. I'm sure the doctor will be with you in a minute. Why don't you go back to your friend and I'll see what I can do."

I head out through the lobby and, amidst a gaggle of smoking medical staff, phone Penny to give her an update.

"Don't worry," she says. "I'm just making a bit of tea. I'm in no hurry."

I consider phoning Ricardo too. I need to hear his voice, and I want to tell him what's going on, but there's so much to tell I can't really think where to begin.

When I get back to Jenny a doctor has finally appeared. Because he looks too young, I check his name tag, but *Doctor Rowney* is what the tag says.

Dr Rowney has a pierced eyebrow, the same as Tom's. Who would have thought that doctors could look this cute? Who would have thought they could be this young?

"Well you seem to be fine now," he tells her with a mild smile. "I can't see any reason why you can't go home. You'll be very tired for a while." He nods at me. "She just needs sleep now."

"Really?" I say. "But what happened? Will it happen again?"

He shrugs. "A seizure. These things happen," he says. "And often as not they never happen again."

"God, really?" I say.

"Just keep an eye on her for twenty-four hours."

"But what causes it? What if it happens again?"

"Do what you did. Recovery position. Make sure she doesn't choke or hurt herself. Phone 999. But it won't."

"God," I say. "If it doesn't happen again then in twenty-four hours we're out of the woods then?"

"I think we can probably say that you're already out of the woods," he says. "Now, I'll get an orderly to take you out to the taxi rank. Back in a tick."

I stand there feeling cheated. If I am supposed to take Jenny home and look after her I need infinitely more information than I have been given. I crouch down beside her. She looks back at me in a vague, unfocused manner.

"How are you feeling?" I ask.

"Awful," she says.

"Do *you* think you're OK to go home?"

"I'm tired," she says.

"OK," I say. "But do you feel OK to go home in a taxi?"

"I want to sleep."

"Right," I say, feeling utterly convinced that this *isn't* the right thing to do, that Jenny should stay in a place where people know what to do if her eyes roll backwards and she starts vomiting.

"And Sarah. At five," she says pulling at her hospital tag as if it's maybe a watch.

I slide my phone from my pocket. I don't tell her that it's already ten to eight. "Sure," I say. "Where is she?"

Jenny frowns at me.

"Sarah? Where is she?" I repeat gently.

"She's at school."

"School?"

"Well, nursery school."

"Right. And after?"

"Next door. Susan's picking her up. I want to go home now. It stinks here. What's that smell?"

"Hospital smell. Disinfectant I think," I say.

"It stinks," she says.

I hear the curtain being dragged open and turn to find the doctor standing next to an asian orderly. "There you go," he says.

"Are you sure this is OK?" I ask. "Because I really don't feel..."

"Oh!" the doctor says, looking past me and furrowing his brow. "*Oh!* You're not fine at all, are you?"

I swivel back to see that Jenny's head has lolled forward and her left arm and leg are juddering exactly as before. The doctor pushes me out of the way and crouches down beside her, and I think, "*Thank God! Thank God it happened here.*"

This second seizure lasts only ten or fifteen seconds, and this time Jenny comes around almost immediately, saying, stumblingly, "What... Did it happen again? That smell!"

This second attack though, is enough to shift her hospital experience into an entirely different gear. Doctor Rowney stops smiling blankly at me and starts chewing the inside of his mouth instead. "We're going to have to keep her in," he says. "Two seizures, *isn't* normal, not by any stretch."

Jenny is wheeled, with urgency, to a ward. She doesn't react to any of this – she just sits there and stares out at us all. She looks like one of those confused old ladies you see being wheeled around in retirement homes.

I sit outside her ward for an hour and watch nurses whizzing back and forth. I play spot the cutest doctor, and check out the corners to see if they are as dirty as people always say. They aren't.

And then my phone shows 21:40 and I decide that I have had enough. I collar the cutest nurse on one of his many strides past. He's a chunky guy in his late twenties with a shaved head, a neat, golden goatee and electric blue eyes.

"Oh God, I'm sorry. Someone should have told you..." he says. "She's fine. We've sedated her. And we've given her anti-convulsants to stop the fits. She'll sleep until tomorrow, and then we'll have to do some tests – try to work out why this is happening."

"And why *might* that be?"

"There's no telling really..." he says. "Sorry."

"No idea at all?"

"Maybe she's epileptic... As I say... It's hard to know."

"Should I stay, or..."

"She'll sleep. Guaranteed. So there's no point. She mentioned a daughter. Do we need to contact social services or..."

"No, I can go and sort her out," I say. "If I don't need to be here, that is."

"No, there's really no point staying. You're better sorting out her daughter."

"Can I give you my number?" I ask. "Just in case..."

"They'll take it at the front desk," he says.

"And tomorrow, I should... what? Call?"

"Sure. After lunch I would say. I doubt we'll know much before then."

"Right," I say standing a little too fast. Just for a second, I think that I might faint – I have to hold on to the wall to steady myself.

"Sugary tea," the nurse tells me with a wink.

"Sugary tea?"

He nods. "Cures all ills. There's a machine at the end of the corridor."

As I head off in search of the drinks dispenser, I think, *"If only it did. If only sugary tea did cure all ills."*

What Other People See

When I get back to the house, Penny, already slipping into her overcoat, opens the front door. "How is she?" she asks.

"Not good," I say. "She had another fit, and..."

"Oh the poor love," Penny says.

"They sedated her. We should know more tomorrow."

"They don't know what caused it then?"

I shrug. "Epilepsy maybe. That's the only word I heard anyone use."

"God."

"I know."

"Sarah's with the woman next door. She came around. She was spitting blood... but I calmed her down."

"Right," I say. "That side? The June Whitfield lookalike?"

"That's the one," she says. "She *does* look a bit like her. You know her then?"

"Not really. We met briefly. You look like you're on your way home."

"I'm sorry love, but yes, it's after ten. I have to go. Will you be OK?"

"Sure," I say.

"I made a big bowl of pasta – it's in the fridge. I thought you'd all be hungry."

"Thanks," I say. "I'm starving."

"You can microwave it. I'm sorry love, but I really have to..."

I nod. "Sure. Thanks so much."

"I've left my number next to the phone. If you need anything."

"Right," I say.

She shuffles around me and then pauses and pulls a face. "What a day, huh?"

I smile feebly. "Yes, what a day!"

Penny opens her arms, and we hug briefly.

"You don't have a key do you?" I ask.

She releases me and wrinkles her nose. "A key? Oh, for *here?*"

I nod.

"I'm sorry love. The truth is, I don't really know her at all."

"Right," I say. "Well, thanks so much."

"Good luck with the little one."

"Yes, I think I'll need it."

"Bye." She gives me a little wave and then walks quickly away.

I take a deep breath, put the door on the catch, and head back to June Whitfield's house. It's her husband who opens the door though.

"Hi there," I say. "I'm, um, looking for Sarah? Jenny said she was here."

"I'll get Susan," he says, vanishing into the lounge as Sarah's head appears at the top of the stairs.

"Hello you!" I say.

She looks at me very seriously, then descends one step and sits, rubbing her eyes. "Where's Mummy?" she asks.

The door to the lounge opens again and Susan appears. "Hello," she says, without much pleasure, "you again." Then to Sarah, she shouts, "And you, back to bed young lady."

Sarah ignores her completely.

"How is she?" Susan asks. "I came around, but she said – a woman answered the door – and she said she's at the hospital."

I wince and flick my eyes at Sarah. "Not in front of you-know-who, eh?"

Susan nods, closes the front door, and with another, "Bed!" directed at Sarah, leads me into the lounge. It's one of those not-redecorated-since-1970-but-spotless lounges, all green wallpaper, cut crystal, and mock walnut.

"She's had some kind of fit," I explain. "Well, two actually. We don't know why yet. They had to keep her in."

"It's not drugs, is it?"

"Drugs?" I ask, astonished. "Why would it be drugs? Do you know something I don't?"

"Well it happens," she says.

"Oh... well, then, no – no it's not drugs."

"Well, good. Sarah can stay here the night if that's any help," she says.

"Sure. I was going to take her home, but..."

"I'd rather she stayed here," she says. "At least until I can speak to Jenny."

"Of course," I say. "You don't really know me, do you. Well it's up to you. I can take her next door or..."

The door pushes open and Sarah's face appears. "I want to go home," she says.

Susan sighs. "I think it's best if you stay here," she says. "Your dad's very tired and..."

"I'm not her dad," I interrupt. "I'm just a friend. A friend of the family."

"Oh, I'm sorry," Susan says, warming up a little. "Oh, God, I'm sorry. I just assumed... I thought you were Nick. And he doesn't have the best reputation from what I hear."

I wince again, and she glances down at Sarah and pulls a face. "Sorry," she says. "So is Sarah happy to go with you?"

"Sure," I say. "You remember me, don't you? Uncle Mark. From France?"

Sarah nods seriously. "You stole Mummy's boyfriend," she says.

I snort, grit my teeth, close my eyes, and rub the bridge of my nose. I don't know whether to laugh, or cry, or faint from hunger and exhaustion. When I open my eyes again, Susan's expression has reverted to grim. "I definitely think she should stay here," she says.

"Where's Mummy?" Sarah asks, her bottom lip trembling. "Is she at the hotel?"

"Yes, she's at the hotel," Susan says, shooting me a glare.

"It's got a baby fridge," Sarah tells me. "Full of chocolate."

I nod. "Wow. Sounds good."

"Yes, but Mummy said you can sleep over," Susan says. "Wouldn't you rather sleep over with Franny and have pancakes for breakfast?"

Sarah's frown fades slightly, just enough to indicate that she might yet be convinced.

"And tomorrow we can go to the park again."

Sarah blinks and rubs her eyes.

"But only if you get straight back up to bed."

Sarah nods and hesitantly vanishes behind the door again.

"God," I say, "you're good."

Susan shrugs. "They love sharing a bed. They won't get any sleep, but..." she shrugs. "Tomorrow's not a school day."

"Does she go to school already?"

"Franny does," she says.

"Right, well, I'll, just, um, leave her with you then."

"I think that's best."

I nod. "Oh, and you don't happen to have a key, do you?"

"A key?"

"To Jenny's place? This was all a bit unplanned, so..."

"No," she says, starting now to look suspicious as well as grim. "No, I don't *have a key*. How well do you actually know her?"

I sigh. "Pretty well. Well enough to fly all the way from Colombia to come to the funeral, anyway."

51

"Colombia?" she says.

"Yeah. South America."

She takes a step forward, forcing me to retreat to the front door. "Yes, I *know* Colombia," she says. "I saw a documentary."

"It's a country," I say, sensing first hand the frustration that Colombian's must feel about their country being persistently reduced to drugs – *nothing* but drugs. "It's a whole, vast, country." I run a hand across my forehead and realise that I'm feeling shaky and angry. "Jees... look... thanks for looking after Sarah. We can sort the rest out tomorrow, eh?"

"I'll call Jenny in the morning," she says. "That's the best bet really."

"They said after lunch. The people at the hospital. They said they wouldn't know anything till after lunch. Just so you know."

"It's Frimley Park, I take it?"

"That's the one."

"OK. I'll call her after lunch," she says, already pushing the door closed.

What other people see, I think, as I head back to the house. From alcoholic father to cocaine-trading-stealer-of-boyfriends in less than ten minutes.

Sliding

I return to the house and pull a salad bowl filled with pasta, tomato sauce and ham from the refrigerator. I reckon that I can fish the lumps of ham out and that, tonight, I actually don't care if I miss one or two. I stick the bowl straight in the microwave.

I sit in Jenny's mother's kitchen and look out at the darkened garden, and think that I don't want to be here, that I don't want to be here at all.

But these moments of sheer emergency leave no room for manoeuvre – they simply *require* that you do this and then *require* that you do that, and you're left just batting away random balls as they fly at you. It's like being in a car sliding across the ice. I can do little but wait to see how far it will skid before my steering wheel gains some traction again.

In spite of my tired state, I barely sleep that night. Perhaps it's because not feeling able to lay claim to Jenny's bed, and not wanting to sleep in her dead mother's room, I opt for the sofa. Maybe it's just unknown house syndrome: the place is full of unfamiliar shadows and strange noises. Nothing truly sinister – just a coat hanging here, a branch moving in the moonlight, the grunting and groaning of a building at sleep, the tinkering of radiators and the wheezing of a gas meter... I'm jet-lagged and stressed as well, of course, but it's mainly the noises and the shadows that keep me awake.

At six, precisely, a milk float enters the close, and that sound, the whirring of its electric motor, the clinking of bottles, is one that is so familiar, so reassuring... I yawn, and think that I haven't heard a milk float since I was a child. I'm so glad they still exist.

When I reawaken, I feel like I have merely dozed off for a few seconds. Initially I'm confused as to where I am, in which country even, but then I remember.

The VCR is showing nine-fifty-four which strikes me as unlikely so I switch on my phone to check the time and realise that I can now phone Ricardo.

A quick scan of the house reveals no signs of broadband – Jenny's laptop has an old fashioned modem plugged into a phone socket – so I text Ricardo with the house number and while I wait, I head through to the kitchen and scour the cupboards for breakfast options. In the refrigerator, hidden behind a pack of chilled toilet roll (does someone have haemorrhoids? I wonder) I find butter, Marmite, and joy of joys, crumpets. And that's what I'm eating when Ricardo phones.

He declares that he can't talk for long, but then patiently remains on the line for over an hour as I tell him about Jenny and the hospital, and then in reverse order of urgency, about the funeral, and Tom, and Sarah, and the neighbour. Finally, I ask him what he thinks might be causing Jenny's fits.

"If it is epilepsy," he says, "it could be anything... tired, stress, flashing lights..."

"But wouldn't she know if she was epileptic?"

"Probably," he says. "But, you know, you don't know you've got that kind of things until you know. And it might be cause by something else, some other illness."

"Like?"

"Best to wait for the results," he says, sounding suddenly doctorly. "No point speculating."

"Right."

"Now I really do have to go, Pumpkin. I'm meeting up with a friend downtown and I'm late."

"You're still in Bogotá?"

"Yes. Going home tonight. I wish I was with you Chupy."

"I'd rather be there with you, I think," I say.

"It's no fun on either side," he says. "Believe me. OK. Gotta go. Bye."

And it's only once the line is dead that I remember that his mother has died as well. I can be so selfish sometimes, it scares me.

I send him a guilty text. "Thanks babe. Sorry about the me, me, me. Love you masses. xxx"

Ricardo immediately answers with, "But if love is never having to say sorry...?"

"Aww... he knows Love Story," I murmur.

After much rather gruesome digging around, I find a front door key in what I assume to be Jenny's mother's handbag. Unable to get any information from the hospital other than the generous visiting times (two-thirty to eight-thirty) I eat another round of crumpets, put my vomit-stained trousers in to wash, and head off on foot towards the town centre.

The grey featureless day does little for Camberley. The pavements look dirty and grey, the houses repetitive and mundane. The town centre with its mall, and its Boots, Body Shop, and Superdrug is so generic it could be literally any town in Britain.

The crisp clean air and scintillating light, the postcard beaches and fragrant forests feel truly an ocean away today. It's never until you leave that you realise what you're leaving behind. And it's never until you return that remember why you left in the first place.

**

I haven't really thought much about what to expect at the hospital. I suppose that if I guessed I would picture Jenny sitting up in bed, looking chipper, and being rude to the nurses. Or perhaps, perched on the edge of the bed waiting to be taken home – irritated because I am somehow, "late."

In fact, she is snoring lightly when I arrive, so I sit and watch her sleeping, and wonder if the greyness of her complexion is caused by lack of makeup or if it reveals something unsettling about her condition.

Some fifteen minutes into my bedside vigil, I glance over and see that she has one eye open. I tip my head sideways and lean into her field of view. "Hello you," I say. "How are you feeling?"

Jenny stares at me in silence. She looks sad. If she is thinking about anything, I would guess that it's the loss of her mother. Poor Jenny, she's really not having a good month. Thinking back to Ricardo, and Nick, and her dad, and her brother, I realise sadly that she isn't having a particularly good *life.*

Suddenly emotional, I swallow with difficulty. "Are you OK?" I ask. "How are you feeling?"

Because she still says nothing, I murmur, "I'll be back in a minute," and cross the ward to speak to a nurse.

"Excuse me, but, Jenny Holmes, she looks awake but she isn't speaking... Is she OK?"

"Her over there?" the nurse asks in a thick Polish accent. "The girl who have seizures last night?"

"Yes. Did she have more?"

She shrugs. "I don't know. I just know she have seizures."

"Right. She's not answering me. Is that normal?"

"She's tiring, I expect," the nurse says. "They always are after seizure."

"Right."

"She just needs sleep," she says.

"Should I just leave her then?"

"Sit with her. I'm sure she like that. But don't expect too much talk."

"Right. And do we know... you know... *why*, yet?"

"Why?"

"Why she's having seizures?"

The nurse shakes her head. "She's book for CT scan at four, so we know more later. Now, I'm sorry, but I have to change dressing, so..."

"Sure, sorry."

I take a deep breath and return to Jenny's side. "Are you actually awake sweetie?" I ask. "Because I'm not even sure if you can hear me."

Jenny rolls her eyes, which I take as confirmation not only that she can, but that the sarcasm centre of her brain is still working.

"Do you need me to do anything?" I ask. "Do you want me to bring Sarah in to see you?"

Jenny's brow wrinkles, her expression shifts to concern. "Sarah," she repeats quietly.

"She's at Susan's. She's fine. Do you want me to go get her? To bring her. Do you want to see her?"

"No," she says.

"Right."

I sit for a minute or so and wonder if she actually wants *me* here. It's not at all clear. "Is Sarah OK at Susan's? Are you happy with that?" I finally ask.

"Susan's," Jenny says, visibly struggling to keep her eyes open. "Yes."

"I think I should just let you sleep," I say. "I'll come back this evening."

I lean in to kiss her forehead, and she says, "Tom."

At first I think she's confused, and answer, *"Mark.* Yes?"

Jenny swallows and says again, "Tom?"

"You want me to call Tom?"

She blinks slowly, so I force a smile and nod slowly. "Of course," I say.

"Thanks," she says, her eyes already closing.

I walk all the way back to town battling with myself to not feel peeved that she wants Tom rather than myself. *"Maybe Tom should come and sort everything out,"* I think, meanly. But as I walk, I manage to calm myself down. Jenny never had a lot of friends, and the fact that Tom was the only person our age at her mum's funeral speaks reams.

In town, I buy more crumpets and some strong cheddar, and then reluctantly head back to the close. I'm not really looking forward to speaking to Susan again, and I'm certainly in no hurry to call Tom.

The entire walk ends up taking well over an hour but the exercise clears my head.

Feeling sweaty but calmer, I head straight to the neighbour's house.

"Hello," she says in a reassuringly neutral tone of voice. "Have you been? Have you seen her?"

I nod. "Yes. Is Sarah...?" I glance behind her.

"They're playing out back," she says.

"Good. She's in a pretty bad way," I tell her. "I just came from there. She can barely answer, 'yes' or 'no.'"

"And do they know what it is yet?"

"No. Maybe later. They're doing some scans or something this afternoon. Is Sarah OK with you? For the moment?"

"Sure," Susan says. "But will Jenny be back tonight? Because I can't look after her tomorrow. We're off to Sutton."

"Sutton?"

"Yeah, my sister's place. I tried to call the hospital, but they wouldn't put me through."

"No, well, as I say... she's pretty ill."

"So if she's not back by tomorrow, well, we'll have to think of something else."

"I'll have to take her," I say. "But that's OK."

"She seems to remember you at least," Susan says, a shadow slipping across her features.

"I've known Jenny for twenty years," I tell her. "We even dated once," I add, hoping that this hint of heterosexuality will reassure her.

"Right," Susan says in a tone of voice which indicates that my strategy probably hasn't worked. "Well anyway, let's just hope she's out by then, eh?"

"Yes," I agree. "Let's hope for that. But otherwise, Sarah will be fine. Really."

Susan nods. "OK," she says, grudgingly. "Fair enough."

As I open the front door to Jenny's house, I think, with some relief, that I don't have Tom's number anymore. But that's too selfish. I can, of course, use directory enquiries. Or I could, if I knew Tom's current address, or even the number for directory enquiries.

On the hall table, though, is Jenny's Nokia. I should have taken it to her, of course. In the recent-call list, I find an entry entitled, *TOM - MOB*.

I sink to the bottom stair, groan and hit the "call" button.

Tom speaks before I can say a word, saying, "Hello beautiful, how are you bearing up?"

It's the first time I have heard this voice – this, normal, happy, *loving* voice, since we split up. The contrast with the way he spoke to me yesterday is so marked that I'm momentarily lost for words. After a few seconds listening to him say, "Hello? Hello? I can't hear you baby!" I hang up.

The landline in the house rings almost immediately. I brace myself and pick up on the third ring. "I couldn't hear you Jen," Tom says. "Could you hear *me?*"

"It's Mark, Tom," I tell him.

"Oh," he says, his tone shifting instantly. "Can you put Jenny on? She tried to call me and..."

"It was me," I say. "She asked me to phone you. She's in hospital."

"In *hospital?*"

"She had some kind of fit. Just after you left."

A shadow appears behind the patterned glass window of the front door. A bunch of letters, presumably addressed to Marge, plop onto the doormat. And then, without a sound, the shadow spookily fades away.

"A fit?" Tom asks. "What do you mean a fit? What kind of fit?"

"We don't know yet. They're doing some tests this afternoon."

"Where is she? Can I call her?"

"Frimley Park – it's here, in Camberley. But there's not much point for the moment. She's virtually comatose."

"Right," he says. "Was it *stress?* Is that the cause? Because, well..."

"We don't know, Tom," I say, cutting him off before he can imply that I am somehow responsible.

I hear him sigh deeply on the other end of the line. "How come you're at her house, anyway? And how come you have her phone?"

"I had to stay. Because of Jenny. And the ambulance guys didn't give us a ten minute window to go around collecting her stuff."

"Ambulance?" he says. *"God!"*

"She was vomiting and..."

"She had a lot to drink."

"It wasn't drink or stress. She had, like, an epileptic fit or something. Anyway, now you know. She wanted you to know."

"Maybe I should call," he says.

"I don't know. You can try, but they probably won't put you through."

"I can't come back up. Not till the weekend. Can you..."

"Yes?"

"Nothing. Never mind," he says.

"Tell her you called? Let you know if there's any news?"

"I suppose," he says. "Both of those."

"Sure. Of course."

"Right."

I can almost hear him struggling to find the largesse to thank me. "Bye Tom," I say, saving him the pain. "I have to go now." I stand and move through to the lounge.

"Right. Yes. Bye," Tom says.

I sink onto the sofa and look around me at the old-lady lounge and sniff the air and think about the strange flowery old-person smell the place has. It's actually making me feel a bit nauseous. Opposite, I spot a potential culprit – a plug in air freshener. I think about Jenny saying that the house, *"had death in it,"* and decide that making the smell of the place a little more neutral, a little less mumsy, can only be a good thing.

I open all the windows, and hunt down three plug-in air fresheners which I stick in a kitchen drawer, and two bowls of really stinky potpourri which I bin.

From the upstairs back bedroom – Marge's old room – I can see Sarah playing in the back garden with the neighbour's daughter. I stand unseen and observe her for a moment as she screams and runs around. She has grown up so much since I last saw her, she looks like a proper little person now. I wonder how well I will manage if I have to look after her tomorrow. I wonder what she eats. I wonder if she goes to the toilet on her own. What I don't know about... God, how old is she even? I squint as I calculate her age: four and a half, I decide. So what I don't know about four and a half year olds, would fill any number of encyclopaedias.

Back downstairs I pull a blanket over my shoulders against the breeze. The blanket too, smells distinctly floral.

I wander around the house with my iPhone checking for wifi and discover that if I lean against the right hand bay window, I can use an unknown benefactor's network. I check the time, and Skype the beach-house but there's no answer, so I text Ricardo asking him to phone me on the landline again.

And then I return to the sofa and lie back and close my eyes. I can vaguely hear Sarah screaming in the back garden, and as I drift towards sleep, I think for some reason that I'm back in Nice and that Jenny and Sarah are in the upstairs flat.

"Chupa Chups!"

"Ummm... God, I was falling asleep."

"You want I call back later?"

"No! No, I want to talk to you babe. Where are you? Are you back home?"

"Uhuh. You don't have caller id over in England?"

"We do, but not in this house. It's all distinctly old-school here. But I found out that the neighbours have wifi. Do you want me to Skype you instead?"

"No, it's fine."

"Skype is cheaper."

"I don't want to mess around with the computer Chupy."

"But I can Skype you on the landline."

"It's *fine.* Are you OK?"

"Sure. And you?"

"Yes. Fine."

"How are you coping?"

"Fine. I *said.*"

"How is Paloma?"

"She's fine. She's fat babe. I think Maria feed her too much. How is Jenny?"

"She's almost unconscious."

"Unconscious?"

"No, well, she *isn't.* But she's really really tired. She can hardly speak."

"Oh, OK. Well, that's normal. After a seizure."

"They're doing some tests – scans and stuff – this afternoon. I'm going back this evening to see if she can come home. I hope she can, because otherwise I have to look after Sarah tomorrow."

"Ah, little Sarah. Is still with the... *voisine?*"

"The neighbour, yes. She doesn't like me much."

"Sarah?"

"No, the neighbour."

"How could anyone not like you Chups?"

"I know. Can you imagine such a thing?"

"And Tom. Have you seen more of Tom?"

"No. He lives a long way away, thank God. I had to call him though."

"What for?"

"Well, to tell him about Jenny."

"Right. What did you say?"

"I just told him she's in hospital."

"Is he coming?"

"I don't think so. I don't think he can. Did I tell you what Sarah said? To Susan, the neighbour?"

Of course it's a mistake to tell Ricardo about Sarah's comment – that I'm the man who stole Mummy's boyfriend. That territory is too emotionally complex for Ricardo, so it merely puts the dampers on our conversation, it merely hastens its end.

I realise too, that I am talking about *me* again, but it's difficult to do otherwise when the only stuff happening in Ricardo's life – namely, his mother's death – is stuff he doesn't seem to want to discuss.

Still, I tell him I miss him and he says I'll be home soon enough, and I hang up feeling desperate for more, which is at least better than feeling like you've had enough.

I toast another round of crumpets. I'm sure I must be putting on weight on my new unhealthy crumpet diet, but when you haven't been able to get hold of a favourite food for years, it's just too hard to resist. Plus, I tell myself that with all that is going on, I deserve a little treat. And then another. And another.

Ricardo: A Potentially Bad Move

My fling with Cristina lasted four and a three quarter days longer than I intended – it lasted five. The sex was good. She was a horny bitch (she claimed that Carlos had gone off sex, but then doesn't every unfaithful woman say that?) and being in Bogotá was a good change for me. I got to see a lot of people I thought I had lost from view, you know, family, school-friends, people like that. And I felt OK about everything really; if I wasn't overly suffering from the disappearance of *mi mamá* it was in part, I'm sure, because Cristina was keeping me so busy. And busy we were.

The end was nearing though. We both knew from the beginning that our story would be a short one because it was limited in time by the return of Carlos on Monday and my own flight to Santa Marta now booked for Tuesday Morning. I would fly back and forget Cristina, and she would forget me, and everyone would be happy.

When I lied to you, I knew immediately that it was a stupid thing to do. You asked me if I was back at home and I did a split-second mental calculation on the current state of the chess board and decided that it was riskier to admit that I was still in Bogotá than it was to lie and say I had returned back home.

But I regretted it the second I said it, Chupy, because as soon as I said that, I had to start calculating all the future moves. I had to think about how you might find out that I lied: if you phoned the house, if Maria told you, if you suddenly found out that you did have caller id after all, and I had to start working out what I would say to cover my tracks if that happened.

That did me good though, because I realised suddenly that I was taking risks, and I realised that the one thing I didn't want was to fuck everything up.

I wish that I had gone back one day earlier though: Cristina made us a romantic farewell roast pork dinner with candles and Champagne, which honestly was the *last* thing that I wanted because I was all about breaking the links, not strengthening them. And then she asked for my phone number, and I said I would think about it, and she got angry and cried and dumped the dinner in the trash.

Afterwards I gave her a wrong number (I swapped two digits so that she might think she had made a mistake) but it made her happy, so we had a farewell fuck and smoked a joint and ordered pizza to replace the pork.

I left Bogotá with a sick feeling in my stomach. I left with an unnerving sensation that somewhere along the line I had made a false move, that I had somehow overlooked a vital corner of the board and left my king exposed to future attack. But then, as I travelled home, it seemed that I had got away with it, and I started to feel better; I started to feel quite pleased with my little Bogotan adventure.

Jenny: Quite Big

I thought that they would tell me something as soon as I came out of the scanner. I thought they would show me the scan, in fact.

They slid me from the machine and helped me down onto the wheelchair, and I asked, as planned, "Did you find anything?"

I had rehearsed that phrase over and over as that terrifying machine buzzed and whirred around me. And I had rehearsed the answer too. I knew with absolute certainty that the reply would come in the form of a joke. *"Absolutely nothing, love. Your head's entirely empty."*

The nurse I asked wasn't apparently the right nurse. He shrugged and nodded at another guy stepping from behind a computer screen.

"Did you find anything?" I asked again.

And he raised an eyebrow and said, "We'll get a doctor to come and explain the results to you."

Which wasn't, of course, how the dialogue was supposed to go.

He didn't look like he was joking. And he *didn't* look like there was nothing.

The doctor took an hour to come along. It's a cliché of course, but that hour was no ordinary hour. Einstein was right – time is not linear.

When the month-long hour was up, a doctor appeared. A tired, grumpy doctor with sprouting nasal hair that I couldn't seem to stop looking at.

He pointed with his chewed ballpoint pen to a vague shadow on a sheet of paper. The pen left marks, and I remember thinking that he should retract it and show some respect for my brain scan.

I asked him how big it was, because that's something people always say on TV dramas, and he said, *"Pretty big, about the size of a golf ball,"* which *didn't* sound like something they say.

I didn't tell Mark when he came in. I pretended to be too tired to talk.

I was still feeling sick and vague and stunned. That was maybe part hangover, or maybe from the drugs, or possibly from the seizures, or perhaps from my "golf-ball." I couldn't really tell which feeling was coming from where.

But mainly, I didn't tell Mark because I simply didn't want to. And there were so many reasons for that.

I hadn't even begun to deal with the information I had just been given. I had a whole backlog of things to deal with from Mum's death to living with Sarah in the house, to... well, Mark turning up.

And it seemed that telling Mark what was wrong with me somehow opened a door to let him in. He would have time to think about what that meant for me, even before I did, and I didn't want that. I didn't trust him enough to let him get there before me. I'm not sure that makes any sense, but it's what I thought.

And then they gave me another round of the pills that made me feel sick, and told me to, "Lay back and try to relax." And I thought, *"Yeah, Right!"*

Under the Circumstances

I'm awoken by the doorbell, and as I fumble and stumble into my clothes, I realise that I have slept well for the first time in a week. Feeling normal because of something as simple as a good night's sleep is an invigorating, optimistic experience.

As I hop into my jeans, I peer out and see Susan and Sarah on the doorstep.

The second I open the front door, Sarah runs past me shouting, "Mum? Mummy? Mum! We had pancakes and strawberries and maypole syrup."

"*Maypole* syrup," I laugh, and Susan smiles at me for the first time ever.

"I told her she's not here," she says. "I said she's at the hotel, but it goes in one ear and out the other at that age. Sorry if this is a bit early, but we have a long drive ahead."

I glance up at the hall clock. "Six-thirty! Wow. I haven't seen six-thirty in a while."

Susan nods. "Your lie-ins are over," she says. "This one goes off like an alarm clock every morning at six."

"*Six?*"

"Sometimes earlier. Will you be OK? She's a bit of a human dynamo."

"I'm sure I'll cope somehow."

Susan hands me a folded post-it. "My mobile number," she says. "Just in case."

I blink slowly at her. "Thanks for that."

"We're back on Sunday."

"Right."

Her husband appears holding his daughter's hand. I nod a "hello" at him and he nods back and then stares at his feet.

"You must be Franny," I say to his daughter. "Hello!"

She too nods and stares at her feet. She's a rotund little girl, which I guess is what having a mum who makes pancakes for breakfast will do for you.

"Shy," Susan says. I'm not sure if she means her daughter or her husband or both. "Did you find the keys?"

"Keys? Oh! Yes."

"Because I *do* have some. I, um, forgot."

"It's fine. I found some. Keep them."

"Right." Then clapping her hands and turning away, she shouts, "OK, let's get this show on the road."

When I close the front door, Sarah is clambering back downstairs. "Where's Mummy?" she asks.

"At the hotel," I say. "Susan told you."

"The same hotel? With the polish machine and the magic fridge?"

"Polish machine?"

"It cleans your shoes."

"Right. OK. And there was a *magic fridge?*"

Sarah nods at me seriously. "Angels fill it up with chocolate when you go out."

I laugh. "Do they? How amazing. I wish I had a magic fridge. No your mum's in a different hotel this time. One where they bring you dinner in bed."

Sarah wrinkles her nose. "In *bed?* Proper dinner?"

"Yes, they bring you a tray with sausages and potatoes and a cup of tea."

"We had sandwiches in bed. And Coke. And chocolate."

"Well it's the same. Only the food's not so much fun."

"I like sausages and mash. Where's Gran?"

I swallow, and clear my throat. "Didn't Mummy tell you?"

Sarah shakes her head, holds on to the bottom bannister and swings one leg around self-consciously.

"Umh, where do *you* think she is?" I ask, stalling for time.

"Mummy says she's gone away."

"Right."

"But Franny says she's died and gone to heaven."

I grind my teeth. May whatever turns out to be truth forgive me for what I'm about to do.

"Well, they're both right," I say. "She's gone away to a place called heaven."

Sarah nods, apparently thinking about this.

"Please don't ask me what heaven is like," I think.

But what Sarah asks is, "Do you want to see my Polly Pockets?"

I laugh. "I'd *love* to see your Polly Pockets."

And so the day passes. We play with Sarah's Polly Pockets – three inch dolls with rubber clothes – for almost two hours.

I ask Sarah what she wants for lunch, and with an expression that reveals that she thinks she's pushing her luck, she asks for alphabet spaghetti. She doesn't seem able to believe it when we head off on a shopping trip to actually look for some.

In fact, I don't think she can believe her luck in general, for, having no idea what to do with a four-and-a-half year old, I become her personal slave, taking her – on order – to the park, to the ice-cream shop, and on a second shopping trip for bangers and mash because she, "Wants to have the same dinner as Mummy."

She asks me repeatedly about her mum and grandma. What will Mummy be eating? Can we go and visit Granny? Do they have chocolate in heaven? (The answer is, of course, *masses* of chocolate.)

But she shows no signs of stress at this strange new situation whatsoever. Her trust in this barely remembered adult called Mark is absolute, and I can't help but think, somewhat nauseously, how easy it must be for bad people to abuse that trust. Suspicion is clearly something we human beings take a while to develop.

There is a single moment, as she eats her sausages, when she suddenly goes quiet. A tiny crease even forms on her forehead. After a day of jubilant monologues and endless questions, the change is immediately apparent.

"Is something wrong?" I ask her. "Don't you like the sausages?"

Sarah looks me straight in the eye and says, "Is Mum with Granny? Is she in heaven too?"

"No, Dumpling. She's in hospital."

"You said she was at the hotel," Sarah says.

"Oh. Yes. Well a hospital *is* a kind of hotel. It's a special hotel where you go when you're tired. That's why they bring your dinner in bed so you don't even have to get up."

"Can we call her on the tephelone?"

"The *te-le-phone*? Of course we can," I say. "We can call her as soon as you've finished your tea."

"And then can we call Granny?" she asks.

I shake my head. "They don't have phones in heaven," I say. "But we can call Mummy at the hospital and wish her goodnight."

We get patched through to Jenny without any problem this time. I listen as Sarah tells Jenny that we had alphabet spaghetti and that Frannie has *three*

Polly Pockets but that I am going to buy her a new one and that Gran is in heaven but we can't phone her because they don't have phones, but they do have chocolate, and, and…

And then I send Sarah upstairs to get her pyjamas on whilst Jenny tells me that I am spoiling her daughter.

"Well, of course I am," I laugh.

"How was she about her gran?" she asks. "I should have told her myself, but I didn't have the heart."

"Fine," I say. "I didn't decide to tell her either. But her friend Franny told her and I couldn't see any point confusing things by saying something different."

"No. You're quite right," Jenny says. "As long as she's OK."

"I don't think she has any idea what it means, actually. She asked me if they have phones in heaven."

"Right," Jenny says. "Do they?"

"Of course they don't."

"No."

"You sound better."

"Yeah, I feel tired still. And these pills they're giving me make me want to puke all the time."

"Poor babe. Have they told you anything?"

"No. Nothing. And nothing about when I can go home either."

"Well don't worry about Sarah," I say. "Everything's fine here."

"I'm sorry Mark. It's hardly fair…"

"Hey. It's fine."

"How long can you stay? I mean, if need be?"

"As long as it takes."

"You don't have a flight booked, or…"

"Not for weeks."

"I'm sure I'll be out by the weekend, but…"

"Really. Don't worry about it."

"Are you coping OK?" Jenny asks. "She can be pretty hard work sometimes."

"Sure. We're fine."

"You can take her to school tomorrow. Ten till four. It'll give you a break and the routine is good for her."

"Sure, no worries."

"She needs a packed lunch or three pounds dinner money. It's just around the corner. She'll show you the way."

"Do you want me to bring *you* anything? Money, or clothes, or your phone?"

"Tomorrow maybe. If they keep me in again. Would that be OK?"

"I could bring Sarah after nursery."

"Sure. That would be nice."

"See you then, then."

"Right."

"Bye."

"Bye. Oh and Mark? If she won't sleep, just lie next to her and read. There's a really boring one about a hibernating dormouse. That usually works."

"No problemo. Bye then."

"Bye – oh, are you still there?"

"Sure."

"Umh, thanks for this. I don't know what to say really..."

"It's fine, Jenny. Honest," I say.

"I feel bad though."

"Well, now we both feel bad. But it's the least I can do. Under the circumstances. Right?"

"I suppose. But thanks anyway."

***

Sarah does indeed wake up at five-thirty the next morning, but all she does is pad downstairs and crawl under my duvet. I'm a bit surprised by this, and can't really decide if it's appropriate, but in the end I'm too sleepy to think about it, so I go with the flow.

"Where's Mummy?" she asks, snuggling against me.

"At the special hotel."

"And Granny?"

"She's gone away."

"Why are you sleeping here?"

"Shhh. Go back to sleep." Which amazingly, for another forty minutes, she does.

As I doze back off myself, I think about how nice this animal warmth is beside me, and how simple our instincts can be. It's such a shame adulthood makes everything so complicated as our desires for human warmth become confused by desire and suspicion and morality. Sarah, with almost cat-like simplicity, wanted to snuggle up, and that's exactly what she did. And her trust in me is more than enough, I now see, to compensate for waking up at five-thirty am.

The early morning calm doesn't last for long of course. At six fifteen she starts to fidget, and at six twenty she starts to talk.

By six thirty I'm in the kitchen thinking about breakfast options.

"What do you *usually* have for breakfast?" I ask her.

"Chocklit biscuits," she says definitely. She's such a bad liar, I laugh out loud.

"Well, I don't think we have any, how does toast sound?"

"With jam?"

"Sure. With jam."

"OK."

But when I open the drawer to take the bread, Sarah's eagle eyes spot the Hobnobs. "See," she says, pulling them out. "Chocklit biscuits."

"Well for each slice of toast you eat, you can have a Hobnob. How does that sound?"

Sarah wrinkles her nose. "But not the crust."

"This bread doesn't have crust," I say.

She points at the vague brown stain around the edge of the loaf.

"Fine," I say. "Without crusts."

I wonder if toast, butter and jam is actually in any way healthier than chocolate biscuits. My guess is that there's not much in it.

She's an amazing kid: funny, helpful, clever... But by the time I leave her at the nursery, I feel as if I have done a full day's work. Boy does she talk! I can feel my brain turning to mush from the simple endless bombardment of kiddy talk. I wonder how heteros manage to put up with it day after day. Maybe it does turn their brains to mush. Maybe a few months of this and I would be buying frozen meals and watching *Who Wants To Be A Millionaire*.

At half past five we get to Jenny's ward and find her sitting on her bed, fully clothed. "God!" she says. *"Finally!* I thought you were coming at four, straight from the nursery."

It's so close to how I imagined she would be yesterday, that I experience a brief unsettling sensation of déjà vu.

"We went to the park, didn't we," I say, lifting Sarah up and putting her next to her mum. "I brought your phone and stuff, but it looks like you're all ready to go."

"Yeah, I'm out of here," Jenny says. "One more over-cooked cabbage leaf and I swear..."

"That good huh?"

"That good."

71

"So what do you think of this hotel?" I ask Sarah who is looking around the ward, wide-eyed.

She shrugs. "Why has that man got tubes in his nose?"

"Because he isn't very well," I say. "The tubes have medicine."

"The other hotel was nicer, wasn't it?" Jenny says.

Sarah nods. "Are we going back there?"

"No, we're going home," Jenny says.

"To Gran's?"

After a silence that lasts exactly one breath, Jenny answers. "Yes. To Gran's."

In the taxi, I ask Jenny what the verdict from the doctors is.

"I don't know," she says. "I have to keep taking the horrible pills."

"Are they still making you feel sick?"

"Yeah," she says. "And really tired too. Well, I *think* it's the pills. I have to go see a specialist on Friday so maybe I can get them changed. Will you still be around?"

"It's entirely up to you," I say.

"Because he's in London, the specialist. So if you could look after Sarah on Friday... Otherwise I can ask one of the neighbours."

"No, it's fine. But why London? And what kind of specialist?"

Jenny turns away to look out of her window. "I don't know," she says. "A woman-who-has-fits specialist I suppose."

"And why London?" I ask again.

"Search me," Jenny says, pulling a circumspect face.

When we get back to the house, I open the front door and Sarah runs straight upstairs. Jenny, for her part, hovers on the doorstep.

"Are you OK?" I ask. "You look a bit pale."

"Yeah," she says.

"Actually, you've gone green. You're not going to faint are you? You're not having another fit?"

Jenny scrunches up her nose. "No. It's just... Look. I haven't been in the house actually. Not since, you know... Not since Mum died."

"Oh," I say thinking back to the funeral and realising that she stayed in the garden the entire time. "God."

"I know."

"Do you want to go down the pub or something, have a pint first?"

"I'm not allowed to drink."

"Oh. OK. You could go back to the hotel for the night maybe?"

Sarah comes back downstairs carrying Polly Pocket. "What are you doing?" she asks as she reaches the porch.

"Nothing," Jenny says.

"Are we going out again?"

Jenny puts one foot upon the doorstep. Her eyes flick down at the hall floor. "No," she says.

I step up beside her and take her hand. "I've been here for the last two days. It's fine," I say.

"Right. On three," Jenny says.

"On three."

"One, two, three, go..." She shakes my hand free and strides along the hall straight into the kitchen where she instantly busies herself filling the kettle and putting teabags in cups. But I catch a glimpse of her face and see that her eyes have a glassy shine to them.

When Sarah heads out into the back garden, Jenny asks, "So what are we telling madam?"

"About?"

"About Mum."

"Oh. Um – that she's in heaven."

"Right."

"I'm sorry. I didn't know what you wanted to say."

"It's fine. I just need to know. So we both say the same thing."

"She's in heaven. And they have lots of chocolate but no phones."

"Oh yeah. I remember now. You told me yesterday. If only, eh?"

"Sorry?"

Jenny shrugs. "I'm not, you know... a great believer in heaven."

"No," I say. "But then again, who actually knows? Maybe it'll turn out to be the best description anyone ever stumbled upon. A land of endless chocolate."

"I should have told her. I should have just said. But I thought she'd be too upset," Jenny says, fishing out the teabags and adding milk. "Sugar?"

"No thanks. I thought she'd freak out too, but she seems to accept pretty much anything. She's a great kid."

"She is."

Jenny carries the two cups of tea to the kitchen table and we sit face to face. "So," she says.

"So."

"I'm going to have to go and have a kip once I've had this."

"Right. I can make dinner, so..."

"I'm ever so grateful for, you know... And I'm sorry I was a bitch."

I shrug. "I deserve it. It's karma," I say.

Tears are clearly visible in Jenny's eyes now and after a few sips of tea, I say, "I'm so sorry about your mum."

She sips her tea and flicks away a tear with one finger. "It's not that," she says. "I haven't even had time to think about it. That's the worst thing. Not having the time to think about anything."

I nod. "Sure. What with the hospital and everything. Still, you can have some time-out now. Just rest and think about everything. Get it all into perspective."

"Yes," Jenny says. "Get it all into perspective. Right."

In a Sombre Landscape

Jenny's life imposes its own new rhythm upon mine. In the mornings, Jenny gets up and gives Sarah her breakfast. She claims to be unable to lie in any later these days anyway, and that certainly isn't a problem I share. At nine, she wakes me with a mug of tea and returns upstairs to bed.

I walk Sarah to nursery and pick up any shopping we need on the way home.

When I get back, I Skype Ricardo – the only moment in our corresponding timezones when this is possible. We talk for at least an hour every day. We discuss Jenny's illness (Ricardo is disgusted that the NHS still haven't given her any indication of what's wrong, something he calls worse-than-third-world-service). We talk about Jenny's mourning and Ricardo suggests that I find a way to get us out of her mother's house – clearly a great idea with no apparent solution.

Because Ricardo brings the subject up, we repeatedly discuss Tom as well. I detect a note of jealousy in his repeated probings about Tom's presence (which so far has been limited to a few crisp phone calls to enquire about Jenny.) Ricardo's jealousy irritates me, but of course it reassures me too.

In fact we talk about pretty much anything as long as it revolves around *my* life rather than his and I'm left wondering if it has always been this way. Anything to do with how Ricardo might be feeling is quickly sewn up with a short sharp, "I'm good, I told you." As ever, I can't work out whether he is selfless, indestructible, or an emotional cripple. But the hours he's prepared to spend talking to me prove his devotion, and I'm never left in any doubt of the fact that he loves me and misses me. Unless he is interrupted by another phone call or the need to go to work, it is never Ricardo that ends our conversation and by the end of our daily chat, even at five thousand miles, I'm always left feeling as loved as I have ever felt. And in the sombre landscape in which I find myself, that love shines like a lighthouse in the distance. The fact that he exists, the fact that he loves me, the fact that he's waiting there to wrap his arms around me makes it all ultimately bearable.

On Thursday, when Jenny hands me my mug of tea, she says, "You should, you know, take the room upstairs. There's a bed going to waste up there. This whole sofa thing is silly."

I sit up, wrap the quilt around me and pull a face. "I know," I say. "But I don't feel that comfortable about... well..."

"I know."

"You won't even go in there."

Jenny nods and slumps on the sofa beside me. "I know," she says.

"It's full of all her stuff."

Jenny nods. "I know," she says again. "I'm sorry, I can't... I thought if it was your room, rather than hers, well, that might help. But I can't clear her stuff. I'm not up to it."

She glances around the room – the same gesture I have seen her do a hundred times. She always looks like she's scanning the horizon for some hidden potential assailant, but this time, because of the context, I understand what she's doing.

"You're not comfortable staying in this house *at all* are you?" I ask.

She shrugs. "It's like you say... it's just all the stuff. I keep checking to see that none of it has moved. And I keep being surprised that it hasn't. Which is weird, I know. It's like it's all waiting for someone who's not coming back." Her eyes are misting and I see her force herself to stop and stand. "I have to go for my kip," she says. "I feel shit."

And so it is that I take on this new task – the gut-wrenchingly sad job of trying to remove as many of Jenny's mother's personal possessions from around the house as discreetly as possible: a cardigan here, some knitting needles there, her underwear from the chest of drawers. As Jenny snoozes, I creep around binning a friend's mother's clothes and moving her clutter to boxes in the attic, slowly but surely erasing the traces of her life.

Jenny notices every single change – I can sense the way each vanished object makes her skin prickle. Occasionally she asks questions such as, "It *was* you that took her toothbrush, right?" and I nod sadly and stroke her arm.

"Good," she says. "Just checking."

My final push to de-grannify the house comes on Friday.

With Sarah at nursery and Jenny insisting she wants to go to her appointment in London on her own, it's the perfect opportunity.

I blitz the house removing as many traces of Marge's personal possessions as possible. Of course this being Marge's house, *everything* was a personal possession, but I try to remove anything that only she would have used and anything someone of my generation simply wouldn't give houseroom to. Out go doilies beneath pot plants, and a few of the plants themselves. Out go antimacassars from chair backs, a flowery pink umbrella, some unfinished knitting, a calendar in the kitchen on which the days had been crossed out, ceasing on the sixteenth of September. From the kitchen I bin half a jar of Horlicks, a mug marked "Grandma" and a copy of *Diet For Life - Live to a hundred by eating nature's superfoods.* I roll rugs and cart them up to the attic. I move furniture to new, less satisfactory but at least different configurations.

In her bedroom I remove everything except the furniture which I inexplicably wash down before rotating the entire contents of the room ninety degrees clockwise. I strip the bed, flip the mattress and put the curtains in to wash before covering every available surface with the few possessions I have in my own bag. Even being in the room still gives me the shivers, but Jenny said she thought it might help if I made it my room, so that's what I attempt to do.

By the time I have finished, the house looks as different as I can make it look without actually redecorating the place.

I sit back and wait for Jenny to return, a little exhausted but pleased at how uncluttered the place suddenly feels. And then I start to worry. I start to think that I have maybe gone too far and that Jenny will walk through the door and have a nervous breakdown.

When Jenny *does* arrive she looks grey and drawn. She looks like she doesn't have the energy for a breakdown.

She looks around, blinks twice, and says, "Can you pay the taxi somehow? I'll get it back to you, but right now I just need to sleep."

As she climbs the stairs to her own unchanged room, I head out to the waiting black cab, fumbling in my wallet and counting the change from my pocket as I walk.

"Alright mate? How much is it?" I ask, working out that I have just under nineteen pounds.

He winks at me and taps the top of the meter. It reads £137.50

I laugh. "You're joking, right?"

"Nope," he says. "No sense of humour, me. You can ask my missus."

I frown at him. "That is... Is that pounds?"

"Nah mate, it's Pesetas," he says.

"Where did she...?"

"London. St Thomas' Hospital. Door to door."

"Right."

"I told her the train was cheaper, but you know women."

"Right. Umh... Jesus."

He beckons to me so I lean in the window.

"I don't think she's well, mate," he says in a confidential tone. "I don't think she could face public transport if you know what I mean. Don't give her a hard time – I don't think she's having a very good day."

"Well no," I say. "No, of course. It's just that, I, um, don't have that kind of cash."

But the cabby takes Visa, Mastercard and just about any other method of payment on planet Earth, so I stick it on one of my cards and wish him a safe journey back.

The taxi dealt with, I peep into Jenny's room to see if she wants to talk, but she insists, quite aggressively, that she needs to *sleep*.

My mind racing as to just how bad her day can have been – and why – I head off to pick Sarah up from the nursery.

The next morning, I'm awoken by Sarah pulling the sleeve of my t-shirt. I open one eye and grunt – despite this being my first night in a proper bed for nearly a week, I have slept just about as badly as I have *ever* slept.

"Why are you in Gran's bed?" Sarah asks with ear-piercing brightness.

"Umh?"

"Who moved everything? Did Mummy?"

"Shhh."

"Where are all the things?"

"Um?"

"All the things. Where are they?"

"In the attic, now come and have a sleep."

"The attic?"

"Up there," I say, pointing at the ceiling as Sarah climbs into bed.

"In heaven?"

"No. Just in a little room up there."

"Why are you in Gran's bed?"

"Why are *you* in here? It's only six. Where's Mummy?"

"She's not getting up today. She said to wake you up instead."

"Did she now?"

"Lazy Sunday."

"It's Saturday. Now, go to sleep."

But there's just no way Sarah is going back to sleep. She fidgets and talks and fidgets some more and within minutes I'm feeling wide awake myself – wide awake and hungry and grumpy. So I get up and make breakfast.

I pour Sarah a bowl of cereal and park her in front of cbeebies on TV. It's the first time I have resorted to the electronic babysitter, and I'm more than impressed at just how powerful and instantaneous the box's hypnotic effect is. Click. Silence!

Sarah suitably paralysed by the Tweenies, I return to the kitchen and watch the sky as it turns from deepest grey to... Actually, it doesn't change much this morning. Maybe from nighttime-grey to daytime-grey. Apparently our run of good weather is over.

I'm feeling a little grey myself – tired and a bit depressed and a little resentful at Jenny's decision to stay in bed. I could do with a cuddle, and I don't mean with Sarah. I'm really missing Ricardo this morning.

At nine I take Jenny a cup of tea, as much as anything, to find out if she has any intention of getting up. But her responses are entirely monosyllabic.

"Are you OK?"

"No."

"Do you need anything?"

"No."

"Fine. I'll see you later then."

"Right."

At ten, as Sarah and I head out the front door, it is starting to drizzle. The temperature has dropped spectacularly too, and I can see my breath. A reminder that we're heading towards winter here. Thank God I will be back in Colombia by the time it hits.

"What's wrong with Mummy?" Sarah asks as I button her coat.

"She's not feeling well."

"Has she got flu?"

"Something like that."

"Franny had flu and I wasn't allowed to go round in case I catched it."

"*Caught* it. Right. OK, come on Miss, let's go."

"Where's the brella? It's raining."

"The *um*brella? It's in the attic."

"Why?"

"We can buy another one in town."

"Why?"

"Because I want to buy one."

"Can we buy a Polly Pocket too?"

"Yes. Exactly. We can find you a Polly Pocket too."

"You have to go to Toys R Us for Polly Pockets. Are we going in the car?"

"No."

"Why not?"

"I'm not insured for it."

"What's in sured?"

"A special thing I don't have."

"Why?"

And so passes our morning. Sarah's questions are constant and random and if truth be told, I don't think she's even very interested in answers. I learn not to exhaust myself going into too much detail.

We take the bus into town – Sarah insists that we travel on the top deck and memories come flooding back of the bus I used to take to school. Upstairs was the smoking section in those days – imagine!

We buy a new "brella" and track down a Polly Pocket without, thankfully, having to brave Toys R Us. And then the three of us – myself, Sarah, and Polly Pocket #3 – walk very very slowly back to the house.

When we get home, Jenny is sitting at the kitchen table in her dressing gown.

"Look Mummy!" Sarah says, bouncing the doll across the table.

Jenny squints at her daughter as if her squeaky voice is causing her physical pain. "That's nice," she says. "Why don't you take her upstairs and show her her new home."

"Are you feeling any better?" I ask once Sarah has bounded obediently away.

By way of reply, Jenny simply shrugs. Her eyes look puffy as if she has been crying, but it could just be lack of makeup.

"What happened yesterday?" I ask her.

"Yesterday?"

"In London."

"Nothing really. They did some tests."

"Tests?"

"Yeah."

"What tests?"

"I don't know really."

"Right... Do you want coffee?"

"No ta."

"How can you not know what tests they did?"

"Oh, actually, if you're making it, I will have one after all."

"Sure. So you must have some idea."

"I was tired, Mark. I was out of it. I have to go back on Tuesday."

"Maybe I should come with you."

"Maybe you should."

I sigh and busy myself with the coffee and wonder if she is being elusive or if it's really possible that she knows so little.

"Why did you get a taxi home?" I ask.

"I'm sorry?"

"You got a taxi all the way home. It cost like a hundred and forty quid. Were you just tired, or..."

"I'll get the money back to you."

"It's not the money. But did something happen? In London?"

"No, nothing happened in London."

"Right."

"Tom's coming tomorrow by the way."

"Ouch. You *are* mean today."

"If you want to vanish somewhere for the day, I'd understand."

"Would you *rather* I vanished?"

"Not really... but I'd understand."

I place the cafetière on the table along with two mugs and the sugar bowl. "Just let it brew for a bit," I say.

Jenny looks up at me. Her eyes are glistening.

"Oh, babe," I say. "Is it your mum? It was bound to hit you at some point."

"Jesus!" Jenny mutters, standing. "Can't you just leave me alone? I mean, it's questions, questions, questions. You're worse than bloody Sarah!"

I watch as she walks from the kitchen and heads back upstairs. "Your *coffee?*" I call after her, pulling a face.

I sit and wonder if my presence in the house is getting on her nerves. Maybe I should leave definitively. There are certainly places I'd rather be. With Tom coming tomorrow I can't think of many places I'd *less* rather be.

Sarah returns carrying her three dolls. "Mummy's grumpy today," she says, thoughtfully.

And I realise that, for the moment, I *can't* really leave. "You're right," I say. "She is, *really* grumpy. Best just to let her sleep. So! Show me those. What's different about the one we bought today?"

One Slap Too Many

On Sunday morning, when I get up, I have every intention of heading straight out and leaving Tom and Jenny to it.

I have spent half the night imagining a cosy love-in with the pair of them and it's not an appetising prospect.

The second I enter the kitchen, though, Jenny stands. "Oh you're up," she says. "I hardly slept, so if you could keep an eye on Madam, I'll head back up for a kip."

"Oh," I say.

"Is that OK?"

"I suppose... I was going to go out. What time's Tom arriving?"

"About twelve, I think."

"And are you still cooking him Sunday lunch?"

Jenny shrugs. "I was going to try to con you into doing it, but if you're out for the day we can just order pizza. No worries."

"Yeah. I didn't think... I mean, I thought it was better that way."

"It's fine," Jenny says, already climbing the stairs. "Really. Just let me get an hour's kip, and you can be gone before he even gets here."

I poke my head into the lounge and see Sarah watching TV. "Move back a bit," I tell her. "You'll hurt your eyes." I pull a face at the realisation that I suddenly sound like my mother.

Sarah points at the TV. "That's Bumper," she says, touching the screen where an image of a dirty rabbit is jumping up and down. "He's very naughty."

I cross the room and drag her six feet back from the screen. "You're too close," I say again.

"Are we going to Tesco's?"

"Tesco's?"

"Mummy said we have to go to Tesco's. For dinner."

And with a smile and a sigh, that's exactly what I resign myself to doing.

My intention is simply to return with the shopping and run away quickly, but Sarah enthusiastically offers to help make dinner, "as a surprise for Mummy," and so we start to peel potatoes and prepare brussels sprouts. And the truth is that with my little assistant, I rather enjoy it all.

Once the food is all ready to roll, I plop Sarah back in front of the cyber-nanny and Skype Ricardo on my iPhone but we have barely said, "hello," when Tom rings the doorbell.

Still holding the phone to my ear, I open the front door. "Two seconds," I say to Ricardo. "Hey Tom," I say, keeping my tone as neutral as possible. "Jenny's gone back to bed, but go make yourself a cuppa and I'm sure she'll be up in a bit."

Tom doesn't take the hint. Instead, he follows me into the lounge and sits next to Sarah, but facing the other way. He sits and stares at me.

"Nice phone," he eventually says. "Where did you get that?"

"Is that Tom?" Ricardo asks.

"Yeah. He just got here. But I'm going out."

"Is that still the phone *I* gave you?" Tom asks.

"Tom!" I protest.

"Only asking."

"It is, and I'm talking to someone on it."

"Why *someone?*" Ricardo asks. "Why don't you say it's me?"

"Is that Ricardo on the line?" Tom asks.

"Yes. Yes, it's Ricardo."

"Ooh. Give him my love," Tom says.

"Put him on," Ricardo says.

"No, I don't think so," I say, looking at Tom's curled lip.

"Are you going to sleep with him?" Ricardo asks.

"Ricardo!" I say, glaring at Tom and heading through to the kitchen.

"Sorry."

"Well, where did *that* come from?"

"He makes me jealous."

"Well, he shouldn't."

"No, sorry. Hey Chupy, I have to go. My mobile ring."

"But Ric..."

I frown at the phone, and then look up to see Tom watching me. "Problems in paradise?" he asks.

"No," I say. "Everything's fine. He had to go. His mobile rang. Work I expect."

"He still in Colombia?"

83

"Well yes."

"It's a long way."

"I'm sorry?"

"Well, you know what they say."

"I have a feeling you're going to tell me."

"While the cat's away and all that."

"I beg your pardon?"

"Nothing," Tom says. He opens the oven and peers inside. "Ooh, roast dinner. Missy has been busy."

"Yeah," I say. "Just stick the oven on when Jenny gets up. And put the veg on twenty minutes before."

"You're not staying?"

"No."

"Shame."

His voice is just neutral enough for me to be unsure if this final comment was sarcasm or regret. Which is just as well, as I'm a hair's breadth away from rearranging his features.

I stomp angrily into town and sit in the window of Pizza Express and in a vague attempt at cheering myself up, I order my favourite pizza Florentine. I watch as the sky darkens and as spots of rain appear on the plate glass window and try not to think about Tom, which is entirely impossible of course. Tom was hardly a bastion of monogamous virtue and his self-righteous attacks are so unfair, so gallingly inappropriate that I'm torn between feeling relieved that I left and wishing I had stayed long enough to punch him.

And I try not to think about what he said about Ricardo. Tom knows nothing about my relationship with Ricardo, but he does know just enough to press my buttons. Like a heat-seeking missile his comments have gone straight to the only existing chink in our armour – the fact that my relationship with Ricardo was born from mutual cheating. Neither of us could claim to be unaware of what the other is capable.

But Ricardo wouldn't cheat on me any more than I would, and if he did, I'm not even sure if I would care. I think about this for a bit and then strike it. I almost certainly *would* care. But the point is that we're *in love*. And I *believe* that people who are *in love* don't cheat. But *beliefs*... How many times in the history of this planet did a man come to the realisation that *they* were wrong?

I make lunch last as long as I can, and then head to the nine-screen cinema complex where Ratatouille brings a dose of welcome relief. I just wish that I had brought Sarah with me. She would have loved this.

When I get back to the close, Tom's Beetle is still outside. I would turn around and head back to the cinema, but it's starting to rain quite heavily now, so I quietly let myself in and begin to creep upstairs to my room.

As I reach the landing, the toilet flushes and the bathroom door opens. No escape.

"Oh, you're back," Tom says, buttoning his fly. "I'm just leaving so..."

He looks unusually sombre. His eyes are bloodshot. He looks, in fact, as if he has been crying.

"Right," I say.

I pass him and head for my room, but Tom grabs the sleeve of my sweatshirt and stops me in my tracks. "Mark?" he says.

I turn to face him, and for a moment I think he is going to hug me. And then I see him look at my lips and I decide that he is going to kiss me. And in that instant, bizarrely, I remember how that *felt*. I remember the exact feeling of Tom's lips on mine, and in spite of myself, lick my lips.

But Tom doesn't move. He swallows. I see his Adam's apple bob. And then he says, *"Look..."*

"Yes?"

"I think you're a prick."

I wonder if he *wants* me to punch him. I snort. "I'm thinking less and less of you as it happens Tom."

"But..."

"But?"

"Well, thanks."

"Thanks?"

"For looking after Jenny for me. I can't be here, and, well, thanks."

The idea that Tom is somehow thanking me makes me sweat with anger before I even know why.

I frown at him and say, "Goodbye Tom. Have a good journey home."

But as I close my bedroom door in his face, I realise why it's so very, very irritating. The fact of his thanks implies that I am somehow doing this *for him*. In fact, he even said that. "Thanks for looking after her *for me*." I sit on the edge of the bed and wrestle with my desire to leave – to throw my things in my bag and walk out the door right now.

After five minutes Sarah knocks on my door and pokes a Polly Pocket through the gap. In a silly squeaky voice which is presumably the voice of Polly herself, she says, "Mummy says there's tea and choklit cake downstairs if you want some."

"Is Tom still here?" I ask.

Sarah pushes the door wide open and shakes her head gravely. "He left."

"Right," I say.

"Do you like Tom?" she asks.

I frown. "Sure. Why do you ask?"

"He made Mummy cry," she tells me. "And now she's all sad."

Downstairs Jenny smiles up at me unconvincingly. She too looks like a train wreck. Certainly something has been playing havoc with her mascara.

"Tom brought all these cakes," she says. "We saved you the eclairs."

"My favourite," I say, sitting down.

"Yes. Tom said so," she says. "Sorry about all that. And thanks for lunch. It was lovely. I'm sorry you felt you had to leave."

"Everything OK between you two?" I ask.

"Sure," Jenny says. "Why?"

"Dunno," I say. "A strange atmosphere. You look like you've been crying, too."

"Nope," Jenny says, swiping at her eyes. "Anyway, why would we argue?"

I shrug. "I don't know. About me perhaps?"

Jenny laughs. "No," she says.

"Why are you laughing?"

"Well, why would we argue *about you?*" Jenny says.

Which though I can't work out why, feels like another slap.

Which feels like one slap too many.

"I'm leaving tomorrow," I say. The words have left my lips before I even know that I'm going to say them.

I'm not sure quite how I expect Jenny to react, but it certainly isn't the way she *does* react. "What time?" she asks.

Ricardo: Speechless

Initially, I was happy to have the interruption of course.
I could hear Tom in the background just waiting to pounce on you, only you couldn't see it Chupy, and he was bound to bad-mouth me too; I could imagine exactly the kind of thing that he and Jenny would be saying about me. Of course I should have thought about that when you decided to go to England in the first place, but I didn't.

Anyway when my mobile rang, I was glad to end the call, but then the voice on the other end sent a shiver right down my spine babe because I couldn't see any possible way she could have got my correct number.

For a moment I was speechless. I just listened to her voice, saying, *Hello? Ricardo? Hello?*

Cristina? I asked, and she replied, *Hola, guapo, – Hello beautiful, God it's good to hear your voice*, and of course I couldn't even ask her how she had got the number because that would involve admitting that I had given her a bad number in the first place, so I just said, *Oh hello,* and tried to pretend that everything was normal.

She told me that she missed me and I had to fight the urge to say the same thing back, not because I *did* miss her (I honestly hadn't thought about her once since I got home) but it's just what you say when someone says they miss you, isn't it? You say, *I miss you too.* Only I didn't. I hoped she would notice that.

To remind her that she had a husband, and that I knew this, I asked her instead if Carlos was back, and she said that, yes, he was but that *he's an asshole,* and that she couldn't stand him touching her anymore and I thought, *Oh Jesus – problem.*

I told her that I was sorry but that I couldn't really talk, and she said that, *of course,* I wasn't alone. *Your girlfriend?* she asked, and I lied and said, *Uhuh,* as if someone was beside me and Cristina sounded disappointed but told me that she understood entirely and that she would just wait for me to phone her back another time.

But I was furious after that Chupy. I couldn't work out which annoyed me the most: you and Tom getting all cosy together, or Cristina somehow getting my number. And I couldn't decide whether to call her back or change my number. And I couldn't decide whether to call you back or not, and what I should say if I did. I couldn't work out what I would have to say to either of you in order to make Tom or Cristina vanish forever.

My first patient was the kind that would usually cheer me up – the kind I would usually laugh about with you when I got home.

He was a sixty year old fisherman with one of those inexplicably wealthy sons, and he wanted to know how best to cure his impotency. He couldn't get it up with his wife, he said, and his dilemma, and he was totally sincere babe, was whether he was better off with Viagra or, as his son had offered, a twenty-year-old Argentinian whore, and I was in such a bad mood that even advising him that combining the two would probably do the trick didn't cheer me up one bit, because you weren't back home for me to tell, and because I now had other things on my mind.

Will It Be Fine?

I have just finished packing my bag when Jenny enters the room and sits on the edge of her mother's bed. A little sunshine is leaking though a complex sky outside, catching flecks of floating dust in its rays.

"You've moved everything around," she says, apparently noticing this for the first time.

"Yeah, as much as possible, I did."

Jenny nods thoughtfully. "It's better," she says.

"Well, at least you can lie in bed and look at the stars now."

"No curtains," she says.

"They're drying. On the line."

"Right. Look. Have I upset you?" she asks. "Because, you know, I'm all over the place at the moment and I didn't mean to..."

I shrug and sit down beside her. I sigh deeply. "It's just... I thought I was helping. But I'm just on the outside really, aren't I? Because of everything that's happened. Which is fine. But you have Tom, and I think I should move on."

"You *have* been a help," Jenny says. "You've been brilliant."

"Thanks."

"And Sarah's loved you being around."

"Yes. I've liked seeing her too. She's a great kid."

"Where are you going now? To France, or back to Colombia?"

"I thought I'd head to the south coast for a few days. Have a look at Eastbourne. Maybe Brighton too, for old times' sake. But don't tell Tom."

"No."

"And then on to Nice. Ricardo wants me to look in on his flat."

"God, does he still have that?"

"Yeah."

"The same one? Overlooking the port?"

"It's rented of course, but yes."

"I had no idea."

"No."

"And have you booked tickets and hotels and stuff?"

I shake my head. "I thought I'd do it as I go along."

"Right."

I frown at Jenny, picking up on some hidden motive. "Why?"

"I... look, I know I haven't been as nice as I should have been, right?"

"Really Jen, it's fine. You've got so much going on."

"But... well... if you could..."

"Yes?"

"If you could stay till tomorrow."

"Tomorrow?"

"Yeah, you know I have to go to London..."

"Oh, yes, right. And you want me to look after Sarah?"

"No, that's not it. No, Sarah will be in nursery and Susan can pick her up."

"Then...?"

"I think I need someone with me."

"In London?"

"Yes. And Tom's working of course, so..."

"Right," I say. I frown and glance a little regretfully at my packed bag. "Is there something specific happening? Is there a specific reason, because..."

Jenny sighs and swallows. "I didn't want to tell you," she says, rubbing her brow and looking out of the window. "It's not fair really. It's not fair on you."

I touch her arm and she looks back at me, watery eyed.

"Jenny?" I prompt.

"It's *cancer,*" she says in a whisper.

"I'm sorry?" I honestly think that I have misheard her.

"It's cancer. A brain tumour."

"You?"

"No the neighbour's cat."

"The neigh...?"

"Well of course *me.*"

"I'm sorry, I mean... *God! Really?*"

"Well, that's what they said anyway."

"And that's the cause of the fits you had?"

"Yes. Pressure on the brain or something."

"God."

"Yeah."

"Did they say anything else?"

Jenny nods and bites her lip. *"Yeah,* they did," she says, her voice trembling and tears welling up. I sit and watch her face swell and wait for whatever's coming next.

"It's in a really difficult place," she finally says.

"What do you mean, a diff..."

"Difficult to operate on. That's why he had to consult."

"To consult?"

"With a colleague." She clears her throat, then continues, "The guy I saw – the specialist – he had to talk to a colleague, about what to do. Because he doesn't think they can take it out because of where it is."

"So what's happening Tuesday?"

"Tuesday they decide. Or at least, Tuesday he *tells* me what they've decided."

"Right. About what?"

"Oh, Mark, look, I don't know..." she says, her voice strangely flat. Tears are streaming down her cheeks though and I'm starting to cry as well. "I'm... I'm *scared,"* she gasps.

"Oh Jen. *Of course* you are. You should have told me."

"I know. And I know it's not fair, but, *can* you? *Can* you come with me?"

"Of course," I say. "You know I will."

"I'm so scared," she says again. "I'm so worried about Sarah."

"Sarah?"

"Well if something happens..." Her body shudders and I turn towards her and take her in my arms. "If something happens to me," she whispers. "What's going to happen to her?"

"It'll all be fine," I say squeezing her as tight as I can and staring outside at the fast-moving clouds.

"Will it?" she asks. "Will it be fine?"

"Of course," I say. "You'll see. It'll all be OK. They do miracles nowadays."

Just Statistics

For some reason, I am expecting Saint Thomas' hospital to be a decrepit old building on the outskirts of London, not a modern mega-complex opposite the houses of parliament. Equally, despite Jenny's warnings, I'm expecting Professor Batt to be a disheveled old man with a friendly bedside manner rather than a posh patronising twat.

Seated in his large, windowless office, he shows us Jenny's brain scan. It's the first time I have seen this and it provokes a sharp intake of breath. I had imagined something like the ultrasound scans they show on TV, where they say, "There, you can see his arm," and the mother-to-be says, "Oh! Yes!" even though quite clearly, no one can see anything at all. But here, the dumpling-sized blob on Jenny's brain scan is terrifyingly, indisputably *there*.

Jenny sits in silence and stares at the blob and nods. "It looks bigger," she says. "Has it got bigger?"

"It's the same scan, dear," Professor Batt says, with barely veiled sarcastic undertones.

"Of course."

"It's a pontine glioma," he says, "but we'll need to take a tissue sample before we can know if it's malignant. We'll probably want to do a spect scan too."

"What does that mean?" I ask. "A pontine glioma?"

"It's where it is, and the type of tumour," he says, leaving me none the wiser.

"And a tissue sample, you say? So that's surgery?"

"Yes, keyhole. A tiny hole, here..." he points to the back of his head. "And then we take a tiny sample to see if the cancer cells are malignant. And if this is the primary tumour or if it has metastasised from elsewhere."

"You mean there might be others."

"There might."

"And malignant is the worst kind, right?"

"Um... Well, malignant just means the cells are dividing and spreading."

"Which is worse..."

"Well, the tumour would be growing in that case."

"Which is worse than if it isn't though?"

"Well, yes."

Jenny nods, and still says nothing, so I scan my sheet of paper for the questions with which Ricardo primed me.

"How many brain tumours do you operate on a year?" I ask. Ricardo was very specific that you should never entrust yourself to someone who isn't doing a *lot* of the specific kind of surgery that is required.

"Here, at the hospital? Or me personally?"

"Um... You, I suppose. If you're doing Jenny's surgery."

"I'm afraid surgery isn't an option here, so..."

"Oh," I say. Which is where Ricardo's questions cease to be useful.

"But I treat a few hundred brain tumours a year, if that's your question. With surgery, radiotherapy, chemo, and sometimes all three."

"And *why* can't this one be removed with surgery?"

"Because of where it is – the pons."

"The pons?"

"It's here," he says, pointing at the scan. "It's the part of the brain that deals with breathing, and swallowing... critical functions. We don't go near it if we can help it. It's just too dangerous."

"Right. But the keyhole thing is OK?" I ask.

"Yes. Well, pretty much... there's always risk, but we can go through the details later. We basically take a sample the size of a pin-head. Well, maybe a little more, but..."

"And if it's benign, she'll be OK, right?" I ask, trying to cling to the positive here.

Doctor Batt grimaces. "Not at all, I'm afraid."

"But there's more *likelihood* that she'll be fine."

"Well, you can die of a benign glioma just the same as we have had patients survive anaplastic gliomas. It's less likely of course, but..."

I glance at Jenny who is looking green and confused.

"I'm sorry, these terms mean nothing to us," I say.

"No," Professor Batt agrees. "No, of course they don't."

"What we need to know really," Jenny says, finally speaking up, "... in layman's terms... is will I be OK? Or am I going to, you know... What are my chances? Of surviving this?"

"A prognosis is impossible at this stage, and useless at *any* stage," he says with a sigh. He sounds smug. He sounds like it's one of his favourite catch-phrases.

"Sure. But she's not going to actually... you know... *die* from this is she?"

"I have a daughter to think about," Jenny says. "A prognosis isn't useless *to me.*"

"Let me try to explain..." the professor says. "It really makes no difference if I tell you that you have a one in ten chance of living another thirty years, or, say, a thirty-to-one chance of living another ten."

"Well it kind of *does*," Jenny says.

Professor Batt shakes his head slowly. "I'm afraid it doesn't my dear. Because that still doesn't tell you whether you'll be the one-in-ten or one of the other nine. Statistics are population based. But they have little meaning for one specific individual. Prognoses are just statistics and statistics only function for the group."

Jenny looks at me. "Do you understand this?" she asks.

I blink slowly. "Yeah, kind of," I say. "He just means that no matter how bad the prognosis you might survive."

"And no matter how good, you could still be one of the ones who dies," he says.

I glare at him. I could kill him for that remark.

"Maybe you can explain that on the way home," Jenny says. Turning to the professor, she continues, "So what happens next? Do I make another appointment?"

"Well, I'm afraid what *doesn't* happen next is a trip home."

"I'm sorry?"

"I don't think that you're going home my dear. Not tonight. Not if we have a bed available."

"But... Oh... My daughter."

"I can sort Sarah out," I volunteer.

"And I haven't even brought..."

"Your tumour is not a candidate for surgical removal, as I said, because of its position. After discussion with Tim at Saint Bart's, we rather agree that time is of the essence here. If we can get you in for the biopsy tomorrow and, say, the spect on Thursday or Friday... Yes. That way, if this *is* malignant," he says, tapping the scan with his middle finger, "we can get you into treatment as soon as possible, maybe even as early as next week. It's up to you of course, but I really wouldn't advise any dilly dallying."

I turn to look at Jenny. She looks like a Madame Tussaude's figure – pale and waxy. She stares back at me and then for some reason, quietly repeats the words, *"Dilly dallying."*

Jenny: No Guilt

I hadn't wanted to get Mark involved, but my feelings were in such a maelstrom that I wasn't even sure why. To begin with, I thought I was keeping him away because I knew I couldn't rely on him – he had betrayed me. Big time.

And then I thought I was doing it for *his* sake, because it wasn't fair to dump all of that angst upon him.

Sometimes I felt like I was avoiding implicating him for both of those reasons at the same time even though that didn't seem to make much sense.

But when push came to shove, I had no choice. If Mum had still been alive, then she would have been there for me. If Dad, or Freddy had lived longer, or if my relationships with Giles or Ricardo or Nick had worked out, or if Tom had been the kind of person who didn't have a full time job, or even the kind of person who could put his friends *before* his job – if any of those things had been different, then I would have had other options. But they weren't, and I didn't.

I knew from my first meeting with Batt that I couldn't do this on my own. I had learnt nothing from that first meeting and I spent the entire taxi journey home trying to work out what questions I should have asked. And crying.

Because the only two questions occupying my mind were, was I going to die from this and if so when? And what would happen to Sarah if I did? That's three questions, I suppose: if, when, what? And apparently my three questions were the three no one could answer, and so they churned and churned in my compromised brain to the exclusion of all else.

So I let Mark in because I had to. And I justified this – because I didn't have the energy to feel guilty on top of everything else – using the exact same reasons that had made me reticent to get him involved in the first place: that it was unfair to dump all this on him, but that he had betrayed me: so he owed me.

That will sound mean I expect, but I *felt* mean. I felt mean and crazy and desperate and all out of options. All I could do was try to find a way through the next day and try to find a way not to add guilt about dumping on Mark to the rest of my worries. But he owed me. And as Sarah's godfather, he owed her too.

Lack Of Expectation

Sarah astounds me with her adaptability. I pick her up from Susan's just after six and announce that Mummy is staying at the hotel again. Sarah's only questions are whether it's the hotel with the magic fridge, or the hotel with the tube-man, followed closely by, can we have alphabet spaghetti again. Even the information that her mum is in a third, different hotel that's too far to be visited provokes little apparent concern.

As I make her tea, I think about this, for clearly, somewhere within lurks a life lesson, and I come to the conclusion that it's this: until you start deciding how things *should* be, until you start having expectations of what *will* happen next, everything and anything is fine.

Which of course means that if you can be childlike and take each day as it comes, or at least engineer your expectations to include the random changes that life constantly throws at us, whatever happens can at least be considered *usual*, if not necessarily desirable. Which, I suppose is what the Buddhists mean when they go on about the origin of all suffering being our desire for permanence. *Because* we expect everything to carry on as today, we suffer every time it doesn't. And we all know that it *doesn't*.

At four and a half, Sarah hasn't yet developed any expectation of permanence, and it seems that it's probably just as well.

On Wednesday I talk to Ricardo for nearly two hours. I tell him everything I know about Jenny's diagnosis and he tells me that he'll look it up on the internet.

"But I think it's pretty bad Chupy," he says. "As far as I can remember it's one of the worst places to have a tumour."

"Yes," I say. "I'm getting that too."

"Who else is around? To look after her, I mean."

"Other than me? And Tom maybe... no one really."

"Family?"

"Her mum was the last to go, I think."

"And no boyfriend?"

"No. There was some guy - Rodney or something, about a year ago. But she hasn't mentioned him and I haven't asked."

"And Tom. Is he around much?"

"He works all week, so..."

"Right."

"We haven't talked about that Ricardo. I think we need to talk about it."

"What?"

"Tom."

"What about Tom?"

"Well, why did you ask me if I was going to sleep with him?"

"It was just a question. Are you angry by my question?"

"Well not really. But you should *know* the answer. I'm not going to sleep with anyone. Ever. No one except you."

"OK."

"Because I love you."

"Me too."

"Well good."

"You know, I bet you won't be able to go to Nice next week," he says.

"I know. I was thinking that. Does it matter? Does it matter if I don't visit your flat?"

"No. Not at all. And I bet that you won't be able to fly back on the twenty-seventh neither."

"Either."

"OK, *either*. Either, neither... it's never the good one."

"No. I've been thinking that too. It depends what they say on Friday I suppose. If it's malignant and they have to start treating her..."

"Did they say what treatment?"

"No."

"Either will make her sick. Radiotherapy or Chemo."

"Yeah. Still, they might still say it's benign. There might not be any treatment."

"They might."

"Would you mind? If I couldn't come back so soon?"

"Of course not Chupy. If you need to stay longer, you must."

At that moment, I realise that one of the things I love about Ricardo is precisely his own childlike acceptance of change. He doesn't seem to have any expectation either, so nothing phases him. It's so relaxing after the drama of some of my past relationships. "You're sweet," I say.

"You're *more* sweet. Maybe you should look at how much for changing the flight though."

"It's unchangeable, remember."

"Oh, yeah. You could still call them. Maybe under special circumstance."

"Sure. But I don't know enough yet. We can think about it at the weekend."

"My back hurts from sitting here. I think the thing I hate the most about you being away is having to sit at this computer all the time to talk."

"I'm sorry babe. Shall I call you on the landline?"

"No. It's fine. But if I got an iPhone, could we both Skype on it? Then I can make breakfast and talk at the same time." –

"But you hate them. All style and no substance. You said they're for fashion victims."

"I know Chups. But if we could *Skype*. Especially if you have to stay longer."

"Well yeah... maybe look into it. I think the deals are quite expensive in Colombia though."

"I'd have to change my number I guess. I'd have to go to Movistar. I don't think Comcell do them."

"No. I don't think so either. But you can take your number with you these days. At least, you can in Europe."

"I'm not sure babe. I'll find out. But I don't care if I have to change numbers anyway. The only person who call me is you and work."

"And make sure you can pick up out there. There's no point if there's no coverage."

"I'll look into it Chupa Chups. OK, I have to go. It's time for work and I didn't even eat breakfast."

"And here it's just about time for lunch."

"Happy eating babe."

"Happy healing the sick."

Headache Doesn't Cover It

On Friday, after dropping Sarah at nursery, I return to London to meet Jenny. When I check the ward, someone else is already occupying her bed, and I am directed to the waiting room.

"You're up already," I say, when I see her look up at me.

"Bed shortage," she says, squinting at me as if the room is somehow too bright. "Hat?"

I pull a red beret from my coat pocket. "I hope it's OK," I say. "Apparently they're *in* right now."

"As long as it looks better than this," she says, lowering her head so that I can see the strip they have shaved.

"Ouch," I say. "Jesus, does that hurt?"

"They cut a slit in my head and drilled a hole in my skull..."

"Enough!" I say.

"Well what do *you* think? *Does it hurt?*"

"I didn't realise brain tumours made people so mean," I say.

"Sorry. Headache," she says. "Though that doesn't really cover this. I have some top notch painkillers though." She stands and takes my arm. "I'll let you have one if you're good. Now can we go?"

"Sure,"

"And I just want a taxi again."

"All the way?"

"I can't cope with anything else."

"Sure."

Once we find a taxi willing to take us to Camberley (and amazingly, considering the cost, this takes three attempts) Jenny fidgets until she finds a position leaning against me that doesn't press on her wound.

"Is that really sore?" I ask.

"The cut? Not really. It's inside. Like a migraine. Only worse."

"I have pretty bad migraines," I say.

"Me too. This is much, much worse."

"You poor thing. Did they say anything?"

"Sorry, but can you talk quietly?"

"Sure, sorry."

"And no. On Tuesday. Apparently."

"God. You have to come back *again?*"

"I know. I *am* sorry."

"What for?"

"All the to-ing and fro-ing. And being a grumpy bitch."

"It's fine. You have a hole in your head. You're allowed."

"Right..."

Within a minute her head starts to loll, and by the time we have left Lambeth Jenny is sawing logs.

Despite the pins and needles in my arm, I don't move for the entire hour-long journey. I know from my own occasional migraines at least a little about head pain, and I figure that my discomfort is nothing if it provides her with a little respite through sleep.

I watch London going past the windows, and think how crazy it is that I should find myself here, today, in a London cab with an ex girlfriend from *way* back, and Ricardo's ex-girlfriend from not so long ago – sleeping in my arms.

And I try not to wonder, where the fuck any of us can go from here.

Jenny wakes up as if by magic, the moment we enter the close.

She squints at me, visibly peering through pain.

"Bad huh?" I say.

"God, yeah. I need more Zamadol, like *now,*" she says.

"Go sort it, I'll get this."

By the time I have paid the taxi and picked Sarah up from Susan's house, Jenny has already retreated behind the closed door of her bedroom. Her failure, after four days away, to even say hello to her daughter I take as proof – if any were needed – of just how bad a post craniotomy headache might feel.

Shooting the Messenger

At eight-fifty on Saturday morning, in an attempt at letting Jenny sleep in, I answer the landline on its first ring.

"Jenny?"

"No, it's Mark. Is that Tom?"

"Yeah. Sorry, can you put Jenny on?"

"She's still in bed I'm afraid."

"I tried her mobile, but it's off."

"Yes, she's still in bed."

"Right. She's usually up by now. That's why I called early. To catch her before she goes back to bed."

"I hear you Tom, but she's *still asleep.*"

"OK. Um. Never mind. Can you just tell her I'll be up your way about twelve?"

"Well I *could*, only I'm not sure it's such a good idea to be honest."

"I'm sorry?"

"She's really poorly Tom."

After a two-breath pause, Tom says, "And when she's poorly, she only wants to see you, right?"

I laugh. "Not at all. She doesn't want to see *anyone. I* haven't seen her since six yesterday evening. Nor has Sarah."

"Is she *OK?*"

"Well no. She isn't. That's why I'm letting her sleep."

"So I can't visit her. You don't want me to come up?"

"Tom, really! Get a grip. This is nothing to do with what I want. She got back from the hospital yesterday. They drilled a hole in her skull. She has the worst headache she has ever had, and she's sleeping. If you come up you'll just end up having to sit and chat to me, and I don't think that's what you want. Is it?"

"Well, no. Clearly not."

"So... When she gets up, I'll get her to call you, and you and she can decide what's best. OK?"

"I suppose."

"Right."

"You promise?"

"What?"

"Promise you'll tell her I called?"

"Whatever, Tom. I promise."

I click the end-call button and grimace at the handset.

"Is Tom coming?" Sarah asks, looking up from a bowl of cereal at me.

"Maybe," I say. "We'll see when Mummy gets up."

"He *isn't*," Jenny says from behind us.

Both Sarah and I turn to see her standing in the doorway of the kitchen.

"This is a no-visits day," Jenny says.

Sarah drops her spoon and runs across to hug her mother's legs. Jenny reaches down and ruffles her hair. "Hello sweetheart," she says.

"You're up," I say, stating the obvious.

"I'm not stopping. I just need some water to take this," she says, showing me a pill.

"How are you feeling?"

"Shocking."

"Some breakfast maybe?"

Jenny shakes her head, prises Sarah off and crosses to the kitchen sink.

Sarah stands a little forlorn in the middle of the kitchen and watches her mother.

"It might do you good to eat something," I say.

Jenny fills a glass from the tap, takes her pill and replaces the tumbler on the counter. "It wouldn't," she says.

"Can you just call Tom and tell him then?" I ask.

"I'd rather not," Jenny says, leaving the room.

"Text him maybe?" I plead. But Jenny is already climbing the stairs.

"She's feeling poorly," I tell Sarah who is standing staring at the now-empty doorway. "Don't worry, she'll be back down later. Now, if you can just finish your breakfast Miss," I say, patting the seat of her chair.

As she continues eating her breakfast, I sit and finger the phone.

I think that I could text Tom, but he would just phone me back, furious. I could maybe email him, but then he might not see it – he might turn up anyway.

"Is uncle Tom coming?" Sarah asks.

"No. You heard Mummy say she's too tired for visits today, right?"

Sarah looks up at me and nods, giving me a better idea.

"Well how would you like to phone uncle Tom and tell him?"

Sarah nods again, simultaneously emptying a spoonful of rice-crispies onto the table.

"You can tell him all about your new doll as well."

"Tom doesn't like Polly Pockets, he says they're boring."

"Well you can tell him all about them anyway."

Sarah spends a good ten minutes rambling on about her dolls before announcing, rather brutally. "Mummy says you can't come. She says no visits today."

But Tom presumably takes this information better from Sarah than he would from me, because Sarah is still smiling when she hangs up.

I shower her and dress her and we spend the morning in the park. It's a grey old day but thankfully dry. I spoil her a little with chocolate from the refreshments kiosk and another round of her obsession – alphabet spaghetti – in an attempt at making up for her mother's pain-induced insularity.

And then I park her in front of the television and call Ricardo.

He tells me excitedly that he has found a reasonable deal for an iPhone and that he's heading into Santa Marta to pick it up later this morning.

"It's a double deal Chupy, that's the only thing, so I have to change the landline number as well," he says.

"Isn't that Federico's though? Surely, the landline isn't ours."

"I checked with him, and he doesn't mind."

And then he tells me what he has found out about pontine gliomas. "Statistically she's going to die," he says with Colombian brutality.

"Jesus babe, don't say that."

"But you need to know. As far as I can see it's the worst prognosis of any kind of brain tumour. I'd say she's lucky if her chances are one in fifty."

I glance at the door to check that Jenny is out of earshot. "God, I can see why the surgeon didn't want to discuss probabilities."

"But don't tell her," Ricardo says.

"Well, no, of course."

"And I might be wrong. It's not my speciality, babe."

"No."

"But everything I can find says that it's usually fatal."

And so, Sarah happily mesmerised by the *Teletubbies*, I sit and try to process this new information, this new concept... That Jenny, currently asleep upstairs, may not be around for that much longer. And I try to work out what that means, for her, for her daughter, for myself.

But there are no answers to be found.

Quarterly Plans

Tuesday is the day everything changes.

I'm not sure if Jenny is paralysed by fear or drugged to her eyeballs, but she remains entirely unemotional as Professor Twat describes the problem and his proposed treatment schedule. This he does with all the tact of a plumber describing fixes to a failing central heating system.

The tumour, he tells us, is grade three. Once I convince him to stop using technical terms which no one understands, he explains that this means that it *is* cancer, and it *is* growing, but at least not as fast as a grade four. He tells us that they would generally use radiotherapy and then follow on with chemotherapy if required, but that because Jenny's is so big, and because of where it's situated, and because she has already had seizures they intend to use both treatments at once. "The advantage," he tells us proudly, "is that we double the chances of actually slowing the bugger down."

"And the *disadvantage?*" Jenny asks – the only thing she says during the consultation.

"Well if it fails, there aren't a lot of other options," he says. "But we can cross that bridge if and when we get to it."

And then he sits and draws Jenny a calendar of the next three months.

Seeing as her new schedule involves radiotherapy every afternoon from Monday to Friday, plus extra appointments at the end of each month for chemotherapy consultations and progress scans, this clearly is going to be *my* timetable as well.

I don't *want* to spend the next three months driving back and forth between Camberley and London, and, if I were to analyse it, it wouldn't even seem reasonable considering my relationship with Jenny that it should fall on me to do so. But there simply isn't any other option, and so I don't think about it. I think instead, *"Oh! I had better tell Ricardo that I won't be coming home."*

Jenny maintains her icy calm during the entire consultation and conserves it as we negotiate the corridors of the hospital.

She even expresses some relief, saying bravely, "Well at least we know. At least now we have some idea."

"Right," I say.

"I mean, at least they're planning for, you know, three months. That's something," she says.

"Yes," I agree.

As I lean over to open the door of the hire car for her, I say, "You know we're going to have to sort your Mum's..."

"Sorry?" she asks, opening her door, fully.

"We're going to have to sort the Nissan out – insurance and stuff."

Jenny climbs in and buckles up. "What do you mean?" she asks.

As I pull out onto the main road, I explain, "Well, if you have to come *every weekday* for *three months*, that's like... sixty trips or so. You can hardly rent a car every time. And you certainly can't take a hundred and twenty taxis."

"No," Jenny says. "But you know they took my licence away, right? Because of the seizures. I told you I got a letter from the DVLC?"

"Sure."

"And I doubt I'd be up to driving anyway," she says.

"Not *you*. *Me*. We need to get *my name* on the insurance."

I'm fully occupied for a minute or so with the mess of traffic around the hospital, but once I get onto the A4 I realise that Jenny has gone very quiet. When I glance over I see that she's staring out of the side window, but that tears are streaming down her cheeks.

I check the mirror and pull into a bus stop.

"Oh babe!" I say, stroking her shoulder.

"I didn't know," she says. "That's all. And I was too afraid to ask."

"You didn't know what?"

"If you'd stay. I didn't know if you'd be able to stay here."

"Of course I will," I say, squeezing her shoulder. "Of *course* I fucking will."

Ricardo: Complications

O h Chupy, what am I to say? Life should be so simple but others work with such devotion to make things complicated!
Though I was missing you like crazy, I started to be relieved as well that you weren't coming back too soon, because as your story with Jenny got complicated over in England so did mine here in Colombia.

Once she had my mobile number, there was no stopping her babe. Her texts flowed like blood from the wounds of Christ, first in drips, little *Sweet dreams* texts at night, or sometimes a *have a beautiful day*, text in the morning, and then like a torrent: Call me babe. Call me today. Call me now.

So I called her. I told her, *Cristina, baby, I had a lovely time with you, but it's now over. O.V.E.R. Over.* The line went dead immediately and I felt some relief that my message had got through. But then, not ten minutes later, my mobile rang again and she left the longest, loudest, maddest message my voicemail has ever had the misfortune to record. I would tell you what she said, but for the most part it was incomprehensible. She was raging, babe. Raging.

I called Movistar the very next morning and reserved myself an iPhone and a new number, but before I could even get there to pick it up she called me on Federico's landline.

"How did you get this number?" I asked her straight off, because that was the mystery that needed to be solved.

"Juan gave it to me," she said.

"Juan?"

"Juan González," she said.

"How the fuck do you know Juan González?" I asked, getting angry now.

"Well, Carlos gave me Maria's number, and Maria gave me Daniela Gómez' number, and she gave me Pepi González number, and he of course, gave me Juan's. He's such a polite boy. Is he cute?"

I was beside myself with anger Chupy. The stupid bitch had climbed my entire family tree and no doubt hung around on a comfortable branch here or there for a chat on her way up. And no matter how discreet she might have been – and I doubt frankly that the appropriate adverb is *very* – Colombian tongues would now be wagging.

At this point, I was still finding the whole thing vaguely amusing, and a little flattering also, so I just told her not to call me; I told her to work on her marriage and to forget me. I lied and said I was moving overseas and that there was no future for us. And when she hanged up on me again, I phoned Juan. He was the only member of the chain I felt close enough to discuss the matter with, and that babe, is when things got *really* scary.

"You have got yourself mixed up with one crazy bitch, Uncle," he laughed. "And if Carlos finds out about it, you're a dead man. You really should know better."

"Why am I a dead man?" I asked him, already shivering in anticipation of the explanation. As you know, you learn to take such phrases seriously here in Colombia.

"Well, for one he's an asshole," Juan told me. "And for two, his business partner is Alejandro Ceballos. And for three he's your cousin."

"He's *not* my cousin, Juan."

"Well second cousin. Or *third*. Or something like that."

"And who the hell is Alejandro Ceballos anyway?" I said.

"The son of *Antonio* Ceballos," he said.

"Antonio Ceballos," I repeated, "I know the name, but..."

"You've really been away too long Uncle," Juan laughed. "Antonio Ceballos. *The Snake.*"

"Shit, from the old Cali cartel?"

"Ah, you see, you do remember your Colombian history."

"But he's dead, right? Antonio Ceballos is dead?"

"Not dead, in prison. Ceballos gave himself up, remember? But his son isn't in prison. His son spends his days with crazy Cristina's hubby Carlos."

"Stop sounding like you think this is funny, Juan."

"Hey, who's laughing?"

"So let me get this right? Carlos is business partners with the son of *The Snake?*"

"Exactly. That sounds like a B-Movie. *Son of The Snake.* Starring Crazy Cristina."

"Oh, fuck."

"Yes Uncle. Fuck."

"And the business?"

"I think they call it import/export these days."

"Shit."

"Oh yes."

"So now I'm changing all my numbers, OK?"

"OK."

"And if that crazy bitch calls you don't give her the new ones, OK?"

"Sure."

"Or the address. Or the town even. Don't tell her where I am either."

"Sure. You have vanished."

"Tell her I've gone back to France."

"Sure. But Uncle Ricardo?"

"Yes?"

"I kinda like my legs, right?"

"I'm sorry?"

"Well try to quiet her down, yeah? Because if *he* asks me... I mean, you know, if *Carlos* asks me... for *anything*... no matter what... well, the answer's gonna be, 'yes.'"

"Sure."

"I mean, if he wants me to suck him off *and* tell him where you are, the answer's still 'yes.'"

"I hear you, Juan. I hear you."

Family Man

As if planning a military manoeuvre, we work out the fine details of who is going to do what and when. Jenny will get up with Sarah at six, and then return to bed for an hour. I will get up at eight, drive us to London, dropping Sarah at nursery en route, and then find some way to occupy myself for the hour that Jenny's treatment is slated to take. On the way back we will pick Sarah up along with any shopping needed.

Our test runs are to be Thursday and Friday when we have to go to London for fittings and pre-treatment consultations.

Of course, nothing goes quite to plan.

Thursday starts badly at half-five when Sarah wakes me from a nightmare by, for some reason known only to her, poking her finger into my ear.

"Ugh!" I splutter, jerking away and trying to focus on her features. "What are you doing?"

"You were talking," she says.

"Um... I was having a dream," I say. "What time is it? *Five?* Where's Mummy?"

"She's snoring," Sarah says.

"God, OK... Go downstairs, and I'll be down in a minute."

I lie and stare at the ceiling for five minutes to give my heart time to slow. I attempt to remember the nightmare too, but other than a house filled with corpses surrounded by a muddy field, it has already slipped into the void. But even that's enough to work out what it was about: I am in a house filled with death, and I can't get away.

Jenny finally surfaces less than twenty minutes before we have to leave the house. "Sorry about that," she says still applying lipstick as I unlock the Micra. "I just couldn't wake up."

Once Sarah has been dispatched, I head for the motorway.

"It's normal," I say. "The routine will take a while to kick in."

"Yeah," she replies.

We drive in silence for half an hour before I say, "You're quiet this morning. Are you scared?"

"Not really," Jenny says. "They said you don't feel anything. And I don't think they're actually zapping me till Monday anyway. No, I'm more scared of the chemo. They said that will make me feel *really* shitty."

"You're a brave little thing really aren't you?"

"No choice," Jenny says. "Having no choice makes bravery that much easier."

"Well, I still think you're brave," I say.

"I was thinking about the car actually. Mum never really used it much."

"No, I saw that. Four thousand miles. It's practically new. Is it weird for you, me driving it?"

"No, not really."

"Rain!"

"Yeah."

I put the wipers on to clear away the spotting on the windscreen. There is something about the sound of those wipers, something so familiar about being in a right hand drive car driving along a motorway beneath a grey drizzling sky with Jenny by my side that is so incredibly, stunningly familiar that my vision mists. I think, *"Of course, this is me,"* and have a sudden feeling of belonging, here, now. It's strange and unexpected.

"No, the car's so new," Jenny continues. "It's just, you know, a car."

I'm surprised that she hasn't noticed my brief wave of emotional turmoil, but then why should she? "Right," I say, the feeling fading as fast as it arrived. "Not like the house then."

"No. I should maybe sell it or something," she says.

"Maybe."

"I would if all this shit wasn't going on."

"Sure."

"God, I haven't phoned that guy back about probate."

"I'm sure it can wait a couple of days."

"You know, I forget about Mum sometimes. Just for a few minutes."

"I think that's normal," I say.

"It's a relief. But then I remember, and it's worse."

"Yeah. I had that. With Steve. It slowly gets easier though. You just have to trust in the process."

"I forget about the cancer too."

112

"That's pretty impressive."

"It's like I can only think about one of those at a time."

"They're both quite big thoughts I guess."

"I suppose. Plus I only have half a brain and a golf ball now, so..."

"Funny girl."

I leave Jenny at the hospital and walk over Westminster bridge and through St James' park. The rain has stopped now, but the grass is wet and fragrant, the air heavy with moisture. I sit at a kiosk and drink a cup of frothy coffee but Jenny phones to tell me that she's going to be two hours, not one, so I drink up and continue across the park. When I realise that I'm on the Mall, I head for the ICA. I love a bit of weird and wonderful, and the Institute of Contemporary Art always has plenty of that.

By the time I pick Jenny up I have watched five of the most peculiar short films I have ever seen, and am almost feeling guilty for having had a nice time.

"God," I say, when I see her expression. "You don't look like *you* had fun."

"They didn't do anything," she tells me, moving towards the exit. "They just made this horrible plastic mask so they can bolt my head to the table."

"Yuck."

"You have no idea. I look like Hannibal the Cannibal."

"To stop you moving your head presumably?"

"To stop me biting anyone I think. And so they don't zap the remaining good bits. Tomorrow I have a mock up session. They put me in the machine but don't actually do anything."

"Right."

"And then Monday, they zap me."

"So Monday is chemo *and* radio?"

"Yip. Presumably Tuesday is when all my hair drops out."

"Really?"

"Nah, they said four weeks or so. Maybe. Some people actually escape it. But I thought we could go wig shopping one of the days next week just in case. I'm going for platinum blonde."

"Oh me too!" I joke. "We can pretend to be twins."

My new life is all-enveloping.

Some days, I don't even find time to phone Ricardo. Some days I worry about the distance between us. Some days I worry he'll meet someone else. And some days I honestly don't *think* about him once.

Jenny's needs, Sarah's needs, combining their double schedules, getting everyone fed and watered and delivered to the correct address at the correct time is a full time job.

I start to understand how it must feel to be heterosexual – to be a family man. I start to understand just how different the experience of life is, when every second of the fabric of the day is wound around the needs and destinies of dependant others.

The lack of options feels reassuring, safe, worthy... And incredibly dull.

I realise maybe for the first time exactly what we gay guys miss out on in the great no-dependants deal. And I realise everything we gain.

I can't help but think that we probably get the better deal.

Jenny: Parental Instinct

The day they made me that mask, was the day it all became real.

Up until that point my cancer was just a story. It was a story born in the hysterical aftermath of my mother's death. It was just a story and it didn't have an ending. I didn't seem able to think about possible endings.

But when they made me that perspex mask, when they bolted my head to the table; when experts in white coats made calculations and marked exposure angles on my perspex prison and ordered that vast machine to glide around me in robotic silence, I couldn't avoid thinking about endings any longer. Because at that moment I couldn't avoid the fact that I looked, and felt, and was being treated, like a woman who might die.

They say that having multiple personalities is an illness, but I think we all have them. Or maybe I have always simply been mentally ill. Whichever it is, one of me, let's call her Marge's daughter, surprised me by not turning out to be that attached to life. When death looked her in the eye on that cold treatment table, Marge's daughter looked back over her life and didn't particularly mind the idea of not being around any longer.

Maybe some people really do have lives full of money and love and support and joy... You see them on TV sometimes, and someone must have written those stories, so maybe they do. But mine hadn't been that way – my life had always been a struggle. A struggle to lose weight, a struggle to find a boyfriend, a struggle to come to terms with my brother's death, to escape Nick's violence, to cope as a single parent. I felt cheated. I felt like this product called life wasn't as it had been advertised. And I felt through with trying to make the reality correspond with the image. Because I was old enough to know now, that it really never would.

But there was another me, Sarah's mother. And Sarah's mother would never give up as long as her daughter needed her. When I thought of my daughter, every cell in my body, cancerous or not, *screamed* in resonance with hers. Sarah felt more integral to me than my own body, if that makes any sense.

If my cancer had been in a leg or an arm or a breast I would have insisted that it be removed if that increased my chances of seeing my beautiful child into adulthood. I would uncomplainingly have had *all* of my limbs removed if that's what it took. That will sound like an exaggeration, but it isn't. I mean every word. And if you don't believe me, then maybe you're not a parent. Because only a parent can understand how intense, how gut wrenchingly total is the need to protect the child.

But my cancer wasn't in a limb. It was in my brain. It was right at the *heart* of *me* and it was right at the heart of my love for Sarah.

So no matter what anyone thought I was thinking about or worrying about – Mum's death, my treatment, Mark or Tom or wigs or probate – I was always thinking about Sarah: I was always stumbling over how I could assure her future. And I only came up with two ideas.

One was quite simple – it was not to die. It was that if I had *any* power over my body, I *would not die*. And if there was any God or any spiritual set up in this life that could be influenced by a woman's love for her child, *I would not die*. It was obvious.

But I had always suspected the universe to be mechanical and unfeeling rather than fluffy and responsive. And I suspected that no one, not even my own brain-cells were going to listen to my prayers.

So the backup plan was to find Sarah's father. My instinct insisted that the DNA Nick shared with his daughter would drag him, no matter where he might be in his life, to exactly where he *needed* to be. My instinct *knew* that once he found out that his daughter was in danger, he would have no option but to be exactly what she needed. This went against every observation I had ever made of Nick's alcoholic, destructive behaviour in the past, and it went against everything my intellect could predict about how he would behave in the future.

But instinct is a powerful master, and parental instinct, perhaps the most powerful of all. And so, secretly, when Mark wasn't looking, I started trying to track him down.

Symbol Of Love

Two weeks into Jenny's double-treatment, my Visa card is refused at Waitrose. I have been paying bills willy-nilly with it, earning nothing, and secretly dreading this very moment. But money is one complexity too many right now, so I have been refusing to think about it.

For the first time, I try to use the card that Jenny gave me instead.

"I'm afraid that's been refused as well," the cashier, announces. According to her badge her name is Cheryl.

I'm not the only person interested in names, though. "Mrs M. Holmes," Cheryl reads from the card. She looks up at me and raises both eyebrows.

The woman behind me in the queue tuts, Cheryl frowns, and I feel myself blush. "It's not what it looks like," I say. "I'm, um, shopping for a friend. She's ill in bed."

Cheryl, looking unconvinced, reaches for her internal phone. "I'm sorry, but I'll have to call the supervisor," she says.

"The shopping's for Mummy," Sarah says, amazingly coming to my rescue. "She's got cancer and she sleeps a lot."

I stroke Sarah's head and watch Cheryl's hand hover over the handset then relax as her eyes mist. "Right," she says, clearing her throat. "Um, do you have some other way to pay for this or...?"

"I don't think I do," I say. "Do you want me to... you know, put it all back?"

"No, that's fine," the girl says. "I'll get someone to deal with it. I'm sorry I can't, you know... but..."

Even the woman behind us in the queue smiles sadly at us as we leave empty handed.

When we get back to the house I find Jenny sitting at the kitchen table. The room smells of cigarette smoke.

"Phaw!" I exclaim, crossing the kitchen floor and opening a window.

"Don't lecture me," Jenny says. "I'm not in the mood."

"I wouldn't dream of it."

"Where's the shopping?"

"Well, we have a bit of a problem."

"Yeah?" Jenny says, raking one hand through her hair. "Me too. Look at this."

She holds her hand up to show me the strands of hair that have come away.

"Oh, already?"

"Yeah. Four weeks my arse. Lying buggers."

"God. Well, we have another little problem too. My Visa was refused."

"What, your card?"

"Yeah."

"But I gave you Mum's."

"Yeah. Well that was refused too."

"That doesn't make any sense," Jenny says, pulling out another handful of hair.

"God, don't *pull* it out!"

"No," she says thoughtfully forcing her hand to the table. "You're right. Did you use the right code? Three-six..."

"Three-six-oh-two."

"That's it. But Mum's account has, like, twenty grand in it. Unless they've put a stop on it."

"I'm thinking they have," I say.

"Shit, I didn't call that probate guy," she says.

"No."

"Do you think that's why? Maybe I should call him now."

"Not on a Saturday."

"No... God. You can try mine, but there's not much in there either to be honest," she says.

"If you want food," I say. "It might still be worth a try."

And so, Sarah and I return to do a complete repeat of our shopping experience. At least by the time we reach the checkout Cheryl has gone to lunch.

On the way home, I stop at an ATM to check Jenny's bank balance and see that she has the princely sum of ninety-seven pounds left in her account.

With Sarah eating, and Jenny sleeping, I text, then Skype Ricardo.

"Chupy!" he shrieks.

"Hi babe, how are you?"

"Happy! I have Saturday off and my Chupy call me!"

"How's the new phone?"

"It's good. I like. I don't like to use it in public so much. In case it get stolen. But yes, I like it. And how are things in England?"

"Oh, OK."

"You sound worried."

"I'm broke actually babe."

"Broken?"

"No, broke. It means I have no money. *Je suis fauché.*"

"Vraiment?"

"Yes. My card was refused. I've been just paying for everything... bills, food, petrol..."

"Well *of course* you have."

"And I haven't even *looked* at my account. I can't seem to access it with the phone, and the ATMs here won't give me a balance, and Jenny's PC won't start up..."

"Your laptop didn't arrive yet?"

"No. Not yet."

"I post it a week ago."

"Well, hopefully soon."

"So how much do you need?"

"Well Jenny has money. Or rather, her Mum did. But we have to go to the lawyer and everything to get that sorted, and what with going back and forth to the hospital, there isn't really time, and..." My voice is running away with itself, and changing in pitch and tone. I realise I'm starting to cry.

"Oh Chups," Ricardo says. "Slow down."

"It's just that, there's, you know, so much to deal with," I say, my voice wobbling crazily. "And now we don't even have any money, and..."

"I know babe. You're doing really well. So. Money. How much? I transfer it today."

"Are you sure? Can you?"

"Of course."

"I mean, you'll get it back. I promise. But..."

"My money, your money. It's the same. So how much?"

"I don't know. I don't even know what's in my account. Nothing I suppose."

"How much? A hundred? A thousand?"

"Can you?"

"Hang on... Look. I'm looking now. Hold on... password... and... here it come... OK. I have three thousand euro in my French account. You want I transfer it now?"

"Are you sure it's OK?"

"It's the rent money. From the flat. Of course I can."

"I'm really sorry..."

"Stop. Either we're a couple or we aren't."

"Right."

"And if we are, it's your money too, so just tell me what you want me to do with your money."

I hang up and dry my eyes and sit on the sofa and think about a whole new set of complex feelings.

I'm relieved to have some money to live on again of course. But I'm also profoundly uncomfortable at having had to ask Ricardo. Our finances have always remained entirely separate and borrowing money from him seems a far from insignificant milestone in our relationship.

And then the discomfort fades a little and is replaced by a wave of love. For the ease with which Ricardo offered to do this, the fact that he is generous enough to not even question my spending on Jenny and Sarah, to not even *ask* when he's likely to get it back; his statement that we're a couple, and that his money is my money... well relationship wise, it's one of the loveliest things that has ever happened to me.

I didn't know that money could be so symbolic. Or at least, I didn't know it could be symbolic of anything wholesome. I didn't know it could be a symbol of love.

Florent Nightingay

By week four we are all well and truly settled into our new routine. It feels, in fact, as if life has forever been like this; it feels as if it will go on like this forever more.

As far as I can tell, Jenny is as solid as a rock. She seems to become tougher and cockier and funnier with each day that passes. I'm sure that most of this must be constructed bravado, but it's truly impressive – inspirational in fact.

My relationship with Ricardo too feels surprisingly solid. The complexities and costs of calling him on weekdays – from London – mean that our daily chats have now reduced to weekends only. But despite that, Ricardo is endlessly reassuring. He continues to offer every kind of support he can from such a distance, and his every word continues to project a future for us both. He is even discussing coming over for Christmas should I still be here by then, an idea I have yet to mention to Jenny. Her cancer has become a trial our relationship simply has to undergo. At least we know it's one that *we* will survive.

As week four is Jenny's second chemo week she has to spend three hours daily at St Thomas' rather than one. And because it's raining, and because it's cold outside, and because I have now visited pretty much every museum in London – or every *free* museum at any rate – I offer to sit with her during chemo. For the first time, she accepts.

When the male nurse appears and starts to insert Jenny's IV he strikes me as instantly familiar, so I sit and struggle to remember where I have seen his face before. He looks like a little bearded blue-eyed angel.

Finally he catches me staring and frowns at me quizzically.

"Sorry, I..." I say, shaking my head. "Do I know you from somewhere?"

"Nice," Jenny murmurs.

"I'm sorry?"

"Original," she says.

I tut and roll my eyes. "Seriously, though..."

The nurse shrugs. "I haven't been here long," he says.

"Hum," I say.

"I was in Surrey before if that helps."

"Ahah! Camberley hospital."

"Frimley Park, that's right," he says tapping Jenny's arm in order to raise a vein. "Nice veins," he says.

"Aw, all you boys say that," Jenny flutters, shaking her new Marilyn wig.

"Being blond is turning you into such a tart," I say.

She laughs. "Says Mister Haven't-I-seen-you-somewhere-before..."

"You know who this is, Miss Clever-clogs?"

Jenny shrugs.

"He's the nurse who looked after you when you had your seizure."

"Really?"

"Well one of them. There was a Polish girl too."

The nurse frowns and nods. "It's possible," he says. "You see so many patients in a day... I'm sorry."

"Hey, don't worry babe. I don't remember you either," Jenny says. "It can't have been *that* good a night."

"Well you *were* unconscious most of the time," I point out.

"There's no telling *what* those nurses got up to," Jenny says.

The nurse blushes and grins, and starts to tape a plaster over Jenny's IV entry point. "Well, well spotted anyway," he says, shooting me a grin.

"Oh Mark never forgets a pretty face, do you Mark?" Jenny says.

"Jenny!" I protest, blushing myself.

"Right, that's you done. Enjoy," he says.

We watch him leave and then Jenny turns to me.

"His name's Florent," Jenny says.

"Florent?"

"It's French, I think."

"He doesn't sound French."

"He isn't. Just his name. Florent Nightingay."

I laugh. "Nightingay, ha! Very good Jen. Is he? Gay, I mean?"

"Well what do *you* think?" Jenny says. "How many straight men have arses like that?"

"How many *gay* men have arses like that?"

"He's like a little cherub, isn't he?"

"He is."

"God I suppose I'm going to have to put up with you two making eyes at each other every time I have chemo now."

122

"Well it's you he's following from hospital to hospital," I point out. "I think it's you he's stalking."

"Maybe this isn't chemo. Maybe he's murdering me."

"Perhaps. Can you feel that stuff going into your veins?" I ask, nodding at her suspended IV bag.

"A bit. It's cold. But not much."

"Yuck."

"But then after twenty minutes I start to feel vomity. It happens every time."

"Nice."

"I know."

I glance over at the door and Jenny says, "He'll be back in precisely forty minutes. Don't worry."

"Jenny... I *am* married."

"Yeah, well... You know what I think about that."

"Not really, but I can guess."

"You could do much better," she says.

"Not a nice thing to say about the man who is putting food on the table and petrol in your tank."

"True," she says. "Still, I should be getting the money from probate soon."

"Yeah."

"A week or two, they said."

"Right."

"And then you can pay him back and hook up with Florent Nightingay."

"Jenny!" I protest, frowning seriously now.

"God," she says. "If you can't even take a joke."

I roll my eyes at her. "I can, it's just..."

"But you actually *could,*" she says. "Do better, that is."

Wednesday Child

Jenny's wit fades again as her week of chemo progresses.

On Wednesday I have to leave the M3 early so that she can vomit in a lay-by, and by the time Friday evening comes around, she looks, with her green skin and vacant expression, like a zombie. Her platinum blonde wig suddenly resembles an absurd stage-prop – she looks like an Almodovar tranny. But of course, I don't say a word.

On Saturday she cancels Tom's Sunday visit which means that thankfully I can stay in. I too am feeling shattered, and with the pouring blustering October weather outside, the last thing I want is to have to vanish for the day. Which is why I'm sitting reading a picture-book with Sarah when the landline rings on Sunday afternoon.

Wondering whether the caller will be my ex or my current, I swipe the phone from the base before it can wake Jenny up.

"Hello?" asks a woman's voice. "I'm, um, trying to get in touch with someone. Jenny Gregory. Or Jenny Holmes. I'm not sure which name she uses now."

"Holmes," I say.

"Yes, of course. My, um, aunty mentioned that she was trying to get in touch with Nick and this is the only number I have for her."

"I doubt that," I say. "I doubt she's trying to contact Nick, I mean."

"Well that's what Joan said. Only Joan doesn't talk to Nick these days so..."

"Right."

"So, sorry, who is this? Because I'm not even sure if this is the right number."

"It isn't really. I'm... a tenant," I say, wondering why I'm lying before I have even realised that I am. "But I can give her a message."

"Oh, OK. Do you *have* a number for her?"

"I'm sorry, I don't. But I'll see her, um, when she comes for the rent."

"Right. It's a bit personal really, that's all."

"I'll make sure she gets the message."

"OK. Well, can you tell her that he's in High Down. Or I suppose I could just leave my number, maybe that's better?"

"High Down?"

"Yeah. It's, you know, a prison."

"Oh."

"What a family, eh?"

"Can I ask what for? Why he's there?"

"Um, well, it was just driving on a ban."

"I see."

"It was drink driving on a previous ban actually. And leaving the scene of an accident, I think."

"Hit and run?"

"Well, yeah. I suppose."

"Nice."

"Yeah. Anyway, if she wants to visit, it's Wednesdays. I'm sure he'd love to see her."

"Right."

"He doesn't get a lot of visitors."

"I bet."

"And not the *first* Wednesday of the month. That's when I go, you see."

"Of course."

"Can you give her my number. Just in case?"

"Sure," I say.

"So it's 0771..."

"0771," I repeat as if I'm writing down the numbers, which I'm not.

"You'll make sure she gets the message then?" she asks once I have finished pretending.

"Oh yes," I say. "She'll get the message."

Because Jenny stays in bed most of Sunday, and because when she does get up she looks so thoroughly dreadful, it's not until we're driving to London that I get a chance to speak to her.

"You and I have to talk," I say, once we're safely on the motorway.

"That sounds ominous," she says.

"It is."

"I thought you seemed funny. What have I done now?"

"Nick," I say, simply.

"Nick," she repeats.

"Your ex."

"Well I know who he *is*," Jenny says. "I just don't know why you're saying his name."

"I think you do," I say.

After a pause, Jenny says, "I'm sorry Mark, but can you stop playing games?" Her tone has shifted from 'amused' to 'irritated.' "Nick. Yes. *And?*"

"You've been trying to contact him," I say.

"Oh that."

"Yes, that."

"It's just a precaution. Anyway, how do you know?"

"A precaution?"

"It's just in case."

"In case of what?"

"Shit the traffic's bad today."

"Yes, it is. In case of *what?* In case you fancy a punch in the mouth, or a kick in the stomach?"

"Look I know you don't like him," Jenny says.

"Don't *like him*," I repeat incredulously.

"OK, understatement. Nor do I."

"So why?"

"Well, he's Sarah's father, isn't he."

"We're talking biologically here?"

"I'm sorry?"

"Well, he knocked you up and then he..."

"We *were* married," she interrupts.

"He knocked you up, and then he knocked you about. If that's a definition of father then it's more of a biological one than a social one."

"Sure. You're right. But he's still her father. He's her biological parent."

"And a violent, alcoholic waster."

"Yes, he was."

"*Is.*"

"Well we don't know that do we?"

"Oh, yes we do. He still is."

"Has he been in touch?"

"His niece phoned when you were asleep."

"Oh, Tara? Excellent. How is she?"

"I have no idea."

"Oh."

"Busy on Wednesdays."

"Busy on Wednesdays?"

"Yeah."

"Mark. Please don't be so cryptic."

"Shall I tell you where wonderful Nick is? Shall I tell you where you can find him?"

"Well that might be an idea. Unless you want me to guess."

"He's in prison, Jenny."

"Oh."

"Yes, *Oh*. But you can try to guess *why* if you want."

"Oh. God," Jenny sighs. "Do I have to?"

"I bet you can."

"Hitting someone?"

"No. Try again."

"Drinking and driving?"

"Bingo! Actually he did hit someone too. Hit and run. Driving on a ban. Drunk."

"Jesus. How long did he get?"

"I don't know. Does it matter?"

Jenny doesn't reply, and so I drive on in silence. It's a full twenty minutes before she speaks again.

"I just needed to know," she says. "Just in case."

"Sure. But I still don't see why," I say. "In case of what?"

"In case I die, stupid," she says. "God, you're thick sometimes."

"Because if you die, what Sarah needs is Nick?"

"It might be better than nothing," Jenny says.

"Might it? A violent alcoholic father in prison? Someone to visit on Wednesdays?"

"Well no."

Another five minutes pass before Jenny says, "I can't believe that idiot is in prison again." Her voice is weak, on the edge of tears.

"I can," I say.

"Yeah. I suppose I can as well."

"He's a drunk. He'll always be a drunk."

"Yeah, I know. I was thinking though, and don't jump down my throat for this, please don't..."

"No."

"No, never mind."

"No, go on."

"Well, I was just thinking that maybe if he knew. Maybe if he found out that Sarah needs him that would change things. Maybe he'd sober up. For her."

"Wishful thinking," I say. "Very wishful thinking."

"You think?"

"He kicked her when she was still in the womb," I say. "You do remember that right?"

"Yes."

"You could have lost her."

"OK. Don't."

"But you need to…"

"OK!" Jenny shrieks. "Just stop!"

I sigh. "If you promise to leave Nick out of it, I'll stop."

"I promise."

"It would be so irresponsible to get involved with him now."

"Right," she says. "I agree."

"Good."

"I just… I'm just… you know. I'm trying to find options."

"Nick's not one of them."

"No."

"Staying alive is."

"Yes. But what if I can't…"

"You will."

"But if I don't… If I die. What happens then? What happens to Sarah?"

"Well what doesn't happen is that she gets to live with Nick."

"No. But what *does* happen? I mean, it's not as if Tom's going to look after her, is it? And it's not as if you could."

"Tom!" I say with a laugh. "Imagine!"

It's a diversion, a distraction from the second half of her question.

"I know," Jenny says. "Imagine!"

And I wonder if she has noticed that I haven't replied for myself. And I bet that she has.

Adulthood

Once in London, I leave Jenny at the hospital and head off in search of a pub with free wifi. As ever, these days, big thoughts require Ricardo's input. I seem to have lost the ability to chew over complex issues on my own.

We chat for a while about life, the weather, London, money, and Ricardo's work, before he asks, "So? Tell me."

"Tell you what?"

"What's worrying."

I laugh. "Am I that transparent these days?"

Ricardo laughs. "It's what you do Chups. You talk about everything else first. And then if you don't hang up, there's some big thing."

"OK. Good call. Well, it's Jenny. Or rather Sarah."

"Sarah."

"Yeah. It's difficult really. But what happens to Sarah if... you know..."

"Jenny is dying."

"Well yes. Exactly."

"You *think* she is dying?"

"No. She's fine. But it could happen."

"Of course."

"And Sarah's not even five."

"You want we take her?"

"Ricardo!" I laugh. *"No!* I just want to talk about what happens to kids who lose their parents."

"Oh, OK. Well Jenny have no family now, right?"

"No."

"No cousins? Uncles?"

"I don't think so, no."

"Nephews, nieces?"

"I don't think so."

"I can't imagine such a thing."

"No, I bet! Not with your lot."

"And the father?"

"Nick? He's horrible. Alcoholic. Violent."

"Yuck."

"Yes, yuck."

"It sound like a TV documentary Chupy."

"Yeah, it is."

"That girl has bad taste in men, babe."

"She chose *you*..."

"Exactly."

I laugh. "She tried to contact him – Nick, the father – but I persuaded her not to."

"Well maybe it's better than nothing."

"It isn't. Honestly. I know him. He's horrible. And he's in prison."

"Prison?"

"Yeah."

"So what does Jenny say?"

"She's terrified."

"What did she *say?*"

"Well nothing really. She just said that Tom obviously wouldn't."

"He wouldn't? But I thought they were friends."

"Well, they are. But this isn't like adopting a cat..."

"No. So that leaves..."

"Well no one really. Except me."

"Us. Yeah."

"But obviously I couldn't."

"I think we should."

"How can you just say that? I can't see how you can just say that. As if it's so simple."

"OK. Calm babe. So what is alternatives? She can go to an *orphelinat?*"

"An orphanage? I don't think they exist anymore. No, she'd go to a foster family I suppose."

"They might not be nice. You read stories."

"Yes."

"Maybe violent too. Maybe worst than the father."

"I know. I mean, I suppose people watch them. Social services and stuff."

"Pff! You trust social service with little Sarah?"

"Well, not really."

"Then it's us," Ricardo says.

I pull a face at my phone. I can't believe that Ricardo is being so matter of fact about this. His reaction strikes me as simplistic, childish even. He once again strikes me as completely alien.

"You should tell her," Ricardo says.

"Sarah?"

"No, Jenny. She must be worry. You should tell her that we make sure Sarah is OK if anything happens."

"I think it needs a lot more thought babe."

"OK."

"And she's fine at the moment anyway."

"OK. You know best Chupy. But you know, I have no problem with it. Now I have to go to work babe."

The conversation over, I sit in slightly stunned silence and nurse my Coke and try to analyse what has to be the strangest conversation I have ever had with Ricardo.

I'm touched, as ever, by his unstinting projection of *us* into the future. An *us* he apparently sees as solid enough to welcome a five year old.

And then again, his simplicity of view strikes me as childish and irresponsible. For in truth, he knows nothing about how long this thing he so easily calls *us* will continue to exist. Sarah will be dependant for at least another thirteen years. And thirteen years, especially thirteen *gay* years, is a long, long haul.

Is it the faith issue again? I have had this thought somewhere before, though I can't quite remember where or when. With Tom maybe. And look what happened there.

But maybe Ricardo is right. Maybe what you have to do in order to stay together for twenty years is simply talk the talk and walk the walk. Maybe you just have to project that it *will* happen, and weave a life that is so rich and complex that it can't be pulled apart. That's certainly what heterosexuals do with their kids and their pets and their mortgages.

But the truth of the matter is that it terrifies me. The idea of being tied to one person, let alone tied to *two* people for a decade or more, is just about the scariest thing I can imagine. Maybe Ricardo *isn't* the one who needs to grow up here. Maybe it's me.

The arrival of my all-day-breakfast distracts me momentarily because it's the smallest cooked breakfast I have ever seen. A single fried mushroom, and single half a tomato, a tiny fried egg, a slice of toast and about ten beans. When I call the barman back to complain, he simply shrugs.

"But it says mushroom-*zz* on the menu..." I point out. "And tomato-*zzz*. Those are plurals, they mean more than one. They certainly mean more than a half."

"Well we ran out," he says, simply, with another shrug.

"And it says a vegetarian sausage."

"Yeah. Like I say, we ran out."

In a state of some annoyance, I eat my breakfast, but when I come to pay, I balk at the total of almost eleven pounds for a coke and a mini-breakfast, so I hand him a fiver.

"No, it's *ten*-ninety-nine," he says.

"Yeah. Sorry about that," I say. "You ran out of food, I ran out of money."

Amazingly, he simply shrugs again.

Three To Six

"That's bigger, isn't it?" Jenny asks as Professor Batt clips Jenny's latest scan to the illuminated board.

"You always say that," I point out, even though something in the professor's solemn manner is making me nervous as well.

"I'm afraid this time you're right," he says. He runs his finger around a vague halo to the right of the grey dumpling on the scan. "All of this is new growth," he says.

"So the radiation hasn't killed it?" Jenny asks.

He moves behind his desk and clasps his hands. It strikes me that the desk is protection for him against our reaction to whatever he's about to say. I hold my breath.

"The fact is that neither therapy seems to be having much effect," he says.

I hear Jenny suck air sharply through her nose.

"Though of course, we don't know how fast the tumour would have progressed without treatment," he continues. "But no. This is not a success story."

"You said before... I mean, I think... you said before..." she says stumblingly.

"Yes?"

"Well, didn't you say that if this failed there weren't any other options?"

"There aren't many," he says.

"What *are* the options?" I ask, turning back to face him.

"Well we can carry on with this treatment. Perhaps adjust the dosage."

"But you don't think that will work," Jenny says.

"It hasn't so far. And I'm worried about your liver function if we up the dosage of the chemo."

"It's worth a try though," Jenny says.

"You've been really ill on the chemo," I point out.

Jenny glares at me as if I have revealed some great secret that's going to stop her becoming school prefect.

"I know that," the professor says. "I can see from your blood work."

"Are there other options?" I ask. "Surgery or..."

"No, I'm afraid we can rule surgery out entirely."

"So basically, that's it?" Jenny says with an incongruous laugh.

I look out at the plummeting October rain and wonder if Jenny will be here to see springtime. I wonder if she is thinking the same thing.

"There is a clinical trial we're participating in," the professor says. "A new drug, nitomazatab. We're combining it with temazilimide to see if it can slow this type of tumour."

"OK, let's do that," Jenny says.

"It might help, and it might not."

"Sign me up," Jenny says lightly.

"But it's a new drug. With all the attendant risks that implies."

"I don't care," she says.

"Well you *need* to care," Professor Batt says. "People die in clinical trials."

"Like those guys who swelled up," I say. "On the news."

"Indeed. This isn't the same type of drug at all – that was a novel type of gene therapy – but yes, bad things happen."

"But without it I croak anyway," Jenny says.

"You really don't seem to be taking this seriously," the professor says.

"Oh I *am*," Jenny says. "But I don't have any other options, do I? Or *do I?*"

"The other thing is that it's a double blind trial."

"Meaning?"

"Meaning half of the group get the new drug..." he says.

"Half?" Jenny says.

"The other half get a placebo," I explain.

"Exactly," Batt agrees.

Jenny frowns. "But I don't want a placebo."

"Well no. But it's how drug trials work. Otherwise we can't tell if the drug is working or not."

"God," Jenny says. "If I slip you fifty quid can you make sure I'm in the right group?"

"I'm afraid no one will know, not even me. It's randomised. That's the point."

"A hundred?" Jenny says.

"No..."

"So it's fifty/fifty," Jenny says. "I get it. But that's still better than no hope at all."

"Well, it's fifty/fifty that you get the new drug or placebo. And it's perhaps fifty/fifty that it works for your tumour. And that's *if* we can get you into the trial."

I frown. "Why wouldn't you be able to get her into the trial?"

"There are criteria. Blood counts have to be within limits. We need to stop your current regime and see if your red blood-cell count goes back up."

"And will it?"

"Hopefully. And you need to not be pregnant of course."

"No worries there," Jenny says.

"Good."

"So let's do it."

"You'd have to stay in for the first forty-eight hours, but then you could take it from home."

"Home?"

"It's in pill form."

"Wow. That sounds better."

"But the side effects are essentially the same. Sickness. Diarrhoea, fatigue."

"Diarrhoea," Jenny says. "Nice. That's new."

"Well not everyone has all of the side effects."

"Yippee."

The professor frowns. "I'm very concerned about your attitude," he says. "This is an incredibly serious situation."

Jenny nods and sighs deeply. "I can cry if you prefer," she says, sounding suddenly bitter. "I can do that quite easily if you want. Or I can do *this*. I'm sorry but they're the only two attitudes in my repertoire right now."

The professor nods. "Of course. I just need to know that you understand."

"I understand," Jenny says soberly. "So how long before we know?"

"If you can join the trial? As soon as we get the blood work back. I'd say end of next week."

"And radiotherapy? Do we continue with that?"

"No. No, this trial excludes that possibility."

"And if it doesn't work? How long before we know *that*?"

"We'd be doing monthly scans. So..."

"So you'd see if the tumour is still growing," I say.

"Exactly."

"And... I have to ask," Jenny says. "What if this doesn't work either?"

"Well we'd have to see if we could come up with something else."

"And if we can't? How long then?"

"How long? You mean mortality?"

"Yes."

"It's impossible to..."

"I know, I know!" Jenny says. "You always say that. But look, I'm being serious here. It's what you wanted. So if this is the last ditch attempt... I have a young daughter. I need to think about what happens next."

"Three to six. That would be my guess," he says. "But it's only a guess."

"I'm sorry," I ask. "But is that months or years? That's years, right?"

"Months. It's months, isn't it," Jenny says.

"Yes," he says. "Yes, I'm afraid it is."

Once a nurse from oncology has filled seven tiny test tubes with Jenny's blood and we're heading downstairs, I try to take her arm but she shrugs me away.

"You were really brave today," I say. "You amaze me."

"Don't," Jenny says. "Just... *don't.*"

"Sorry," I say.

"And stop apologising."

"Sor... right."

I look away and pull a face.

We walk through the rain to the car park in silence, and then Jenny smiles unconvincingly over the roof of the car. "Can you do me a really big favour?" she asks.

"Sure," I say. "Anything."

"I know it's pissing down and everything, but could you chuck me the keys and fuck off somewhere for half an hour?"

I nod. "Sure. But what... you're not going to drive or... or do anything daft are you?"

"I just need a moment," she says. "I just need a moment alone in a soundproof box. I... I have to let something out."

I swallow with difficulty and throw the keys to her.

"Now go, and don't come back for half an hour, OK?"

I smile and nod and blink back tears. "Sure. Half an hour," I say, turning on one foot and marching away.

I hear her unlock the car, and I hear the door close again.

And even from fifty feet, even from within her soundproof box, even over the sound of the rain, I hear her wail. But I don't look back.

I could do with a soundproof box myself.

Something Good

With Jenny's treatment (and our trips to London) suspended, her energy levels rise visibly with each passing day.

She slots into her old life as if she has never taken a day off, walking Sarah back and forth to nursery, doing the shopping, and all of this despite the rain.

She claims that this is to "give me a break" but I think we both know that it's more profound than that. She doesn't know how long she'll be able to do these things, and she doesn't know how long she'll be around to spend time with her daughter. And she isn't going to miss a minute.

This all leaves me with a lot of time on my hands to realise both how artificially I have slotted myself into someone else's life, and how much I miss Ricardo and, yes, Colombia. If part of my reason for coming to Britain was to see if I wanted to move back, this much is clear: *I don't.* Other than the need to be here for Jenny and Sarah, the delights of being back home have long since faded to vanishing point. Above all it's the weather that I simply can't bear. It has been raining for weeks now, and this running from house to car to supermarket to car to house has left me feeling like a caged animal. Some mornings when I open the curtains and see the raindrops sliding down the pane I could scream myself.

There is still a possibility, of course, that the South of France will convince me to stay if I ever manage to get *there*, but right now I just want to be back at the beach house; I just want Ricardo to wrap me in his arms and tell me that this particular adventure was nothing but a bad dream.

I even start hunting the web for cheap flights so that I can perhaps grab a quick cuddle before Jenny's next phase of treatment starts, but it only takes Ricardo's reminder of the dire state of our finances to convince me to look for work instead. Within twenty four hours I have pulled two small freelance translation projects from the agency list and so, as Jenny bursts in and out of the house shaking umbrellas and cursing, I sit at the kitchen table and translate European disability regulations from French to English.

By the middle of the second week I'm feeling grey and washed out, whilst Jenny is looking flushed and buoyant.

"I know," she says when I comment on this. "I think it's being up and about. I think it's getting out of this bloody house."

And then we stare at each other for a moment during which I'm pretty sure we both think exactly the same thought: that it's barely possible to believe that she has a brain tumour right now. And that it's totally impossible to imagine that she might die.

***

The letter from St Thomas' hospital arrives on the same day as the cheque from Jenny's solicitors.

She looks at the hospital envelope and then opens the other one. "Hey, I can pay you back!" she says, brandishing a cheque at me. "I must owe you three or four grand."

I nod and smile. *"And I can pay Ricardo back,"* I think. *"And I can maybe fly home to see him."*

And then Jenny opens the second letter, but hands it to me. "I can't bear to look," she says.

I scan the letter. "You're in! Wow! It starts on Monday," I say, disguising my disappointment that any possibility of a brief trip home is now terminated.

The way Jenny whoops you would think we were discussing her entry into the Star Academy rather than an experimental cancer treatment. But of course, her inclusion in the trial provides a smidgin of hope. And sometimes a smidgin of hope is all anyone needs.

That night we celebrate with a decent bottle of wine (for me) and a bottle of *Appletise* for the girls. We also order an obscenely huge pizza.

Because we can't explain it to her, Sarah has no idea what's going on. But the fact that she is allowed to dance around the lounge holding a slice of cheese-dribbling pizza is proof enough that – after weeks of misery – something good is afoot.

Jenny: Safe Haven

T he disclaimer was the moment that the euphoria ended.

It ran to twenty three pages and the doctor Stevens running the trial, a young serious man I had never met before, insisted that I read and sign every single page.

These pages described, in detail, the side effects the drug had had on rats, rabbits, dogs and monkeys. The drug had, it seemed, already inflicted a great deal of suffering on many others before me. It struck me as particularly unfair that they had had no choice. In the case of the dogs these side effects were not good – not good at all.

The contract held "harmless" St Thomas Hospital, UK Medtrials Ltd and GSB Inc for all and any effects the drug might have on me *up to and including* sickness, disability and death.

They left me alone with the paperwork for an hour which was just as well, not because I needed an hour to think about whether to sign it – as far as I could see, I had no choice – but because I needed a moment to think about Sarah. Because these documents were saying something unusually concrete. They were saying that this new molecule might kill me. They were saying that I might die *today*. And dying today might be something a twenty-year old med-student being paid for a trial is able to have a laugh about, but as a mother, it shook me to the bone.

Forgetting that it would be in pill form, I asked if I could have Florent administer the drug – he was good with IVs – and surprisingly they agreed and paged him.

When he arrived, I asked Florent for a sheet of paper and a pen, and together we wrote a letter to my solicitor, the one who had dealt with my mother's estate.

It said that in the event of my death, all of my possessions and all of my money should go to my daughter Sarah. It said that under no circumstances

139

should her biological father be given custody and why. And it said that every decision concerning the management of property or finances, and every decision regarding Sarah's wellbeing, should be taken by her godfather, Mark, who I hereby named as her legal guardian as well.

Neither Florent nor I had much of an idea whether this was sufficiently legal – whether it would, as they say, stand up in court. And I certainly had no idea what Mark would have thought about it had he known. My guess is that he would have run screaming back to Colombia.

But I had no time. And I had no choice. And so I signed the sheet and the lovely Florent witnessed it, and then I signed the twenty-three pages of the disclaimer.

Florent brought me a tiny beaker of water and three pills, and I swallowed them and lay back to see what, if anything, would happen next.

For the first half an hour Florent sat with me, so to pass the time I told him how wonderful Mark was and what a good friend he had been, because that is what I was thinking about. I was thinking about how, amazingly, I had gone from hating him to loving him as deeply as I have ever loved any man. Because when push came to shove, he was the only safe haven for my daughter, my darling angel, who I loved so much it hurt my chest to think about her.

And Mark was the only person on the entire planet that I could trust to make sure that, in one way or another, she would be looked after.

Lovely Florent nodded and um'd and ah'd in all the right places, and I thought again, that he and Mark would make a good couple, and so, just in case I was dying, I told him that he could do a lot worse than get to know Mark himself.

He um'd and ah'd some more but in a less convincing way this time, and I guessed that Mark wasn't his type, or he already had a boyfriend, or maybe he didn't want to get involved with someone about to inherit my four-and-three-quarter year-old daughter.

I felt sleepy and asked if that was normal, momentarily terrified that death was creeping up on me, and Florent patted my hand and stroked my head and said, "Sure, you have a little sleep now, I'll see you later."

And I wondered if he would.

An Agreed Narrative

The relief of not having to go to London every day is profound, and the fact that Jenny tolerates her new treatment so well gives us both a fresh dose of much-needed optimism.

During her chemo she is still tired and nauseous – even more so than before – but this is clearly a plus, not a minus. As Jenny declares as she struggles not to vomit up the pills, "If these are a placebo then I'm Marilyn Monroe."

"Well you do have the hair," I point out.

But within twenty-four hours of ending her chemo-week her energy levels rocket sky-high. Whether this is a result of not being dosed daily with radiation, not having to trudge back and forth to London, the optimism borne by the knowledge that she has ended up in the desired half of the trial, or perhaps even a sign that the treatment is working, is unclear. But we tacitly agree to decide that it is this last explanation that holds true.

Whatever the real cause, Jenny has energy to spare. She deals with every aspect of Sarah's schedule, cooks beautiful meals for the three of us, and even starts to repaint the hall. "Whether I end up getting rid of this place or dying in it, I still don't want a green hall," she declares.

It's a phrase that sticks in my mind; a phrase I rehear every time she mentions any aspect of her painting project.

I sit in the kitchen and translate incomprehensible marketing babble from French to English and listen to the sound of Jenny climbing up and down the metal step ladder. I alternate between the cold November air blowing through the cracked window or the stench of paint inside the house when I close it. And I think about that phrase, and wonder again how to get Jenny away from this house. Because that troubling phrase seems to reveal that if she is to stay alive, she, at least, believes that it will be elsewhere.

One Thursday afternoon, I pick Sarah up from nursery. It's the first time I have done this for two weeks. Jenny is in the middle of painting the skirting boards and has declared herself sick of it: she is determined to finish today.

It's a crisp, dry November afternoon and the fumes from the gloss paint are eye-watering, so I'm happy for the excuse to take a break.

Sarah is surprisingly perturbed by the change in routine. "Where's Mummy, is she sick?" she asks me even before she has finished crossing the playground.

"She's fine," I say. "She's at home. She's painting."

Sarah's face relaxes and she takes my hand as before, but it's a rare indication that she is aware of her mother's illness. And so as we walk towards the shops, I wonder how much she understands and how often she thinks about it.

I wonder too if she realises that her Mum might disappear entirely in the same way her grandmother has, and what she thinks might happen to her if she does. Which raises, of course, the original question of what *does* happen to Sarah if Jenny dies?

It's not a subject Jenny or I have ever mentioned again. With our new agreed narrative that the treatment is "working" it has become almost a superstition on my part not to say anything that suggests that any other outcome is possible. Perhaps faith is important, I think. Perhaps belief *does* become reality. And if that's the case then the last thing I want to do is sow seeds of doubt.

And it suits me not to discuss it too, because I still don't have the slightest idea how to resolve my own thoughts on the subject. Ricardo has mentioned it twice now by matter-of-factly asking me if I have told Jenny *yet* that we're prepared to look after Sarah. The implication is clear: he sees this answer as the only solution to the dilemma – he sees it as an evident truth, as a no-brainer. And yet it still seems like a complete impossibility to me. Though I can't see how I could refuse, and though I can't come up with any other solution, imagining such a future requires a series of images that my brain simply refuses to conjure up.

As we turn into the close, Franny appears breathlessly at Sarah's side and without introduction of any kind starts blathering on about school and birthday parties and fireworks on Monday. Something about this relationship between five-year olds and its independence from we superfluous adults makes me grin.

"Mum says you can come to our Guy-Fawkes night and sleep over if you want," she tells Sarah, glancing behind.

I follow the line of her gaze and see Susan walking briskly to catch us up.

"Hello you," she says when she reaches me. "No Jenny today then? Is she not well?"

"No she's fine," I reply. "You two run ahead, we'll catch you up," I tell the girls.

Once they are out of earshot, Susan says, "Sorry. I keep doing that, don't I?"

"It's OK. It's just that we try not to discuss it in front of her. It's not like it's a secret – Jenny has told her and everything, but... well, we try to control the flow of information. Because you can't tell what she understands and what she misunderstands. You know how it is."

"Sure. I'm sorry. So how is she?"

"She's doing well. She's painting the hall actually."

"God," Susan says. "Are you sure that's wise?"

"It's not really up to me," I say. "But I think it makes her feel better to be productive. And it puts her stamp on the house too."

"Is she getting ready for viewings? Because she said she'd like to sell up. It can't be easy, it being her mum's place and all."

"No, it's not. I think it's really hard for her to be honest. But no, she's not selling. Not yet."

"I wouldn't want to stay, I don't think."

"Well no. She'd love to get away, but we're kind of stuck here," I say. I frown and start to think about that use of the word, 'we.'

"I suppose moving would be too much upheaval," Susan says.

"Well, selling and buying... it's stressful at the best of times," I say. "I don't think that now is really the right time."

"Do you want me to carry one of those?" Susan asks, gesturing at my carrier bags.

"Nah – they kind of balance each other out," I say. "But thanks."

"Well," Susan says, sucking hard through her teeth. She seems to hesitate a long time before continuing, and I wonder what on earth she's going to say.

"You could always use our place I suppose. If you wanted to get away for a bit."

"Your place?"

"Sorry. Yes. Not here... In Pevensey. We have a holiday house down in Pevensey Bay."

"Pevensey near Eastbourne?"

"You know it?"

"Sure. I come from Eastbourne. Well, originally I do. I used to ride my bike along to Pevensey when I was a kid."

"Right. I didn't know. So yes, we have a beachfront place. It's only small, and it's a bit of a mess. We only go there in summer really. Well, we used to.

We thought we'd spend more time there when Ted retired but it hasn't really happened... We should sell it really but you know how it is."

"It's not one of those places right down on the front is it?"

"Yeah that's it. Two stories, two bedrooms. Pebbles in the front garden."

"That must be amazing."

"Well, it's pretty great in summer."

"I bet the view's fab though, isn't it?"

"Well, it's a view of the sea, so I suppose if you like the sea – when you can see it that is. I always seem to spend the whole time cleaning salt off the windows. And you'd have to keep an eye on Sarah. Keep her away from the water. Anyway, if you wanted a weekend away, well, it's nice down there. And Eastbourne's not far away. And Brighton's just down the coast."

I glance at her to check her expression. The words seem to have been said with meaning. I almost expect her to continue and explain that there are lots of "my type" in Brighton. But she doesn't, and her expression reveals nothing. And I think that were Tom not there, Brighton would definitely be an attraction.

"Well thanks. I'll mention it to Jenny. If you're sure?" I say.

As we near the house I hear Jenny scream from within the open door. "You stupid little shit!" she shouts. "How could you?"

Susan looks shocked.

"Oh God," I say. "That sounds bad."

"Yes, it does," she says, opening her own front door and pushing Franny inside, "good luck."

Inside Jenny's hallway I see the cause of the outburst. Sarah is squashed against one wall, her face swelling, tears, if not a full-blown tantrum, clearly on the way.

Jenny is frozen at the bottom of the stairs looking red and outraged. "Look!" she says. "Just look."

From the upturned tin, a vast pool of white paint is gloopily spreading across the hall carpet.

Because of the gloss-paint nightmare – a crisis we spend most of the evening trying to resolve before simply untacking and rolling up the hall carpet – I forget to mention Susan's offer.

Only once Jenny has gone to bed do I remember it. I sit and think about how nice a weekend at the seaside would be. And I sit and think how awful what would inevitably become a weekend with Tom would be as well.

In the morning, I mention it as soon as Jenny gets up but she seems fairly unenthusiastic about the offer, saying simply, "Oh, how sweet of Susan to offer. But I don't really know her that well."

As breakfast progresses, however, Jenny's pace speeds up.

I can see the idea taking hold and energising her until she whizzes through her own breakfast even refusing her usually "essential" second cup of coffee. She showers and dresses with unusual efficacy and by nine she is back from Susan's with a big smile and a bunch of keys.

It's the first time I have seen her really grin since I got here. I suddenly notice how much weight she has lost and am shocked to the core. It's something to do with the way her teeth protrude from her face when she smiles this broadly.

"So what about it?" she asks, jingling them at me.

"Well, I'm just about to take Sarah to nursery," I say, now checking her waist and seeing that her jeans are scrunched up by the big belt holding them in place.

"You don't want to go to nursery *do you?*" Jenny asks Sarah.

Sarah frowns. Clearly she *does*.

"Wouldn't you rather go to the seaside and make sandcastles?"

"Today?" I ask, a little incredulous at the sudden change of plan. But one look at their two faces is all that is needed. I have never seen mother and daughter look more alike. And I have never seen them look so excited.

"You really do want to go *today?*" I say.

Jenny shrugs. "Sunshine, seaside, sand, out of this house... what's not to want?"

"It's pebbles," I say, wrinkling my brow. I'm sure that there's a good reason not to go today, but she just isn't giving me time to think of it.

"Oh, come on! Where's your sense of adventure?"

"OK..." I say vaguely. "If that's what the ladies want."

"It is," Jenny says. "You pack your stuff and sheets for all of us. I'll do Sarah's and a big box of food. We could be there for lunchtime if we get a move on."

I laugh, starting to get swept up in the wave of excitement. "Jen, I get that you're keen, but let's not rush this. Let's pack and have lunch and then leave this afternoon."

"No way!" Jenny says. "I want fish and chips on the beach. That's the lunch I want."

"Fish an ships," Sarah shrieks, wiggling up and down as if she needs the toilet or perhaps is attempting the twist for the first time ever.

By ten our bags are packed.

Jenny locks the house and I throw mine and Sarah's bags into the tiny boot of the Nissan. I'm about to start the engine when I see Jenny heave her own bag onto the rear seat beside Sarah.

"You're sure this is for the weekend?" I laugh.

"Sure," Jenny says. "Why?"

"Well that's one big bag."

"Well we don't know what the weather will be like, do we?"

"You're *sure* I don't need my laptop?"

"You won't work, not at the seaside. You know you won't."

"And we'll be back Monday?" I ask.

"Well yes, of course."

I wrinkle my nose, unconvinced.

"Come on," Jenny says, sounding almost hysterical now. "Let's go."

I start the engine and then turn it off again. "You know what," I say, releasing my seatbelt and reaching for the door-handle. "I'm gonna take it anyway."

As we wait for a gap in the traffic at the exit of the close, Jenny says, "God, I'll have to phone Tom," and starts to fumble in a bag at her feet. "It'll be so much easier for him, won't it? Brighton's how far away?"

"About forty minutes I think," I reply, looking, then frowning at a local taxi waiting to turn into the close.

Because Jenny is bent double looking for her phone she doesn't see what I see, and I make an on-the-spot, and thoroughly dishonest decision *not* to tell her.

As I accelerate away, Jenny straightens and laughs, "God, from not being keen, someone's in a hurry to get to the seaside."

"I am," I say, wondering if he recognised me, and wondering if the taxi is right now turning around to follow us. "I can't wait."

Compared with a visit from fisty-Nick, the seaside, even *with* Tom, suddenly does seem extremely appealing.

Fast-Moving-Moods

As Camberley fades into the distance, I start to accept that we're not being followed. In fact, by the time we join the motorway, I am doubting that I saw Nick at all. From such a fleeting glance, it's hard to remain sure – the image of his face is already fading from my mind's eye.

Sarah is as good as gold in the back, playing i-spy, asking endless questions about the beach and what we will do there, and whether there will be ice creams, and if we can buy a bucket and a spade...

I listen to the chatter and try to work out why I'm feeling increasingly peeved. It's obvious that a trip to Pevensey is preferable to yet another day in Camberley, so what's with the bad mood, I wonder.

For a while I think it's to do with Nick, but Nick, if he ever *was* there, is now way behind us.

Perhaps it's because of Tom's proximity to Pevensey and his inevitable omni-presence at the house this weekend (Jenny has already invited him for dinner this evening.) But after thinking about this for a bit, I have to admit that this is not the cause either. I'm getting quite used to Tom's sarky irritation, almost learning to enjoy our regular sparring sessions.

"I hope someone has wifi for the internet junky," Jenny says, pulling me momentarily from my thoughts.

"Yeah, me too," I say, thinking that without broadband and without a fixed phone line, I won't be able to chat to Ricardo at all. The thought makes me feel truly angry, and this in turn enables me to zoom directly in on the cause of the bad mood.

Because though going to Pevensey is nicer than staying in Camberley, I didn't choose it... and it's *not* what I would have chosen. What *I* want is to go home – to *my* home. I want my bed and my boyfriend and my cat upon my knees. Fuck Pevensey Bay.

I think about my use of the word "we" yesterday, and feel even worse. For what has happened here is that my life has been hijacked. I have become the de-facto husband of a possibly dying woman, and the de-facto father of a possibly-to-be-orphaned little girl, and here I am driving my new de-facto family to the fucking de-facto beach. And as much as I love them both – and I *do* – none of it has anything to do with what *I* want *at all*.

As I join the M23, Jenny touches my arm but I instinctively pull it away. It strikes me as yet another brick in the new family edifice. Today, right now, it strikes me as a bloody liberty.

"Are you OK?" she asks. "You seem really quiet."

"I'm just driving," I say in the warmest tone I can manage, which isn't, it has to be said, very warm.

"Is it me? Have I upset you?" she asks.

"No," I answer. I think it's a lie, but I certainly couldn't identify anything Jenny has done to annoy me; I certainly couldn't explain.

"Are you missing Ricky?"

"Ricky," I think. No one calls Ricardo *Ricky* for the simple reason that he hates it.

"Ricardo," I say. "Yes, that'll be it. I'm missing Ricardo."

"Aw," Jenny says. "Do you think he's missing you the same way?"

I frown at her.

"Of course he is," she says, grimacing. "Sorry."

We drive in silence for a moment and then Jenny says, "If you want to go back. You can you know."

I'm not sure if she means to Camberley or to Colombia. Either way, it's clearly a lie. "Just... find some music or something, will you?" I say. It's as much as I can do to resist telling her to shut up.

I try really hard to mellow out, but for some reason it's exceptionally hard today.

As Jimmy Sommerville and Jenny duet to Smalltown boy, and as Sussex glides by beneath an increasingly luminous sky, I think about what Jenny is going through. I think too, about how fragile her little daughter is. I remember that her mother died not so long ago as well, and try to remind myself how brave she's being.

But today, none of it helps, because like a three-year-old, all I really want to do is stamp and scream until someone gives me what *I* want – until someone gives me my life back.

***

Thankfully no mood of mine could ever resist that first glimpse of sea.

As we come over the downs, Sarah shrieks, "See the sea!"

"Well done, you were the first to spot it," Jenny says, "so you win an ice cream."

"Wow!" I comment, not even noticing that every ounce of my bad mood is at this second being sucked from my body by that incredible vista of grey sea and blue sky, by the whitecap waves and the fluffy clouds skimming east to west, by the smell of iodine and salt, by the sensation of my eyes focussing, for the first time in months, on the horizon – on infinity.

"God it's good to get away," Jenny says, touching my arm again.

And I turn and smile at her. "It is," I say. "It really bloody is."

Because it's getting late, and I'm worried that they will close, we stop to pick up fish and chips the second we reach Pevensey Bay. And then, the car filled with the seeping odour of fish and fat and vinegar, we drive on to the beach-front car park, deserted on this windy Friday in November.

"Bracing," Jenny says as she climbs from the car.

"That's what they call it," I laugh.

Jenny releases Sarah from the rear and wraps her in a thick parka.

"Shall we leave the bags for now?" I ask.

"Yeah. Just bring lunch."

The sun is shining and only a few clouds remain now, but the wind is strong and gusty enough to make the cables on the small beached boats slap against the masts.

"It's all stones," Sarah says.

"Yes, pebbles. They're called pebbles."

"You said we could make castles."

"But pebbles are great for throwing into the sea," I tell her.

She nods as if seriously considering the pros and cons of pebbles versus sand.

We battle fifty yards along the beachfront and then Jenny points at a small seventies originally-white-but-now-weatherbeaten cube of a building and says, "That's the one I think."

I look at the tiny house. The beach truly does end at the building's south-facing bay windows. "No!" I laugh. "Really?"

"It looks nice," Jenny says.

"I'm not usually a fan of americanisms," I say. "But it's fucking awesome."

Jenny pulls a face and nods at Sarah.

"Sorry Sarah," I say. "But it had to be said."

"You don't say that word," Jenny says.

"Awesome!" Sarah says, giggling.

"Let's sit behind that wall and have lunch before it goes cold," Jenny says. "We can move the stuff in and park the car somewhere else afterwards, OK? I'm ravishing."

I laugh, my bad mood now entirely forgotten. "Sure. I'm ravishing too. Mmm, fish an ships, Sarah! Fish an ships!"

There doesn't seem to be any way to get out of the wind which doesn't also involve getting out of the sun, so we only manage to eat half of our meal before I give in. "It's f'ing freezing," I say. "I'd rather get into the house and reheat the rest later."

"Sure," Jenny says, standing. "Me too. Can you stop with the f'ing though?"

"Sure, sorry. I thought the censored version was acceptable."

"It isn't."

"Fair enough," I say, wondering why Jenny is suddenly getting all Mary Whitehouse about my language. She has never mentioned it before.

The locks on the house are so stiff that we think for a moment that we are maybe trying to break in to the wrong house and look nervously around in case an owner, or police, or security guards are about to pounce on us.

But then Jenny re-reads the instructions and, both agreed that this *is* the right house, and that this *is* the right key, I stick a piece of wood through the keyring and manage to lever the lock open. "Must get some oil on this bugger," I say.

Jenny steps in first, and immediately turns to me and pulls a face. "Ooh! Musty!" she declares.

'Pooh!' Sarah says, copying her mother's fanning gesture.

Inside, the house is unrenovated seventies time-warp. Not swirly wallpaper seventies, but sleek, white, minimalist seventies. The people who built it and furnished it had money and taste – once upon a time.

"Susan apologised about the furnishings. Apparently it all came with the house thirty years ago."

"I like it," I say, taking in a white lampshade suspended on a chrome arc and a vast orange sofa. I cross the room and run my hand through the dust covering a sleek, walnut Bang & Olufsen music centre. "God, talk about time-travel – this has a built in eight-track," I comment.

"What's eight-track?" Jenny asks.

"Oh, just a stupid seventies format that didn't catch on. Before cassettes. This is probably a collectible now," I say. I flick through a couple of records stacked in the cabinet below the music centre and see Nancy Sinatra's *Greatest Hits*, Simon & Garfunkle's *Bridge Over Troubled Water*, and *Odessey and Oracle* by the Zombies. This last album has an amazing psychedelic cover which I hold up to show Jenny. "Look, even the records match..." I say.

"Oh yeah," Jenny says, feigning interest.

"I like it."

"Me too," she says. "I'm not liking that smell though."

"No," I agree. "It smells like something died in here."

This new thought prompts a nervous exploration of the remaining rooms.

There are only two rooms per floor, so it doesn't take long. Behind the reasonably sized lounge with its stunning beach view, is a blind windowless kitchen complete with yellow formica kitchen units. Upstairs has the same layout with a large bedroom, again with an entire wall of glass, and a smaller one above the kitchen with a tiny side window. It's from this last room that the stench is clearly emanating.

"Don't go in Sarah," I say. "Mould isn't good for you."

"Leaky roof?" Jenny asks, nodding at the huge furry patch of mould covering one wall.

"Leaky roof," I agree. "It's a flat roof too which explains it."

"Why does that explain it?"

"Well... Flat roofs *always* leak. They were a great sixties idea. Not." I close the door and we return to the bright front bedroom.

"We *can* stay here, can't we?" Jenny asks.

"It's not very healthy," I say. "And it really does stink."

"Yeah," Jenny agrees with a sigh.

The smell truly *is* overpowering, and the sensation of clammy damp in the air is most unpleasant. She crosses to the bay window and runs a hand across it. The outside is frosted with salt, backlit by the sunlight.

"I can see what she meant about the salt on the windows," I say.

"Uh?"

"Oh, you weren't there... Susan said you spend the whole time cleaning the windows here. That looks like frosted glass"

"Yeah. I bet the view's fab if they're clean though," Jenny says, unclipping the window, and sliding it open.

The room is instantly filled with the buffeting sea breeze and the noise of the waves crashing on the pebble beach.

"Wow," I say.

"Yeah. Look at that. I suppose that's why there's no television here."

"You're right. I hadn't noticed, but you're right."

"Don't!" Jenny says, pulling Sarah back from the rusting railings by her hood.

I test them and declare them, "Rusty, but safe," and she releases her again.

"Oh *please* let's stay here," Jenny whines.

"How?" I ask. "It stinks."

She sighs. "I know," she says. "But couldn't we just seal that room up or something?"

"I could sleep downstairs," I say. "The sofa looks fine."

"Oh yes. Please?"

"Like it's up to me," I laugh.

"Yes!" Jenny says victoriously.

"Tell you what, I'll go get the bags in, and you two look and see if you can find bleach. We need to wash that mould away. And open all the windows. And see if you can get the heating on."

"There's a shop up the road. For bleach. If we need it."

"Yeah. And sponges. And rubber gloves."

"And air freshener."

"And window cleaner."

And so to the sounds of the Mamas and the Papas, we spend our first day at the seaside scrubbing mould from walls, smothering carpets in cleaning products and drenching every porous surface with air freshener.

By the time the sun vanishes and it becomes too cold to keep the windows open, it seems as if we have beaten the smell into submission, but then again we may just be getting used to it, a theory bourn out by the expression on Tom's face when he arrives at the front door.

"What an amazing place," he says. "Phew, a bit pongy though, eh?"

In the end, we eat at the Beach Tavern – a family pub at the end of the road. Sarah finds this late-night treat terribly exciting, and the novelty and the alcohol somehow make my own time with Tom less intense than usual. In fact there are even a few moments when we forget that we hate each other and have a few minutes of normal conversation – a most unsettling experience.

Jenny and Tom order beef-burgers, and Sarah and I share another portion of fish and chips, Sarah by choice, and myself because it's the only non-meat option on the menu.

After lashings of bitter I scoop sleepy Sarah from a corner seat and we walk back to the car park. The wind has dropped, but it's now cold enough to see our breath rising like puffs from a steam train.

Jenny kisses Tom goodbye and asks him, "Are you sure you're OK to drive?"

152

For a terrible minute I think that she is going to invite him to stay, which would certainly create some who-shares-with-who issues. But Tom declares himself fit, and promising – or threatening – to see us again tomorrow, climbs into his Beetle and drives away.

As we crunch across the gravel, Jenny links her arm through mine. "It was nice seeing you two being civil," she says.

"Yeah, well..." I say. "Don't expect too much of it. It's not easy you know."

"No," she says. "I do appreciate it, you know."

"What's that then?"

"All this. Everything," she says. "I do realise that you'd rather be elsewhere."

"Hey it's cool," I say, pausing to look out at the broken reflection of the moonlight on the sea. "Isn't this place lovely?" I say.

"Yeah," Jenny says. She points to a lit pier in the distance. "Is that Brighton?" she asks.

"No, Eastbourne," I say. "Brighton's further around. I tell you what though... It'll be amazing here on Monday."

"Monday? Why Monday?"

"The fifth of November. You'd be able to see the fireworks all around the coast."

"Oh *yeah!* Maybe we should stay an extra night."

"Maybe. This one has a party though, doesn't she?"

"She won't even remember if you don't tell her."

We both look out at the view, and for a moment take in the sound of the waves falling on the pebbles and dragging back out to sea.

"It sounds like it's breathing," I say.

"Mmm?"

"The sea going in and out. It sounds like it's breathing in and out."

"Yeah. Well, maybe it is," Jenny says quietly before turning to head across the pebble garden to the house.

When she opens the door she pulls the face again. "Phew!" she says.

"Still bad?" I ask.

"Worse I think."

I step inside and screw up my nose. "Oof! Mould plus floral air-freshener equals..."

"Equals yuck," Jenny says. "Still, maybe it'll get better tomorrow if we open all the windows again."

"Yeah. Maybe," I agree.

I don't close the curtains that night.

I prop myself up on the big orange sofa, and lie and stare out at the moonlit beach and the vaguely fluorescent waves as they come and go.

I listen to the sea breathing in and out and think how amazing it is to suddenly notice that the physical world is so stunningly beautiful, and I wonder what purpose that has, what evolutionary function humans finding their environment beautiful can possibly serve. Maybe it's supposed to make us respect it better.

Wishing that Ricardo was here to share it with me brings tears to my eyes – tears which, I now remember reading, contain exactly the same percentage of salt as the sea. Scientists say that this is just a coincidence, but then scientists say all sorts of things...

Snapshot

On Saturday morning, I awaken to the screaming of seagulls. This is a real snapshot from the past because it's the sound I used to hear every morning as a child in Eastbourne. I close my eyes and smile as I listen, and then a strange cry makes me frown and open my eyes. The off-key seagull is in fact Sarah, who has entered the room and is copying the cries of the gulls as best she can.

At seven am – quite a lie-in these days – it's barely light and way too cold to eat outside, so we move a fold-out table in front of the window and set breakfast up there.

The sky is still pink from the recent sunrise, a crazy contrast against the sea, momentarily pea-soup green. We sit and sip at mugs of tea and stare out to sea, all three of us mesmerised by the view.

By the time we have finished our bowls of cereal, dark clouds are appearing on the horizon. "We'd better get out and make the most of it," I say. "I don't think the weather is going to hold."

"You and Sarah go," Jenny says. "I'm happy just pottering here."

Wrapped against the cold, I attempt to teach Sarah to skim stones, but she's too young and merely manages to chuck one at my head, to fall flat on her face, and to get soaked up to her knees by a wave. But she doesn't care about any of it, and as she tears up and down the steep pebble beach chasing birds, and as she clambers on the crumbling wooden breakwaters, she doesn't stop smiling for one instant. And I remember, with thanks, my own childhood. I wonder what London kids do all day long.

Back at the house, Sarah plays with a pile of pebbles I have brought in from outside, and Jenny and I sit side by side and stare at the view some more, this time with cups of coffee.

"It just changes all the time," she says.

"I know."

"Even while you were out with Sarah, the sky went from pink to blue to green. Now it's grey."

"It looks like a Rothko," I say.

"A Rothko?"

"Oh, a painter. Russian, I think. He did big modernist things that are just swathes of colour. Have you seen how dark it is though? It looks upside down."

"Upside down?"

"Yeah, the sky is darker than the sea. It should somehow be the other way around."

"I suppose," Jenny says pensively, supping her coffee. "It's going to piss down though. Are the views as good back in Colombia?"

I swallow and pause considering my answer. Discussing Colombia or Ricardo with Jenny has always seemed like a minefield to me, which is why, up until now, we have scrupulously avoided both subjects.

"It's different," I say. "The sky is less... changing... I suppose. It's more just blue in the dry season, and grey in the wet season."

"What's it like there? Otherwise, I mean?"

"It looks like a holiday brochure really. You know, palm trees and white sand."

"Sounds good to me."

"Yeah," I say. "And the house is amazing. It's wooden, on stilts. Oh, I sent you photos didn't I?"

"Yeah."

"There's no big window you can sit behind like this, though. Which is a shame. But Colombia is very beautiful."

"I'm sensing a 'but,'" Jenny says.

I frown, and wonder if she's hoping for some dirt on my relationship with Ricardo. If so this could yet turn sour.

"No, not really... it's just that it's Colombia," I say.

"Is it sort of third-worldy?" Jenny says.

"God don't say that. They hate that."

"Yes, I suppose they would."

"No, it's just a very different society."

I tell Jenny about the parties and the beach bar and the influx of tourists in the summer. I do my best to explain how joyous and open people are. And then I tell her about the stories of kidnappings and police informants having their legs chainsawed off, and men with machine guns in the boot.

"God, it sounds terrifying," Jenny says.

"For the most part, they're just stories you hear," I say. "But yeah, it's unsettling to say the least. You're always a bit on guard."

"But Ricky takes care of you?"

"Ricardo? He hates Ricky you know." The truth is that I hate it even more. Ricky is Jenny's Ex. Ricardo is all mine.

"Yes. Ricardo, then," she says. "Sorry."

"Well, he's Colombian. So he knows how things work, so..." I say. "It's reassuring to have him around."

"Did you find any wifi to Skype him?" Jenny asks.

"No," I say. "No, none at all. And it costs a fortune from my mobile, one pound fifty a minute, I think. I only have about a fiver left, so..."

"Well, you can use mine if you want."

"Nah, thanks. You're all right," I say, thinking that using Jenny's phone to call her ex would somehow be just a bit *too* weird.

Jenny sips her coffee and looks back out to sea. She sighs deeply. "You do love him though?" she asks.

I wrinkle my brow and wait for her to look back at me.

When she does, she too frowns. "I just mean... you know... it's real."

I nod vaguely. "It's real."

"That makes it more understandable somehow," she says.

I nod and lick my lips. "No, it's real," I say again.

"Mummy, look," Sarah says. We both turn to see that she has piled up five of the stones.

"Very good," Jenny says. "Try and get one more on the top. How about that big one?" Then she glances at the time on her mobile. "And what about Tom?" she asks. "How do you feel about Tom these days?"

I shrug. "It's difficult," I say. "But you know that."

"Yeah..." Jenny says. "But you loved Tom too, right?"

I nod and shrug simultaneously.

"But you love Rick... Ricardo more?"

I laugh lightly. "They're very different Jen," I say.

"You don't sound very sure."

"Why are we discussing all this anyway?"

Jenny shakes her head. "No reason. If you don't..."

"It's not that. It's just a bit strange. I mean, with you."

"I'm just trying to... you know... relax a bit about it all. Understanding things helps. Maybe."

"Right," I say. "Well, I suppose they're so different it's hard to compare. I guess that's what I would say."

"Right."

"I mean, if you could pick and mix, you could make up this perfect partner with all the ideal character traits," I say. "Sexy, and funny, and easy going and... But you can't... so there are things that I loved about Tom..."

"Like his sense of humour," Jenny says.

"Well, yes. Exactly. He's very witty. He is actually sharper than Ricardo, wit-wise."

"Right."

"But there are things that drove me insane about Tom – things that meant that we simply weren't compatible."

"Sure."

"And with Ricardo, nothing we've come up against yet is a deal breaker. So... it continues."

Jenny frowns. "And is that... you know... enough?"

"Enough?"

"Well it sounds like you're saying you just haven't found a reason to dump him yet."

I laugh. "I'm sorry Jen... it's hard to explain. Especially to you. I tend to... you know... tone things down. For your sake. But he's sexy and solid and reassuring. He's generous and a good cook and..."

"OK, OK. So you do love him."

I shrug and nod vaguely. "Well yeah. What are you gonna do?"

"I still think Tom is kind of... well... more straightforward."

"Well in some ways he is. He's very direct about what he is and what he thinks. But if you don't see eye to eye, there's no compromise possible."

"Yeah. I know what you mean. But you're exactly the same."

"Maybe that was the problem," I say. "And Tom is from the same culture. Ricardo's, you know, more exotic."

"Harder to read."

"Exactly."

"But that's quite appealing too," Jenny says.

"Well, exactly. Mystery is quite sexy too."

"Yeah. I know."

"Well yes. Of course you do."

"Anyway, enough of that," Jenny says, clapping her hands and standing. "I'm, um, going to get started on lunch."

"Oh!" I say, surprised at the quick-change of rhythm. "I think I'll give the boy a quick call after all."

"Use mine if you want," Jenny says.

"No. I only want to say, 'hi.'"

I step beyond the bay window and phone Ricardo.

In a rush and a gush I tell him that I don't have much credit but that I love him and that we're at the seaside and the view is amazing. He tells me that he's missing me too and that Paloma is on his knees and that it's a lovely sunny day. The entire conversation must last less than three minutes.

When I step back inside, Jenny is fussing with Sarah's hair. She looks up at me with hair-clips between her teeth. "That was quick," she mumbles.

"Yeah, well, as I say. At one-fifty a minute... I just said I was fine and that we're at the seaside. I tried to describe the view. Have you seen how dark the sky is now?"

Jenny gazes at the sky beyond the window. "Wow," she says. "Amazing. Can't you send him a photo with that amazing gadget of yours? A picture's worth a thousand words and all that."

"Not without wifi. Oh, actually, I can," I say. "Of course I can. I just can't use Skype."

I step back from the window and set up the shot, and then I hesitate and wonder whether to ask Jenny and Sarah to pose in front of the window. I'm sure Ricardo would be interested in seeing how big Sarah has grown, and for that matter, how different Jenny looks in her Monroe wig. But then again, sending my boyfriend photos of his ex is, perhaps, a little bit too much.

As I look at the image on the screen and try to decide, Tom knocks on the front door which settles the matter once and for all. I'm certainly not sending poor Ricardo a photo containing *both* of our exes, and so as the first spots of rain hit the window, I simply snap a shot of our seascape view and send it on as quickly as I can, before Tom gets involved and starts asking what I'm up to.

Ricardo: Ghosts In The Corner

With no phone line and no broadband either we could only talk for a couple of minutes. I understand why you sent me that email, babe, I know you *meant* well. The picture was supposed to reassure me. "I miss you. Look at the view!" the accompanying text said.

But because I was missing you so much I *did* look at the view. I looked at it a little too hard.

To start with, I sat on the balcony with Paloma on my lap, and we looked at it on my iPhone. I compared the English sea with the Caribbean before me. And then, a little bored and keen to play with my new toy, I downloaded it to the computer so that I could look at it on the big screen.

I sat and looked at the strange grey sea, and the black horror-film sky, and the boats on the beach, and I imagined you in the distance over the horizon and I missed you as much as I ever have. And then I noticed the whispy reflection in the corner, a family of ghosts, reflected in the window.

Once I enlarged it, it became heavily pixelated, but I could still tell it was you, holding your phone up to take the photo. And I could make out Sarah facing sideways watching you, and Jenny beside her touching her new blond hair, as if she somehow knew she was in the picture.

But there was a third adult in that picture babe, and it wasn't just anyone: I was pretty sure that it was Tom. And you hadn't said anything about Tom being there – not one word. Which got me to thinking.

Despite everything you had told me about how irritating Tom was being, I started to get angry, because that reflection was a secret photo within a photo: it was a portrait of you and Jenny and Sarah, and *Tom*. It was a *family* photo babe, and I saw suddenly that you were in the exact same configuration as when I first met you, and I realised that something was happening here: you were being sucked into your old life. And I was becoming an outsider again.

160

As my boring Saturday went by, I kept going back inside and looking at that photo. I kept looking at it and feeling sick, and wondering what I needed to do.

As if that wasn't a bad enough start to my weekend, the phone then rang, and thinking it was you, and that maybe I could ask you about Tom and you could reassure me, I swiped it from the base and sank onto the hammock.

But it wasn't you Chupy was it? It was Carlos.

He was polite and friendly. He asked how I was. He asked me *where* I was. He reminded me that we had met at Maria's baptism twenty-five years ago and asked me if I still saw her. And then, as if it was a question like any other, he asked me why I didn't want my nephew to give my phone number to his wife.

Cristina had phoned Juan, it seems, and when Juan lied and said that I had gone overseas that crazy bitch had gotten Carlos to make the call instead.

"She's just worried about you, man," Carlos said, "What with your mother dying and you living out in the sticks on your own."

I lied in the only way I could think of. I said that I was trying to forget about *mi mamá's* death, and that it was hard enough to do so without all these calls from family to check up on me. I said the concern was sweet, but that it was just a constant reminder, that kept dragging me back. Which sounded, even to me, like a load of bullshit.

I told him that I wasn't on my own, as well. I said that I shared the house with Paloma. Carlos assumed that Paloma was a "chiquita" and laughed and called me a dirty old so and so, all very man-to-man.

He seemingly bought all of my bullshit, but with a guy like Carlos, you never can tell, because with a guy like Carlos, that would always be his reaction. No matter what he was thinking, he would always seem cool and unruffled, right up to the moment when his henchmen turned up to slit your throat.

The problem that then arose was that only three people ever phoned me with hidden numbers: you when you used Skype, Cristina – obviously to trick me – and Carlos of course: in his line of business you don't dish out phone numbers lightly.

And so, from that point on, every time the phone rang and no number showed, instead of grinning and assuming it was you, my hand started to hesitate. Sometimes late at night, it trembled.

Because what to say if it was Cristina, babe? I had no plan, you see. Her getting Carlos involved was a threat, and a clever, efficient one at that.

And if Carlos phoned again – it would be to arrange to meet me. He would have some innocent pretext, like catching up for old times' sake or a business proposition, but it would mean that he had worked out exactly what was going on.

But it never *was* them, Chupy. From that point on, it was always you.

And that made me worry even more. Because the fact that Cristina never did call meant that Carlos *hadn't* given her my new number.

And that too, meant that he *knew*. And if he knew it was only a question of time before he decided to do something about it.

It was a mess babe. It was a big scary mess and I couldn't think of a way to sort it out.

Kiss Of Death

The effect of the view on every one of us is profound and unmissable. The house feels zen, calm, healing even.

As the four of us sit at the table and the beach darkens beneath the advancing rainclouds and the first raindrops slip down the pane, we all slip into an unusually gentle mood of benevolent chatter. Even Sarah sits calmly as we eat dinner, staring at the beach and occasionally pointing out a man with a dog or a seagull perched on the garden fence.

It's as if with such a magnificent view, the need for any of us to impress is removed. And so we sit, chatting quietly in almost hushed tones.

Tom and I manage to laugh at each other's jokes – a first since our break up. In fact, Tom has both Jenny and me laughing out loud with his stories about the renovation work in his new apartment. Most of these stem from communication problems he's having with the Lithuanian builders his uncle sent.

Jenny tells me at some length what happened to Rodney, a stockbroker she had been dating last summer. That initially promising relationship ended, she reveals, when he turned up with a gift of handcuffs, whip, and gimp mask.

"Sounds quite fun to me," Tom says predictably.

"Well, to be honest," Jenny laughs, "I wouldn't have minded that much if it had been for *him*. But he thought he was going to whip *me*. I mean, as if..."

Once dinner has been cleared away Jenny produces a stack of board games she has found in the sideboard and the three of us set up a game of Risk. I also simultaneously play Snakes and Ladders with Sarah, which explains why Jenny, in unusually aggressive mood, manages to stomp all over me so quickly. At least, that's my alibi. The fact that Sarah thrashes me at Snakes and Ladders is perhaps harder to justify.

As the remains of the day slip into the sea, I go around the lounge switching the various small lamps on. I put the Isley Brothers on the turntable and turn to see Sarah "driving" a pebble across the sofa and Jenny and Tom laughing in front of the now black sea-scape. It looks warm and safe and gorgeous. It looks like something from a furniture catalogue – perfect people in a perfect interior having a lovely time. I feel a pang of unease that we will soon have to leave this place and return to Surrey.

After a three hour battle of nerves, Jenny wins the game and heads off to the kitchen to "rustle something up."

"Now that's what I call a modern woman," Tom says.

"I'm sorry?"

"Well, she can conquer the world, *and* make tea."

I laugh, ruffle Sarah's hair and carry the empty Risk box to the table.

I become aware that Tom is sitting staring at me whilst I put the plastic pieces back in the box. He doesn't help, he just sits and stares. I decide that he is probably trying to think up some stunning put down.

But as I reach across the table for a final stray soldier, he half stands, leans forward, and steals a peck on my cheek. I jump so hard that I almost knock the Risk box back onto the floor.

"What the fuck?" I ask, straightening up, pulling a face and rubbing my cheek.

Tom grins at me smugly and shrugs. "I felt like it," he says.

"Well don't," I say, popping the lid on the box and crossing the room to the sideboard. "Don't *feel like it.*"

"Oooh," Tom says, childishly.

I close the sideboard and glare at him. "Right," I say. "I'm going out for a quick walk. I need a breath of fresh air."

"I'll come with you," Tom says.

"I'd rather you didn't," I reply, hastily grabbing my coat and, even before I have put it on, opening the front door.

It's not that I want to be mean, it really isn't. It's just that the kiss took me by surprise. And it's just that, despite myself, I rather liked it. I'm worried that the unexpected stirring in my loins will be visible if I stay. I'm not sure I trust myself to go for a walk along the beach with him either. Oh lord.

"Don't be too long," Jenny calls from the kitchen. "This'll be ready in fifteen minutes."

Outside, the pebbles are glistening from the recent rain.

The air is icy and damp. I shiver and button my coat and crunch off across the beach, my mood already shifting from surprise to a mixture of flattery, embarrassment and anger. In the end, it's the anger that ends up being the dominant emotion. Tom and I have to spend time together for Jenny's sake. And today is the first time we have managed to do so in a civil manner. And now he has messed it all up – now he has made it all complicated again. And that, frankly, is something I could do without.

"Mark!"

I hear Tom's voice behind me, and think, *"Shit! What now?"*

"Mark!"

I pretend not to hear and walk quickly across the beach, but then I hear the crunch of his feet on the pebbles just behind me. He grabs my sleeve. "Mark," he says panting.

I turn to face him and shake my head. "What's *wrong* with you?" I ask.

And then he grabs my other sleeve and launches his mouth at mine.

For a few seconds I resist, essentially by keeping my lips tightly pressed shut.

But the truth of the matter is that it just feels so good, it's been so long since anyone kissed me, and even longer since anyone kissed me with this passion, and so, despite myself, despite the screaming of my brain, I melt into him and open my mouth to his.

He links his arms behind me, effectively locking me in, but the shabby truth is that I don't try to escape. His mouth is warm and sweet, welcoming and full of memories of all the other times we kissed, times when I was totally enamoured with everything about him.

He moves one hand to the front of my jeans, and then pulls his head back to look me in the eye. "I still have the same effect on you then," he says, grinning.

There's no point even trying to contradict the statement that my dick is so eloquently making.

"I want to fuck," Tom says, before launching himself at my mouth again.

A shiver runs down my spine, and I think, *"Oh, God, so do I."*

"But someone's coming," I say, pulling away and nodding up the beach.

"Here! Over here," Tom says, pulling and then bustling me up the beach towards some beach-huts.

"Tom this is madness," I say. "We both have boyf..." and then he pushes me into the gap between two huts and starts to kiss me again, simultaneously unbuttoning my fly.

"Tom stop," I say. Even *I* realise that I sound unconvincing.

He sinks to his knees and slips my dick between his lips. It feels warm and soft and irresistible. It feels indescribably wonderful, in fact.

"Oh, Tom..." I groan.

"I want to fuck you," he says, pulling away and looking up at me.

"We can't," I say.

"Exes don't count," he says. "Everyone knows that."

I shake my head and gasp in exasperation. I'm not sure if I'm exasperated because I *can't* have sex with Tom, or because I'm *going to*. The roulette wheel is still spinning.

Tom stands and turns me around. "No," I say. "We..." And then he nuzzles my neck and then starts to lick it. The one advantage exes have of course, is that, whether they are trying to piss you off or seduce you, they know exactly which buttons to push. "Oh, God..." I groan, melting against him.

And then I feel the head of Tom's dick against my arse, and a tiny voice struggles to be heard. As his spits in his hand and lubricates himself it takes every last ounce of willpower for me to let that tiny voice be heard above the others. Forcing my mouth to speak the words, "Tom, no. Not without a condom," is one of the hardest things I have ever done, and yet the statement makes me feel like a complete slut, for in fact, it is an admission of intention. It is proof that – condom permitting – I have accepted the inevitability of what comes next.

"Have you got one?" he asks, licking behind my ear.

"No, of course I haven't," I say.

"Well, it's fine. It's still fine," he says.

"No," I protest, turning around. "No it isn't *fine*, Tom."

He kisses me again, and then tries to forcibly turn me around again.

"No," I say. "Stop."

"But I'm negative," he says. "You know I am."

"Maybe I'm not," I say. "How would *you* know?"

"Oh of course you are," he says. "You're Mother Teresa."

Thirty yards away, a guy is crossing the beach. His beagle appears at the corner of the beach-hut.

This momentary intrusion of reality enables me to break free and take control. "Stop this now," I say, pushing him away and then pulling my jeans back up.

"But..." Tom says, then, at the dog, "Shoo! Go away." He picks up some pebbles and throws them and the dog yelps.

"What have you found, boy?" the dog owner calls, now climbing the beach towards us. "Is someone there?"

"I can't do this Tom," I say, slipping out from in front of him and running to the road on the other side of the huts.

Tom runs after me, simultaneously buttoning his jeans. "Mark!" he says. "Jesus."

"I can't do this," I say. "It's crazy."

"What's crazy," Tom says, almost jogging to keep up, "is how seriously you fucking take everything. Jesus, it's just sex. It's just a bit of fun. I'm not going to ask you to leave saint Ricardo or anything."

"I have a partner Tom. So do you. That might not mean anything to you..."

"It didn't mean much to you when *we* were together," he says.

"Don't let's dig all that..."

"Well it *didn't*. Don't be such a hypocrite."

"You weren't faithful either," I say, stopping and turning to face him.

"But I'm not the one getting all prissy," he says.

"I'm sorry, I can't."

"Why? Why now?"

"It's just... different."

"Why?" Tom says.

"I..." I say, lowering my head and staring at my feet. The reasons: that I love Ricardo more than I loved Tom, that my future is with Ricardo, and that even if it isn't, it certainly isn't with Tom – are too cruel to be spoken.

Without me saying a word, Tom, somehow gets the gist. "Oh, *right*," he says. "Thanks."

"Tom... I'm sorry," I say. "I just can't."

"Yeah, right," he says. "Well, if you'd had a condom, you would have. So you can get off your high horse."

I shake my head. "I'd like to Tom, I mean, I'm still attracted to you, but..."

"Yeah, whatever," he says. "Cheers for the grapple eh?" And then he slaps me on the shoulder and heads off across the beach.

"*Tom!*" I shout.

But he doesn't answer, and because I don't know quite what I would say if he did, I passively watch him leave.

I walk down to the breakwater and stare for a moment at the reflection of the cloud-blurred moon on the sea, and then turn to the right and continue to head west. To my left the sea is calm and glassy, and shimmering with moonlight. To my right the straggling houses of Pevensey Bay look dark and abandoned.

***

Two hours later, I get back to the house to find Jenny sitting at the table smoking. "Is that a joint?" I ask, sniffing the air.

"Yeah," she says. "Sarah's in bed. Tom left me a couple. What happened between you two?"

"Happened? What do you mean?"

"Well, one minute everyone's all lovey dovey and the next you're both stomping off across the beach, and now Tom has gone home."

"He went home?"

"Yep. He didn't even stay for tea. Yours is in the kitchen by the way. You can just heat it up."

I hang up my coat and join her at the table. "I'll have a toke on that first if I might."

"Sure," she says, handing it to me. "So?"

I shrug and take a drag. "Nothing."

"Nothing?" she says.

"Nothing."

"Well whatever your nothing was, it was the kiss of death to my little dinner party."

I frown at her, wondering if she knows after all.

"What?" she asks, grinning.

""Sorry," I say, "about dinner."

"Well, it's only macaroni cheese, but all the same... So nothing happened *at all?*"

"I don't really want to go into it," I tell her.

Jenny chuckles, and then slips into an outrageous, dope-fuelled fit of laughter.

"What?" I ask.

"Well, you two," she says, tears in her eyes. "You're like twins."

"Eh?"

"Well that's what Tom said too," she says, still grinning. "I don't want to go into it," she repeats, putting on a pompous voice.

"Sorry," I say. "But..."

Jenny waves one hand in the air. "Whatever," she says. "Keep your little secrets."

"I will."

"What do I care? Now. To macaroni cheese, or not to macaroni cheese. That is the question."

"Oh yes," I say, handing the joint back and standing. "Oh yes. Macaroni cheese indeed."

Once I have eaten, Jenny heads upstairs to bed, and I sit and smoke one of her cigarettes and stare out at the shimmering sea and try to remember what was so wrong with Tom that I left him, and for that matter what was so right about Ricardo that I chose *him*. As time goes by, those memories are becoming less and less clear-cut. So much for absence making the heart grow fonder.

Sticking Around

On Sunday, the sky and the sea are such a uniform grey that it's impossible to see where the one ends and the other begins. "It looks like someone has drawn a big grey curtain," I comment over breakfast.

"Yeah, but I like it even when it's grey," Jenny says.

After breakfast we walk about a mile to the east alternately looking at the sea and peering into people's living rooms, and then we walk most of the way back and decide to have lunch in the second pub, a far darker more traditional place, all red velour and carved wood.

"It's weird the way you change towns and suddenly you're going for walks and having pub lunches," Jenny comments, sipping her Coke. "I mean, we do *have* pubs in Camberley. And there *are* places to walk."

"It's because it's the seaside. It makes you think you're on holiday."

"Well I like being on holiday," Jenny says.

"What do *you* think Sarah?" I ask her.

She looks up from a plate of fish fingers which she is busy mashing up with tomato ketchup. "Very nice, thank-you very much," she says, making us both laugh.

"Such a polite little girl."

"Takes after her mother," Jenny says.

When we finally step back outside, we realise that it has started to rain heavily. "Shit, when did that happen?" Jenny says.

"Shit?" I say. "Is that now on the acceptable word list?"

"No," Jenny says. "It isn't."

"Do you want to wait, or..."

"I don't think it's going to stop," she says, pulling up Sarah's hood. "Anyway, it's not far. We can run for it."

I move to the other side of Sarah so that we can each hold one of her hands, and then I count, "One, two, three, go!" and we run out into the rain and along the sodden tarmac, alternately running at Sarah's pace and suspending her between us for extra speed.

We burst through the door into the house in a big sodden, laughing huddle.

I bend down to unbutton Sarah's coat and I ask her if she is OK.

Her reply, *"Awesome,"* provokes a fresh round of laughter.

"I told you not to use that word," Jenny laughingly scolds her.

The afternoon rain is constant and uninterrupted. It's the kind of day that usually drives me to distraction, but behind our glass wall, it doesn't feel so bad. Jenny digs through the record collection and chooses classical – first an irritatingly twiddly bit of Mozart, and then, rather aptly, Debussy's La Mer. I build Sarah a house of cushions to play in, and then for want of anything better to do, open my laptop and resume work on my translation.

Over breakfast on Monday morning, we decide to go to Eastbourne. I want to go back and look at my childhood home and Jenny to take Sarah along the pier.

But in the end, the truth is that neither of us want to move from the house. Its hold over us is almost magnetic, and so we simply read/play/translate all over again.

In the evening we bake potatoes in silver foil and prepare a big salad to accompany it, and then, as the sky flames red, we sit behind our window, coats at the ready, and wait for darkness to fall and the fireworks to begin.

I pour myself a glass of wine, and Jenny, who can't drink, vanishes occasionally around the side of the house to alternately smoke cigarettes or joints out of Sarah's sight.

"So no Tom then?" I ask finally, a question I have been scrupulously avoiding until it's too late to influence events.

"Well it doesn't look like it," Jenny says, glancing at her wrist and then, realising that she doesn't have a watch, at her phone instead. "I can call him if you want."

"Noooo," I say. "Not on my behalf."

"I didn't think so," Jenny says, a lopsided grin on her face. "What *did* happen between you two?"

I tut and shake my head.

"Tell me," she says. "I mean, if things are this awkward, maybe I *need* to know."

"You don't," I tell her.

"OK," she says. *"Jesus."*

"He kissed me, OK?"

"He *kissed* you?"

"Yes. It was just a peck. But yes, he stole a kiss."

"He *stole* it?"

"It means he did it without my perm..."

"I know what it means, it just sounds so... so *Brideshead,*" she says, slipping into a grin.

"It's not funny Jen," I say. "It was very awkward."

"I bet it was," she says. Then she repeats again, in a whisper, "He *stole* a kiss."

"Stop it," I say. "I know you're stoned, but..."

She bites her lip and pushes her tongue into her cheek. "Sorry," she says. "It's just..."

"Yes?"

"Well, it's ironical, I suppose. *Ironical?"*

"I think plain old ironic does the trick. But why, anyway? Why ironic?"

"Well, Ricardo stole you... or you stole him... or whatever..."

"Your point being?"

"Well, now Tom's trying to steal you back. By *stealing* kisses." She snorts again.

"Is he?" I ask. "Has he said something?"

"Lord no," Jenny says. "In fact the only thing he said to me that was vaguely relationship related was how happy he is with Sven."

"Sven?"

Jenny pulls a face. "Sorry. Oops. Yes, Sven the bodybuilder."

"Sven?"

"He's Swedish, I think." And then she snorts again. "I'm not supposed to mention him either."

"Why?"

Jenny shrugs. "I don't know," she says.

"And you will not discuss this with Tom, OK?"

"No. Absolutely no mention of the stealing of kisses," she says.

"You're impossible."

"Yeah. I know. Was it nice though? Was it a *nice* kiss?"

"I think you can probably deduce the answer to that if you think about it," I say.

"Oh I can," she says. "I hereby deduce that you liked it more than you're prepared to admit, but that you'll pretend to the death that you hated every minute of it."

"Every minute? It was a peck Jenny. It lasted an eighth of a second. We didn't snog," I lie.

Thankfully, at that instant we're interrupted by the first flash of colour over Eastbourne pier.

"It's happening, quick," Jenny says, just as the bang reaches us. She jumps up and pulls a startled Sarah through the roof of her makeshift house.

We button our coats and run out through the bay window and down over the gravel to the sea.

It's not a huge firework display, and the distance makes it even smaller, but symmetrically reflected in the oily surface of the sea, it is unreasonably beautiful.

I lift Sarah onto my shoulders.

"Beware," Jenny sniggers in my ear. "She wet herself with excitement last year."

"You have to go *oooh* when the rockets go up," I tell Sarah, "And *ahhh*, when they explode. Like this... Ooooh. Ahhh!"

"Do you?" Jenny asks, sarcastically.

"That's what I was taught when I were a lad," I say, for some reason in a mock west-country accent. "Many many years ago that were."

And so, we stand, and the three of us shout, "Oooh, and Ahhh," just like when I was a kid. The whole thing makes me feel so happy I'm almost in tears by the time it finishes.

When the climactic finale is over, I say softly, "God, I love fireworks."

"Me too," Jenny says beside me.

"Me too!" Sarah shouts, piercingly in my ear.

Because Jenny's voice was cracked, I turn to look at her and see that her eyes are watering. I put an arm around her shoulders and pull her towards me. "Ahh, you feeling all emotional?" I ask.

She wipes her face with her sleeve and slips an arm around my waist. "It's just so beautiful," she says, her voice crumbling even further. "It makes me want to stick around so much it hurts, you know?"

I pull her tighter and say, "Well, call Susan. Maybe we can stay *another* day."

Jenny pulls away. "That's not what I meant," she says quietly, turning and heading back up the beach.

It takes me a moment to realise what she *did* mean.

I sigh sadly and watch for a moment as residents along the coast release their own straggly rockets into the air, and then I take a deep breath and remember that Sarah is still on my shoulders.

I jiggle her up and down and say, "So! Some baked potato for you?"

"Yesss!" she says.

"With or without alphabet spaghetti?"

"With!" she says, clasping my head so hard it hurts.

"OK. One, two, three... off we go!"

Post Holiday Blues

On Tuesday morning, Sarah wakes me up with her unique finger in the ear technique. I gasp and pull my head away. "Jesus! Don't *do* that," I say, dragging myself from a rather sexy dream and struggling to focus on her grinning face.

"Mummy says she's ever getting up again."

"What?"

"Mummy says she's ever getting up again," Sarah repeats.

"Never."

"Never ever."

I blink repeatedly in an attempt at improving my grungy vision.

"She says she's going to stay in bed for ever and ever," Sarah says.

I groan and roll onto my back so that I can look out at the view – this morning a vision of blue, wall to wall.

"Are we going home today?" Sarah asks.

"Yes. I'm afraid we are."

It takes a while for me to get up, but I still beat Jenny to it. I make tea and set Sarah up with toast and orange juice, and then, seeing that it is now gone nine, I take Jenny's mug of tea upstairs.

The sun is illuminating her bed and she is propped up on pillows with her eyes closed. "Are you sunbathing or sleeping?" I ask in the doorway.

"Both," she says. "How cool is that?"

"Sarah says you're not getting up, not never."

"That is correct," Jenny says, shielding her eyes and looking over at me. "I've decided to stay in bed for a year and eat toast. Call it a clinical trial if you want."

"I think they've already tested that therapy," I say, crossing the room and putting her tea down on the bedside cabinet. "They tried it in America a thousand times."

"Does it cure cancer?" she asks.

"No, but they need a crane to get you out at the end."

She shrugs and reaches for the tea. "Who cares?" she says.

"You remind me of..."

"Yes?"

"Never mind," I say, retreating to the landing.

I had been about to say that she reminded me of Tom when we visited the gîte in Chateauneuf D'Entraunes. It had been impossible to get him out of bed on the last day as well. But considering everything that happened when we *did* get back from that trip, I decide that it's better not to continue.

I peer into the mouldy room and pull a face: it still smells pretty bad despite our bleaching attempts. And then I close the door and head back downstairs to where Sarah is still laboriously working her way through the same slice of toast.

Jenny finally manages to drag herself from her bed just before ten.

"The sun moved off the bed," she explains. "The trial required constant sunlight, so..."

Despite the beautiful weather, we are all subdued as we collect our things from around the house and load up the car. No one puts any music on the record deck this morning. I don't think any of the records are sad enough.

By the time I drive away – the two girls straining their necks to look back at the fading view – it feels like the end of something wonderful. It feels, in fact, like we're heading to another funeral.

As if to push the point home, Sarah asks, "Will Granny be there?"

"No darling, she won't," Jenny replies, catching my eye and raising an eyebrow.

Silence reigns through most of the journey. Sarah sleeps in the back and Jenny stares from a side window and, I notice, wrings her hands together.

"Such a waste," she says at one point.

"What's that?"

"This weather. Such a lovely day," she says. "We should have stayed and driven home this evening."

After the beach-house, the house in Camberley feels dark and oppressive.

Jenny parks Sarah in front of the television and heads outside for a cigarette whilst I make us all toasted cheese sandwiches. I am just serving these onto plates when the doorbell rings.

"Jenny, can you get that?" I call. "Front door."

"So?" Susan asks a minute later, as she and Jenny enter the kitchen. "How was it?"

"Oh amazing," Jenny says. "We loved it, didn't we."

"Absolutely amazing," I agree.

"The furniture's all a bit tacky," Susan says, "We keep thinking about replacing it all, but it doesn't really matter for a holiday home, does it?"

"I loved all that actually," I say. "The seventies is my favourite era. The records were great too."

"Not *my* taste," Susan says, "that's for sure. They all came with the house too. We bought it at the end of the eighties in an auction – Ted had a friend who was an auctioneer and he told us about it – it's pretty much as it was then. The owners went to Australia and decided not to come back, so they just sold the place and everything in it. It was almost like they were on the run or something. Still, it was a pretty good deal at the time."

"Well we absolutely loved it," Jenny says. "Everything about it. All of us."

"Well, now you know where it is," Susan says, taking the keys from Jenny's grasp. "Anytime."

"There is one problem we need to tell you about though," I say.

"Oh yeah," Jenny says, pulling a face. "The roof."

"The roof?"

"It's been leaking," I explain. "The back bedroom is completely mouldy."

"It's always been a bit damp," Susan says.

"I'm afraid it's *more* than a bit damp now," Jenny tells her. "The whole wall has gone green. We tried to bleach it, but it didn't help much. Mark says it's the flat roof leaking."

"Oh God," Susan says. "We'll have to get someone in to fix it then. I wonder how much that will cost. It means going down there too, of course."

"Don't you *like* it there?" Jenny asks, incredulously.

"It's OK," Susan says. "I used to really like it. I was always keener than Ted. But then... well, nowadays it... it reminds him of things. *You* know what I mean, I'm sure," she tells Jenny, somewhat mysteriously.

"Right," Jenny says vaguely.

Susan coughs. "Plus Ted likes his home comforts. It's hard to convince him to go anywhere these days to be honest."

"I wonder what happened in the beach-house," Jenny says once Susan has left.

"I bet he cheated on her," I say. "A summer romance."

"Or she on him," Jenny says, "Maybe there was a sexy neighbour."

After lunch I head upstairs for a sleep. I doze off quickly and dream that I am back on the beach. When I wake up an hour later, I jolt with surprise at the sight of the green wallpaper around me.

I wash my face, and head downstairs to find Sarah seated, exactly as before, in front of the television.

In the kitchen, Jenny is still at the kitchen table too – staring out at the garden. "The view's not the same, is it?" she says when she becomes aware of my presence.

"It's not bad," I say. "But no, it's not the same."

"How are you feeling?" she asks.

"Better," I say, taking a seat beside her. "I was feeling a bit washed out to be honest."

"Yeah. I feel quite... well... depressed really," she says.

"Post holiday depression syndrome," I say.

"I suppose."

"Sarah's happily catching up on all the TV she missed. She doesn't mind."

"Yeah. I was thinking about that too. It's funny really. She didn't even miss the TV down there."

"Too busy with pebbles," I say.

"Yeah. I suppose. I think I prefer that, though. It seems healthier for her."

"Sure," I say. "Still, back to nursery tomorrow."

"Yeah. I almost took her for the afternoon, but to be honest, I just couldn't summon the energy to walk there."

"You should have told me."

"You were asleep."

"You could have woken me."

"It doesn't matter anyway."

I yawn and stretch. "So how long can Sarah stay off before you get into trouble?"

Jenny turns to me and frowns. "What do you mean, *get into trouble?*"

"Well, it's like school isn't it? Surely she has to attend a minimum number of days."

"Not at all. No, it's a private thing. I *pay* for her to go. It costs nearly two hundred quid a month. There were no places at the state one by the time we moved."

"Wow. Really?"

"Uhuh."

"Why?"

"Why what?"

"Well, why take her then? I mean, it's not like you're working at the moment."

Jenny shrugs. "Mum thought it was a good idea. Which I suppose it is. They learn to make friends and stuff. It gets her ready for school next year. And she watches less TV that way. Also, the plan was, of course, that I would find a job."

"Fair enough," I say. I sit and think about this for a bit and then say, "You know, I thought she *had* to attend."

"No. As I say. It's optional."

"But if she *doesn't*... well then there's no reason why we have to be here at all, is there?"

"What do you mean?"

"Well, why don't you ask Susan if we can't use the house longer term. We could offer to fix the roof or something... repaint that room for her. We could do a deal."

Jenny turns sharply to look at me. She looks suddenly very business like, very professional. "You mean *live* there?" she asks.

I shrug. "Why not? For a few weeks. Or a few months. I don't know. Why not?"

"Wouldn't *you* mind though?" she asks.

"Me? Why? I *love* it there."

"Oh," Jenny says. "I thought you preferred it here."

"Why would you think that?"

"I don't know. You have a room here, at least."

"But if we fixed up the spare room. If we mended the leak."

"And you can call Ricardo here... there's no phone line is there. *And* no internet."

"Sure, but... Look, don't take this the wrong way..."

"Go on," she says.

"Well I hate it here to be honest."

Jenny laughs sourly. "Well join the club," she says.

"And London's not too far from Pevensey for checkups and stuff. And it's not like you have to go every day now..."

"No."

"So we could get organised. You could get the post redirected. We could maybe get the phone down there reconnected if it's not too expensive. I saw that there's a socket."

"And you wouldn't mind?"

"I'd rather be there than here," I say with a shrug.

"Right."

"Are *you* sure you don't mind Sarah dropping out of nursery though?"

"I think it's good for her to be elsewhere to be honest. Running around on beaches and all that."

"So..." I say.

"It all depends on Susan though really, doesn't it?" Jenny says, standing.

"It does. Where are you going?"

"To ask her."

"Right now?"

"Yeah. Right now."

Less than a minute later, Jenny returns. She looks glum.

"No go then?" I say.

"She's not in. They've gone out."

"Oh well."

"God. I so want to do this," Jenny says, breaking into a smile. "I hope that she says, 'yes.'"

"Me too."

"I'll be gutted if she doesn't."

"Maybe we need to look for something else in that case."

"Yeah. Maybe we do."

Pancake Therapy

The good news comes on Tuesday afternoon: Susan is so happy for us to use her beach-house over the winter that Jenny wonders if our presence next door doesn't perhaps offend her in some way. Whatever her reasons – and I think it's probably got more to do with her hopes that we will fix the roof – we can barely contain our excitement. Jenny starts running around the house randomly grabbing things to take, and Sarah, infected by all the elation, follows her from room to room shrieking.

Jenny, predictably, wants to leave immediately, but I persuade her to wait until the weekend. "Let's do it properly," I argue. "Let's take the time to think about everything we need to take, and everything we need to do. Otherwise we'll have to come back in three days because we have forgotten something."

We redirect the post, request that the phone line be reconnected, and empty the refrigerator. Jenny makes vast lists of everything that we might need, and then rampages around the house fetching things and putting them in piles.

Fitting this eclectic collection of stuff into the Micra takes almost as long again, but on Saturday morning, in a mood of boundless optimism that is entirely disproportionate to a simple house-change, I drive out of the close.

"Goodbye misery, hello happiness," Jenny says as I attempt to coax the heavily laden car into pulling away. I only hope it turns out to be that simple.

The omens are good, though – the traffic is as fluid as the day is bright. Man, woman and child driving a car loaded with luggage to the seaside feels somehow primordial – like some ancient ritual handed down over generations. Never have I felt so hetty.

The only thing missing is a bank-holiday traffic jam, and so by eleven thirty I am bumping back over the beachfront car-park again.

"God I'm so happy to be back," Jenny says. "Is that weird?"

I turn off the engine and push my door open against the buffeting breeze. I stand and scan the horizon, taking in the vista which stuns me anew.

180

The sea is a deep dark blue today, topped with frothy whitecaps. The low winter sun is sharp and warm, its intensity doubled by the shimmering ripples of the sea.

The air is shockingly cold and unusually clean and transparent. The result is that all of the colours look brighter than usual, as if someone has upped the saturation.

I take a deep breath.

Jenny releases Sarah from the child-seat and looks at me over the top of the car.

A gust of wind ruffles her hair and she slaps a hand on top of her head to hold her wig in place and breaks into a grin. "Nearly had a carry-on moment there," she says.

I smile back. "Wow," I say. "It's just irresistible, isn't it?"

We spend Saturday moving stuff from the car to the house and shuffling it around. Because our stay here is less temporary we also move some of the furniture around to better suit our needs. Specifically, we turn the vast sofa so that we can sit side by side and face our nine feet of seascape telly.

"Tomorrow I'll scrub that wall upstairs again," Jenny says as she butters bread for lunch. "If we can make that room usable it would be much better for you."

"Yeah," I agree. "I'll get up on the roof and try to see what's wrong. Stopping the leak is the first thing."

"And then I think you should get out and about," Jenny says thoughtfully.

"Out and about?"

"Yeah, get yourself over to Brighton and have some fun before my next chemo session. You haven't had a night out since you came over from Colombia."

I frown. "Hum," I say vaguely, thinking that I'm not sure I want to bump into Tom. Brighton's gay scene may be consequential considering the size of the town, but it's my experience that it's impossible to spend a night in Kemptown without bumping into someone you know.

"If you're worried about bumping into Tom," Jenny says, efficiently reading my mind, "we can synchronise. I can invite him over for the evening, and leave you with Brighton all to yourself."

I nod slowly and chew my lip. "Maybe. It's not just Tom though," I say, thinking back to London and how incapable I was of enjoying the gay scene there without Ricardo. And then I realise that London now feels like a very long time ago, and that since then, I have learnt to live without Ricardo quite efficiently. Which strikes me as a far from reassuring thought.

Our broadband arrives on Tuesday and, because of these concerns, I make a concerted effort to speak to Ricardo daily. This campaign ironically coincides with it becoming increasingly difficult to catch Ricardo in – the arrival of the dry season in Colombia means that I rarely manage to call at a time when he is within hearing distance of the phone.

After a week of frustrated messages on answer-phones, we agree that it's easier if he just Skypes our landline daily instead, and this slight change has its own perverse side effects. Because fifty percent of the time Jenny answers the phone, she ends up having to speak to Ricardo.

The first few times this occurs, the shock is evident – she throws the phone at me as if it is a grenade about to explode and runs, blushing, from the room.

As the days go by, however, she learns to execute this first with elegant nonchalance and then to actually relax enough to exchange civilities with him.

On our second Wednesday in the house, I return from having tar-taped the split in the roof and find Jenny slouched on the couch, apparently in the midst of one of her long friendly chats with Tom.

Once I have showered and changed I return to the lounge to find her still on the phone.

I'm just considering asking her to wind up her conversation (it's time for my call from Ricardo) when she hands me the phone. "It's Ricky," she says, casually, "he wants a quick word with you."

Ricardo's opening phrase – *I can't talk for long, Chupy, I have to go out,* does little to stem my rising tide of jealousy.

I spend all day, in fact much of that week, wondering what they talked about: their past together? Jenny's illness? Me? A couple of times, I even open my lips ready to express the question forming on my tongue. But I never *do* ask. For some reason I never quite find the right way or the right moment.

Other than Jenny's resurrection of "Ricky," though, those first weeks at the beach-house are perfect. The cold, crisp weather continues, the tar-tape seemingly holds, and the wall in the spare room dries. By day I work on my translations and run along the beach with a screaming Sarah on my shoulders, and by night we sit and listen to our seventies time-warp record collection and stare out at the phases of the moon.

Most importantly of all, Jenny looks as well as I have seen her since the end of radiotherapy. She even starts to put on a little weight – an unsuspecting subject of my own secret Susan-inspired clinical trial of cooking her pancakes every morning for breakfast.

Whitehawk Argy Bargy

It's spitting with rain by the time I get to Brighton on Friday night. It's not ideal for wandering around on my own, but with Tom and Sven invited to dinner, it's hardly an ideal moment to stay at home either.

I head down to the pier and buy myself a donut. As I walk across the wooden planks biting into a delicious mixture of sugar and fat, the smell of the donut mixed with the salty sea air, and the flashing lights of the amusement arcades provokes a flurry of memories from my childhood. I remember playing air-hockey with my dad at the end of the pier, the feeling of having candy-floss stuck to my nose, an aunty sneaking me out of the house to play the slot machines on the sea-front.

Feeling melancholy, I stride briskly to the end of the pier, look down into the swelling depths below and then, as the spots of rain intensify I march even faster back the other way.

When I reach Kemptown, I glance at my watch. It's just eight-o-clock, dinner time really, only – no doubt thanks to the donut – I'm no longer hungry.

As a time-wasting strategy, I head into my old haunt, Red Roaster, for a coffee.

Inside three people are sitting alone eating and reading newspapers. The atmosphere is quiet and studious, like a library.

I take a seat on one of the leather sofas and feeling a bit sad and a bit homesick, and even a little home*less*, I look out at the rainy street and sip my cappuccino as slowly as I can manage.

My brother Owen – now in Australia – used to have a house in Brighton, in fact I even lived there for a while with him after my accident. Red Roaster feels like a flashback to a previous life – I could almost imagine Owen or Tom appearing in the doorway now and smiling and joining me for coffee. I sit and remember the past and think about Owen on the other side of the world and Ricardo on the *other* side of the world and how much I miss them both, and how much I miss my father, and strangely even Tom. I think about this for a moment and then change my mind. No, Tom is definitely better an hour's drive away. If I hang around Tom too much I will end up sleeping with him, and that wouldn't do anyone any good.

In that instant, my life seems to me to be one huge fuck-up. A great, deep, dark cavern filled with fading memories of better times. I wonder how long it will be before Jenny vanishes into the same void – before Ricardo joins my army of exes.

Realising that I'm sinking into a melodramatic fug, I reach for a newspaper, determined to distract myself before it gets out of hand.

An hour later, having read the Guardian cover-to-cover I leave Red Roaster and head up Saint James' Street towards the Bulldog.

The rain has stopped but the streets are shiny and wet – the air temperature can't be that far above freezing. Winter is truly upon us, and I still don't even have a date by which I can imagine leaving.

Halfway up the hill, a queue for the cashpoint is blocking half of the path – a line of punters waiting for Friday night beer-tokens.

As I draw level with the bank, a girl appears from a side-street. She's in her late teens, and heavily made up. She's wearing a pink puffa-jacket over a very short T-shirt that nowhere-near meets her low waisted jeans. Her diamanté belly-piercing twinkles in the orange light from the street lamp. My first thought is how cold she must be – truly a fashion victim.

She reaches the narrowest stretch of the pavement at exactly the same moment I do, but because she is holding three large paper shopping bags in her left hand, and has a big pink handbag wedged over her right arm, there isn't enough remaining room for me to get by without stepping into the road.

I glance behind me and see two buses heading up the hill, and so it is that we grind to a halt, face to face.

She's yacking into her mobile when her eyes focus on mine for the first time. "Yeah," she says, "Yeah, yeah, I know, he's a prick."

I wait for her to move the bags or even just turn sideways a little so that I can squeeze by, but she simply stands there, staring at me and talking into her phone.

I glance behind and see the first bus is now about twenty feet away, so stepping into the road is out of the question.

"I know," she says into the phone. "Yeah, I know. Hang on a minute Mum can you?"

I shrug and smile at her and wait either for her to make the slightest effort so that we can pass, or for the bus to move on up the hill.

What happens instead, is that she says, "Yeah. Hold on a minute Mum, there's some cunt in front of me who won't fucking move."

My mouth drops open in shock.

"What's your fucking problem?" she asks, addressing me directly now and pressing the phone against her chest, as if to protect her mother from this second round of expletives.

"None," I say, perplexed. "None, except the width of your shopping bags."

At this, she sighs and barges past, toppling me into the road. Luckily I stumble into the gutter during the gap between the passing of the two buses and am safely back on the pavement by the time the huge wing mirror of the second bus whistles past my ear.

I look down the hill to see her marching onwards but still looking back at me. "Fucking poof! Like it up the arse do you?" she shouts back at the top of her voice. "I'll bet you do. Fucking queer." And then she quite calmly resumes her phone call. "Yeah Mum, some poof, anyway..."

"Nice," a guy queuing for the cashpoint comments.

"Jesus!" I exclaim.

"Whitehawk trash," he says.

"Whitehawk?"

"Council estate," he says, nodding up the hill.

"Right," I say, giving him a nod, and heading, less enthusiastically, onwards.

Inside the Bulldog, I order a pint of beer to calm my nerves and take a bar stool against the far wall.

A motley crew of clients are dotted around the place tonight. To the left of the bar, two guys are chatting up a younger third. All three look like their drug cocktails haven't been treating them too well. In fact their sunken complexions remind me of Jenny when she was on her initial chemo, and it suddenly strikes me that this is what these drugs are – chemotherapy for life. Perhaps if they called it that instead of a "cocktail" it wouldn't seem quite so attractive to all the idiot condom-allergic youngsters.

At the rear of the bar, on the exact spot where I first spoke to Tom, a cute bearded guy in his thirties is flicking through a magazine. I fix a benevolent half-smile and watch him, but when he finally does look up at me he simply wrinkles his nose and turns away. *Ouch.*

The only other couple in the place are two twinky-twenties in the midst of an animated and theatrically public discussion about whether Diesel jeans are cut better than G-Star or not, so I reach for an abandoned free-sheet and start to flick through myself.

185

It's been a long time since I visited the scene and I ponder that I couldn't feel much less at-home if I were to go to a Mormon prayer meeting.

The door to the bar opens and the guy from the cashpoint appears. He nods at me and raises one eyebrow then heads straight for the bar. He's a fit-fifty, cute, balding, blue-eyed – a little over-built for my tastes but at least he has a friendly smile. Once he has paid for his drink he comes straight over to talk to me. "You survived the Whitehawk argy-bargy then," he says.

"Only just," I laugh. "She nearly pushed me under that bus."

"Classy bird," he says. "A proper little potty mouth."

"She was on the phone to her *mum*," I say, grinning at the *potty-mouth*. "Swearing like a trooper she was."

"Nice," he says.

"I'm just wondering where all that aggro comes from. I mean, straight into homophobia, like a reflex."

The guy shrugs. "Living in a shit council estate with no money and no future and walking past a load of affluent poofs every day helps I expect."

"You did *see* all her shopping bags?" I say. "*And* she was on an iPhone. She wasn't *that* skint."

He laughs. "All on tick, I expect. She'll be up to her pierced navel in store-cards, out spending every Saturday in an attempt at shoring up her crumbling self-image."

I push my lips out and nod to express how impressed I am. "Detailed analysis there," I say.

He grins and holds out one hand. As we shake, he says, "Billy. Social worker to the great unwashed of Whitehawk."

"Ah!" I exclaim. "I'm Mark. Good to meet you. That must be one tough job."

I chat to Billy for nearly two hours. I realise that he's probably hitting on me so I quickly make clear that I have a boyfriend but he seems unfazed. Were I single, I'm pretty sure that I would end up in bed with Billy tonight – he's funny and clever and fit. Luckily, the fact that I have to drive back to Pevensey means that I can't get so drunk that I forget what I'm about.

At ten-thirty Billy glances at his phone. "I'm going over to Schwarz," he says. "You fancy tagging along?"

"Schwarz?"

"The club below Legends."

"The leather place?"

Billy shrugs. "You'll be OK with me," he says, looking me up and down. "I know the doorman."

I hadn't been referring to the dress code; I was thinking about the fact that what usually happens in a place like Schwarz isn't something I should be participating in.

"I'm sorry," I say. "But... I don't... you know..."

"No, not really," Billy says. *"What* don't you... you know?"

"Well, we're faithful. We don't play around."

"A rare and splendid thing," Billy says. "But I don't think you *have* to have sex in Schwarz. At least you didn't have to last time I was there."

I laugh. "Right."

"And you know what they say," Billy continues. "It doesn't matter where you get your appetite as long as you eat at home."

I laugh again. "I like that," I say. "Yes, very good."

"So?" Billy asks, downing the dregs of his pint and pulling on his jacket.

I shrug. "Oh, what the hell," I say. "Just don't let me do anything I might regret."

A Bill Clinton Moment

Schwarz feels like any other bar – initially at least. It's redder, and darker, and the music has more base than the Bulldog. It's actually considerably busier too and the thirty or so guys here cover the full spectrum from clean-shaven youngsters to bearded granddads.

The only thing most of them have in common is the bar's imposed dress code: shiny boots and leather jeans abound.

Billy and I head straight for the bar. "So are you into the whole leather thing?" he asks once we have paid for our bottles of beer.

"Not like some of *these* guys," I say. "I mean, I've never bought a leather *tie* for example... Or leather underwear... But I've nothing against it. Which is ironic."

"Ironic?"

"Well, yeah... I'm vegetarian."

"Really?"

"Yeah. Well, I eat fish, so..."

"But you wouldn't want underwear made of fish, would you?" he says, restraining a smirk. "They'd be all smelly."

I laugh. "Exactly. Leather's much better."

"Well, I rather like it myself," he says, stroking the sleeve of his own jacket. "I think it's very sensual."

"Yeah," I agree. "I have been known to dabble... I had a motorbike for many years which is always a good excuse for wearing a bit of cow-hide."

"Hum, biker, nice," he says, then swigs at his beer. "And your bloke?"

"Yes?"

"He a biker too?"

"No," I say.

Billy looks disappointed, so I add, "He was a fireman though, when I met him. He had the shiniest boots in town."

"Hum," Billy says again. "Biker gets off with fireman. Now there's an image to wank over. ..." His final words are lost in the music – a remix of Unkle's *Reign* getting louder by the second.

"Eh?"

"I said that's *hot,*" Billy shouts. "I'm into uniforms too."

"Right," I say. "I love this track."

"Yeah," he says, disinterestedly. "It's a good one. I'm, um, off for a wander down yonder. You want to join me?"

"No, I'll stay here," I say.

He winks at me and turns and crosses the room, vanishing behind a partition.

Because I feel self conscious without him, I drink my beer over-quickly, and then remember that I can't order another one without going over the limit for driving. I feel even more self conscious once the barman whisks the empty bottle away. In the old days, of course, that's what smoking was for – a displacement activity, a way to occupy flailing hands.

Because I'm feeling awkward but also because I'm intrigued, and partly even to avoid the cloying glances of the guy with the new-romantic flop-top beside me, I follow Billy's path across the room and position myself against the first partition where back-room meets bar.

In the depths, out of sight, I can hear someone groaning.

A guy with a shaved head and a goatee enters and positions himself beside me, raising one knee and leaning against the wall. He's wearing leather jeans and a t-shirt which he quickly removes and stuffs into his rear pocket. His chest is muscled and furry, with just a hint of beer belly – made to measure in order to test my endurance, the bastard.

I glance at him and he nods towards the interior and then turns and vanishes, assuming that I will now follow. In a very Bill Clinton kind of way, I stand and argue with myself about what exactly constitutes sex, what I could maybe get away with that *wouldn't* count as cheating.

Sadly, what I *would* like to do with him clearly falls beyond the remit, and so I sigh and stay put, noting a vague butterfly sensation in my stomach that I once naively believed meant *love*. I just hope Ricardo appreciates my sacrifice.

A text-book scene happens before my eyes: a tall fit-fifties rather Village People leather man leads his younger "boy" past me on the end of a dog-lead. The older guy is wearing high-top boots, leather jeans and shirt. The younger guy is short, blond, and has porn movie pecs and a washboard stomach. He's wearing nothing but a black leather posing pouch, chaps and a thick dog-collar.

The older guy pushes him against the first interior wall and says, "OK, boy, *now* you can come."

"Thank-you sir," he replies in a foreign accent.

I watch as his master unzips him and his pierced dick springs forth. I'm amazed that such a perfect porn-scene should be happening in such a mundane way, and barely out of sight of all those guys casually drinking their beer to my left.

As I watch, the master starts to squeeze his boy's nipples and the boy himself masturbates frantically. I try to work out whether this is what people call sexual liberation, and therefore something we should be proud of, or man reverting to chimpanzee: our basest desires laid bare and an embarrassment to us all.

What I *can't* deny is how arousing the scene is.

I watch the cliché porn-scene for a moment and start to feel seriously horny myself. There's a reason, of course, why clichés are clichés, and the master ordering his more than willing boy around is intrinsically hot, especially when they are both so very, very pretty.

A hand slides over the bulge in my jeans and I look right to see Billy grinning at me. "They're sexy aren't they?" he says. He leans in and whispers in my ear, "I've had the little guy. He's hot, don't you think?"

"They both are," I say, struggling to decide how to react to Billy who is right now pushing his hand down inside *my* jeans. How I *should* react of course is obvious enough, it's just that it feels so good... I'm rapidly losing control of whatever part of my brain needs to say 'no' here.

Billy grabs my belt and I let him tug me further inside. He pushes me back against the wall next to the boy with the dog collar, and sinks to his knees to unbutton my fly.

Beside me the blond guy is crying out and wanking frantically as his master pummels his nipples. Daddy catches my eye and smiles dirtily, and removes one hand from his boy and slides it under *my* sweatshirt.

As Billy slips his lips around my dick, I'm momentarily lost in the moment, and it is heavenly. "Oh God," I say.

I think, *"Shit, now that really does count as sex,"* and, *"you can't even say you were drunk."*

But then it is heavenly no more – his blow-job hurts more than any blow-job should. "Hey, be careful," I say.

Daddy frowns at me and I open my mouth to say, *"not you,"* but then I can take Billy's teeth on my dick no longer. "Ouch! Fuck!" I say, which regrettably causes Daddy to release my nipple and return his attention to his own partner, who, I note, is still frantically masturbating. He seems, in fact, to be having considerable trouble coming.

190

"Sorry," I say, pushing Billy's head away. "Sorry, but... this isn't working for me."

Billy stands and smiles and shrugs before wandering off into the shadows.

I button my fly and re-enter the bar. Having to refasten my belt with at least five people staring at me makes me feel as cheap as I ever have felt, and sensing that to top it all I am now blushing, I head directly for the exit.

As I climb the stairs, I have a final reassuring thought. That maybe if you don't come, maybe *then* it doesn't count as sex?

It is almost one a.m. when I get back to Pevensey Bay so Jenny has already gone to bed.

Wide awake, I creep upstairs and check the wall in the spare room which, despite the downpour, seems to have remained dry, then I return downstairs to sleep.

But I don't sleep. Instead, I lie on one side and stare out at the almost full moon glimmering through the thinning layer of cloud and think about my evening, because what happened tonight doesn't feel insignificant.

The reason for that, I decide, is that it is an omen – a glimpse of the future. Unless I make a determined effort to engineer it otherwise what will happen is that I will slowly forget Ricardo – it's happening already – and then one night I will meet someone new and without ever really having decided it, my time with Ricardo will be over. It's clearly not beyond the realms of possibility that I could slip back into a relationship with Tom.

The fact that neither of these scenarios strikes me as unappealing demonstrates how far down this path I have already gone.

As a mental exercise, I force myself to think about Ricardo. I force myself to remember what he looks like and what his body feels like next to me in bed. I think about his qualities and all the reasons I love him. And as I fall asleep, I reaffirm that letting this relationship slip into the void – when it came after all at such cost – is not what I want. It's not what I want at all.

In the morning I half wake up as Jenny and Sarah, whispering loudly, slip out of the front door, but fall quickly back to sleep. It's almost ten when they wake me up for the second time.

"I got all the stuff for a proper cooked breakfast," Jenny says. "We even found you some veggie sausages. Pevensey has everything."

"Sausages," Sarah says, "sausages!"

She sounds like a talking dog that was on TV when I was a kid. Sausages was all it ever said.

"So how was Brighton?" Jenny asks, once breakfast is served. "Did you have a nice time?"

"Yeah," I say. "It was good. I met a really nice guy called Billy and we spent all night chatting."

"*Billy*," Jenny says, as if trying the name out for suitability. "So? What's he like? *Billy*."

"Oh nothing, you know..." I stammer. "But, um, really interesting. He's a social worker so he had lots of funny stories."

"Right," Jenny says. "But not your type, or...?"

"Jenny!" I protest.

She shrugs. "I just thought it would be nice if you had a bit of fun," she says.

"So now you think cheating is *a good thing?*"

"No, but it would be nice if you found someone who wasn't ten thousand miles away," she says. "That's all I meant."

"Five," I say. "Five thousand."

"OK, five."

I frown and analyse this phrase as I eat my Quorn sausages. There is something so *wrong* about Jenny saying this to me but for a moment with my morning brain-fog I can't work out what exactly the problem is. And then it comes to me. *"He's only five thousand miles away because I'm looking after you,"* I think. It would seem too cruel to point that out to a woman with cancer, and so I attempt to look unruffled and change the subject instead.

"How was *your* evening?" I ask. "How was Tom's mystery boyfriend?"

"Still a mystery, I'm afraid. He couldn't come – work or something. So it was just the three of us."

"Just me, Mummy and Tom," Sarah says.

"Oh," I say. "That's a shame."

"Yeah, I was looking forward to meeting him. I'm quite intrigued really. Tom seems very in love anyway, so that's good. It's lovely the way he has unexpectedly stumbled on a whole new chapter like that, don't you think? It means there's hope for the rest of us."

"Yeah," I say. "Did you see that the wall stayed dry?" I ask, rapidly changing the subject.

"Yes, I did! I checked it this morning."

"It looks like my repair worked."

"Yes. I thought I'd phone Susan today and ask her what colour she wants."

"Just white again, hopefully," I say.

"Well, it's up to her really isn't it?" Jenny says.

Jenny: Pushing and Pulling

Of course I knew that I was playing mind games. And of course, part of me knew that it was wrong. But I couldn't seem to stop myself.

My motivations were complex. On the simplest level, I was beginning to see Ricardo, rather than my cancer, as the cause of all the guilt I was feeling over Mark's forced presence. If Ricardo vanished, my logic went, then Mark would be perfectly happy to stick around, and Lord knows, I needed him to stick around.

But it wasn't only that Ricardo was an obstacle to satisfying my own and Sarah's needs. I had dated Ricardo, I *knew* Ricardo, I had myself *trusted* Ricardo. And I knew that he was an able liar and a deceitful cheat, and nothing in my new unexpectedly relaxed conversations with him convinced me that this was anything other than a permanent way of being for him. The holes in his stories, the gaps in what he would relate about the simplest of things were black holes within which sordid truths lurked – I was sure of it. This felt like a woman's intuition, but perhaps it was just my ego insisting that the failure of our relationship had nothing to do with me... Either way, I was convinced that he would make Mark no less unhappy than he had made me. I just kept waiting for Mark to see the same truth.

Try as I might – and perhaps through bad faith, I didn't try hard enough – but try as I might, I couldn't envisage a happy future for them together and I honestly did want Mark to be happy. It was just that every time I imagined Mark happy the image I created didn't include Mark dating Ricardo. I imagined him dating the nurse in the cancer ward, or a guy I had seen at the fish and chip shop... I pictured him dating someone new he would meet on a night out in Brighton, someone funny, someone a lot more like Tom than Ricardo.

And so, on autopilot almost, I found myself trying to push wedges between he and Ricky; I found myself encouraging him to go out; trying to create a space where he too would imagine a better future for himself.

I was feeling suddenly energetic and optimistic beyond any logic to do with my circumstances, and I wanted Mark to feel the same way instead of simply resenting being stuck here with me. A new love interest would do that for him.

Perhaps, above all, I wanted a way for him to be happy that was compatible with my own needs and maybe that *was* wrong of me. But when I sat down and analysed it, I couldn't see much that was right about his current relationship either and so I thought, what the hell. I'll be successful and he'll be happy, or I'll fail and he'll go back to Ricardo. And no-one actually dies either way.

The Case Of The Missing Daughter

On Tuesday lunchtime, I send off my latest piece of translation work and begin to clear the spare room ready for redecoration.

Both the mattress and the carpet stink of mould and so I resign myself to finding cheap replacements and dump them outside in the rain.

In order to enable me to carry it alone, I remove the drawers from the dressing table and in the final drawer, discover a photo album. I sit on the newly bared floorboards and, feeling something of a voyeur, flick through the pages.

These are typically poor quality snaps from that era: everything that happened to photography in the seventies – Polaroids, 110 compacts, – was to do with speed, size and convenience, and nothing to do with quality. This batch looks bad enough to have been taken with the worst of all formats, a Kodak disc camera.

There are blurred, low resolution photos of Susan and Ted looking young and surprisingly wealthy on Eastbourne pier, and another of Ted standing proudly in front of a shiny new car. There are photos of Ted giving baby Franny a bottle, and images of him opening the door to this house, presumably for the first time.

When I reach the end of the album, I flip it shut, but then, having spotted something wrong with the chronology, I frown, and open it up again.

At that moment, I hear Jenny open the front door, so I take the album downstairs to show her.

"God the garden looks like a gypsy encampment," she says.

"I'll call the council and arrange to have it picked up," I say as she removes Sarah's coat.

"Why is the bed outside?" Sarah asks.

"I told you," Jenny says. "It's because it's smelly."

"Why is it smelly?"

"Because of the leaky roof," Jenny replies.

"Why is the roof leaky?"

"Hey Jen," I say, interrupting what I know will be a never ending list of questions. "Look what I found."

She takes the album from my hand and crosses to the sofa. Sarah and I sit either side of her as she flicks through.

"God that's *them* isn't it?"

"Yeah," I say.

"Who are they?" Sarah asks, pointing.

"The people from next door," Jenny explains. "Franny's mum. But a long time ago. He was handsome wasn't he?"

"And she looked like Dietrich."

"Yeah. And who's that?"

"It's too long ago to be Franny."

"Yeah. These must be twenty years ago at least."

"Thirty, I'd say."

"Yeah, but at *least* twenty. God, look at that car. A friend of mine's dad had one of those."

"Austin Princess," I say. "Horrible huh?"

"But posh. They must have been loaded."

"Well, yeah... buying second homes as well... So, who *is* that?" I say pointing at the toddler again.

"Yeah. She'd be twenty or thirty now."

"I thought it was Franny for a minute."

"It looks a bit like her, but, no, of course not. I always thought they seemed a bit old to have a six year old actually. I mean, I know people have kids later nowadays, but all the same."

"So maybe Franny is their grandchild," I say.

"Yeah, that's what I was just thinking."

I am about to say that this leaves the mystery of the missing daughter, but it crosses my mind that she may have died. "Anyway," I say, instead. "Are you gonna phone them and ask them what colour this room needs to be?"

"Sure," Jenny says. "But you know we have to go to St Thomas' to pick up my chemo tomorrow?"

"Yeah. Precisely," I say. "I thought we could buy the paint on the way home."

"OK, I'll phone her today," Jenny says, still looking at the photo. "Do you think I should mention these?"

"No," I say. "No, I don't."

196

"I suppose..." Jenny says wrinkling her nose and snapping the book shut, "if they left them here, well, it was for a reason, wasn't it?"

"Exactly."

***

The trip to London goes without surprises. The hospital staff extract a few tubes of blood for tests and hand Jenny a fresh batch of pills – the whole thing takes less than an hour.

On the way back, we call into B&Q and pick up tools and pots of paint. Sarah, who refused to eat lunch in London, turns, unusually, into a screaming devil child halfway around B&Q and maintains a war on our eardrums during the remainder of the journey home.

When we get back I find our first pile of redirected mail lying on the doormat.

Jenny busies herself with Sarah's tea, and I carry the paint in from the car before slouching on the sofa to leaf through the mail in case any of it is for me.

One hand-written envelope is bizarrely addressed to *Jenny Gregory* – her old married name. I glance back towards the kitchen, and then hold it up against the table lamp beside me. Seeing that the letter inside is handwritten, I slide it down the side of the sofa and a few minutes later hand Jenny the remainder of the pile.

"Bill, bill, bank..." she says, leafing through them. "Oh!" She rips open the final envelope and says, "Oh. Well, at least that's good news. They've granted me incapacity benefit. Four hundred and eighty quid a month."

"Nice," I say.

"Yeah..." she says. "It's better than a kick in the arse isn't it?"

It's not until she retires that night that I retrieve the hidden envelope from the side of the sofa. Dreaming up plans of how to redeliver the letter should I need to do so, I open it as carefully as I can and extract the single sheet of notepaper and smooth it open. In almost unintelligible scrawl, it reads:

Dear Jen,
Tara said you tried to contact me. Ive been a way but now I'm back you can write me or phone me if you want to.
I tried to call in but no one was home.

If you need money, Im afraid its all gone now and Im skint again, so your out of luck, but for anything else you know Im always happy to help. I hope the baba is doing OK.

Love Nick.

"Always happy to help," I mutter, refolding the letter and slipping it into my backpack. "Useless, drunken loser."

Grumpy

The next day is sunny and once Jenny has headed off with Sarah across the pebbles – subtly encouraged to do so by myself – I text Ricardo and ask him to phone me when he gets up. Nearly an hour later, he finally calls.

"Hello babe," I say. "You're late today."

"It's the weekend," he says. "And I was tired."

"It's Thursday," I point out.

"Well, it's *my* weekend."

"Sure. Look, I need to talk to you. I did a bad thing."

"Really bad?"

"Yeah, pretty."

"If you sleep with someone I don't think I want to know," he says.

I frown. "That's a joke right?" I say. It's hard to read his voice this morning.

"Why? *Did you?*" he asks.

"Well, no," I say. And that's it. The decision to not tell him has apparently been made – just like that. At least I'm not lying. I didn't *sleep* with anybody. And after all, what decision was there to be made? It's not as if there's any reasonable way to tell your boyfriend that you have been *half* sucked-off twice, once by your ex and once by a random stranger.

"OK. So what you do?" Ricardo asks.

"I intercepted a letter."

"Sorry?"

"I stole a letter. To Jenny. From Nick."

"Ahh. What did it say?"

"Nothing really. It just has his new address and phone number. Now he's out of prison."

"OK, so?"

"Well, do you think I should tell Jenny or not?"

"Tell her that you steal her letter?"

"No. I mean, do you think I should *give* her the letter?"

"I don't know," he says.

"You sound funny. Are you OK?"

"Yes."

"But you... don't have any opinion?"

"No. I just wake up."

"Maybe you should wake up more and call me back later," I say, starting to feel annoyed at his terse attitude.

"Do what you want," he says. "Give it, don't give it."

"Ricardo!" I whine.

"Well..." he says.

"But if I give it to her she might get back into that whole thing of giving Sarah to Nick."

"Then don't give her," he says.

"You're not being very helpful today," I point out.

"Look, babe..." he says with an audible sigh. "Either you agree we should take Sarah, or you let her contact Nick."

"How can it be that straightforward for you?"

"It's not so complicated either," he says. "Either we agree to take her or we don't. If not, I agree with Jenny that Nick isn't the worst thing that can happen."

"Well that's because you don't know him," I say.

"Look... just do what you want," he says.

"Why can't we discuss this?" I say. "Why does every phrase have to be the definitive answer?"

"I'm discussing," he says.

"No you're not. You're saying, 'do it,' and then 'don't do it,' That's not a discussion."

"Because you don't listen maybe."

"I don't *listen?*"

"Yeah. You do what you want. So I'm bored with the talking."

I take a deep breath before replying. "OK babe," I say. "So, what do *you* think?"

"I *tell* you already," he says.

"Then tell me again. This time I'll listen."

"I think you tell Jenny that *if* anything happen, we will look after Sarah."

"Right."

"Now I have to go."

"But we've only been talking for five minutes."

"Yes, but a car arrive outside."

"I don't believe you."

"That's nice. Very nice. Thanks."

"Well, we never have visitors up there. Who is it?'

"I don't know."

"Look, why don't we have nice long talks anymore? And why don't you call me Chupy anymore?"

"Really Chupy. You're just grumpy today. And I have to go."

"And don't just *Chupy* me to get rid of me."

"You see. Grumpy."

"You know what's happening here?" I say. "We're drifting apart. This isn't good."

"Yes babe."

"Yes?! If we carry on like this we'll end up splitting up."

"And that's *my* fault?"

"Well, no, it's nobody's fault but..."

"OK, talk tomorrow. I go now. Goodbye."

"Bastard!" I mutter as the line goes dead. And then I see Jenny hesitating beyond the bay window.

"How long have you been there?" I ask once I have slid the window open.

"About a minute," she says. "Why?"

"No reason."

"Have you two been arguing?"

"No."

"You so have. Do you want to talk about it?"

"No, I don't."

"Fine. Come on inside Sarah. It's OK. Mark's just grumpy."

"I am *not* grumpy."

"OK. Mark *isn't* grumpy," she says rolling her eyes.

Ricardo: Fading Options

I think that was the first time ever that you didn't believe me about something, Pumpkin. I was hurt and annoyed about that, not least, because what I was saying was true. A taxi *had* just pulled up in the car park, and as I put down the phone a booted foot was descending from the rear door.

By the time I got outside, the taxi was already receding into the forest leaving a trail of dust in its wake, and Cristina was standing there like a shop-dummy, smiling and glassy eyed.

What a beautiful place – those were her words Chupy, as if this was a perfectly normal visit. I asked her how she had found me, and she said that she had got the address from Carlos' computer, which got me worrying right off about why Carlos would have my address in the first place.

She looked strange though. It was something about the way her eyes didn't match her smile, like a lying politician or a photo-fit police picture. I asked her what the hell she was doing up in Tayrona, and she told me she had left him. *He hit me,* she said, and I could see that her cheek was a little red where she had been slapped.

I grabbed her arm and bustled her inside the house and out of the sight of Carlos' spies who, my imagination insisted, were already gathering in the forest around the house.

Once inside she tried to kiss me but I pushed her away, and she told me again that he had hit her and that she had walked out with nothing but the clothes on her back to avoid suspicion. She said that now, finally, we could be together.

I did my best to talk reason to her babe. I told her that I had a wife who would be home tomorrow. I reminded her that Carlos would kill us both if he found her here, but it was like talking to an automaton. She was dosed up on Valium and vodka, and she just kept on repeating that she didn't have any other option but to come here, and I felt sorry for her, I really did, because I know how, once you get involved with someone like Carlos for business or pleasure, your options just shrink and shrink until there are no options left at all. I myself was only involved with his wife, but already I could feel my own walls closing in.

I tried to book her on a flight back to Bogotá that day so that she could be back before he even noticed, but there were no flights available, so I made up the spare room just to make it clear what was and wasn't happening here. The idea of one final fuck did actually cross my mind, but the thought that Carlos or his men might turn up at any moment and catch us together played like a horror film in my mind so that idea went no further.

She took another Valium and I served her a nice big glass of wine and parked her on the balcony and she just drifted away babe. She sat, all afternoon, staring out at the waves and talking quietly to herself. Paloma, who I think thought she was being wooed, took a shine to her and jumped onto her lap, and neither of them moved for the entire afternoon.

That evening as I cooked dinner, she tried again to seduce me. She put on a baby Marilyn Monroe voice and pouted and said, *Baby Ricardo, don't you want to look after little Cristina?* and I pushed her away and understood exactly how Carlos had come to hit her, because she was so irritating I wanted to slap her myself.

As we ate she said little, just muttering occasionally in a random, crazy kind of way, but even the few random factlets that she thus released into the ether were more than I wanted to know. I thought about putting my fingers in my ears and singing a song, but I didn't babe, and so I heard when she said that Carlos spied on her and that he listened to her phone calls. It sounded like paranoid schizophrenia, but, well, as they say, just because you're paranoid doesn't mean that they're not after you, especially when you're talking about the likes of Carlos.

I heard too, when she named a few well known government officials who came to the house and these were names that were big enough that even I knew them. These were names that I *really* didn't want to hear.

She asked again if she could stay, and I told her again that she couldn't. I said again that Carlos would kill us both if she did, and then suddenly babe, it was over. At that moment, she had some kind of revelation – I saw it happen. I saw her fall out of love with me.

You're scared of him, she said, and I replied that, of course I was fucking *scared of him.* And it's true babe. Thinking about how Carlos was hanging out with not only the secretary to the minister for the economy but also the assistant to the CIA head of *Plan Colombia,* and that, thanks to Crazy Cristina, I now *knew this* was making my hands shake. I had been sitting on them to hide the fact, but now I saw that it was my escape route and so I held them up to show her instead.

I thought you were more of a man, she said, and I agreed that it was a shame that I wasn't and, just like that, her love affair with Ricardo was over.

After dinner, she went off to the spare room of her own accord, choosing Paloma not me as her sleeping partner and I sat and watched the forest for headlights and then at first light drove her to Santa Marta.

At the airport she said, *you're all bastards really aren't you,* and I agreed that we mostly were. Sending her back to slap-happy Carlos I felt like a bastard too, but, as I say, by this point she had no options.

Outside, I bought a packet of cigarettes and smoked one to calm my nerves and I watched and waited to see that she didn't change her mind and reappear.

A short guy came up and asked me for a cigarette and I should have said no and walked away, but I never was very good at avoiding trouble Chupy.

He lit his cigarette and then asked me if I was Federico's cousin.

"So who's the girl?" he asked.

"Just a friend," I told him.

And he nodded slowly at this and said to give Federico his love.

As he walked away I realised that he hadn't said who he was, and as he crossed the car park he looked back at me babe, and something about that look wasn't right. I couldn't explain exactly what was wrong, but the hairs on the back of my neck stood up on end and even though it was a beautiful sunny day, I shivered.

Star Signs

If astrology truly worked there would be days when the horoscope would simply tell you to stay in bed and keep your eyes closed.

Jenny looks hers up every morning. I can tell, because when I open my laptop it's sitting there on the screen announcing that she's going to have an "active day," or "get in touch with long lost friends," when all that actually happens is that she takes three colourful pills and spends the day in bed feeling sick.

I don't generally bother looking at my own, but when I do it's a sure fire sign that something serious is wrong and that I can't work out how to fix it – I use the dose of daily platitudes as a starting point to try to help me think about my problems rather than as any kind of answer to them.

On Monday, for example, my horoscope tells me to get "out and about" (it's pissing with rain), to "communicate with loved ones" (Ricardo isn't answering phones, sms or email), and it warns me that work colleagues will be demanding (when of course, I don't have any).

Now clearly, for most people, on most days, these are three nigh-on universal truths – universal truths that simply happen to have no bearing on my life, here, today.

These neutral horoscopes and the miserable reality continue all week. The rain continues to lash against the bay window; Jenny continues to feel sick and to sleep. Ricardo has either been unexpectedly murdered or is ignoring my calls, and without a nursery where I can take Sarah, or a TV in front of which I can park her I am unable to work on my translations, or paint the spare room, or, in fact, do anything useful at all.

And so I sit and play games with Sarah and stare out at the rain and alternate between worrying about my relationship with Ricardo, and worrying about Ricardo himself.

On Friday Jenny's horoscope promises that "modern technology will bring good news," and indeed the hospital phones to speak to her – a first.

I leave her bedroom door open but what I overhear doesn't sound very upbeat to me. Indeed, when the conversation is over I return upstairs and she hands me the handset saying, "So much for the good news."

I sit on the edge of the bed and take her hand. A week of chemo has entirely undone my weeks of pancake-therapy and she looks grey and translucent.

"I wish you'd eat something," I say, stroking her hand.

"Not hungry," she says. "Apparently my creatine levels were all wrong."

"Which means?"

She shrugs. "Something to do with my kidneys. I have to go back on Monday."

"Right," I say. "Why were you telling them you've been fine?"

"Were you spying on me?"

"Not really," I lie, "But I overheard you saying how well you've been."

"Well..." she says, "I'm OK really."

"You're *OK?*"

"Well... I suppose I don't want to be bumped off the trial," she says.

"Right," I say. "Of course. But I don't think you should lie to them. It might be dangerous."

"Yeah, well, so might being bumped off the trial," she points out.

"Yes," I say. "Point taken. Well, it's up to you, I suppose."

Downstairs, I attempt to phone Ricardo to ask him what creatine is, but he's still apparently filtering my calls and so I look it up on the internet instead and learn merely that it's a "reliable" measure of kidney function.

I slump onto the sofa beside Sarah. "I'm bored," she says.

"Me too," I agree. "Let's look up our stars again. Here, yours says... *the bad rain outside is a perfect opportunity to do some drawing.*"

"OK," she says, brightly. "What does yours say?"

"Mine says exactly the same," I tell her, "so it looks like we have to do some drawing *together.* Go get the crayons."

What my horoscope actually says is that all things must come to an end, and that if I look carefully I can already see the first signs of what the coming changes might be. Sadly, it doesn't tell me whether it's referring to Jenny's participation in the trial, my own continued presence in Pevensey Bay, or my relationship with Ricardo, but it does say that it's time to dream about what comes next.

Sarah draws a picture of Jenny smiling and surrounded by flowers, and I draw a picture of a beach-house with a cat and two men on the balcony, and as if in answer to my own dream, my phone finally beeps with an SMS from Ricardo.

"Sorry Chupy, V busy for a week. Will explain. Text me your new address if you want a surprise. Love you."

'Hum, that's more like it," I say, tapping my reply. "Technology brings good news," I murmur, already conveniently forgetting that that was Jenny's horoscope, not mine.

***

Because we have Sarah with us, Jenny goes to her consultation with Professor Batt alone whilst Sarah and I visit the Natural History museum. We discover here, that Sarah has a previously unrevealed passion for dinosaurs.

When we return to pick Jenny up two hours later she is nowhere to be seen, and it takes almost an hour of wandering around oncology before I manage to collar Professor Batt's secretary. She informs us that Jenny has been settled in a general ward.

"What's up sweetie?" I ask, when we finally track her down.

"Don't worry," Jenny says, reaching out with her free hand to ruffle Sarah's hair. "It's not as bad as it looks."

But Sarah *isn't* worried. "Mummy we saw dinosaurs. We saw a tyrosauris rex and a diplodogpuss..." she burbles.

"A Ty-rann-o-saurus Rex," I enunciate. "And a Dip-lo-do-cus."

"They're like monsters," Sarah tells her wide eyed.

"So what's all this?" I ask her. "It took us ages to track you down. Your phone off?"

"Yeah, they're not allowed in here. Didn't you get my text?"

"Uh-huh," I say.

"Oh, sorry. I sent one anyway."

"So what's with *that* monster?" I ask nodding at the machine.

"It's dialysis," she says.

"Dialysis?"

"Yeah. Nothing serious. But they reckon my kidneys need a holiday. Especially because that's how Dad, you know..." She nods at Sarah.

"Family precedent," I say.

"Exactly."

Frustratedly unable to judge how much of Jenny's upbeat attitude is theatre for Sarah's benefit and how serious this new development really is, I ask, "And the trial?"

"Um, should be OK," Jenny says, catching my eye. "Probably OK."

"Probably."

"Yeah... Anyway..." she says, swallowing and licking her lips.

"And how long does this machine have to whirr for?" I ask, nodding at the dialysis machine.

"Oh, I have to stay in. Till Wednesday."

"Ah! So you were right."

"Yeah," she says. "Good job I packed that bag."

"Shall I go and get it?"

"I guess," she says, then to Sarah, "Are you staying here with me? Or..."

"Yes," Sarah says, definitely.

"OK. But only until Mark gets back with my bag. Then you have to go with him, OK? Mummy has to stay here for two days."

"OK," Sarah says, with almost insulting ease. "What are those tubes?"

"They go to that machine," Jenny explains as I start to walk away. "They take the blood out of my body and that machine gives it a good scrub and then puts it back."

"Is it dirty?"

"Apparently, yes. Apparently it is."

When I return, someone has pulled the curtains around her bed, so they don't see me approach.

Inside, I can hear Jenny saying, "OK, you like them all but who do you like best?"

"Um, Tom," Sarah replies definitely.

"Tom?"

"No Mark," she says.

"So Mark?"

"No Tom!" Sarah giggles.

Jenny laughs. "OK, you like them both," she says.

"Mark plays games better," Sarah says.

"So Mark?"

"But Tom gets those special cakes."

I stick my head through the curtain and Jenny averts her gaze and blushes.

"What's with the curtains?" I ask.

"Oh, it's just this one mucking around," Jenny says. "Can you open them for me?"

"No!" Sarah shouts.

"Hey Missy, you're coming with me now. So we have to open these, otherwise Mummy gets into trouble."

I open one side, and then, as I open the other, Sarah closes it again.

"Is she on a sugar rush?" Jenny asks.

"Nope," I say. "Just dinosaurs."

"Just leave them closed," Jenny says. "The nurse can do it once you've gone."

But now that she is authorised to leave them closed, Sarah decides to open them after all. Once she has done so, I grab her hand.

"OK then. We need to get going," I tell her. "We have to get food for tea on the way home."

I wink at Jenny and say, "I'll call you tomorrow," and she winks back.

As I lead Sarah away, she asks me, "Where's the new book?"

"The dinosaur one? In the car."

"Can I look at it?"

"Sure."

As we reach the doorway, I glance back at Jenny and see her watching us. She looks profoundly sad, and I suddenly realise that though it's reassuring to see her daughter more preoccupied with dinosaurs than her mother's illness, a bit of affection clearly wouldn't go amiss.

"Blow mummy a kiss," I whisper, "and tell her you love her."

And, bless her, that's exactly what Sarah does.

Out in the car-park, thinking, *Anything Tom can do, I can do better,* I ask, "Shall we buy some cakes too. For after tea?"

"Yess!" Sarah says.

"What's your favourite?"

"Choklit."

"Chocolate eclairs? The ones with the cream in the middle?"

"Yess!" she says.

"Those are my favourite too."

"Oh," she says, suddenly frowning. "Maybe we should get two then."

Making Love

Sarah's strange excitable mood continues during the drive home, throughout Tesco, and long into the evening.

For only the second time ever, I have to re-read her bedtime book because she hasn't yet fallen asleep. Only when, amidst much protest, I switch from the far-too-exciting dinosaur book back to *Derek the Sleepy Dormouse,* does she finally calm down and drift off.

As I creep downstairs, I check the time on my phone and see that it's nearly ten. The lounge is in darkness, and the beach beyond the bay-window looks eerily luminous.

I cross the room and look out at the full moon. It's almost as bright as daylight out there and I wonder if this is why Sarah has been so hyper.

I stand in the darkness and think about Ricardo. I wonder if I'll be able to call him tomorrow. I wonder why he's so busy. I wonder how long the post will take to deliver whatever it is that he is sending me.

Just as I start to turn back into the room, a figure appears on the other side of the glass, literally inches away. The shock makes me gasp in surprise.

And then he waves at me in an old familiar way and I realise who it is, and reach out to release the window catch. "What the hell are *you* doing here?" I ask.

Tom shrugs, grins, and steps into the lounge. "This," he says, grabbing my head with both hands and kissing me.

"Jesus Tom!" I splutter, pulling away. "What's got into you?"

He looks around the darkened room. "Jenny's in hospo right?"

"Well yeah."

"So no one needs to know."

"Yeah, but... Well, Sarah's upstairs."

"Asleep."

"Well yes, but..."

Tom steps towards me forcing me further back into the room. "Tom!" I protest. "What on Earth?"

I back up again, but my shins make contact with the couch, and as I glance behind me, Tom takes advantage and pushes me so that I end up losing my balance and sitting. But as he fumbles with his big duffle coat, I slip out sideways and return to the open window which I close before turning back to face him.

"Tom, this is crazy," I say as he throws the coat onto a chair, and fiddles with his cuffs Prince-Charles-style.

He's wearing a grey checked suit, brogues, and a big turquoise tie. Fetishes are absurd I know, and who could ever explain where any of them come from? But absurd or not, I never could resist Tom in a suit. I take in his rigid cutaway collar, the bulge forming in front his silky trousers, the shiny blue knot of his tie, and my mouth starts to water, and my own dick hardens.

Tom sees all of this and grins smugly as he unbuttons his jacket and smooths his tie against his chest, and I decide that he probably changed into these clothes specifically for the purpose of seducing me. And it's working, damn him.

"Fuck you look good in a suit," I say, shaking my head.

Tom winks. "It's new," he says, crossing the room. "Hugo Boss."

He slides his hands around my waist, and kisses me tenderly on the lips. "It's a virgin suit," he says. "Sven doesn't get the whole suit thing."

"No?"

"No," he says, kissing me again.

"Shit Tom," I say. "You have a boyfriend. I have a boyfriend. This is crazy."

"Exes don't count," he says.

"You keep saying that," I mutter, pulling him against me and looking over his shoulder, in fact to avoid kissing him.

But the hug feels great too. He nuzzles my neck with his beard making me sigh, and as he pulls me tighter I can sense his dick against mine. I can feel his buttocks through the suit trousers.

I push him away just far enough to look into his eyes. "Sacré Tom!" I say.

He shrugs. "It's just a hug," he says.

"Only it isn't, is it?"

"Oh for fuck's sake," he says. "When will you just relax about sex?"

I shake my head and look into his eyes.

"You want it, and I want it, and no one ever needs to know," he says. "So where's the problem?"

"Hum..." I say, doubtfully.

"If I tell anyone, you can tell Sven," he says.

"Only I don't know Sven."

"Well no. That's better isn't it? You don't need to feel guilty."

"Maybe," I say. My dick is doing its best to convince me to cave in here. "It still doesn't seem right," I say weakly.

Tom laughs.

"Shhh!" I say. "You'll wake Sarah. Are you stoned?"

"Of course," he says, pulling a funny face and sinking to his knees. "Better put something in my mouth to keep me quiet."

"Not here," I say, suddenly aware of the expanse of glass behind me. I take his hand and pull him through to the kitchen.

I close the kitchen door and Tom pushes me back against it and kneels before me again. Just as before, my resistance melts at first contact. *The power of sex. Never underestimate it,*" I think. "Oh yeah," I say, as he flicks his tongue around the top of my dick.

"Uh, Umm," Tom murmurs, pulling a condom from his pocket and holding it up for me to grasp.

He stands and his trousers crumple around his ankles – he's not wearing any underpants.

And then he turns to face the yellow formica counter top.

And there, in the windowless kitchen, still in his shirt and tie, but with his trousers around his ankles, I fuck him, and much as I would like to say otherwise, it feels heavenly. It feels as warm and intimate, as dirty and exciting, and as animal and sexy as it ever did.

We come together, me inside him, and Tom all over his brogues, and then, suddenly awkward, I'm wrapping the condom and stuffing it to the bottom of the bin, and Tom is mopping up with kitchen roll and straightening his tie.

Looking for all the world as if he has just sold me some insurance, he pecks me on the cheek and returns to the lounge for his overcoat.

I follow him through.

"Sorry, early start tomorrow," he says, his hand already on the front door. "But I'll call you."

Once he has gone, I sit and stare at the moonlit beach and shake my head in disbelief at what I have just done, and wonder what this now means.

I wish my emotions were more simplistic, more masculine. I wish I could just *fuck* instead of making love, but it's a separation I have never been able to manage.

And having *made love* with Tom, all I can do now that he has gone, is sit and stare at the view and wonder what to do with all this love that I have made.

212

The End Of The Line

Come Wednesday, Jenny travels back from London on the train alone. She insists that she has never felt better, and indeed, when Sarah and I pick her up at Eastbourne station she looks brighter-eyed than I have seen her in a while.

It's not until Sarah is in bed that evening, that we are able to discuss her treatment.

"So?" I ask her as she returns from the kitchen with two mugs of hot chocolate.

"So?" she repeats.

"The verdict from professor Twat?"

"Oh," she says, wrinkling her nose and sliding into the seat opposite. "Well... you know I'm on two combined drugs?"

"Yeah."

"Well, one of them is... nephrotoxic I think it's called. Or nephratotoxic maybe. Anyway, it attacks the kidneys. Some people more than others."

"Right."

"And I'm one of the unlucky ones. Apparently my kidneys had almost packed up, which is why they put me on dialysis. But they picked up again once they got a break, so..."

"So what now?"

"They've changed my drug regime. Two thirds the dose, but more often. They reckon some people tolerate it better that way."

"And if you don't?"

"Then they drop it to half the dose, which is as low as they can go."

"And if..."

"Look Mark, there's no point going there. Really."

"No."

"Let's just take it all one step at a time."

"Sure."

"But of course, the answer is that if it still isn't working for me then I drop out of the trial. That's pretty much the end of the line."

"Right. Shit."

"Yeah. Shit indeed," she says. "And you have to help me drink masses of water. I have to drink a minimum of three litres a day. I hate water, that's the thing. Stupid but true."

"Maybe get some cordials," I say.

"Yeah, I suppose. Maybe a mint one. I used to like that when I was a kid."

"Hey, can't they just give you the non-toxic drug? I mean, if they need to change something?"

"I asked that. But no. It already failed in a previous trial. Which is why they're combining it this time."

"Right."

"We just have to wait till next week and see how I do on two pills instead of three."

"Sure."

"Anyway, what about you?"

"Me?"

"Yeah, presumably you have some news to share."

"Do I?" I ask, frowning and wondering what Tom has told her.

"I presume you two *have* actually spoken to each other since."

"Um... no, not really," I say, trying to stifle my mounting anger. *"Sven, whoever he is, is sooo going to hear about this,"* I think.

"You haven't talked about it at all. But that's like, a week isn't it?"

"Oh!" I say. "Oh, Ricardo, right. Um, well, no... Yes, I mean. He texted me. And we spoke briefly yesterday."

Jenny frowns at me. "What did you think I meant?"

"Nothing," I say.

She shakes her head in confusion and stands. "OK, well, I'm going to go for a quick walk along the beach."

"Now?"

"Yeah. I've been in bed for three days. I missed it actually. Plus the forecast is for rain."

"I thought I might paint the spare room tomorrow," I say.

"Yes," she says mockingly scolding me, "well, I thought it would be done by now, Mark."

"Huh!" I exclaim. "I've been a slave to your daughter."

"Sure. Well, we can do it together."

"I think it'd be easier if one person looks after Sarah whilst the other one paints. You remember the pot of gloss paint and the hall carpet, right?"

214

"Sure. We can take it in turns. And any news from the other one?"

"The other one?"

"Yeah, the stealer of kisses."

"Oh, Tom? No," I say, wincing at the unconvincing sound of my own voice.

"I wonder if they're still coming on Saturday," she says.

"Saturday?"

"Yeah. Tom phoned and said he was bringing the mythical Sven to dinner again, though to be honest I'm doubting that he really exists. What are these?" she asks, picking up a pile of photos.

"They're my seascapes. I bought a photo printer in Tesco the other day. It was only forty quid."

"They're lovely," she says, leafing through. "A bit boring, but lovely."

"I thought I'd take the same photo every day, and then make a huge picture out of them all. Like a mosaic."

"Right," she says, doubtfully.

"Just imagine a whole wall filled with them. All the same, but every one different."

"You'd need a lot to fill a wall," she says.

"Yep. Hundreds."

"Well, hopefully you won't have to stay here for that long," she says. And then she wrinkles her nose and puts the pile of photos down. "Maybe I hope that you *will* have to be here that long..." she says, thoughtfully. "Anyway..."

She slides open the bay window, and then smiles weakly at me from the other side. As I watch her head off across the beach, slowly becoming cloaked by the night, I realise that there are only two ways out of this for either of us. Jenny either gets better or she dies. And either of those could take a very long time.

It's stupid of me, I know, but it really hadn't dawned on me until now that this situation could actually take years to resolve itself. Which means that my relationship with Ricardo is, to all intents and purposes over. This is the end of the line for us as well, despite our pretence otherwise.

I stare unblinkingly at the window and let this new thought take over my mind. I wonder if Ricardo has already realised this. I wonder which of us will be the first to say it out loud. *Jesus!*

Cornered

I fully intend to be out by the time Tom and Sven arrive on Friday night, but the final coat of paint in my bedroom-to-be takes longer than I imagined and getting the paint out of my hair and fingernails takes even longer.

When I come downstairs I can see by the fading light that it's later than I intended. I glance at my phone to check the time just as I hear Jenny say, "Anyway, do come through," and realise that they have already arrived.

Jenny appears from the kitchen carrying a tray of nibbles, followed by Sarah who is shyly hanging onto a corner of her mother's cardigan.

Behind her follow Tom and Sven.

Jenny must notice me gaping at Sven, because she mutters, "Don't stare now," as she passes.

Tom pauses and kisses me on the cheek, and I shake hands with Sven, who doesn't appear to recognise me.

"Anyway, I'm off now, so have a lovely evening," I say.

"Oh please stay," Tom says. "You don't have to run off just because..."

"Honestly," I interrupt. "I've been within these four walls all week. I'm looking forward to my night on the town."

"Just have a drink," Jenny says. "Just, you know, to be polite."

"Yes, just a drink," Sven says, in a thick Swedish accent. "I heard so many things about you."

"Did you?" I ask, catching Tom's eye.

"Oh yes," he says, saucily.

"Go get Mark a glass will you?" Jenny asks Sarah. "They're on the drainer. But walk back with it, don't run."

"So you got rid of the smell," Tom says, removing his jumper to reveal a peace-symbol t-shirt, and sitting down on the sofa. "Now it just stinks of paint."

"Yes, we finished it," Jenny says. "I did the first coat and Mark did the rest."

"*Maybe*, finished," I say, hesitating about whether or not to sit next to Tom – he hasn't left much space. "I think the stain is seeping through again," I add.

"Well, it's certainly better than it was," Jenny says.

"I think you had better show me," Tom says, jumping back up. Something in the way he maintains eye contact me makes me think that there's a reason for this – that he needs to tell me something, and thinking that it might be about Sven, I lead the way, saying, "It's only white really, but..."

Behind us I hear Jenny ask Sven, "So, what are you doing here in England Sven?"

Upstairs in the spare room, Tom closes the door with his arse and reveals that his hidden agenda is simply to kiss me.

"Tom!" I laugh, "Stop."

He releases my head from between his hands and shrugs.

"Honestly," I say. "Not with Sven downstairs. Actually, not *at all*."

"I find it pretty exciting myself," he says.

"Yeah, well. I don't."

"So this is the room," Tom says. "Jenny got the better deal."

"Yeah. The front bedroom is amazing, but... still, at least it doesn't stink now."

"Sure," he says. "We'll be needing a bed though."

"Yeah..." I agree, before I realise. "Tom!"

He laughs and reaches for my arse, but I pull away and head out onto the landing and then, on the spur of the moment, I say, "I need to pee," and take refuge in the bathroom. The door safely locked, I stand and try to work out what is happening here. Tom seems to be assuming that he now just *can*. Does that mean that he thinks we're now back together? And if so, *are we?* It's too much to process. It's too much, too fast. And I can't help but think that it's probably all some dreadful mistake. And yet, my heart is pounding.

Once I hear Tom return downstairs, I rearrange my arousal-indicator so that it can't be seen and head back down.

"Mark's right," Tom is saying through a mouthful of peanuts. "It does still show." It takes a few seconds before I realise that he's talking about the wall.

"I think it needs a final coat of some kind of special paint..." Jenny says.

As the conversation continues, I attempt to steal glances at Sven to make sure, but I'm certain, he is definitely the guy I saw in Schwartz, the "boy" who was led past me on the end of a dog lead.

After half an hour or so, Jenny heads through to the kitchen to check on her pie, and Tom follows her, so I am left with Sven.

"Anyway," I say, standing. "I suppose I'd better get a move on."

"It is closed," Sven says. He pronounces closed, *clo-said.*

"What's that?"

"Scwartz," he says. "They clo-said it for renovation."

"Right," I say, crossing the lounge for my jacket. "Well, I wasn't actually going there anyway, so."

Sven snorts so I turn to look at him. "What?" I ask.

"He thinks you are such a good boy," he says.

"Um, why don't you go see if you can carry something for Mummy," I tell Sarah who is watching this exchange a little too acutely for my comfort.

Once she has left the room, I say, "I'm sorry Sven?"

"Tom, he thinks you are so nice. Such a *good* boy."

"Well, that's just a joke," I say. "Tom knows me pretty well."

"No," Sven says, lightly. "No, no joke. He thinks you are like the Mother Teresa."

I shrug and force a smile, but Sven isn't smiling back.

"Maybe I tell him," he says. "Maybe I tell him about the real Mark."

"Well, you can if you want," I say flatly. "But you know, people who live in glass houses..."

"I'm sorry. What? Grass houses?"

"No, it just means... look, I don't mind *what* you tell Tom, we're not together anymore. But if you do, you'll have to tell him you were in Schwarz too."

"Oh Tom don't care about me!" Sven says. "He only worry about little Mark."

"He *knows* you go to Schwarz with that guy?"

"Sure," Sven says.

"On a dog lead?"

Sven shrugs. "I'm not with Tom," he says. "All this is just to impress."

"Right," I say. "Well, anyway, tell anyone whatever you want. I'm outa here."

As I reach the front door, Tom surfaces from the kitchen and grabs my sleeve. "Oh don't go. Stay for dinner," he says.

"No," I say. "No, not tonight. Really. You three just enjoy each other's company. Sven, by the way, is *fabulous.*"

Once outside, I find that I don't have the slightest desire to drive to Brighton, so I simply walk to the end of the road and settle in the farthest corner of the Bay Inn. Here I eat fish and chips, watch an excellent jazz-band comprised entirely of over-sixties, and wonder who exactly Tom is trying to impress by bringing a bitchy Swedish body-builder to dinner.

Drama Day

By Tuesday, it is clear that Jenny's new drug regime isn't working any better for her than the old one. She spends the entire day in bed, her only movements regular trips to the bathroom to evacuate the litres of mint cordial I am forcing her to drink.

Wednesday at lunchtime I hear her retching and decide that it's maybe time for her to inform the hospital. I phone Ricardo first to discuss it, but as usual these days, the best I can do is leave a message on his voicemail.

"You just finish that," I tell Sarah, who is busy colouring-in a fluorescent pink dinosaur, "and I'll be back in a minute."

Jenny looks up weakly as I enter her room and sit on the edge of her bed.

"Someone's not having a good day," I say.

"No," she says, simply.

"Are you going to phone Twat and tell him?"

Jenny pulls a face.

"Are you wearing fake tan?" I ask.

Jenny frowns at me incredulously, so I lean to one side to get a better look. "I think you're going yellow sweetie," I say. "That's a kidney thing isn't it? You definitely need to call Twat."

"You have to stop calling him that," she says, smiling vaguely. "I nearly asked for Professor Twat at reception last time."

I take her hand and stroke it. "It makes you smile though," I say. "It makes you grin every time. So?"

"So?"

"Will you call Twat or shall I? Because you really are a bit yellow."

"Let's just wait till Saturday. I want just to get through one week and see," she says. "Maybe I'll be fine by Sunday."

I sigh. "You think he'll take you off the trial?"

"That's what they said."

"Frankly Jenny, you look like shit," I say.

"Thanks."

"Well, you do. And you looked great until you started taking the pills again."

"What did you think of Sven?" she asks, clearly changing the subject.

"Sven?"

"Yeah."

"He seems nice enough," I lie.

"Yeah. I thought so too," she says. "He was brilliant with Sarah."

"Really?" I ask, genuinely shocked.

"Yeah. He played with her all evening. It was like having a nanny."

"That's sweet," I say, thinking that it was probably Sven's strategy for avoiding discussing the true nature of his relationship with Tom.

"It made me think about asking Tom," Jenny says. "You know, about Sarah."

I push my lips out and shake my head vaguely to indicate that I don't understand.

"I thought I could ask him how he would feel about looking after her, just in case," she says.

"Tom?"

"Well, now he's in a relationship."

"They've only been together a couple of weeks," I say, wondering whether to reveal that they maybe aren't together at all, or at least, not in the sense that Jenny means.

"Sure," Jenny says. "But I think it might last. Call it woman's intuition."

"Really," I say. "Is that what you call it?"

"Careful, you sound jealous."

"No," I say categorically. "No, I'm not at all."

"You're not having doubts then?"

"Doubts?"

"About Ricardo. About Tom for that matter."

"No."

"I saw Florent again last week by the way... did I tell you?"

"No."

"Well, he asked after you."

I shrug. "Good."

"You don't seem to talk much anymore – you and Ricardo," she points out. "Are you sure everything's OK?"

And it's undeniable that we don't. My phone calls to Ricardo have gone from an hour every day to ten minutes once a week. Ricardo insists that this is simply because it's the dry season and he's out at Max's all the time. But even though I can understand the logic of this, and even though I realise that

221

Ricardo can't spend all his evenings alone staring at the cat, it would be dishonest to say that it hasn't crossed my mind: maybe he *has* met someone new.

Were Ricardo gay of course, this would be more unlikely. Colombia is a pretty homophobic society and as far as I know there are no options whatsoever for meeting other gay men in Santa Marta, let alone in Tayrona. But of course, Ricardo *isn't* gay, he's bisexual. So the whole *world* is his oyster.

I haven't asked him outright yet, but I think that the day might be coming when a direct question will slip unexpectedly from my lips. Because nothing Ricardo has said or done over the last month – other than his continued view that we should take Sarah – provides any proof that there is a joint future for us. And in the light of what I can only admit is a failing, *fading* relationship and in view of the inability of either of us, under the circumstances, to do anything to fix this, even his views on Sarah are anachronistic at best. At worst, they may just be lies intended to placate me.

"Yes," I say. "Yes, everything's fine."

"That was a long pause," she says.

"Was it?"

And then Jenny pulls a face, pales even more than usual, and pushes me aside so that she can retch into the bucket beside the bed.

"Jesus Jen," I say softly.

She makes a deep, weepy breathing noise and then retches again.

I stroke her back and chew the side of my mouth. "Don't you just end up vomming up the pills?" I ask.

"Not now," she says.

"Sorry," I say, standing.

"No," she says, drying her mouth with some tissues. "No, stay! I meant not this late in the day. If I throw them up immediately I wash them and take them again."

"Yuck."

"And if it's during the first hour I have to take another dose. But this late in the day it's fine."

"Poor you."

She lies back on the pillow and blows through her lips. "Fun, fun, fun," she says.

"And they said this is normal?"

She shrugs. "It can't be that *ab*normal," she says. "No one batted an eyelid when I threw up in hospital. God, I feel so dizzy today though."

She pats the bed and I sit back down. "Lovely day out there," she says, looking out at the horizon.

"It is," I agree, studying the yellow tinge to her skin and wondering if I should phone the hospital of my own accord, and then wishing Ricardo would phone me back, and then thinking about her asking Tom to look after Sarah, and realising that we're suddenly using Sarah as a cypher to discuss the possibility of Jenny's death again, and thinking that this definitely is *the* moment where I should step up to the mark and tell her that I will take Sarah if need be. All of these thoughts rush through my mind.

"Um, about Sarah," I start. But then my mouth dries, and I can't go through with it.

"Yes?" Jenny asks.

"I... I thought I'd take her out for a walk this afternoon," I say. "She made me promise. I think she's getting a bit stir crazy."

As I watch Jenny's face, I see her look puzzled and then slip into a frown. Finally she raises one hand and points to the beach. "I think she's already... that is... what's she *doing?*" she asks.

I follow her gaze and see Sarah wobbling her way along the top of one of the breakwaters. Because of the way the tides have pushed the pebbles the beach is much higher on one side than the other, in fact, to the left, the way she is looking, the top of the wooden construction is almost level with the beach. Behind her though, the drop down to the lapping waves is at least two meters.

"Jesus!" I mutter.

I have the strangest experience, almost like an acid induced hallucination. I feel a wave of cold air and my scalp prickles and I think that I know that not only that she is about to fall, but also that she is about to *drown.*

In less than a tenth of a second, before Jenny has even pulled her gaze from the view, I am sprinting from the room. I take the stairs in two enormous bounds, almost breaking my neck in the process. I jump over the coffee table and almost run into the closed section of the bay window – only a last minute reflection from a standard lamp saves me, and I skid to a halt and crash up against it before squeezing through the opening and sprinting barefoot across the beach as fast as I have ever run anywhere.

As I reach the crest of the beach, Sarah comes back into view, still wobbling on the breakwater but now hearing me, she turns to look and starts to wobble and topple backwards her arms flailing. I rocket across the beach and reach the water's edge at the very second that her bottom breaks the surface of the sea, and I dive towards her and lift her back up and out at the exact moment that the water first touches her cheeks.

She's standing on dry land before she even realises what has happened.

I double up, dripping and panting beside her and that's when she starts to scream.

When I finally straighten up I see Jenny at the open upstairs window, nodding slowly.

Unable to control a sudden bubble of anger, I shout at Sarah. "What the fuck are you doing out here!" which of course, only makes her scream the louder.

Sarah calms down as soon as she is showered and dried. In fact, I think that the most upsetting element of the day was, for her, the fact that I shouted at her. She spends most of the day sitting upstairs on her mother's bed.

Jenny, bizarrely, makes no comment on the drama whatsoever. At first I think that she is simply too ill to pass comment, but there is something new about the way that she looks at me, something deep and important that I can't figure out.

Every time I catch her eye, I end up trying to work out if she is angry with me for shouting, or if perhaps, as I have wondered myself, she thinks that the only reason Sarah fell was because of my dramatic sprint across the beach.

Whatever the dark pools of her regard are hiding, she's not letting on, maintaining instead a crisp veneer of normality as if today is a day like any other. And perhaps that's it. Perhaps it is a day like any other. Perhaps parents get used to these brushes with mortality, and I am over-dramatising and over-analysing.

Late that night, when they are both in bed, I Skype Ricardo's landline despite the late hour. I intend to leave him a short message to ask him to call me when he wakes up, but as I start to speak, the emotion of the day and the bottle of wine I have downed combine to produce an unintended message from hell.

"Hi babe, it's me," I start, quite reasonably.

"You must be asleep. I hope this doesn't wake you. But if it does, please come to the phone. I *so* need to talk to you. Are you there? No? Oh... It's been a horrible day. Sarah fell in the sea. She could have drowned. I ran really fast and saved her. But it really made me think about the responsibility babe. It seems stupid talking to an answer-phone, but we never seem to talk anymore. The thing is, I agree really, with what you say about Sarah, but I don't see how I can take her on when you're so distant. And it's getting to the point where I'm going to have to say something to Jenny. We hardly talk these days. Jenny's going yellow – did I tell you that yet? I don't know whether to phone the hospital and tell them or not. I mean, what if she dies? What if her kidneys fail because I didn't call? And if I do call then they might take her off the trial, and what if *that* kills her instead. It's not fair that I have to worry about all this on my own. And if you were there you'd just say, call them, don't call them. God, I don't feel like we're a couple anymore. And I'm scared about that. You're turning into just some guy who's five thousand miles away. Someone who never calls. Someone who's never in. Someone who doesn't have an opinion."

"I mean, what happened about Christmas? It's just over three weeks away. Do you remember saying you'd come over? But you haven't booked a flight. You haven't even mentioned it. I don't even know what I'm rambling on about... I'm sorry. I don't mean to... I mean, I know this isn't your fault... But it's just, I *really* need to talk to you today babe. Where the fuck *are* you? *Are* you even there? The phone always used to wake you up. Maybe you sleep better nowadays without me. Look, God... All I want to say is... call me. Please. I need to talk to you today. So if you still really do love me then call me. Anytime. Because otherwise, well, I guess I know what that means. I guess we both do."

"Anyway, God, you'll hate this message. It's everything you detest. I wish I could wipe it but I don't know how. You're not going to pick up are you? No. Oh well. Sweet dreams."

I hang up and then shake my head, incredulous at the message I have just left.

"That'll do it," I mumble. "He'll probably never phone ever again."

And then I sigh, and think that if that's what's meant to happen next, then maybe it's for the best that we just get on with it all. And that, I realise, is exactly why I left the message in the first place.

Ricardo: Guardian Angel

I honestly did work a lot that week babe. Esteban was off sick so I got no days off, and a bout of gastroenteritis had all the locals shitting in their frocks and me running around dishing out rehydration salts and Loperamide tablets. It was so bad, we even had a government guy come in to confirm that it wasn't another Cholera outbreak like the one in ninety-six. Anyway, to be honest I preferred to be busy because every time I stopped I got this strange nervous feeling.

Too tired to cook by the end of the day, I would stop off at Max's for a bite to eat, and that should tell you how tired I was Chupy, because Max too had succumbed to the exploding arse-hole bug, so eating there was a damned risky business. But I followed each meal with half a bottle of rum to kill the bugs, and that seemed to do the trick, it seemed to keep me safe. Safe from food-poisoning, anyway.

Every night I got home and saw your address on the back of an envelope, and realised that I still hadn't worked out what I could possibly send you that would reassure you. I thought of a ring maybe, but I never saw you wear jewellery. And I thought of a pendant, but they only had crosses, and I know how you feel about those... What I really wanted to send you was a plane ticket, but I knew you couldn't come because of Jenny, and if not because of Cristina, and I knew this prolonged separation was turning into a big big problem.

The following Tuesday, Esteban returned, looking tanned and relaxed – I suspect that he had simply been on holiday with that coconut bimbo of his, but I didn't care, because, as I say, without my Chupy to play with, and with my worries about Cristina and Carlos just waiting to trouble me, I had been happy to be out of the house and dealing with other, more material, more literal shit.

But on Tuesday, there he was, tanned and relaxed, and ready to take over my diarrhoea rounds, and so I went home and sat on the balcony, and for the first time I let myself think about everything that had been going on.

Paloma, as ever, came and sat on me, and I stroked her and thought about the fact that there had been no news from Cristina, or Carlos, or anyone else, and that maybe, just maybe, that meant that this stupid, stupid business was now over.

But I couldn't convince myself babe. You know I'm a scientific kind of guy pumpkin. You know I'm no great believer in the metaphysical. But some part of me *knew* that this was far from over, and sure enough, as if my own doubts had summoned up daemons, Federico rang that very evening.

Federico, my man, I said, thinking that maybe he was planning one of his rare weekend visits.

I need you out of the house, he replied. That was his opening line Chupy.

I'm sorry, I said, *you what?* and he said it again babe, *I need you out of my house.*

Hey, Cous' I laughed, *what's up?* But of course, In a way, I already knew.

I'm really sorry Ricardo, but there are behaviours that just aren't... acceptable, he said. He sounded like he was going to cry.

I told him that he was making no sense to me, that I had no idea what he was talking about, but that just made him angry, and I could see why, so I just shut up then and let him talk.

I'm not going to discuss this with you Ricardo, he said, *and I don't want to know who you have been fucking, or where you have been fucking, or how often, or since when, because frankly, I already know way more than I want to. But if you can't control where you stick your dick I need you out of my house.*

I told him I understood, but that it was over, and he told me that, *no, it wasn't over.*

I'm really sorry, Ricardo, but I... I don't know how to help you, he said. *Everyone up there knows about it. And that house was my mother's you know, and that house is made of wood. Do you hear what I'm saying?*

I told him that I heard what he was saying, but that it might take me a while to organise things and he told me that the less time it took the better it was for all of us.

Once he had hung up, I returned to the balcony and stared out at the horizon. The phone rang twice but the number was hidden so I didn't pick up. I wasn't going to let anyone know that I was here, alone, waiting.

As the daylight faded I sat and tried to work out what I would do now, and felt really upset because I wanted to talk to you Chupa Chups. I wanted to ask you how to fix the stupid mess that I had made.

But I couldn't tell you and I couldn't work out what to do, and you wouldn't have had an answer anyway, because there was none. I couldn't decide where to go, or how to explain it to you and I got a huge lump in my throat which was part fear and part regret that I had fucked everything up so spectacularly.

I thought about my mother's place which still hadn't sold, but just down the road from Carlos and Cristina, it was hardly a better option.

I was still sitting there, albeit a bit drunk, when you phoned Chupy. I had decided that the best solution was just to sit and wait for them to come for me. It was stupid drunken self pitying rubbish of course, but that's what I had decided, for the simple reason that I felt paralysed by lack of other options. Luckily they didn't come that night.

I didn't pick up because I didn't know who was calling. I sat and listened as Federico's answer-phone clicked in and you uploaded your own batch of problems into the machine. And then I didn't pick up because I didn't know what to tell you babe.

Once you had given up and ended the call, I missed you so much, I missed that simple happiness that we had had for a while so powerfully that I actually did cry a bit, and lord knows you know I don't cry much. But I thought about you and Jenny, and all *your* problems and felt submerged by them all, because I couldn't fix my own let alone help you with yours and it seemed that everything – like the words in that song you kept playing when we met – truly was shit. And then, like a gust of air when the wind changes direction, something came over me, and I realised that you were an angel – that you Chupy, were my *guardian* angel and that your message was a message from God because it contained everything I needed: a plan of action, a reason to act, and an alibi to explain it all afterwards. I have never loved anyone more than I loved you at that precise moment for leaving that precise message.

The Day After

The next morning when I wake up, I can't quite remember the full text of my answer-phone rant, but I do remember this: I remember asking Ricardo to phone me back, and I remember having said that we would both know what it meant if he chose not to. But as I lie here listening to Sarah drive what is apparently a two-stroke engined teddy across the back of the sofa, I don't know what it means at all. Or maybe I do. Maybe I just don't want to admit it.

Jenny doesn't get up at all this morning, so I bundle Sarah up against the cold and thinking that we both need a change of scene, I drive her to Eastbourne.

The temperature can't be much above freezing today, but the air is crisp and clean and the sky is an almost Mediterranean blue. The pebble beach and the sunshine make me think about my old life in Nice. It all feels like it happened centuries ago. It feels like everything was simpler back then, but I guess it wasn't really.

At the end of the pier, I sponsor numerous costly attempts by Sarah to win a furry blue dinosaur by manipulating a seriously flawed crane mechanism, but eventually even she realises that the machine is a con. "It doesn't work properly," she declares, already looking around for the next distraction.

We buy a bag of chips and squeeze together in a weatherbeaten snug to share them.

"I'm sorry I shouted at you the other day," I say.

She looks at me blankly, so I explain, "Do you remember? When you fell in the sea?"

She nods solemnly. "Mummy says I'm lucky I didn't get a smack," she says. Then she offers me a chip and says, "Do you want this one? I don't like that brown stuff."

229

"Mmm, brown sauce," I say, taking the chip. "I love it. Yes, it was a bit naughty. Because the sea is very dangerous."

"That's the sea, down there," she says, pointing through a tiny gap in the planks below our feet.

"That's right," I say. "It is."

"If the floor breaks," she says. "We'll fall in."

"Yes, if it did, we would. But it's quite strong I think. I might teach you to swim when it gets warmer, though. In summer. That way you'd be safe if you ever fell in again."

Sarah sucks the tomato ketchup off a chip and throws it to a seagull. "Can Mummy swim?"

"Yes," I say. "Your Mum's a very good swimmer."

"I never seed her swim."

"I never *saw* her swim. Actually, you did. It's just you were very little so you don't remember." I grab her hand to stop her throwing another chip. "Don't," I say. "We'll end up with all the seagulls coming to ask for chips."

"All the seagulls in the world?"

"Yes."

"Every one?"

"Yes."

"Are you sure?"

"OK, maybe not all of them," I say. "Anyway, I haven't finished eating yet. When we've finished, you can give the rest away."

"OK," she says, looking between the remaining chips and my face as if she doesn't believe that there will be any. She's probably right. "Can *Mummy* teach me to swim then?" she asks.

"Sure. Don't you want *me* to?"

"No," she says, quite definitely, making me laugh.

And then it crosses my mind that Jenny might not be here come summer to teach her daughter anything. Which leads me back to wondering what happens to Sarah. And on to Ricardo. And onto that whole chain of thoughts.

But today, things take a different route, which is a surprise. Today, I realise that, *of course* I can take Sarah without Ricardo by my side, and in a way, I am already doing this. And I think that if my relationship with Ricardo is ending and there is no need for me to return to Colombia (other than to get my stuff and my cat back) then nothing could be more logical than to stay here and look after Sarah.

It's an unexpected turnaround in my thinking because today I honestly can't work out what I have been worrying about. If Ricardo and I stay together, then it's fine, because he has repeatedly said that we should take her.

And if we don't then I don't need anyone else's approval or commitment anyway.

"Now you can throw them," I tell her, sacrificing the final eight chips.

Of course, living with Sarah would mean lots of sacrifices. It would mean the end of internet dates, and the end of trips around the world. It would be the end of my nights on the town, and of one night stands. But in a way this has already happened. And in a way, none of these "losses" matter, because they're all about trying to find someone to love, trying to find a reason to be, and strange as it may sound, Sarah is all of those things. Times ten.

"Do you *love* Mummy?" Sarah asks, and I wonder momentarily if I have been thinking out loud.

"Of course I do," I say.

"Me too," she says. "Look. No more chips."

"Come on then," I say standing, and lifting her onto my shoulders. "Gosh you're getting heavy. It must be all those chips."

When we get home, Jenny is still sleeping and there are no visible signs that she has been up. In fact, it's not until I have put Sarah to bed that she finally appears at the bottom of the stairs in her dressing gown.

"You're a bit out of kilter, aren't you?" I ask, looking up from one of Susan's dreadful Mills and Boon romance novels.

"Yeah," she says, sleepily rubbing her eyes. "My sleep patterns are all skewed. It's like jet lag. It's the pills I think... I can't do anything much but sleep once I've taken them. And then this is the only time of the day I feel normal."

"Could you take them at night?"

"And spend all night vomiting?" she says, crossing the room and slumping beside me.

"No, I suppose not," I say.

"Have you been out?" she asks. "Sarah's hair smells of the sea."

"Wow," I say. "Very good Sherlock. Yes, we went along the pier. Could you smell the chips she ate too?"

"No, just sort of salty. Was she good?"

"Perfect as ever. Have you eaten?"

She wrinkles her nose.

"You must eat *something*."

"Maybe some toast. And a cuppa."

"Breakfast then," I say, standing.

"Breakfast," she laughs. "Thanks, you're a sweetheart."

When I return with a plate of toast and two mugs of tea, Jenny says, "A weird thing happened today. I almost forgot. It's almost like I dreamt it."

"Yeah?"

"Yeah," she says, taking her mug. "Guess who phoned?"

"Oh, thank God!" I exclaim. "What time?"

Jenny frowns at me. "I don't know. About three. It was Susan though."

"Susan?" I say, trying to disguise my disappointment.

"Yeah."

"Why is that weird?"

"Well, we had a long talk and you'll never guess what?"

I take a mouth of toast and a mixture of butter and Marmite dribbles down my chin. "So?" I ask, wiping it off with a finger.

"Well Franny's adopted."

"Adopted?"

"Yes. And their own daughter – the one in the picture..."

"She drowned," I say.

"Exactly. God, how did you know that?"

"Bizarre," I say. "I don't know... I just sort of did."

"Yeah," Jenny says, nodding slowly. "I kind of did too. It's peculiar. I mean, I *didn't*, but it didn't surprise me at all. She fell off the breakwater, just like Sarah."

"So that's why Fred doesn't want to come here anymore?"

"Exactly. And that's why Susan kept warning us about the sea."

I nod, taking this in.

"She was *Fred's* daughter I think..." Jenny continues. "Not Susan's. I'm not sure about that bit, but that's the impression I got."

"How does *that* work?"

Jenny shrugs. "A first marriage maybe. I didn't ask. Susan was a bit weird about it."

"They look pretty young in the photos."

"Yes. But she kept saying, *'Fred's daughter.'* Never, *'Ours.'* And she said she couldn't have kids, which is why they ended up adopting."

"God, how awful."

"I know," Jenny says.

"I'm sorry I shouted at her, by the way."

"What?"

"When she fell in. I swore at her."

Jenny laughs. "Don't be daft. You were perfect. God knows what might have happened if you hadn't been there."

"She might not have fallen in at all," I say.

"Oh, she would have," Jenny says.

"I thought... it's just... Well, I thought you seemed funny afterwards."

"Funny?"

"I don't know."

"It just made me think about things, I suppose," Jenny says.

"I thought maybe you were angry with me or something."

"Angry? Why?"

"I don't know."

"Well, no, I've been sick. And you haven't exactly been a bundle of joy either."

I shrug.

"Is it Ricardo?"

I shrug again.

"You thought it was him didn't you?"

"Who?"

"When I said someone had called. You hoped it was Ricardo."

"Yeah," I say, with a sigh.

"So what's going on?"

"Nothing," I say.

"Tell me, Mark," she says.

"Well... You think he's awful anyway."

"But it's not my opinion that counts is it?"

"Maybe not," I say.

"Have you two fallen out?"

I pout and shake my head. "Not as such," I say. "But we talk less and less. I left him a nightmare message last night because I drank too much of that Bordeaux. And he hasn't phoned back of course."

"Phone *him* then," Jenny says.

"No, I think I'll just wait," I say.

"Sounds like game-playing to me."

"It's not," I say. And I try to think how to explain to Jenny where we're at without making her feel guilty. Which is, of course, entirely impossible. I swallow hard and sip my tea, and I see her glance at me sideways.

"Are you crying?"

"No," I say. "My eyes are just watering, that's all."

"Right," she says, then after a moment, she adds, "God! It's being here isn't it?"

"I'm sorry?"

"I'm so wrapped up in my own shit."

I shrug. "It's not your fault," I say. "But, you know... three months. It's a long time."

"Is it really three months?"

"Almost," I say. "Mid September I arrived."

"For Mum's funeral. Of course it is," she says, tutting and reaching out to rub my back. "God, I'm sorry."

I shrug again. "It's honestly not your fault. And it's not mine. And it's not Ricardo's either. It just is. But it's, you know, unsustainable."

"Is he still coming for Christmas?" Jenny asks. "Because he was, wasn't he?"

"I don't even know," I say. "He stopped mentioning it, and I'm too afraid to ask. Though I think I probably did in my magic drunken rant."

Jenny sighs and rubs my back again provoking a fresh batch of tears to well up.

"Oh, poor you," Jenny says with a deep sigh.

"I just miss him," I say, screwing my face up and biting my lip.

"Of course you do," Jenny says. "I guess we need to do something about that."

I snort. "Like what?" I say.

"I'll ask Tom," she says. "I thought about it already, but, no, I'll definitely call him tomorrow."

"Ask Tom what?"

"To come over here at Christmas. To come and stay."

"How does that..."

"God, I can't believe I've been so selfish. I'm so sorry Mark."

"You haven't. Really. But I still don't see..."

"You've been looking after us, and I haven't been looking out for *you*. And that's enough. I'm buying you a flight to go see your man."

"Jenny, I..."

"No, it's decided." she says. "If Mohammed won't go to the mountain... or whatever."

"It's not practical Jenny. Tom's working, flights for Christmas cost a fortune and..."

"He's not," she says. "Tom has two weeks off. And he doesn't have to come every day anyway. It'll be fine."

"But..."

Jenny shakes her head. "Don't argue. It's decided," she says. "We'll sort it tomorrow."

Jenny: When Doubts Vanish

T
he day my daughter fell into the sea, I had a new feeling that was so big it took me a while to work out what exactly it meant. But even as it happened, even before I found the time to analyse it, I could sense that almost everything had changed.

The progression of illness may be essentially linear, but you notice it in stages – the need to cut a new hole in a leather belt, the first time your gums bleed as you brush your teeth, the first – and last – clump of hair to fall out.

The fact that I was now too sick to run to save my daughter was a ghastly new revelation. But it was counterbalanced by the incredible knowledge that I didn't *need* to run because Mark could, and Mark did.

I have honestly never seen anyone move like that. Perhaps time was distorted by the nature of what was happening, or perhaps my illness slowed my own thinking down, but the speed at which Mark vanished from the bedroom, the time it took before he reappeared sprinting across the beach – it seemed like a physical impossibility. It was as if everything else – myself, my thoughts, Sarah's slow toppling motion, even the gulls swooping their huge wings as they scrambled to get out of Mark's way as he streaked across the beach – was slowed down.

I knew that she would be fine. I knew that he would save her, and that knowledge gave me a big warm feeling that I didn't know what to do with.

And when he swore at her, I recognised his anger instantly for what it was, fear. I saw at that moment that he had become her parent. The bond between them was now such that no other solution for Sarah's future would be thinkable. My guess was that though he didn't realise it yet, Mark wouldn't even allow any other arrangement. His reaction to my attempts at contacting Nick, were, I suddenly saw, a demonstration of this.

Over the next few days, I watched them together and everything I saw confirmed this view, and, between vomiting fits, I started to wonder if the time was right to bring the subject up. I knew from experience how resistant Mark could be to any idea he didn't think had originated in his own head. Any heterosexual woman will tell you that the most useful relationship skill a woman ever learns is to make men think that everything and anything was *their* idea, and Mark, bless him, was no different: he needed to come to this realisation of his own accord. But the problem was that I wasn't sure how much time we had for him to get there.

I could tell that the chemo was doing bad things to my body, in fact, I can honestly say that I have never felt so ill. And just as food poisoning from fish can put you off fish for months, my body knew that these pills were bad – it was becoming increasingly difficult to even swallow them, and it could only be a matter of time before they bumped me off the trial altogether. Beyond that it would presumably be a matter of months before the golf-ball in my brain resumed doing whatever it was going to do to me. Amazingly, no one had actually told me how I might die yet. I didn't know if it would be silent and painless, or a slow agony, and I hadn't found the courage to ask. But though it still seemed like an abstract, absurd concept, I was starting to get what remained of my brain around the fact that I was probably going to cease to exist, or at best, cease to be able to look after Sarah in any meaningful way. My failure to sprint across the beach indicated that this process was perhaps more advanced than I wanted to admit.

So I started to imagine Mark and Sarah ten years down the line. I imagined him looking at the rude adolescent that she had become, and feeling love tainted with sorrow at my departure. And then I imagined him remembering Ricardo as well – remembering everything he had given up to look after her.

Because what if Mark *never met anyone else*? Lord knows, I can vouch for the fact that love doesn't hang around on every street corner. So what if Ricardo was Mark's last chance for love and he felt he had had to choose between Sarah and Ricardo? What kind of shadow would that cast over their relationship?

I couldn't let that happen. Even if they were to split up at some point in the future, I had to make sure that it could never be said that it was my or Sarah's fault.

I told Mark I would buy him a ticket back to Colombia. I would just have to pray that he returned.

The next morning, I awoke with a headache and a fever. Every joint in my body ached like I had a bad case of flu. I lay there listening to the sounds below trying to summon the energy to organise what needed to be organised and wondering how I would survive a fortnight, possibly longer, without him.

And then I hear the doorbell ring. I stopped breathing to listen as Mark opened it.

A familiar voice rang out, and though I'm not sure, I think I heard Mark gasp.

I felt angry and jealous and cheated all over again. I felt apprehensive and excited and thankful too.

Surprise Delivery

I wake up just before five a.m. Initially I simply need to pee, but by the time I get back to the sofa my mind is racing with thoughts about a potential trip to Colombia and the state of my relationship with Ricardo. He has been so distant lately, I'm not even sure he *wants* me to visit.

Deciding that this is probably a burst of five a.m. paranoia, I phone him to get reassurance, but as so often these days, he doesn't answer. Having learnt my lesson, I leave the shortest cutest message I can muster and sit and wonder where he might be at eleven p.m or what I could possibly have said that he no longer wants to answer my calls. One thing is for sure, though. Until I manage to speak to him there's no point even thinking about flights.

At six Sarah pads downstairs. She doesn't even attempt to wake Jenny these days.

"Are you coming in here with me?" I ask.

"I want a drink," she says sullenly.

"Please."

"Please," she repeats.

I make us both breakfast and sit and alternate between watching the sunrise and helping her identify dinosaurs in her book. She has mastered all of the main ones now, though what use that could ever be to anyone I can't help but wonder.

Out of the blue she says, "Is Tom coming today?"

"No," I say. "I don't think so. Why?"

"I just wondered," she says, which makes me grin. *Just wondering* strikes me as a terribly grown up thing for a five year old to be doing.

"Do you like it when Tom comes?" I ask.

"Sometimes," she says. "Do you?"

"Sometimes," I agree.

"You don't like Sven though," she says.

I laugh. "What makes you think I don't like Sven?"

Sarah shrugs. "Is this a Tenontosaurus?" she asks.

"Nope, that's that one. It has stripes, remember?"

Her intuition about who likes who is apparently more advanced than her dinosaur vocabulary.

At nine I take Jenny tea and toast for breakfast. She accepts the first and refuses the latter with a queenlike wave of her hand.

"That's your last batch of pills today, right?" I ask.

"Yep," Jenny says. "For now anyway. Good job too."

"Well you just rest and get healthy in time for Monday," I say. "I want you looking like a Bay Watch babe by the time we get to the hospo."

"I want to look at flights with you later," she says ignoring my attempts to be upbeat.

"I need to check dates with Ricardo first, OK?" I say.

I return downstairs and sit and eat Jenny's toast, something which is becoming a habit. Every pound she loses is turning into one that I gain.

Thinking about the ratio of calorie intake to expenditure, I ask Sarah, "How do you fancy going for a nice long walk later?"

"Where?" she asks suspiciously.

"How about Eastbourne? We could go around the pier again."

She wrinkles her nose, unconvinced by the idea.

"We could get a donut," I say, thinking even as I say it that this has the potential to ruin the original calorie burning aim of the walk.

Sarah still looks unconvinced.

"Um... we might win one of those blue dinosaurs," I say.

"OK," she says. Deal clenched.

Behind me the doorbell rings. I glance at my phone and frown. It's nine-fifteen and the only person who has ever visited – Tom – never calls during work hours.

I cross the room and, bracing myself to fend off Jehovah's Witnesses, I rest my hand on the latch. And then I realise that it's probably the postman and yank the door open.

The surprise of seeing who is on the doorstep makes me inhale sharply. I blink twice to check that I'm not imagining things. Tears push instantly at the backs of my eyes.

I had completely forgotten how beautiful he can look, especially when he grins this way.

"Chupy!" he exclaims opening his arms to hug me. "I think I have the wrong house but..."

A huge lump forms in my throat making it momentarily impossible to speak.

I think, *"I love you,"* and *"I have missed you so much,"* and *"I'm so happy,"* but "I..." is all I manage to say.

"T'es comme Paloma," he says in an amused voice. "T'as pris du poids." – *You're like Paloma. You've put on weight."*

"I... I can't believe that you're here." I say.

Ricardo holds me at arm's length so that he can look at me. "You happy though?" he says peering into my eyes, wrinkling his brow.

I shake my head and work my mouth before I manage to say, "You have no idea babe."

At that instant the entire weight of being separated from him, of worrying about our relationship, of the responsibility of looking after Jenny and Sarah on my own, the stress of what's been happening with Tom... it all wells up causing tears to slip down my cheeks. I suddenly realise how alone I have felt without him.

Ricardo's face is split in two by his grin and as I start to breathe again I can't help but copy it, so I end up crying and grinning at the same time.

Ricardo looks bemused. "Monkey birthday?" he says.

"I'm sorry?"

"That's what you say when it rains and sun at the same time, no?"

A fresh wave of tears wells up and I lean in and hug him tightly, breathing his scent as deeply as I can. I can still smell Colombia on him.

"God I've missed you," I say. "I've missed you so much, I had *forgotten* how much."

Ricardo frowns, and I shrug and laugh. "Come in, come in," I say, dragging his huge wheeled bag over the doorstep.

"Jenny! Guess who's here!" I shout before I realise that she is just beside me at the base of the stairs.

"Hello," she says in a strangely controlled, yet almost amused tone of voice. "It's been a long time."

He turns his sun-like grin on Jenny but as they hug it vanishes momentarily and he pulls a worried grimace at me.

"God, come in here and see Sarah," I say.

"My you are so big now," Ricardo says as she looks seriously up at him and nods wide eyed. "You remember me?" Ricardo asks.

"Ricky," Sarah says with a frown, and a ghost of the past drifts through the room.

"Yes, Ricky, Ricardo, Ricky, Ricardo," he says, blustering through the moment. "This is me!"

He pulls his coat off and Jenny takes it from him and hangs it in the hall. "Shall I make tea?" she asks. But Ricardo and I are too busy staring at each other to reply, so she shrugs and vanishes into the kitchen.

"God, I still can't believe it," I say, touching Ricardo's furry arm and noticing how hot his body feels – something I had forgotten. "How long are you staying? It's so brilliant to see you babe. Are you here till Christmas? This is such a brilliant surprise. Is this why you wanted the address? I thought you were sending me a postcard..." I burble.

"I decide to send me instead," Ricardo says. "And I'm here as long as you want."

"You got an open ticket?"

"Um, sort of," he says.

"But what about your job?"

"I quit," he says.

"You *quit?*"

Ricardo beams at me again and blinks slowly. "My Chupy say he needs me here," he says. "So here I am."

I gasp and hug him again and shed a few more tears. How could I have forgotten how brilliant this man is? How could I ever have doubted this relationship? *How?*

That day with Ricardo is probably the most beautiful we have ever spent together. It feels even more intense that the three days we stole before running off together.

Jenny, who seems a little paralysed by Ricardo's presence, returns quickly to bed, and Ricardo and I eat brunch under Sarah's watchful gaze before taking her to Eastbourne where I'm hoping we can find a mattress for immediate delivery.

I'm struggling to believe that Ricardo really is here beside me and find myself unable to resist pecking him on the cheek every time Sarah looks the other way. The fact that Ricardo was once her mother's boyfriend makes me twitchy, but even if I avoid kissing him in front of her, I'm sure she gets the idea from the simple fact that I can't stop grinning. I have never felt more in love than today, and it feels wonderful – and that's something I just can't hide.

As we walk from the car to Eastbourne Pier, Ricardo looks up at the Victorian facades and says, "It's really beautiful Chupy."

"You sound surprised."

"I think I am," he says. "It's like a dream to get on a plane and suddenly be here."

"I can't believe that you're not tired," I say. "I slept the second I arrived."

"But I'm a doctor babe," he says. "I take a sleeping pill. I take two actually. I sleep for fourteen hours during the flight."

I glance down at Sarah who is walking along beside me. "Are you OK?" I ask.

She nods, silently. I think she is in some way in awe of Ricardo. Perhaps it's his effect on me that's shocking her. Certainly the amount of effervescent joy suddenly filling the air must be hard to understand after these past weeks of sadness and worry. Whatever the cause, as we walk along the pier today, Sarah even forgets about the blue dinosaurs.

In the town centre we head for a furniture store I have previously spotted. The fact that the salesman has an eastern european accent makes me hopeful that he's going to be more resourceful than your average English bed-salesman, and sure enough, he tells us that for twenty quid extra (cash) a friend of his will deliver it this very afternoon.

In the car home, Ricardo rests his hand on my leg provoking an instant erection. "It's a shame we don't have a bed yet," he tells me in French – moving his hand to indicate that he has noticed.

"Well you'll just have to wait until it arrives," I say, glancing back to check that Sarah is unaware.

I look over at him and he grins and says, "What?"

"I still can't believe you're here," I say. "I have to keep checking. Did you really quit your job?"

"Jobs are easy come, easy go," he says. "You remember how long it took me to get that job, right?"

"Sure. About ten minutes. All the same. I'm really grateful."

He squeezes my leg. "I'm so happy to be here, Chups," he says.

"Is Maria feeding Paloma?"

"Um, yes, of course."

"But she'll get lonely on her own. She can't stay like that forever. We'll have to bring her back over fairly soon if we're staying here."

"Well Federico might be using the house. That's what he said."

"I thought he had a dog?"

"Yes. So this is why I tell Maria to take Paloma home if he come."

"Right. Poor Paloma! She won't know what's hit her. I'm not sure she'll prefer Maria's kids to Federico's dog that much."

"She'll be fine Chupy."

"Do *you* remember Paloma, Sarah?"

"The cat?" she says.

"Gosh, you do."

"She licked me."

"Amazing," I say. "I can't believe she remembers that. I don't remember anything from when I was three."

"Well, you're not five," Ricardo says.

"No, I suppose not."

"Makes you wonder what *else* she remembers," Ricardo says in French.

"You know I was going to buy a flight today? To come and visit you?"

"Really?"

"Really."

"Great minds think the same," Ricardo says.

"I was so worried that I was losing you. Especially when you didn't call back."

"Coming is better, no?"

"Oh yes!"

"You see, I'm very hard to lose."

"Well good. I'm glad about that."

"Jenny a l'air vraiment très malade," he says. - *Jenny looks really ill.*

"Yes. Well, she is."

"Can I come and talk to her doctor on Monday? She said you have to go on Monday."

"God, I would love it if you did," I say. "It has just felt like everything's on my shoulders, you know?" My voice is wobbling, so I stop.

Ricardo squeezes my leg again. "It's all OK now Chupy," he says. "We can share it all. The good things and the bad things."

The Luckiest Guy Alive

When we get back to the house, I make a big salad for everyone and heat a frozen pizza to share.

Jenny comes downstairs and joins us for lunch for only the second time this week. She's even wearing makeup – presumably an effort to look healthy and normal for Ricardo. But she eats little and says virtually nothing. I can sense her discreetly watching Ricardo and me. My guess is that she has a whole raft of feelings to work through about Ricardo, their previous relationship and this new, strange situation. She's doing pretty well considering.

Sarah, perhaps influenced by her mother, returns to being quietly awed too, and so it falls to Ricardo and me to make the conversation. Still, we have plenty of catching up to do, so we yack excitedly about Tayrona and Bogotá and London and life here in Pevensey Bay.

Ricardo clearly senses the strain of the situation because when Jenny asks what we have planned for the afternoon, he tells her that he doesn't know yet but that maybe he should look for somewhere to stay nearby.

"But you must stay *here*," Jenny says. "I thought you two had a bed coming."

"We do," I say, trying not to show that I'm aghast at Ricardo's suggestion.

"I think maybe you're not so comfortable," Ricardo says. "If Mark and I could stay nearby then perhaps…"

"That won't work," I say in rapid French designed to be unintelligible to Jenny. "I have to be here to look after Sarah. You haven't grasped the setup."

"L'atmosphère est à couper au couteau," he says equally rapidly. "On ne va même pas pouvoir niquer." – *You could cut the atmosphere here with a knife. We won't even be able to fuck.*

Jenny frowns. "Despite your efforts, I think I understood the gist of that..." she says. "Look, why don't you go away for the weekend. I understand you need to catch up and you know... stuff."

"I don't want to leave you on your own."

"I'll be fine."

"Sorry, but no," I say, thinking about Sarah watching her mother vomiting, and all that could go wrong whilst Jenny sleeps.

"I'll call Tom and get him to come over then," Jenny says.

"Yeah, that might work."

As Jenny heads off to phone Tom, Ricardo winks at me and I grin. Every inch of exposed skin is calling to me and the desire to rip his clothes off and squash my body against his is almost unbearable. It feels like we're two magnets, and it's taking all my efforts to keep us apart.

As we wait for Tom to phone back, I realise that Ricardo's right – with Jenny in the next room we're not going to be able to do any more than cuddle. Silently. I struggle to force memories of Ricardo's trademark "good hard fucks", from my mind.

But Tom never *does* phone back, so once Jenny has returned to bed, Ricardo and I simply sit on opposite sides of the table with Sarah in the middle keeping the two magnets from snapping together.

At two, I convince Sarah to go and have a siesta with her mum and Ricardo and I manage to have a cuddle and a kiss on the sofa, but the frustration of not being able to undress in case someone comes downstairs is almost worse. Less than an hour later Sarah returns and Ricardo and I spring apart.

"I'm sorry," I say. "It just feels peculiar in front of her."

"I agree," he says. "We can wait till tonight."

The mattress arrives at six and Ricardo, visibly overcome by jet lag, soon makes his excuses and heads upstairs.

I sit and do colouring-in with Sarah and try not to think about his naked body between the sheets until finally, at eight, Jenny gets up.

She crosses the room to the table where we're sitting and nods at the stairs and says, "Just go."

"I'm sorry," I say, already standing. "I know it must be uncomfortable for you."

Jenny shrugs. "It is," she says. "But go anyway. Go before I go and climb in with him myself."

It's an attempt at introducing a little humour to the situation, but a frown must flicker across my brow because Jenny laughs and says, "Joke, Mark!"

"Right, well," I say, standing. "Don't. Don't joke."

"Where are you going?" Sarah asks.

"Mark's very tired," Jenny tells her. "He's going to bed for a sleep."

Upstairs, I find Ricardo snoring lightly. He is splayed across the bed with one arm, one knee and one buttock peeping from beneath the white quilt.

I close the door quietly and stand and stare at the vision. Just his presence in the room makes my heart race, and I try to work out what it is about his body that I find so very very sexy. For Ricardo is no Brad Pitt, and he's no athlete either, in fact, like myself, he's currently packing a few extra pounds, but these do nothing to reduce how sexy he looks.

I look at the swirls of dark hair covering his arms and legs and note that, irritatingly, without doing any sport he's still naturally muscly.

I look at his long trunk and stubby legs and decide that it is above all that ratio of upper body to lower body that I find unbelievably cute. And then I grin and think, *"No, it's just all of it. It's just him."*

I swallow the saliva forming in my mouth and lay myself as gently as I can on the bed beside him. He doesn't stir.

I roll onto one side, and edge backwards until my buttocks just touch his knee, and he groans, rolls onto his own side, and then shimmies behind me so that his knees are behind mine. "Chupy," he murmurs, laying a heavy, hot arm over my waist.

Within seconds he's snoring again, but I don't mind. Just this is perfect; just the unexpected presence of my man behind me here, now, is ecstasy.

I lie there, grinning stupidly and think about these forgotten sensations: his hairy chest against my back, his dick against my buttocks as it hardens and softens in sleep. I think about his smell, about the familiar weight of this arm around me and how safe that feels. I notice how brilliantly our bodies fit together, and think how, despite all my doubts, our lives continue to fit together too, for the simple reason that we have decided that they will.

I listen to Jenny and Sarah retiring next door, and a lump forms in my throat and tears well up at the thought that despite all the shit going on around me, and all the challenges and perhaps sadness to come, I really am the luckiest man alive.

Your Time Will Come

On Saturday morning Sarah wakes me up by prodding my elbow. The second I open one eye, she starts to climb onto the bed, but I move my arm to block her path. "Go downstairs," I say forcefully, "and I'll be down in a minute."

She pushes her bottom lip out but does as I say anyway.

Ricardo, who is squashed against my back (I'm not sure if we have moved back into this configuration or maintained it all night) says, *"Qu'est-ce qu'il y a ?"*

"She wanted to get into bed for a cuddle."

"That's OK, isn't it?"

I snort and move his hand down to my dick. "Not with that going on," I say.

"Ah, no," he laughs, squeezing it gently. "That is mine."

"Don't start," I say, slipping from his grasp. "I have to get up and make breakfast."

"But when babe?," he asks.

"If Tom phones today," I say, pulling my jeans on. "Maybe we can get some time away."

Ricardo pushes the quilt away and stretches and yawns. I look at the line of hair down the middle of his chest and at his erect dick and lick my lips. "God you're sexy," I say.

"You sexy," Ricardo says with a wink. "Do they go places?"

"I'm sorry?"

"Jenny and Sarah. They go out sometimes?"

"Oh. Not much when she's on chemo," I reply quietly, aware that she is next door. "But next week, once she's been off it for a few days, yeah... she'll be almost like normal."

"She is on chemo now?"

247

"Yesterday," I say. "Not today."

"I don't want to wait a few days babe," Ricardo says.

I grin at him. "Don't worry. We'll find a way."

Just as the three of us are finishing breakfast, Jenny joins us.

"You're up early today," I comment.

"Yeah, well," she says. "No horrible pills to take today. You two can go out if you want."

Thinking, *I'd rather stay in,* I ask, "Any news of Tom?"

Jenny pulls a face. "Only an SMS I'm afraid. he can't come."

"Oh."

"Says he has his own shit to deal with."

"Oh. Did you tell him Ricardo's here, because..."

"Nope. So that's not it. But I'll be fine. I was thinking that if you took me to London on Monday, you two could head off somewhere and Sarah and I could come home on the train."

I pull a doubtful expression. "Well, let's see how things go, eh?"

"I can't wait till Tuesday," Ricardo whispers, once she has gone.

I laugh. "You won't have to babe. Your time will come. Your time *to come* will come."

In fact, we don't have to wait too long. After her mid-day snooze, Jenny tactfully announces that she is feeling "tons better," and wants to take Sarah for a nice long walk.

"Ah, a walk would be good," Ricardo agrees.

I nudge him and roll my eyes, and he looks at me and then suppresses a grin and yawns and feigns tiredness instead. "Or maybe a sleep. Time difference," he says unconvincingly.

"Right, well... come on Miss. Let's get you wrapped up," Jenny says flatly. "It's freezing out."

Ricardo and I sit and stare at each other as Jenny and Sarah get ready, and mere seconds after they have closed the door we slip into stupid grins and race each other upstairs.

We dump our clothes on the bedroom floor and, still laughing, press our bodies tightly together.

"Mmm," I say. *"That's* what I wanted."

We kiss for a moment, and I say, "I had forgotten what a good kisser you are."

"Shh," Ricardo says, kissing me again.

His dick, pressed against mine, stiffens and twitches.

"How long she go?" he asks.

"Sorry?"

"You don't understand me now," he says. "My English is so bad?"

"No," I say. "I just need to get used to your accent again I think."

"So how long do we have?"

"Oh," I say. "Um, I don't know. Half an hour? An hour."

Ricardo nods seriously. "OK, then we kiss after," he says. "You have condoms?"

"Sure, in the top drawer."

"OK, give me one."

"But I wanted to fuck *you*," I laugh, as he turns me around and pushes me down onto the bed.

"Me too Chupy," he says, spreading my butt-cheeks. "That's why we need to be quick."

Getaway Plan

When we get to the hospital on Monday morning, Sarah and I head off to the park leaving Ricardo and Jenny at the hospital.

Leaving the two of them alone together seems unnatural and I can't help but feel paranoid that they will talk about me – though what evil plan they might possibly hatch, I have no idea.

Still, Ricardo wishes to talk to the professor. He seems to think that doctors are far more forthcoming amongst themselves.

The grass in St James' park is covered with such a thick layer of frost that Sarah thinks it has snowed.

"It's just frost," I explain as she runs and jumps and looks back at her footprints.

"Mummy said it might snowed," Sarah says.

"*Snow.* Well, it might *snow.* But it hasn't yet. Careful you don't slip."

"It's very slippy. Do you like snow?"

"Yes, I do."

"I hope it snow."

"I hope it *snows,*" I correct her.

"So do I."

"But it hardly ever snows at the seaside because the sea is too warm. So don't get your hopes up."

Sarah frowns at me as if she thinks that I'm telling a big fib.

"It's true," I laugh. "You can ask Mummy."

"But you said it was cold."

"Ah - it's too cold to *swim.* But it's too warm for snow."

Sarah twists her mouth sideways. Clearly she thinks I'm talking rubbish. We walk on across the park for a moment, our feet crunching on the icy grass, and then she says, "Do you mind having Ricardo in your bed?"

I clear my throat. "I'm sorry?"

"Having Ricardo in your bed. Do you mind?"

I stifle an embarrassed grin. "Well, no, not really. Why?"

"Well, he's a bit big. I share Mummy's bed, but I'm only little."

"Ah. Well, it *is* quite a big bed."

"Two boys is too big for one bed though."

"Well," I laugh. "It's a good job you only have to share with Mummy, isn't it."

"Can we have ice cream?"

"Don't you think it's a bit cold?"

"No."

"Maybe then. If the shop's open. And if he *has* any ice cream in December."

When we get back to the hospital, I find Jenny alone in the waiting room. She is clutching her bag of chemo pills indicating that she is all done and ready to leave.

"Where's Ricardo?" I ask her.

"Dunno," she says. "He wandered off with Florence. They were blathering on in French. You wanna keep an eye on that one."

"Ricardo or Florent?"

"Both. Especially together."

I grimace and plonk Sarah down next to her mother.

"What's that around your chops?" Jenny asks her.

"Ice cream," I say.

"In *this* weather? Aren't you cold sweetie?"

Sarah shakes her head.

"Your daughter would want ice cream at the North Pole," I say. "Which way did they go?"

Jenny points towards the corridor, so I head off saying, "I'll be back. Don't move."

I criss cross the entire floor before I finally glance out of a window and see Ricardo and Florent smoking below.

"I can't believe you guys," I say, when I reach them. "You should be ashamed." My blustering introduction is mainly intended to disguise my jealousy.

"Chupy!" Ricardo says, stepping back a little, I notice, from Florent.

"Honestly! A doctor and a cancer nurse *smoking*."

"It's his fault," Florent says. "I only smoke other people's nowadays."

"*You* have cigarettes?"

Ricardo rolls his eyes and pulls a Colombian pack of Marlborough from his pocket and points it at me.

I pull a face. "I don't smoke anymore," I say. "You know that."

"You do sometimes," he points out.

"Well, when I'm drunk. But..."

"Anyway, I don't give you one. I say look at the packet."

I take the pack from him and peer inside. "So?"

"I bought a week ago," Ricardo says.

"Right. And?"

"Sixteen. So I smoke one last week and one today because I want to give Florent one."

"Oh, OK," I say, ignoring that particular double-entendre. "Whatever. So what are you two plotting?"

"Plotting?"

"What are you talking about?"

"Ahh!" Ricardo says, wiggling his eyebrows. "Good thing. Clever thing."

"Right..."

"Ricardo asked me to come to Eastbourne," Florent says.

I frown. *"What?"*

"He is a nurse Chupy."

"I *know* he's a nurse," I say, opening the palm of my hand towards him to point out that he *is* wearing a nurse's uniform.

"Ricardo asked if I would come down to look after Jenny," Florent says.

"Why? What for?"

"So we can go to Nice for some days," Ricardo says. "You need to get away you said. And I want to see my apartment... so... It could be nice. In Nice. Ha!"

"Oh!" I say, my jealousy cloud lifting. "Oh, *right.*"

"It's an amazing... you know... coincidence," Florent says. "I'm on holiday all next week. But I'm too skint to go anywhere. This way I don't have to spend all week listening to my flatmate wanking off."

I pull a face at that image. "Right."

"What you think?" Ricardo asks. "Is clever, *non?*"

"Jenny won't like it," I say.

"Chupy can convince her. Chupy can convince anyone anything."

"Nah," I say. "She'll hate it. It'll make her feel like an invalid."

"She did already invite me," Florent says. "Ages ago."

"She *did?*"

"Yeah, she said you needed a drinking buddy and that you could show me the sights in Brighton or something."

I shake my head. "God, that girl is out of control," I say.

"Anyway," Florent says. "I could make it look like, you know, a sort of social visit."

"I said we will pay to cover expenses and things," Ricardo says.

"So I get a holiday by the sea, and you two get to have your break..."

"And Jenny gets her favourite nurse," Ricardo adds. "It's good! Tell me it's good babe."

"I do really like her too," Florent says. "We have a real laugh together. Well, as much as you can during chemo."

I shrug. "Well... maybe. If she goes for it. Only she won't."

"Leave it to me," Florent says. "I'll call her later, as if I just thought of it..."

"I tell you, if she gets any hint of this..." I say. "She'll be furious."

"I'll be careful," Florent says. "Anyway, I better get back. This is my last shift."

"Do you want her number?"

"Jenny's?" Florent asks. "I have it."

"You do?"

"Yep. She gave it to me ages ago. Yours too."

I shake my head. "Unbelievable."

"OK, see you soon hopefully."

Once he has slipped behind the doors, Ricardo touches my chin so that I look him in the eye. "You're not happy?" he asks, genuinely concerned.

I shrug. "I don't know," I say. "It's just... well, we don't really know him, do we?"

Ricardo raises his shoulders. "Jenny does," he says. "She tell me he is the favourite nurse. That's why I talk to him. I can't find professor Twat."

"*Batt*. It's *Batt*. Twat means... it's an insult."

"Oh. I think I say *Twat* to the secretary," Ricardo says.

"Oh my God! You didn't!"

He shrugs. "Not sure. Anyway, he's not in, so I talk to Florent."

"What did he say?"

"About Jenny? It's not good. But you know that. He say that surprises happen. You know, miracles. But... well... pfff."

"Pfff?"

"Yeah."

"Anyway, I'm still not sure about inviting him into our home."

"Jenny already did," Ricardo says. "So... *Où est le problème ?*"

"I suppose. I didn't know about that. That's very cheeky of her."

"And he seems very nice."

"Yeah, he does."

"Sexy boy."

"Ricardo!"

Ricardo raises one eyebrow and nudges me. "I think Ricardo arrives just in time, non?" he says with exaggerated gravity.

"Enough!" I say. "Come on. Jenny and Sarah are waiting."

***

Back at the house the atmosphere becomes a little more tense with each hour that passes. It's not that any of us are truly failing to get on. It's simply that every act, no matter how simple, seems loaded with unspoken sub-texts.

Whether it is Jenny remembering that Ricardo likes his eggs fried on both sides, or the choice of who sits next to who at the dinner table, the constant stream of knowing looks and mid-sentence pauses inevitably leaves everyone's nerves frazzled.

In fact this contributes to making sure that Ricardo's plan works perfectly. By Wednesday lunchtime when Florent phones, Jenny jumps at the idea that his visit might enable Ricardo and me to vanish for a few days.

"That was Florent," she declares when the call is over.

"Florent?" I ask, trying to modulate my voice to express exactly the right amount of surprise.

"Yeah. We've become quite chummy. Anyway, he wants to come and visit for a few days."

"What, *here*?"

"Yeah, he's on holiday, the poor dear, and he can't afford to go away. I suggested a few days at the seaside."

"Do you think there's room?" I ask, wondering if this isn't pushing my theatrical envelope a little too far.

"Well exactly," Jenny says. "You two could do that trip to Nice you mentioned. And don't tell me you don't fancy a couple of nights away somewhere."

"But you don't know him, do you?" I ask.

Jenny shrugs. "I will by Sunday."

I pull a face. My last, convincing stand before I cave in.

"Oh go on," Jenny says. "When else will you two get the chance to get away?"

"I suppose..." I say, looking at Ricardo. "What do you think?"

"Sounds good to me," he says. "When does he come?"

"Tomorrow afternoon," Jenny says.

"Tomorrow!" I say.

"Can you look at flights?" Ricardo asks. "With, you know, the orange one."

"Easyjet," I say. "Yeah, but they'll be expensive for *tomorrow*."

But of course, I have already looked and though they *are* a bit more expensive than I'm used to paying, mid December isn't high season either. They aren't beyond our reach.

On Thursday lunchtime, I pick Florent up from Eastbourne station and drive him back to the house.

During the short drive he tells me that his aunt died of cancer and that's how he realised he wanted to go into nursing. He still strikes me as incredibly cute, but beyond that I realise that he really is a rather lovely guy too. He's polite and funny and has a sort of scrubbed-clean perfection that's hard to nail down. He tells me that he's thirty-five, which is actually a good seven years older than I would have guessed and I ask him only half jokingly, what kind of skin cream he uses.

Though I know it makes me guilty of the worst kind of stereotyping, his dismissive reply – that he doesn't use *any* kind of cream – makes me wonder for the first time if he perhaps isn't gay after all.

On the drive to the airport, I ask Ricardo about this. "Maybe he's like me," Ricardo says.

"You mean bisexual?" I ask, wondering if Ricardo is going to accept the label for the first time ever.

"No. I mean, maybe he doesn't use skin cream," Ricardo says without irony.

It's raining when we arrive in Nice, which, though predicted by the weather forecast, is a huge disappointment.

"Yuck," I say, staring from the window of the shuttle bus at a couple of bedraggled joggers on the Prom.

"Tomorrow Chups," Ricardo says. "They said the sunshine is for tomorrow."

We alight in front of the magnificent hotel Negresco and walk through the drizzle to our own far less ostentatious choice, *La Petite Sirene*.

The Swedish woman at check-in looks momentarily concerned. "This is a double room," she says.

"Yes, I know," I say with a forced smile.

"With one big bed."

"That's fine."

"We have a twin if you'd prefer."

"Maybe," Ricardo says, clearly uncomfortable at the confusion.

"We're together," I explain. "We're a couple. We always sleep together."

"Oh," she says, breaking into a huge grin of relief. "I'm sorry, I didn't realise. You don't... anyway... here are your keys. Third floor. Three-O-Two."

Once in our modest room, Ricardo says, "Pourquoi tu lui as dit ça ? Ce ne sont pas ses oignons." - *Why did you say that? It's none of her business.*

"Why did *you* say that a twin was OK?" I retort.

"I think maybe she is embarrassed by us," he says.

"She's Swedish. Of course she wasn't. You could see that she wasn't."

"I guess."

"Anyway," I say, steering us away from potential conflict. "What do you want to do first? Visit your old flat? Go have a drink? Shag?"

"The flat," Ricardo says.

"Really?" I ask, somewhat taken aback.

Ricardo nods seriously. "I'm not in mood now."

I understand exactly why Ricardo isn't in the mood. It's the direct consequence of his brief flush of embarrassment at being in a gay couple. But there's no point going there... no point at all.

"OK", I say with a sigh of disappointment. "Let's do that then."

The rain has stopped when we get outside so we walk down to the seafront. The sky is still dark and loaded with rain to come – this is clearly just a temporary pause.

"Look at the sea," Ricardo says as we cross the road.

"Yeah," I say. "It's because of the rain."

"The rain?"

"Yeah, it washes white silt from the mountains into the sea. That's what makes the sea go that milky turquoise colour."

"I didn't know," he says, so I point out how the sea is whitest at the point where the river Paillon floods out into the bay. "It's what makes the Côte d'Azur azure," I explain.

We continue along the wet seafront. As we reach Castel Plage, Ricardo says, "It's a nice place too. Nice."

"Yeah."

"Would you come back to live here?"

"Yep," I say. "Sure. No problem."

"Me too."

"But you'd rather live in Colombia."

"I don't know babe. I'm not sure now."

"*Oh,*" I say, shocked. "Right."

We continue around Rauba Capeu and past the war memorial, then cross to the entrance to Ricardo's building. He repeatedly rings the intercom, but when there is no answer, he looks at me slyly and says, "Maybe we have a look?"

"I don't think you should," I say. "It's not your flat now."

"Just quick," he says, unlocking the street door. "You can watch the stairs."

Which is exactly what we do. I stand at the top of the stairwell and peer down whilst Ricardo lets himself in behind me.

As he opens the door, thunder cracks outside, and rain starts to plop onto the glass roof of the stairwell.

"Chupy, come see," he says.

I cross the landing and peer in through the door. "I thought you wanted me on lookout," I say. "Jesus! What a mess."

The sofa-bed is still in "bed" configuration. Every inch of the remaining floor is covered in a mixture of newspapers, discarded clothes and books. The ashtray is full to overflowing.

Ricardo looks at me and nods wide eyed from the other side of the room. "And I thought *you* were the messy boy."

"I'm not messy," I protest.

He takes in the room and shakes his head. "Well no," he says turning to look out of the window. "Great view still."

"Yes," I agree. "It is."

"You remember what happened here?" he asks, just as I am remembering exactly that.

"Of course," I say.

"And Jenny came."

"And I hid on the balcony."

"In the rain, like today."

"It was the same time of year," I say. "Anyway, come on. Let's get a move on before they come back." I *am* nervous about their return, but more embarrassingly, these memories are giving me a stiffy.

"Maybe we can live here again one day," Ricardo says.

"Sure," I say. "Why not?" I don't mention that if we end up looking after Sarah, this flat would be too small.

As we descend, Ricardo says, "They're very messy people."

"They are," I say. "Are you worried?"

He pouts and shakes his head. "No. As long as they don't burn the place. As long as they pay the rent."

"Have you met them?"

"No. The agency did it all so..."

Down in the hall, I open the frosted glass door onto the street and am startled by the presence of two guys on the other side. One of them is fiddling with his keys.

We step aside and they smile and pass us. We step out into the rain and just as the door closes, I glance back and see them both peering back at us.

"Happy boys," Ricardo says.

"Yes. Gay boys," I say quietly. "Cute boys too. Maybe your renters."

"Maybe," he laughs. "I hope."

"So what now?"

"Nice in the rain?"

"Yeah..."

"I think it's time to go back to the hotel for a siesta."

"You're *tired?*"

"No Chupy. You know what I mean when I say siesta."

"Ah!" I say, slipping into a grin. "*That* kind of siesta."

A Different Kind of Gay

The sex back at the hotel is of the *wham bam* variety, but to be honest I have always rather liked it when Ricardo is in one of his *short-sharp-shock* moods.

Afterwards we have a long, reassuring cuddle and then despite agreeing that we aren't tired, drift off to sleep.

By the time we head out for dinner the sky is clearing, so we have a couple of beers beneath the gas heaters of the open-air brasserie *La Civette* before eating in a favourite restaurant of mine in the old town, *La Ville De Sienne*.

Once we have finished our identical plates of *gnocchi Sorrentina*, Ricardo slides one leg between mine and beams at me.

"What?" I ask.

"Happy," he says, simply.

"You think you could live here again then?"

"Yes," he says.

"So when did you change your mind about Colombia?"

"I did not."

"Well, you said you were less sure about going back."

Ricardo nods and sighs. He stares from the side window for a moment then looks back at me and shrugs. "I think it was when those guys shoot the dog," he says.

"Right. Well. That freaked me out too."

"I don't mind so much for me, but it makes me feel guilty for you."

"Guilty?"

"Responsible maybe," he says.

"Sure. Well. I'm, you know, a big boy," I say. "You don't need to feel responsible for anything."

259

"I love Colombia," he says. "But I think maybe it's still a bit... hairy? Is that what you say?"

I laugh. "Yeah. Hairy works. Why did you leave in the first place? I don't think you ever told me why you moved to France."

"I wanted a change," he says. "And I had a cousin in Nice, so it was easy. It was bad in Bogotá too then. It was good to get away."

After dinner, Ricardo wants to go to a gay bar, but when we reach my first choice – *L'Ascenseur* – it has been re-branded *The Eagle* and is no longer a bar but a sex club. You now have to pay just to get in. I have a feeling of deja vu as if I already knew this but had simply forgotten.

"Let's go anyway," Ricardo says, already pulling banknotes from his wallet.

"You won't like it," I say.

"Let's go," he says, handing the money over. "I want to see."

The last time I was in l'Ascenseur, it had been packed red-wall to red-wall. The ever smiling Gilles who had been behind the bar for almost twenty years would introduce me to anyone I hadn't already met around the pool table.

This time when we are buzzed in, it is into a near-empty room with black walls, sticky floor and a camouflage-netting ceiling. The music is industrial and ugly, and five unhealthy looking chaps are the only clients. Each of them is propped, unsmiling, against a separate section of wall.

I peer through to where the pool table used to be and see that it is now a pitch-black back-room.

Ricardo looks around slowly and then says, "You're right Chupy. I don't like it," and so I nod towards the door, and laughing we push straight back out onto the street.

"Abandon hope all ye who enter here," I say outside.

"You used to come here?" Ricardo asks.

"It was totally different. There was good music and a friendly barman and a pool table," I say.

"Hum," Ricardo says, sounding unconvinced.

"Let's try Smarties. That'll be better."

We walk along for a minute in silence then Ricardo says, "You know, when I see a place like this one..."

"Yes?"

"I don't understand."

"Well no."

"That's when I say I'm not gay, you understand?"

I shrug. "Well in that case, neither am I. It's horrible in there."

"You wouldn't go there then? Even if you were single?"

"No," I say, shuddering at the thought that the differences between the Eagle and Schwarz maybe aren't as great as all that.

"There's no fun. Those guys, they wait for what?"

"Well, for someone to go into the back room I suppose."

"Yes. That's what I think too."

"And then they follow them in."

"They should try talking to each other," Ricardo says. "Less boring."

"Yes," I agree. "They should."

And then Ricardo, ever unpredictable, takes my hand.

We walk hand in hand for thirty seconds before I give his hand a squeeze and release myself. I never have been very at ease with holding hands in public, and I'm amazed that Ricardo – who can't even ask for a double bed – suddenly feels comfortable with it.

When we get to Smarties the atmosphere is much better. The seventies' interior gleams and twinkles with enticing colour, and a DJ is mixing some unctuous electro beats. A few women are mingling amongst the essentially male gay crowd.

"This is nice," Ricardo says once I have ordered our drinks.

"I knew you'd like it," I say.

"Yes."

"And it's gay too," I point out. "It's just a different kind of gay."

"OK," Ricardo says, winking at me and grinning. "Well, then maybe I am just a different kind of gay."

I laugh. "Well that's beyond discussion," I say as we clink our glasses together.

"It's better, no?"

"Oh, much better babe."

An Ill Wind

When we get back to Gatwick on Sunday afternoon it is three degrees and sleeting.

"I think I prefer Nice," Ricardo says as I slip the ticket into the slot.

"Me too," I say. "Jesus! Sixty quid!"

"Let me," Ricardo offers, already feeding his credit card into the machine.

"Thanks," I say. "Fuck it's cold."

"It is, babe."

Not a word is spoken as I head down the M23 and then onto the A27. The price of the parking ticket has left me totting up the cost of our mini-break and thinking more generally about money.

Ricardo, of course, is no longer working, and I haven't taken on a single piece of translation work for three weeks now. I know that Ricardo has some rent coming in from his Nice flat, and that somewhere down the line, he will receive his share of the cash from the sale of his mother's place, but neither of those are going to cover our needs long-term. Living off your remaining capital has never been a good strategy for wealth or happiness because of course once it's gone, so have all your options.

I open my mouth to discuss it a couple of times, but I can't quite find a way to frame the question because it's one of those situations where everything depends upon everything else. How long will we need to stay? Will Ricardo and Jenny get on well enough to make this house-share tenable? Will he want to return to Colombia when it's over? Will Jenny even survive, or will we have Sarah with us? The questions are endless – it's a puzzle of mind blowing complexity and for the moment it's simply too early to even begin to sort through it all.

As we come out of Eastbourne, I ask Ricardo what he is thinking about.

"Nothing," he says quietly. "Everything."

"Like?"

"The way the English drive. So polite. And Jenny and Sarah. The weather..."

"Right."

"That I'm happy, here now."

I look over at him and he smiles broadly, and I know exactly what he means. Love has this amazing ability to make everything right, no matter what else is going on.

On arrival, my heart sinks at the sight of Tom's Beetle. Amazingly, *stupidly*, I had altogether forgotten about Tom these past few days.

I park as far from the Beetle as I can and switch the engine off.

Ricardo reaches for the door-handle and then hesitates. "You OK Chupy?" he asks.

"Yeah," I say. "I'm just, you know... not in a rush for this moment to end."

"The end of the holiday."

"Yes. Something like that. God it's windy." The car is shifting from side to side as the sea wind buffets us.

"Yes. Come on. You have to take Florent to the station, remember?"

"Sure."

I open the door and it is nearly ripped from the car by the force of the wind. "Wow!" I shout. "Be careful."

We pull the bags from the hatchback and head across the car park towards the houses. "Just when you think it can't get any colder," I say.

As we near the first of the beach houses, Tom appears coming the other way. I feel a prickling of stress tempered by a wave of relief that at least we won't now have to sit and chat together.

"It's Tom?" Ricardo asks.

"Yes."

"Right," he says. He sounds apprehensive, so I glance sideways at him and see that he looks as worried as I feel. But then I see him fix his doctor's smile. "Tom!" he says enthusiastically as we come face to face.

"Hi Tom," I say, kissing him on the cheek.

"Hi, he replies, to me alone. He looks pale and flushed, the way he looks when he's really angry, but it could of course just be caused by the cold wind.

"Hi Tom," Ricardo says again, holding out his hand, but Tom just glances at him and then looks back at me. "I didn't know you had gone away," he says.

I hear Ricardo sigh as he slips his hand back into his pocket.

"You were in Nice then," Tom continues.

"Yeah."

"Nice?"

"Very. Did you meet the lovely Florent?"

"Yeah," he says.

Ricardo nudges me and shrugs. "I see you indoors," he says, as he continues on across the pebbles.

"Yeah, sorry babe," I say. "I'll be in in a sec."

"I have to go too," Tom says, smiling falsely.

I sigh and watch him walk away, and then I start to follow Ricardo. I have taken only two steps though when Tom calls my name so I pause again and look back to see him facing me, walking backwards across the beach. "If you, you know, fancy another fuck," he shouts.

I wince and glance back at Ricardo who is hunched up hurrying towards the house. He doesn't react, so I assume that he hasn't heard.

"Tom," I plead.

"Just give me a call," he says, then at the top of his voice, "dial a fuck. That's me." And then he spins and strides on to his car.

I look around just in time to see Ricardo turn towards the house. Just before he vanishes behind the neighbour's shed, he glances back at me, and I try to work out if anything in his blank expression indicates that he has heard Tom's words. The noise of the blustering wind would seem to make it unlikely.

Nervously heading indoors, I find Ricardo standing in the doorway to the kitchen and Jenny and Sarah at the table in the lounge.

"You want tea?" Ricardo asks.

"Yeah, I'm gasping," I say, analysing his voice for signs of tension. He seems a little aloof, but that could be simply from bumping into Tom.

When I enter the lounge, I see that Jenny too looks red-faced and wired. "Hi babe, everything OK?" I ask.

"Sure," she says unconvincingly. "How was Nice?"

"Brilliant," I say. "It rained all Friday night, but Saturday was amazing, you know, one of those blue sky, blue sea days you get after the rain."

"I remember," Jenny says.

"Where's Florent?"

"Upstairs having a quick snooze. He was up really early with Sarah, so..."

"And how are you, quiet little girl?" I ask Sarah.

She looks up from her puzzle. Even she looks tense this evening. "OK," she says – an uncharacteristically terse response.

I head upstairs to the toilet, and as I come out of the bathroom, Florent appears clutching an iPod – not from our room as I expected but from Jenny's. "Oh, I didn't hear you arrive," he says. "I had this on. You have a good time?"

"Great thanks. Brilliant. And you?"

"Yeah, it was great. Well, except for that... has he left? That Tom bloke?"

"Yes. Just now. Why, what happened?"

Florent glances at his iPod. "Actually, could you take me straight to the station? There's only one train an hour, at five to, so..."

"Sure. I'll just tell Ricardo."

Once we're in the private space of the car, I ask Florent again what happened with Tom.

"I don't know," he says. "He came around for lunch and everything was cool. And then I went for a snooze with Sarah. There was a funny vibe so I sort of left them to talk... And then I woke up about an hour ago, and they were shrieking at each other. Do they do that a lot?"

"No," I say. "No they don't. Never really. Did you hear what they were saying?"

"No," Florent says. "I hate arguments. My parents used to shout a lot. I just put my iPod on I'm afraid."

"Weird," I say, pulling a face. "I wonder what it was about."

"Dunno," he says. "But it was a biggy. But other than that it's been great. Jenny's been fine. She's pretty robust really isn't she."

"Yeah, when she's not on chemo, she's fine."

"I really like her actually," he says. "We had a riot."

"And Sarah's a good kid."

"Yeah, she's brilliant. She thought I was staying tonight and wanted to know if I was sharing with you and Ricardo or her and Jenny."

"She's very intrigued by who sleeps where," I say, struggling to push that first, rather appealing image from my mind.

When I get back to Pevensey Bay for the second time, I find Jenny and Ricardo cooking a prawn curry. Though perhaps a bit stilted, the atmosphere seems essentially calm.

"So what was Florent doing in *your* bed missy?" I ask Jenny.

"Ha!" she says, looking up from the pan. "Wouldn't *you* like to know?"

"Did you have a wild weekend of dirty sex?"

"Of course," Jenny says. "We went hang-gliding too. And kite surfing."

I laugh. "Of course you did. Well good. Exercise is important. All kinds. We, um, saw Tom on our way in."

"That's nice for you," Jenny says.

"It wasn't," Ricardo replies.

"Everything OK?" I ask her.

"Sure," Jenny says. "Fine. So Ricky tells me you had a fab time in Nice."

"Yeah. We did."

"T-shirt weather, or so he *claims*."

"On Saturday – at lunchtime – yeah. It was gorgeous."

"Well, I'm dead jealous," Jenny says, standing back from the cooker and wiping her hands on her apron. "It's been pissing down here. Right, that just needs to simmer for a bit," she adds, handing the stirring spoon to Ricardo.

Once Jenny has left, I ask Ricardo – who seems to be avoiding eye-contact – if he's OK.

"Sure," he says without looking up. "Why wouldn't I be?"

I frown. He does seem a little brittle, but then so does the entire household. "Florent says Jenny and Tom had a huge argument," I say quietly. "Did she say anything?"

Ricardo shrugs. "No."

"I wonder what it was about."

Again he shrugs. "I'm not so interested in Tom," he says.

"Sure."

"I think he likes to cause trouble sometime."

"Yeah," I say. "Yes, I suppose he does."

The next morning, I offer to take Sarah for a romp along the beach. It's an icy-cold yet sunny day and waves – driven by the strong winds – are crashing magnificently against the breakwater.

Ricardo predictably announces that he will come too, but Jenny says, "Actually Ricardo, would *you* mind taking Sarah instead?"

Ricardo, still chewing his toast, grins and says, "Yes. I say. I go too."

"No I mean, would *you* take her and leave Mark here. I need to have a private talk with him. Would that be OK?"

So many people I know would be instantly offended by that, but Ricardo just shrugs and nods. "Of course. You want to come walk with Tonton Ricardo?" he says to Sarah. She looks spectacularly doubtful about the prospect.

Once they are wrapped and ready, Jenny slides the window closed behind them and tells me, "I'll just make another pot of coffee and we can get down to it."

I sit and watch Ricardo and Sarah head off across the beach and wonder what exactly it is that we are going to, "get down to."

When she returns, Jenny places the French press on the table and sits opposite me with a heavy sigh. "So," she says.

"So," I repeat.

"So how are you?"

I frown at her. *"How am I?"*

"Yes."

"I'm... um, fine. But what do you want to talk about? You're making me nervous."

Jenny laughs. "There's no need to be nervous. Well. Probably not. Hopefully not."

"Hopefully not. *Now* I'm feeling all reassured," I say.

She sighs and wipes a hand across her mouth. "I've got a few things I need to talk to you about. It's just than none of them are particularly easy. I wish I had a joint to smoke first."

"Didn't Tom leave you any?"

"No," she says. "No, he was going to, but he went off in a bit of a huff, so..."

"Yes, I kind of noticed that," I say.

"You did?"

"Yeah. The atmosphere was pretty tense here when we got home."

Jenny nods and starts to press the plunger down on the coffee pot. "I wasn't sure where to start first, but I suppose we'll have to start with Tom then," she says.

"Tom?"

"Yes. You slept together," she says.

"I'm sorry?"

"You had sex. With Tom."

I widen my eyes and stop breathing for a few seconds.

"He told me," she says.

"Jesus!" I mutter. "The tosser."

"It's none of my business Mark," she says.

"No, it isn't. I can't believe that he told you."

"Well, it *shouldn't* be any of my business, except..."

I grimace at her. "Except *what?*"

"Except that, well, were you safe?"

"I'm sorry?"

"Did you have, you know, safe sex?"

I frown at her.

"Jesus Mark," she says. "It's not that complicated a question."

I shrug and shake my head in disbelief. "No, it isn't Jen. I just can't work out what business it is of yours."

"But did you?"

"Of course we did. Of course we had safe sex."

"You're sure?"

"Of course I'm sure. Jesus Jenny, what is this?"

She exhales deeply. "Thank God for that," she says.

"Why on Earth?"

"No, I shouldn't have said anything. And now I don't need to, so..."

I pull a face and then look at her slyly. "Well, you kind of *have* said something," I say. "But I'm not sure what it is. Because Tom is negative. Tom is HIV negative like me. So..."

"Sure. Well, just forget I said anything," she says. "Now, the other thing..."

"Stop. Stop right there," I say, raising one hand. "Why are you asking me this?"

"I really shouldn't..." Jenny says.

"You can't just chat about something like that and then change the subject. We did have sex – safe sex. We nearly *didn't* as it happens, but I insisted. So?"

"You nearly didn't what?"

"We nearly fucked without a condom. But I insisted."

"Jesus!"

"Why 'Jesus' Jenny? What's going on?"

"He's not," Jenny says.

"He's not what?"

"Negative. Tom isn't negative."

"No, he *is*," I say. "He told me so just the other day."

"He only just found out Mark," Jenny says.

"Really? But how? He can't. A week ago he was negative."

"A week ago he *thought* he was negative," Jenny says.

I rub my brow. "I don't believe you," I say.

"I didn't believe it either."

"God that's dreadful. Does he know how he, you know, caught it?"

Jenny shrugs. "That's the worst bit."

"How?"

"I shouldn't really..."

"Jenny!"

"He's been going to these... I don't know... sex parties I suppose you'd call them. With Sven."

"Tom?" I ask, incredulously.

"He's been taking some drug too and they all you know... shag..."

"What?!"

"I know Mark. It's crazy."

"But Tom has *always* been safe."

"He says he doesn't know what he gets up to. He blames it on the drugs."

"And *what* drugs?"

"I don't know Mark. It's like speed or something, but different. Anyway, I just wanted to make sure *you* were OK."

I cover my own mouth with my hand. "Well yeah. We were pretty safe."

"Pretty safe?"

"Well, we used a condom. But we had oral sex too."

"TMI Mark. Anyway, oral sex is fine isn't it?"

"Yeah... it's pretty low risk. But Jesus! Poor Tom."

"I know. Stupid Tom, more like."

"He tried to as well. He *wanted* to fuck without a condom."

"Really?"

"Yeah."

"But you didn't?"

"No. But all the same."

"Well he didn't know. He was really shocked."

"Plus I can't believe he told you..." I say.

"Well, we were talking about my cancer and what to do with Sarah and stuff so his health obviously came up..."

"No, I mean about *us*... He shouldn't have told you."

"Oh. No. You're right. He shouldn't have."

"God," I say. "This is just bullshit."

"It's awful isn't it."

"You were talking about Sarah you say?"

"Well yes."

"What, did you ask him to look after her then?"

"Not as such. I was just, you know, exploring the terrain. I said I didn't know how long I might be around, and Tom sort of fell apart. Because, well, neither does he now."

"That's a bit dramatic," I say. "The drugs are pretty good now..."

"But all the same."

"Well yeah. Jesus. I want to feel sorry for him but I just feel angry."

"I know. Me too. I mean, here am I struggling to stick around..."

"And it's not like he didn't know. It's not like he's in fucking Africa with no TV or anything. It's not like we're in nineteen-eighty-one and word hasn't got around yet."

"No."

I shake my head, momentarily lost for words.

"You're sure you had safe sex," Jenny asks.

"Yes! I even have safe sex with Ricardo, but..."

"Well seeing as you're not faithful with each other that's probably just as well."

"Yeah," I say, then, "what do you mean *with each other?*"

"Well," Jenny says. "Ricardo's no angel either is he? You know that."

"Do you know something that I don't?" I ask.

"No," Jenny says. "No. Absolutely not. But, well..."

I take a deep breath then say, "I don't think we should, you know... go there."

"No," Jenny says. "Sorry. I didn't mean anything."

"Fuck though. Poor Tom. Is he, you know... OK?"

Jenny shrugs. "He only just found out. So he's in shock I think. He's going to see a specialist next week, so... Anyway."

"God!" I say again. "So that's what you wanted to discuss?"

"Sort of," Jenny says.

"Sort of."

"Well, the other thing is, um, how are you and Ricardo doing?"

"How are we *doing?* What do you mean, *how are we doing?*"

"Well you seem good together. Solid."

"We are."

"And he doesn't know... about Tom?"

"No. *You* won't tell him, will you?"

"Of course not. It's just... I know some of you guys have open relationships."

"We guys?"

"Yeah. Gay guys."

"Well we don't."

"Well, you sort of do actually, but you don't talk about it."

"Jenny, for fuck's sake, we do *not* have an open relationship. I slipped up and had a quickie with my ex. I was feeling lonely and miserable and... but that's all it was."

Jenny raises the palms of her hands at me. "Mark! Stop!" she says. "I'm really not... I'm not trying to judge or upset you or criticise or anything."

"Well good."

"All I'm asking is, do you see your future with Ricky or not? Long term, I mean."

I wrinkle my nose at her. "You're really getting on my tits Jenny," I say. "Of course I do."

"I know. This is all going wrong. Maybe we should try another day."

"What's this about? Do you want him back or something?"

Jenny laughs sincerely. "As if!" she says.

"Then I really don't get where you're coming from."

"It's about Sarah," Jenny says. "I need to make arrangements. Proper arrangements. And I want to ask you. And I don't know if I'm asking you alone, or you and Ricardo."

I stare at her.

"You see now? It's complicated."

I nod and exhale through my nose. "Sure," I say, my tone already softening. "I'm sorry. I think it's just all this shit about Tom winding me up. Fuck. I can't believe that he's positive."

"I'm sorry. Maybe I shouldn't have said anything. But I was worried about you two."

"No, you did good. As far as Sarah's concerned, I don't think you should be thinking about the worst case scenario though."

"Don't," Jenny says. "I know how I feel. I know what the chemo is doing to me. So please don't tell me what I need to think about."

I nod. "I'm sorry. You're right."

Jenny rolls her eyes. "It's... it's just that people keep telling me that I'll be fine. And it gets really irritating, because you can't go any further with that discussion."

"Sure."

"So what I'm asking is, and I know it's a huge ask... But if something happens to me, would you... you and Ricardo, I suppose, well, think of..." She coughs.

"Of course we would."

Jenny nods and works her mouth silently before saying, "I'm talking about actually *adopting Sarah* here."

"I know."

"And you *would* consider it?"

"Yes."

Jenny covers her mouth with one hand and pinches her nose between her thumb and forefinger. Her eyes are glistening. "I've been so scared to ask," she says. "You have no idea."

"No, it's fine Jenny. Really."

"And what about Ricardo then?" Jenny says. "Do you think that he could be convinced? I mean, if you're going to be together a long time it affects you both."

I laugh lightly.

"What?" Jenny asks.

"It's just we discussed it already. Quite a lot actually."

"You *did*?"

"Yeah. And Ricardo always says the same thing."

"Which is?"

"He always says 'yes.' Like it's completely obvious."

"Really?"

"Yep. It's taken *me* longer to get used to the idea in fact. But Ricardo always says, *doh. Of course.* Like it's the most natural thing in the world for him."

Jenny nods but says nothing for almost a minute. She looks taut and shiny with the effort of withholding tears. She sits and stares into my eyes.

"Are you OK?" I ask.

"Yeah. So you'll think about it then?" she says.

"We have Jen," I say. "And if the worst comes to the worst... if... you know... then of course. It's already decided."

She stares at me in silence for a moment, nodding slowly. Her skin looks taut, her eyes watery. She slips a hand over her mouth and makes a puffing noise as her lungs spasm.

Then she clears her throat and says, "I thought you would, but I've been too scared to actually ask."

I reach out and take her hand across the table. "There wouldn't be any other option really would there?"

"No," she says. "That's why I was so scared."

"But it won't happen Jenny. You're going to be fine."

"Uhuh," she says.

I squeeze her hand in mine and notice how boney it has become.

"They're going to kick me off the trial," she says.

"You don't know that."

She scrunches up her nose. "I think I do actually, but we'll see."

"In the meantime, you honestly don't need to worry. Not about Sarah, anyway."

"And you're sure Ricardo agrees?" she says.

At that moment, Ricardo and Sarah round the neighbour's shed and run towards us across the gravel. I slide the window back and they rush in and push the window closed again.

"God, I can feel the cold coming off you," I say.

"Freezing Chupy," Ricardo says, then, "Oh! You two very serious."

"Yeah," I say. "Hey, Jenny watch. And concentrate."

In slow, clear French that I think Jenny will understand (but which Sarah won't) I say, "Ricardo. A serious question."

"OK," he says, doubtfully.

"If something happened to Jenny... how would you feel about us adopting Sarah?"

272

"Bien sûr, je te l'ai déjà dit mille fois," he says. – Of course. I already told you a thousand times.

At which Jenny makes a peculiar snorting noise and crumbles into a mess of tears.

Sarah looks up at Ricardo in horror and runs to her mother's side.

"Mummy's fine sweetie," Jenny says, stroking her hair. "Mummy's just happy that's all."

Rewriting History

That evening, once Jenny has gone to bed, Ricardo moves from the dining table where he has been reading, and sits cross legged beside me on the sofa. "So Chupy," he says. "So quiet this evening."

I nod and turn to face him and sigh. I have been thinking obsessively about Tom's HIV infection and the infinitely small risk of transmission through oral sex. And even if those risks are, and I quote, *so low as to be "virtually theoretical"* – they are still too high. So I need to get tested again. And I need to warn Ricardo somehow.

"I love you so much," I say, my voice cracking as a wave of love and regret wells up.

"Me too pumpkin," he says.

"I've been thinking about Tom all afternoon."

Ricardo pulls a face. "You love me but think about Tom," he says. "I'm not sure..."

"Jenny told me something yesterday. Tom just found out he has HIV."

"Tom?"

"Yes."

"Jesus Mary."

"I know."

"He doesn't know about condoms or what?" Ricardo asks.

I shrug. "I know. It's stupid."

Ricardo nods slowly. "Poor Chupy. Worried about his ex."

"The thing is..." I say.

But Ricardo raises his hand to interrupt me. He looks soulfully into my eyes, then licks his lips, clears his throat and says, "I know babe."

"You *know?*"

"Sure. You worry that maybe he have it before, when you were together."

I frown at him.

Ricardo shrugs. "It's OK babe. But we always use condoms. It's not so easy to catch, you know."

"Right."

"And you use condoms with Tom too, right?"

"Yes. But they say that, you know, oral sex..."

"No. The risk is infinite babe."

I nod and smile weakly, almost unable to believe that Ricardo has just provided me with an acceptable narrative. "If I *did* have it, I'd hate to pass it on to you," I say.

"Yes, so we both do new tests. It's best. But you know, I'm really not worried."

"Right."

"That Tom is a bit crazy, no?"

"Yes."

"And a bit stupid."

"Well, yes."

"He is lucky they have better drugs now."

"Well, yeah."

"But it's still no fun. You have to be careful Chupy," Ricardo says, sounding suddenly very serious.

"We always are, aren't we?"

"Yes, but I mean if you ever, you know... do something... outside of us. You would be safe, yes?"

"Of course. But, well, I wouldn't."

Ricardo nods and swallows. "Yes, I knew it was a lie."

"I'm sorry?"

"What Tom said. Yesterday."

"You heard that?"

Ricardo nods. "Yes. But it's OK because it's not true."

I frown at him. It sounds like a statement rather than a question.

"I mean, why would you sleep with Tom?" Ricardo says. "You already go there and decide you don't like it so much. It makes no sense."

I nod. "Well yes. Of course."

"So it's a lie."

I take a deep breath and sigh.

Ricardo laughs lightly.

"What?"

"This is where you say, yes Ricardo. Tom tell a lie," he says.

It feels like Ricardo is dictating a script to me, a script I have no choice but to follow to the letter. I feel the blood drain from my face. "Yes. He lied," I say.

"Good," Ricardo says smiling broadly and opening his arms. "Come here."

I move across the sofa and lay back against his chest and he folds his arms around me.

Luckily he can't see my confused expression.

"You're so lovely," I say after a while.

"Not *all* bad eh?" Ricardo says.

"You're so trusting."

Ricardo snorts. "If I choose not to believe my Chupy, there is only unhappiness," he says, tightening his arms around me. "What other choice?"

We lie like this and stare out at the shadowy beach and I try to work out what just happened. I can't work out whether Ricardo did believe me or whether he actually doesn't care. It feels like we have just agreed on the only narrative that can get us through this. We have re-written history.

Sometimes, in the past, I have exaggerated a story or changed an ending to make the tale funnier or more dramatic, only to find, years later, that I'm not sure what really happened anymore. I wonder if that is what will happen here. If we just keep up the pretence that I didn't cheat on Ricardo will that ultimately become the remembered truth? I hope so, because, as Ricardo says, the reality brings no good to anyone.

Ricardo fidgets behind me and then nuzzles my hair and squeezes me in his arms again and I think again about how readily he has accepted the idea of bringing Sarah up, and how easily he has chosen to ignore Tom's words. I think about him appearing here at the very moment I needed him most, having given up his job and his country to join me here in the middle of this maelstrom. I think about his constant, unfailing projection of our future together, about his unique ability to narrow his field of vision to the point where he simply refuses to see anything that could spoil that future.

And I decide that I really am dating an exceptional man here. It's probably time that I started acting like I appreciate that fact.

Feline Phantoms

The next morning, I wake up snuggled tightly to Ricardo's back. Apparently my subconscious is as loved-up as my waking mind.

"God I'm glad you exist," I say, kissing his neck and breathing in his odour.

"Mmm," Ricardo groans, pushing back against me.

"It's nine thirty," I say.

"I hear Jenny downstairs."

"She's doing the early shift then. She must be feeling better."

"Yes, she's good now, huh?"

"As soon as she comes off the chemo, it's hard to remember she's ill."

"If she's good today, maybe you and me can go out for lunch together," Ricardo says. "I want to see more of this place."

I lift the curtain and peer out. "Sunny," I say. "I might take you to Beachy Head. Or Cuckmere Haven."

"Cockmere what?" Ricardo laughs.

"Cuckmere. There's an amazing river there. A natural oxbow. You'll see."

As soon as we get up, Jenny heads back upstairs for a sleep, so Ricardo and I take Sarah for a walk along the beach.

We each take one of her tiny hands and swing her along the beach. It's only the second time the three of us have done anything together, and I can't help but wonder if this is how things are going to be from now on. It actually feels rather lovely.

It's a beautiful December day and the wind has dropped. In the sunshine it feels almost warm. I glance at a tree in a neighbour's window and realise that Christmas is almost upon us. "Is it the fifteenth today?" I ask.

"Seventeen," Ricardo says. "No, sixteen. No, sorry seventeen. Definitely."

"You realise Christmas is in a week's time?" I point out.

"I know. So quick."

"It's not having TV," I say. "The world just slips on by. We need to get a tree."

"Would you like a Christmas tree, like that one?" I ask Sarah. "Fuck!"

"Chupy?"

"On a zappé son anniversaire," I say. – *We've missed her birthday.*

"Qui?" – *Who?*

"Sarah. On a oublié son anniversaire." – *Sarah. We've forgotten her birthday.*

"Non!"

"Si."

"Can we have a silver one?" she asks.

"Uh? Um... no. Not *exactly* like that one. A real one. A big green one."

"With pressies under it?" she asks.

"Of course."

"OK then. Can we have a sparkly one like that?"

"No. They're horrible."

Sarah pushes her bottom lip out making me laugh.

"Girls!" I comment.

When we get back Jenny still isn't up from her morning nap, so I wake her with a mug of tea.

"Hi sweetie," I say.

"Morning," she says, rubbing her eyes and sitting up.

"The neighbours have got a tree in the window."

"A tree?"

"A Christmas tree."

"God, *Christmas!*" Jenny says.

"It's in a week's time."

"Ugh. I've been trying not to think about it."

"You know what we forgot last week?" I ask.

Jenny frowns and shakes her head as she sips her tea.

"Your daughter's birthday," I whisper.

Jenny spits her tea out. "Oh my God," she says.

"I know."

"God... that's... It was her fifth as well," Jenny says shaking her head. "What a terrible mother."

"Well you were pretty ill. And we *all* forgot."

"I know, but..."

"Shall we do it late? Do you want me to buy a cake and balloons and shit?"

278

Jenny sighs and thinks for a moment. Then she pulls a face. "I think it's best to just skip it this year. She won't even notice now. She'll get all excited about Christmas next, so..."

"Ricardo and I are off out, so shall we get a tree while we're out or do you want to go on a special tree-hunting trip?"

"Just get one," Jenny says. "God, I can't believe that I forgot!"

"I want to come," Sarah protests from the doorway.

I lean in close to Jenny and say quietly, "She didn't hear did she?"

Jenny looks over at Sarah and frowns. "Nah," she says.

"OK," I say loudly. "As a special treat, we'll come back and get you, and we three can go and choose a tree together. How does that sound?"

"How long will you be?" Jenny asks.

"It's just for lunch, so..." I say, feeling guilty for not offering to take them with us. But the idea of spending a couple of hours alone with Ricardo is truly irresistible this morning.

"Can you get some cereal while you're out?" Jenny asks. "And bread?"

I drive Ricardo over the downs and on to Cuckmore Haven.

"Gosh, incredible," Ricardo says as the vast green panorama of the valley comes into view. "And the river."

"I know, it's great, isn't it?" I say, glancing over at the sunlit sparkle of the water. "It's called an ox-bow. The river carves the sides away and it becomes more and more rounded. The pub is lovely too," I say.

I park the car and then as we pass through the entrance arch and up the stairs to the Golden Galleon, Ricardo laughs, "So English, Chupy!"

Despite the sunshine, it's too cold to sit outside so we push into the warm interior of the pub. "Look," I say, nodding to the left. "A real fire."

"But so quiet," Ricardo says, following me to the bar. Only one other client is in the room, sipping a pint over in the far corner.

"It's Wednesday," the barman says. "And the week before Christmas. Everyone is spent out on Christmas."

"Yeah," I say, nodding at Ricardo. "We still have to do all of the Christmas shopping."

We order food and then retire with our drinks to a table near the fireplace.

Ricardo sips his pint of IPA – ordered on my advice – and pulls a face. "Funny beer," he says.

"Don't you like it?"

"I think it's a bit old," he says. "It has lost its... *bulles.*"

"English beer isn't fizzy," I tell him.

He wrinkles his nose and sips it again. "It tastes OK, but I think I like it fizzy."

"I love pubs like this," I say looking around. "They're the one thing I really missed in France."

Ricardo nods. "Yes. So cosy."

"It's weird," I say. "Because in England you go to any village and there's a cosy pub with a real fire. And in France it's always a freezing bar with formica and strip-lights."

"Yes. The French don't do cosy so well. How do you say cosy in French?"

I shrug. "Chaleureux maybe."

"*Warm,*" Ricardo says.

"Yeah. It's not *quite* cosy... I don't think they have a word for it either."

"Maybe that's why they don't do it so well. Because they don't have a word."

"Maybe."

"But you know, it's not so cold outside in France. Maybe that's why."

"It's pretty cold in the middle of France in winter," I point out. "I think it's just cultural."

"Like English food being terrible," Ricardo says.

At that instant, the barman arrives with said food. A veggie chilli for me and a pork chop for Ricardo. "It looks OK," I say, once he has gone.

"Yes," Ricardo says lasciviously licking his lips. "Not haute-cuisine, but it looks tasty."

"You're such a carnivore," I laugh.

"Hey, I don't eat meat since Colombia," he says. "Well, since Madrid."

"Do you miss it?" I ask tasting my chilli. "Mmm, this is good actually."

"Not at all. But I'm happy to eat this little piggy," he says, raising a cube of pork to his lips.

The pub cat, up until now asleep on a bench seat, smells Ricardo's pork and stretches to cross the room.

"The cat knows what is good," Ricardo says.

"Yeah. I wonder how poor Paloma is doing," I say.

"She'll be fine."

"I think I'll give Maria a call when we get back."

"It will be too late. She'll be at work," Ricardo says. "So, we have to find a tree then. Where do you buy trees in England?"

"Yeah... Actually," I say, ignoring him and nodding at a *Free Wifi* sticker, "I can Skype her from here. I'll do it in a minute."

"I'm sure she'll already be out," Ricardo says.

"Well, it doesn't hurt to try," I say.

"Better to call her in the evening."

"Don't you *want* me to call her?" I ask.

Ricardo frowns at me and half-smiles. "Not at all babe. I just say it's better to call her in the evenings. She rush around a lot in the morning."

"OK," I say. "I'll call her tomorrow when I get up."

We eat our meal in silence to the vague sound of Culture Club drifting from the bar speakers and the occasional chirruping of a slot machine.

I finish before Ricardo and pull my phone from my pocket to check my email.

"Don't Chupy," Ricardo says, sounding annoyed. "She won't be in."

I wrinkle my nose and stare at him. "I wasn't going to actually. But why don't you want me to call?"

"I'm just saying that she won't be in," he says, through a mouthful of potato.

"OK then," I say. "Well if she isn't, it doesn't matter, does it? Let's see."

I connect to the wifi successfully and, aware that something is going on here – Ricardo is watching me like a hawk – I select Skype.

"OK," Ricardo says, suddenly dropping his fork. "I'm sorry. I should have told you."

I lower the phone and look up at him, noting the grave tone his voice has suddenly taken on. "*What* should you have told me?"

"I didn't want you to worry," he says.

"About?"

"Paloma. She isn't with Maria."

"She's still at the beach-house?"

"No. She run away babe."

I stare at him in horror. "She *what?*"

"Paloma run away."

"*Ran* away."

"Yes."

"Paloma ran away?" I ask again in disbelief.

"*Yes.*"

"When? How?"

"After you left. A month maybe."

"But... but you told me she was fine. You said she was getting fat. You told me she was on your lap."

"I know. I don't want you to worry. You have so many things to worry about here."

"But *how?* She wouldn't even go outside the house. Did you look for her?"

"Every night babe. You remember how I was never in when you call. Well, it's because I walk around calling Paloma, Paloma, Paloma."

"But she was scared of the sand," I say. "She wouldn't set foot on it."

"I know."

"God. My baby Paloma," I say, aware that I'm sounding a bit naff. "You should have told me."

"I know. I'm sorry," Ricardo says reaching for my hand across the table.

But I pull my hand away. "How? I mean, when did you last see her?"

"I go to work one morning, and I forget a window. And in the evening, she is gone."

"God, I can't believe it," I say. "I love that cat... I lov*ed* her."

"I know. But she's probably OK babe."

"How? How could she be OK? How can a cat that's scared of sand, lost on a beach, be OK?"

"Maybe she find another house and someone is feeding her."

"The nearest house is miles away."

"Or she hunts perhaps. Mice. There are lots of mice. And big juicy rats."

I tut. "Paloma wouldn't hurt a fly. She plays with spiders but even those she lets go. She's ancient Ricardo. She must be seventeen or eighteen. That's like being sixty or seventy or something."

I imagine Paloma in the Colombian rainforest calling out to me, lost and alone. My vision mists with tears. "I'm sorry. I know it's stupid," I say. "But I'm really fucking upset about this. I saved her from the cat's home. She's lived everywhere I ever lived. She's known all my boyfriends. God, I shouldn't have left her. I shouldn't have taken her to Colombia in the first place. She must have thought I'd abandoned her. She probably went looking for me."

Ricardo stares at me wide-eyed. He looks shocked. "I'm sorry babe," he says, reaching out and stroking my shoulder.

"Well I hope you looked bloody hard for her," I say, my voice quivering slightly.

"I did," Ricardo says. "Believe me. I did."

I cup my hands above my nose and stare miserably into the fire.

"We'll get another cat one day babe," Ricardo says.

I give him a look of utter hatred. I think it's the stupidest thing he has ever said.

Ricardo: One Grief To Replace Another

You seemed so sad Chupy and to be perfectly honest, it started to irritate the hell out of me. Because, sure, you liked Paloma, and sure, you had had her for a long time, and sure, she was a very nice cat. But Jesus babe, she was *a cat* and in the great scheme of things, compared with what happens on fur farms and in abattoirs, and in pharmaceutical labs worldwide – let alone the misery of humans – I just couldn't see what all the fuss was about. It seemed out of all proportion. If you're going to get all bent out of shape babe, then worry about something big – worry about war or famine for God's sake.

Of course, I knew that you'd be upset. At the moment I put her out on the porch and locked the front door it crossed my mind that I was storing up some kind of trouble for the future. But I thought you'd be disappointed and I thought that I would come up with some reassuring story about neighbours or mice and that somehow I would talk that problem away.

But I had been running around like crazy babe. I had moved our excess stuff into storage and packed cases for my trip; I had quit my job and found someone to replace me at the health centre; I had booked tickets and transferred funds. And all of this whilst watching the car park in case Carlos' men turned up to cut my dick off.

I had so much on that the brutal truth is that I didn't think about Paloma until the minute I was leaving the house, and even then I didn't think about her for long.

If I had, I could easily have come up with a better solution. That's what's so stupid. I could have taken her to Maria's place, I could even have left her with Max. But I didn't babe. I put her on the porch and waved her goodbye as I drove off.

In that week before Christmas I tried to see her through your eyes. I tried to understand. I didn't have a choice because no matter what we were doing – buying a Christmas tree, or filling stockings at Poundland, or driving Jenny to London or emptying her sick bucket, you looked sad. And whenever I asked you what was wrong it was always the bloody cat. You were imagining her slowly starving to death on the porch. You were picturing her hiding from predators in the forest. You were thinking about her crying at the door to come in, waiting eternally for your return. My guess was that she would have died in the first couple of days. Lost animals don't die of hunger babe, they die of thirst, and that doesn't take long, especially not in thirty-five degrees. I couldn't work out whether telling you that would make things better or worse, so I said nothing.

And though such fuss seemed like a crazy over-reaction to me, I could see that your sadness was real, and I could see that I had let you down, so I phoned Maria and asked her to go out to the house to look, and though she, like me, thought it was a lot of fuss for a cat, she did – three times I think. But she didn't find any sign of Paloma, sun-dried or otherwise.

And all I could do was sit and watch you with your long face, and try not to get too angry about it. All I could do was to be as nice as I could and wait for you to forget about the stupid cat.

The way Jenny's health deteriorated once she started chemo, my guess was that a far bigger grief would soon be pushing Paloma out of the picture and though that wasn't in *any* way something I wanted, I did feel a certain sense of relief that the coming grief, at least, wouldn't be my fault.

Christmas Miracles

As bad luck would have it, Christmas week coincides with chemo week. Jenny starts taking her pills three days before christmas, and by mid morning on the twenty-second, she is green and sickly and confined to her bed.

Ricardo, who, up until now, has had only my word to go on, is visibly stunned by just how quickly her health fades. "It's not right babe," he keeps saying. "We need to talk to Professor Twat."

I remind him that both Florent who administers the same treatment to a number of patients, and Batt himself seem to consider these side effects to be normal. "Plus," I tell him. "As soon as it's over she's fine again." But Ricardo's concern exacerbates my own, and this added to everything else leaves me feeling sometimes that my back is about to break beneath the weight of it all. Because on top of Jenny's illness, which dominates every moment of the day, I am also trying to work out what exactly we need to do to legally ensure that I, or perhaps *we*, get Sarah should Jenny actually die. And that's a hell of a complicated business. And one hell of an emotionally loaded one.

In addition, Tom's illness is playing on my mind. Now that a few days have passed, my anger with him has become tempered with concern at how he might be coping. I can't help but feel that I should, in some way, be there for him. And with Ricardo by my side, I can't see any way that I can.

And as if all that wasn't enough there is, of course, Paloma's shadow. It's cast right across my brain. I do my best to push it away but the image of her, skinny, scared, alone, hungry, thirsty, and above all waiting, trusting, convinced that, like every time before, I will come back for her is a tough one to shake.

It strikes me as absurd and perhaps even shameful – considering the struggles and sorrow around me – that it should have such leverage over me. Jenny's illness is clearly catastrophic by comparison. Sarah's future is more important. Tom's troubles are more life-destroying. But Paloma is special precisely because Paloma is – or perhaps was – a dumb animal. Though that should perhaps make her troubles less important, it makes my responsibility for them total. She has no reason or understanding of her situation. She has no options. Her life experience as a pet was one of total dependency and her trust in my ability to look after her absolute. I can't help but be convinced that no matter what efforts Ricardo may have made, if only *I* had been there I could have found her. And by not being there I have fundamentally betrayed that trust.

The contrast between the dark shadows filling my brain and the manufactured fun around me couldn't be greater though. With the unspoken acknowledgement that this could be Jenny's last winter, Christmas has taken on a terrifying poignancy and Ricardo and I compete to try to make it the most perfect Christmas anyone could have.

We buy the biggest most expensive tree that we can physically fit inside the lounge. We smother it with lights and baubles and garlands of every colour, transforming it into a gaudy mess beyond Sarah's wildest hopes. The neighbours' silver tree looks positively zen by comparison.

And we buy Sarah so many stocking fillers that we have to switch from stockings to pillow cases to hold them all.

There's something undeniably hysterical about the whole frenzy of preparation, and though no-one mentions it, I'm pretty sure that we're all suffering from the same *Perfect Christmas Syndrome.* If it's to be Jenny's last Christmas then it has to be perfect. If it's to be Sarah's last Christmas with her mother then the memories have to be as big and as shiny as possible. And there's a superstitious feeling which is hard to nail down that perhaps, if we can just make Christmas perfect enough, then everything else will be OK. If we can just get the tree and the gifts and the food *just so*, then Jenny will be fine, won't she?

Maybe when there are things you can't control, it's normal to get really obsessed with those that you can.

On Christmas Eve Jenny comes downstairs looking surprisingly fresh.

"Hum, someone's having a better day," I comment.

"Amazing what a bit of Christmas cheer will do for you," Jenny says. "Well, what a ton of makeup will do. I do feel OK though."

"So, what do you think?" I ask, waving towards the tree.

"Amazing. Have you added *more* decorations?"

"Just some presents. The ones that wouldn't fit in the stockings."

"In the stockings which are pillow cases?"

"Yeah."

"You're crazy."

"Sure. But it's all cheap tat. Kids love opening presents. Anyway, I did when I was a kid."

"She'll love it," Jenny says, smiling. "Where is she by the way?"

"Out with Ricardo. They went to the corner shop. He suddenly realised that we don't have any chicken soup."

Jenny pulls a face. "Chicken soup?"

I shrug. "Apparently you can't possibly have Christmas without chicken soup. Not if you're Colombian."

"Yuck."

"I know."

Jenny crosses to the tree and rearranges a garland. "Actually I wanted to ask you something," she says. "A favour."

"Sure. Anything."

What Jenny asks for is to spend the evening alone with her daughter. She loves Christmas Eve, she says. She loves how excited Sarah gets. And she feels an unexpected need to spend it alone with her daughter. As this is clearly another symptom of *Perfect Christmas Syndrome* I agree immediately.

"As long as you feel well enough, I'd love to get out for a Christmas pint," I say.

After high-tea of sandwiches, scones and mince-pies, plus added chicken soup for Ricardo, we walk up to the Beach Tavern. Were it not for the risk of bumping into Tom I would have headed into Brighton, but there is no way I'm going to risk having Tom neutron-bomb our Christmas Eve. At least this way I can drink.

The pub is packed with a young raucous crowd. It's not until we have been served that I realise that virtually no-one is speaking English.

Ricardo, sipping a pint of lager, frowns. Noticing the same thing he asks, "They speak English Chupy?"

"No. Something eastern European. Polish maybe," I say, hearing a guttural 'R' sound behind me.

"Yes," a guy beside me laughs, raising his glass to me. "Tonight you are in Warsaw."

"How brilliant," I say, feigning enthusiasm. "I always wanted to spend Christmas in Warsaw."

In fact, despite my own prejudices – which are mainly to do with the old Pope and Poland's rich reputation for homophobia – they turn out to be an open friendly crowd. Richard – spelt somehow with a z – introduces us to his twin brother André - equally spelt with a z - and within minutes we are surrounded by half a coach-load of Poles, inexplicably in Pevensey Bay for

Christmas Eve. Seeing us ironically as "local" colour, they surround us and bombard us with questions about the region.

At eleven-fifteen, I am fighting to get to the bar when someone blows a whistle and shouts something in Polish and within a minute, the crowd at the bar has vanished. It's as if someone has pulled a plug.

Ricardo and I take our drinks to a window-seat and watch as the coach, filled with waving arms, manoeuvres and pulls away.

"Nice guys," Ricardo says.

"Yeah."

"I feel a bit drunk. It's nice," he says.

I grin at him. "Me too. It's been a while, hasn't it? Those z-twins were sexy weren't they?"

Ricardo wide-eyes me and nods.

"Straight, but sexy," I say.

"You think?" he asks.

I shrug.

"Not so many girls on the bus," Ricardo points out.

"No. But definitely straight. What a weird trip though."

"Yes. Why here?" Ricardo asks. "Why this little place?"

"The barman's wife is Polish..." I say with a shrug.

"The pregnant one?"

"Yeah. So I guess she arranged to cater for them all or something. Crazy that they're all off to church though. I mean, imagine being on a coach trip that includes midnight mass. That's just bizarre."

"Well, it's an important one," Ricardo says.

"Midnight mass?"

"Yes. The miracle of the virgin birth Chupy," Ricardo says with a shrug. "If you're Christian, they don't come much bigger."

I laugh. "Yeah. I wonder if any of them actually believe it though." Ricardo frowns at me, so I say, "The virgin birth, I mean. Nowadays."

"I think it's quite well documented babe," he says.

I grin at him, convinced that he's winding me up. "Yeah, right," I laugh.

"You don't believe?" he asks, dead-pan.

"Well of course I don't. I'm not Catholic."

"OK, but you're Christian. So it's the same."

"I'm not!"

"OK. You don't believe *now*. But you *were*."

"Never," I say. "I'm not Christian, and I never was."

"You were baptised though."

"No I wasn't. Or christened. Or anything else for that matter."

Ricardo frowns at me as if this is some shocking new revelation for him.

"Anyway *you're* not Catholic anymore," I point out.

"I'm always Catholic. You don't just stop."

"But you don't go to church."

"Well no."

"So you don't believe."

"Not in everything. But the birth of Jesus... I mean..." he shrugs in a way that indicates that this is clearly beyond discussion, even for me.

I frown at him and shake my head. "You're bizarre," I say.

He laughs. "You're the one doing so many things for Christmas," he says. "You're *more* bizarre I think."

When we get back, the lounge is lit only by flickering candlelight. Jenny is sitting at one end of the sofa and Sarah is asleep at the other end.

"Sh," Jenny says. "She only just fell asleep. She was so excited."

"Do you want me to take her up?" I ask.

"If you're sober enough to negotiate the stairs," Jenny says.

"Just about," I giggle.

Sarah groans vaguely but doesn't wake up as I carry her somewhat stumblingly upstairs to the front bedroom.

"She was so excited," Jenny says again when I get back. "She was worried sick about how Father Christmas is going to get in."

I look around the room. "No chimney," I say. "Ouch."

"Exactly. I said he has a magic key these days. Because so many people don't have chimneys."

"A magic key. That's good."

"I want tea Chupy," Ricardo says. "You want?"

"Yeah. Please."

"Jenny?"

"Nah, I'm fine thanks."

Once he has left the room, Jenny adds, "He's becoming very English isn't he?"

"The tea?"

"Yeah."

"Oh, that's my influence. I drink a hundred cups a day. Wherever I live."

"Tom phoned by the way," Jenny says. "With good news."

"Yeah?"

"Yeah. Amazing news actually. His test – his first test – was wrong apparently."

"It was *wrong?*"

Jenny nods. "A false positive or something."

"His *HIV test?*"

"Well yes. Amazing huh? He says it's a Christmas miracle."

I frown and turn to Ricardo who has just returned from putting the kettle on. "Is that possible Ricardo?"

He raises his chin to show that he hasn't heard, so I explain, "Tom says his HIV test was wrong. A false positive. Can that happen?"

Ricardo gives a rather splendid gallic shrug and makes a "pff" noise.

"Well *you're* the doctor here."

He pushes his lips out. "I don't know about HIV tests babe," he says. "But if Jenny says so..."

"Is he *sure?*" I ask Jenny. "I mean, how could you be sure if..."

"Apparently they redid it three different ways and they all came out negative."

"God, that's outrageous," I say. "I mean, you could go and top yourself on the back of that."

"I know. He's over the moon though," she says.

"I'll bet. That's brilliant news. I hope he'll be more careful now though."

A lump forms in my throat. It only lasts a second, but my relief that Tom isn't going to have to face a life on HIV meds is momentary tear-provoking.

"Oh, I think he will," Jenny says. "I gave him a good talking to. Not that I think he needed it but... Anyway, how was the... which one did you go to?"

"Uh?"

"Which pub?"

"Oh. The Beach Tavern. It was full of Poles."

"Poles?" Jenny looks shocked.

"Polish people."

"Oh! I was thinking of poles and pole-dancers for some reason. Why?"

"A coach load. Dunno. They had all eaten a buffet there."

"How weird."

"I know. The owner's wife is Polish I think, so there's some kind of family link. And then the coach came back and whisked them all off to midnight mass," I say.

"*Really?* I love midnight mass," Jenny says.

I roll my eyes, and check that Ricardo is out of earshot in the kitchen. "You know that Colombian geezer. He only *believes* in the virgin birth!"

Jenny rolls her eyes. "You haven't been arguing about religion, have you? Not on Christmas Eve for God's sake."

I laugh.

"What?"

"I don't know really. Just something about arguing about religion. On Christmas Eve. For God's sake."

"You're drunk," Jenny says.

"You're right," I laugh. "I am."

Jenny: Secret Charades

Of course there was a perfectly good reason that I felt so much better over Christmas: I had stopped taking my meds.

Partly this was a conscious decision because I wanted to enjoy Christmas with my daughter, and I wanted her to remember it as wonderful, not as a time when Mummy had her head in a bucket. But mainly it was because I couldn't actually stomach them anymore.

Ironically, it was the pills that made me feel like I was dying, and this time around, that felt worse than the fear of *actually* dying if I didn't take them. So I promised myself that I would catch up once Christmas was over – or I wouldn't – and that would be fine.

The house looked amazing. We had the biggest, best decorated tree that I have ever seen. You could have put it in the lobby of the Ritz and it wouldn't have looked out of place, that's how good it was. And Mark and Ricardo bought hundreds of gifts. There were so many we had to have a rota to get them all wrapped.

On Christmas morning, we sat like some weird kind of extended family – with all the love and all the angst that the word family englobes – and we sipped our drinks and watched Sarah rip her way through the mountain of packages.

I had been off the meds for three days by then and I was feeling absolutely fine. Well, relatively. Perhaps it had simply been so long since I had felt absolutely fine that I couldn't remember how that was supposed to be anymore. But I felt good. I honestly felt optimistic and despite being tired, full of fun. I laughed a lot and that, particularly, felt healing.

And feeling good and being surrounded by friends and watching my daughter almost wetting herself with excitement made me feel, at the same time, very strange indeed. Because I felt *so* well, *so* normal, that it seemed, just for a couple of days, like a complete impossibility that I might die.

In the light of what had happened to Tom I sat sipping a tiny glass of strictly prohibited sherry and wondered if I might not have a little Christmas miracle for myself.

Maybe my cancer had mysteriously vanished, I figured. Maybe they had got the diagnosis completely wrong. Maybe there had been a blur on the lens of the scanner machine and I was as fine as I suddenly felt.

It was all rubbish of course. I remained, deep down, entirely unconvinced. But as we span plastic helicopters into the air, or pulled barking dogs with tinny voices from boxes; as we cooked Christmas dinner and played charades, I was so happy that I repeatedly had tears in my eyes. And because it felt too good to interrupt, I decided to go with it. I decided to let myself pretend that it had all been in big, silly mistake.

That was my secret charade. That was my Christmas gift to myself.

Harsh reality could wait until after Christmas.

Post Christmas Comedown

On Boxing day, Ricardo, Sarah and I are eating a breakfast of boiled eggs when Jenny plonks a bottle of pills on the table.

"That's *my* breakfast," she says.

"What are you doing with those?" I ask. "You're not on chemo this week."

"I cheated," Jenny says. "I stopped taking them over Christmas."

"Ahah!" Ricardo exclaims.

"All is revealed," I say. "We thought you seemed unusually chipper."

"A bit naughty, but I needed a break."

"It's snowing," Sarah says, pointing, and all three of us turn to look out at the beach where, indeed, a few flakes are drifting from the matt grey sky.

"It is," Jenny says.

"Can we make a snow-man?" Sarah asks.

"I think you might need a bit more snow than that," I laugh.

"If it snows more then?"

"If it does."

"So," Jenny says, waving the bottle. "Can you two assume snow-man duties, or whatever, if I do my missing three days of pill-hell?"

I nod and glance at Ricardo. "Yep," I say. "We're cool aren't we?"

Ricardo purses his lips and winks at Jenny. "We are very cool," he says.

"Well then," Jenny says, standing. "It's goodbye from me."

"And it's goodbye from him," I say, completing the TV catchphrase.

***

Two days later, Ricardo enters the kitchen with Jenny's untouched breakfast tray.

"Oh," I say, reaching out to steal a slice of toast. "Back to normal huh?"

Ricardo nods and sighs. "She's not good babe," he says.

"I know," I splutter through a mouthful of toast.

"The pills are killing her," he says.

"Yeah, I know," I say. "So, what do you want to do today? I thought we could go to Beachy Head and have a walk. Get a breath of fresh air."

Ricardo glowers at me. He looks, for some reason, like I am a profound disappointment to him.

"What's wrong with you?" I ask.

"I just say that the pills are killing her," he says. "Did you hear me?"

I swallow and lower the remaining bread to the plate and kick the kitchen door shut to make sure that Sarah won't hear us. "I thought you were talking metaphorically," I say. "They *always* make her ill."

"Not metaphor," Ricardo says. "She looks really bad. When does she go to the hospital for the checkup?"

I sigh and wonder if I have become so used to seeing Jenny ill that I am missing something. "Next Monday," I say. "But I honestly don't think she's much worse than usual. And she was fine over Christmas."

"Next Monday..." Ricardo says, wrinkling his nose. "So they don't see her bad, like today?"

I shrug. "No. It's the way the cycle works. They do the blood tests a week after the end of the cycle. So you're right. They never see her like this."

Ricardo shakes his head. "I don't think she should take them," he says. "She looks *hepatique* to me."

"That happened once," I say. "They put her on dialysis for two days."

"I think she needs something now," he says. "But maybe more for her liver than the kidneys. But she says she don't want to phone the hospital."

"They changed the dosage already," I say. "So if it's too much for her this time she'll be off the trial I think. So she's scared."

"It's maybe better," he says.

"Don't say that babe," I tell him. "She has a brain tumour. Without the drugs they only gave her three to six months."

Ricardo wrinkles his nose and sighs.

"That's your *very* unhappy face," I say. "What is it?"

He shrugs. "Maybe I'm wrong," he says. "But I've seen people die. From kidney fail and liver fail... they look a certain way... the skin, the eyes." He points at the ceiling. "They look like her."

A lump forms in my throat and tears well up from nowhere clouding my vision without warning.

"I think the pills maybe kill her faster than the cancer," he continues.

I pinch the bridge of my nose. "Please don't..." I say. "Don't say that."

"Did you call the man?" he asks gravely.

"The man?"

"About Sarah?"

"The lawyer? For the guardianship will?"

"Yes."

"They're on holiday until the fifth as well."

Ricardo stares into my eyes and sighs. "I think you need to get this done quickly," he says.

I chew my finger as the realisation of what he is saying dawns on me. I stare at him and he shrugs and nods gently to emphasise that he is totally serious.

"And I think you should go convince your friend that she need to go to the hospital so they can see her like this," he adds.

And then, as I start to cry, he opens his arms and steps towards me. "Come here," he says. "Poor Chupy. Maybe I'm wrong. I just think we should get her checked out."

When I enter her room, Jenny is asleep.

I circle the bed to get a better look and observe her in silence.

And yes, she looks ill. The grey winter daylight leaking through a gap in the curtains isn't helping, but, yes, I think she even looks worse than usual. Her skin has the same yellowish colour it had before, but beyond that it has a green papery death tinge to it as well. It's impossible to believe that three days ago she was laughing and playing charades.

"Jenny?" I say. "Jenny? Are you awake?"

She groans and rolls onto her side and squints at me. "Mmmm? What?"

"We think you need to go for a checkup," I say.

Jenny frowns at me. "You woke me," she says.

"You don't look well."

"I don't *feel* well," she says.

"OK. Understatement. You look like before. When they gave you dialysis."

"It's next week. The checkup is next week," she says wearily.

"I know. But both Ricardo and I think you need to see someone sooner."

Jenny slides a hand from between the sheets and covers her eyes with it. "Mark," she says, sounding irritated more than anything else. "It's my last day, I feel like shit, but I'll be fine tomorrow."

I sigh and sit on the edge of the bed and try to take her hand but she pulls it away.

"I'm worried about you," I say. "We both are."

Jenny groans. "Mark. Just... I'm sorry... but... you know... fuck off and let me sleep will you?"

The next day Jenny is still sickly. This is more or less par for the course. But when the following day – New Year's Eve – she is *still* ill in bed, Ricardo beckons me into the kitchen. "It's time," he says.

"You want to call the hospital?"

"I want to take her in. I want her to see someone."

I nod in reluctant agreement.

"We go tell her together, yes?"

"OK," I say, following him to the door.

Jenny is lying on one side facing us as we enter. "Hi guys," she says. "Both at once huh?"

"We need to talk to you," I say.

"I know," she replies. "You want me to call Batt."

"We want you to go see him."

She blinks slowly to show her acquiescence. "Bring me the phone," she says with a sigh. "I'll call him and tell him what's going on."

Because it's New Year's Eve, Batt is unavailable, but eventually the doctor covering for him phones us back. Ricardo sits with her during the call to make sure that she tells him how sick she has been, and probably because Jenny isn't his patient and as such, he isn't taking any risks with her, he asks her to come in immediately.

By two in the afternoon, I am driving Jenny up the motorway, and by six I am heading back the other way alone.

When I reach the house I see Ricardo and Sarah through the bay window. They are reading a picture book together, and both look warm and homely by the light of the orange table lamp. I creep up to the window and watch them together for a moment. Ricardo's face looks animated and funny. He looks as beautiful, in fact, as I have ever seen him, and I am overcome by a powerful surge of love for them both, but particularly for him in this new fatherly role.

I rap on the window, and he looks up and his features transform into a no less pleasing, but entirely different configuration – the one he uses when he smiles at me.

He hikes Sarah up and crosses the room towards us. "Chupy!" he says, as he slides open the window. "How did it go?"

"Pretty much as I said on the phone," I say.

"I mean the drive."

"Oh fine. I was listening to a thing about eighties music on the radio and no traffic, so yeah, fine. And how are you miss?"

"I'm good," Sarah says. I laugh at this. *I'm good,* is Ricardo's stock response. Sarah has now picked it up as her own.

"I made some tomato sauce for pasta," Ricardo says. "Well, we made it, didn't we."

Sarah nods. "I helped. When's Mummy coming home?"

"On Saturday," I say. She frowns at me so I say, "In two sleeps," and she looks into the middle distance, thinks about this for a minute, and then asks Ricardo, "can we finish the story?"

Once Sarah is in bed, Ricardo and I sit to eat our tomato pasta.

"So," he asks again. "What did they say?"

"I honestly didn't get much more than I told you," I say. "They got her to pee on a stick and put her straight on dialysis."

"So we were right to make her go."

"Apparently so."

"And did you ask about the yellow skin?"

"Yeah. They said the dialysis will help."

"I don't understand that," Ricardo says, twiddling spaghetti around his fork. "It's a liver problem, not kidney. The liver is why you go yellow."

"I know," I say. "I asked Florent for you."

"He was there?"

"Yeah. He was all over Jenny. I think he's in love with her or something."

"Serious?"

"No. But he really likes her. Which is great. Anyway, he did tell me but it was a bit complicated to be honest. Something to do with the drug affecting the liver, and enzymes from the liver affecting the kidneys. So dialysis helps. If that makes any sense."

Ricardo pouts and wobbles his head from side to side. "I guess," he says. "Everything is connected so..."

"Exactly. Florent said internal organs are like dominos. If you let one fail then they all fail."

"Right."

"God, it's New Year's Eve," I say, checking the clock. "Have we got any alcohol? I could do with a drink."

"I'm sorry," Ricardo says. "By the time I remember the shop is shut."

"You're forgetting the pub," I say.

"But we can't. Not with Sarah."

"But I can go get something and bring it back here. Wine, or cans of beer."

"It's a good idea," Ricardo says. "We can't have New Year without a drink."

But two bottles of Meadow Creek can't save this particular New Year's Eve. I lay back against Ricardo's chest and we stare out at the frosted beach and sip our pretty-disgusting wine in almost total silence. I'm thinking alternately about poor Jenny hooked up to a dialysis machine for New Year's Eve, and Paloma lost or dead on another distant beach. I used to give her salmon on special occasions like today. I wonder what, if anything she's eating tonight. I wonder if she's still alive.

At midnight, I say, "Happy New Year," and Ricardo replies with a yawn.

"You too babe," he says. His voice resonates in my rib cage.

"I hope it's better than last year," I say.

"It will be," he says. "I think it will be a good year."

"I'm tired," I say.

"It's all the driving."

"Yeah."

"I'm tired too," he says. "Sarah all day."

I laugh. "I know this is a bit... you know... old married couple... but."

"We go to bed?"

I laugh and twist my neck to look back at him. "Yeah," I say. "Can we? Can we forget about New Year and just go to bed?"

Levels of Intensity

Two days later, we have planned to make a "family" trip to London to see the sights and pick Jenny up. But Jenny, who has different ideas, insists that it should be me alone that makes the trip. "I've been thinking," she tells me on the phone in a clipped officious voice. "Sarah's seen enough of hospitals. I don't want that to be her enduring memory of childhood."

"Plus," she adds, in a more ominous tone, "we can talk that way."

She is looking pale and drawn when I meet her in the waiting room, but I lie and tell her that she looks better.

"Sure," she says. "Whatever. Let's go."

There's something rigid about her demeanour, something controlled about her tone of voice that makes me nervous and so I say nothing. But after ten minutes with only the sound of the windscreen wipers and the engine, I can take it no longer. "So," I prompt, glancing across with a sober smile.

"So," she repeats.

"Did you see Batt?"

"Na. I saw Stephens."

"The young guy."

"Yeah. I'm off the trial."

"You are?"

"Well, suspended. Pending further investigations or something."

"Further investigations?"

"Yeah. Blood tests and scans."

I negotiate a roundabout and then glance across at her. "And how do you feel about that?"

Jenny shrugs. "Depressed. And relieved that I don't have to take any more of those bloody pills."

299

"So what happens next?"

"I'm not sure really," she says. "Nothing much, I think."

"Nothing much."

Jenny sighs.

"Look Jen," I say. "Can you just go through everything they said, because this is turning into a really irritating sort of question and answer session."

She sighs again, more deeply this time, and looks out of the side window for a moment before clearing her throat and saying, "Sure, sorry. You're right. So. Start again Jen."

"You have an hour and a half, so..."

"It won't take *that* long," she says.

"So."

"So. I'm off the trial. If the blood-work comes back normal in a month or so, and if the tumour starts to grow again then they might put me back on it, but..."

"So the tumour *hasn't* been progressing?"

"No. Not at all apparently. Quiet as a mouse."

"So that's good news."

"Yes. I suppose. But they think it will probably start up again now I'm off the chemo."

"Is that what they said? *Probably?*"

Jenny pauses and then says, "*Very possibly,* I think he said. Whatever that means."

I nod. "And if it does you go back on the chemo."

"Only if my blood work is OK. But they think my liver and kidneys have both taken a hit, so it probably won't be."

"And if you can't go back on chemo, then...?"

"Well if the tumour kicks off again and my blood counts are still bad then basically that's it I think. I croak."

I wipe the inside of the windscreen, but in fact most of the irritating mist is not on the windscreen but in my eyes. "Shit Jenny," I say.

"I know. It's shit, isn't it. But for now, I have a month off. No scans, no pills, no visits."

"Cool. So you get a proper rest."

"Yes. Well, I still have to take the anti-convulsants, but that's it."

"A month seems a long time between scans. Are you happy with that?"

Jenny shrugs. "They said that there's no point doing it earlier because they wouldn't see anything. And if they did they couldn't do anything because of my liver."

"Fair enough."

"So I want to get some balls rolling."

"Balls rolling?"

"Yeah. We need money, so I'm going to flog Mum's place."

"Well we can talk about that."

"Talk all you want. I've decided. I'm putting it on the market. And we need to get the legal guardian thing signed and sealed too."

"I'm going to see him on the fifth," I say.

"That's, what, Monday?"

"Yeah."

"I'll come. If we can get it all signed and sealed in one go that's better."

I frown and drive in silence for a moment before asking, "You're not... thinking of leaving us *just yet* are you?"

"I got all the info this time. And it could happen anytime Mark. In fact it could have *already* happened anytime."

"Jesus Jenny."

"It might be gradual. Lots of side effects, fits, eye problems... all kinds of shit. Or it could be sudden. I might just, you know, *stop*. Or not wake up one morning. They said that was the most likely."

"I," I say. But my voice fails.

"Please don't start," Jenny says. "And of course, it might not happen at all. But we need to get the paperwork sorted."

I turn onto a slip road and merge out onto the M23.

"Mark?"

"Sorry, I... I don't know what to say."

"Are you having second thoughts?"

"About?"

"About Sarah? Because I could still ask Tom."

"No! Of course not."

"And Ricardo?"

"No. They get on really well."

"They do don't they? I'm quite surprised about that. I don't know why."

"I caught him reading to her the other day. They were so cute."

"He's all-right really isn't he?" Jenny says.

"Yeah. He is."

"Not perfect..."

"No."

"Some quite big faults really."

"Perhaps."

"But a big old heart as well."

"Well yes."

"But then who *is* perfect?"

"Me?" I ask, glancing at her and smiling weakly.

Jenny wrinkles her nose. "You're not perfect sir. Not by any means. But you're all-right too, I suppose."

"Thanks."

She reaches out to put the radio on and then pauses, her hand hovering over the knob. "It's weird isn't it?" she says. "Being able to talk about all this now. You get used to anything really."

"I'm not sure about *that*," I say. But I know what she means. Because although my eyes are watering and I have a huge lump in my throat, I never thought I would have been able to discuss a friend's potentially imminent death with the friend in question whilst successfully negotiating the M23.

"You just can't live at that level of intensity," Jenny says.

"I'm sorry?"

"You can't live at that level for so long. You simply can't run around screaming for months. So I think your brain just adjusts somehow."

"You're right," I say. "It does."

"It's amazing really."

"You're right," I say. "It is."

"Anyway, who cares what the doctors say, huh? Florent did my I-ching. Far more important."

"The Chinese thing with the sticks?"

"Yeah. Only he does it with coins."

"Do you believe in that stuff?"

"Not really, but I'd like to."

"Why, what did it say?"

"Difficulty at the beginning leads to supreme success," she says.

"Difficulty at the beginning..." I repeat.

"Leads to *supreme* success," she says.

"I've heard that before," I say. "I dated a guy who was into the I-Ching. It was *years* ago." I decide not to tell her that the relationship with the guy in question turned out to be a catastrophic disaster rather than a supreme success. "Anyway, it sounds good and positive," I say.

"Yeah," she says. "I think that's why he's my favourite nurse."

A Good Lawyer

On Monday morning, we leave Sarah and Ricardo playing with Lego and head off to Brighton to see the specialised guardianship lawyer. It seems, as I drive over the downs and past Cuckmore Haven, as if a lid has been slapped on all of the emotional turmoil that would normally be whipped up by today's fraught programme. I feel cold and efficient, and Jenny looks the same. But it feels as if one false move might result in the lid popping off and both of us collapsing into tears.

I park the car up on Brighton seafront and we walk side by side towards the town centre.

"What an amazing day," Jenny says.

"It is," I agree, looking out at the horizon. It's proof of my preoccupied mood that I'm only now noticing today's spring-like weather. "We've been pretty lucky this winter," I say. "We've had quite a lot of sun."

"You're right," she replies. "We have."

We get to the Lanes a little early, so we head to Café Nero for coffee.

"Cute dads," Jenny says once we are seated, and I glance over to see a sporty, trendy, bearded dad carrying a toddler Sarah's age.

"You only get dads like that in Brighton," I say.

"Yeah," Jenny agrees. "I know. Maybe I should have moved here. I might have caught one for myself."

And I sit and think about that. Because of course all of our lives would have been different in innumerable ways if we had just decided to live somewhere else. An infinite number of different lives are spread out around us, but until we choose one, until we move and find out who we end up meeting because of where we live they're all unknowable. Other than the fact that you're far more likely to meet a sporty, bearded ad exec in Brighton than in Huddersfield, it really is a lucky dip.

And then I note the past tense of Jenny's phrase, and say, "You still *can* you know."

It's been so long since she made the comment, she says, "I'm sorry?"

"You say you *should have* moved here. You still can."

"Oh yeah," she says vaguely. "Of course."

Five minutes before our appointment we head over to Statton and Houghton's swanky offices in Prince Albert Street.

A fairly attractive woman who I think is trying to look like an old-school lesbian-librarian shows us through to the waiting room but no sooner have we sat down than a voice booms out and we both turn to see a vision of elegance grinning at us from the doorway.

Peter Statton, it transpires, is an extremely good looking man. He is in his late thirties, is tall and dark with a pleasant tan – no doubt from a recent winter break. He is also the most incredible dandy and is wearing a stunning checkered suit and has the biggest knot in the pinkest tie I have ever seen.

"Please, take a seat," he says, fixing his cuffs and slithering behind his desk.

I sit and listen as Jenny explains the situation in a controlled, business-like manner, and I wonder how it must feel to be Peter Statton. I wonder how it must feel to have been born that good looking, that well bred, to be that self confident. I wonder how it would feel to wear that suit, and, somewhat inappropriately I wonder how it would feel to kiss those lips.

The guardianship will turns out to be fairly straightforward. It has to record Jenny's wishes regarding the future of her daughter and must be witnessed by two independent witnesses. Because Nick is alive and could reasonably contest the will, it also needs to state as many reasons as possible that she wants it to be me, and as many reasons as possible that it shouldn't be him.

Once we have listed these, Stratton stands and smooths his tie, continuing the movement of his hand until it strokes his crotch. And then he shakes hands with us and ushers us from his office.

Whilst we wait for the paperwork to be printed I have to place my coat over my lap to hide a rather absurd hard-on. It's the strangest thing that this should be happening here today because the context of the visit has made me so tense that my neck muscles are actually hurting.

Once the will is printed and signed in triplicate and we have paid the outrageous two-hundred pound fee, Jenny and I step outside.

"Can we go and have lunch somewhere?" Jenny asks. "I could do with some time to decompress."

We wander down to the seafront and after take window-seats in Alfresco.

"Are you OK?" I ask.

Jenny nods. "Yeah," she says, smoothing one hand over the envelope. "I'm just trying to convince myself that the words in here don't change anything."

"How do you mean?"

"Well it's sort of in writing now, isn't it. It almost seems like it's inevitable."

I sigh. "I know what you mean," I say, "but you mustn't think like that."

We sit and stare at the view until the waitress takes our orders. Once she has left, I say, to fill the void as much as anything, "Two-hundred quid though!"

"I know," Jenny says. "Still, he knew his stuff. It's reassuring to know that it's worded just right."

"I suppose."

"And they do store a copy forever included in the fee."

"Sure. Though I think his prices have more to do with his taste in suits than storage costs."

Jenny nods and sighs. And then her expression changes. "Is it just me, or did he... you know... *ooze* sex?"

I slip into a smile, my first today. "No. He's a stunner."

"I kept looking at his lips," Jenny says.

"Yep. Me too. So kissable."

"I know! And did you see how... No. Never mind."

"What?"

"No, I'm just being pervy," she says. "I haven't had a shag for too long... I expect that's it."

"I saw him give his packet a good stroke before he shook hands at the end," I laugh.

Jenny's face lights up. She slips into a broad grin. "I know!" she says. "I saw that too. The dirdy birdy."

"I got a bit hard actually," I say. "That's why I was sitting with my coat on my lap."

"I think I got a bit wet," Jenny whispers.

I pull a face. "Jenny!"

She rolls her eyes. "Honestly," she says. "You gay guys. Any mention of..."

"Please don't," I say, raising one hand. "I've ordered mussels."

Jenny's mouth drops in amused outrage. "That's *so* rude," she says. "You have no idea."

I wrinkle my nose. "No," I say. "I do have an idea. I remember."

I smile at her. A bit of humour and a change of context and she suddenly looks almost normal.

I watch her fiddle with the edge of her wig as she laughs. You could almost forget that she has cancer. Almost.

A Different Set of Rooms

When we get back to the house, Jenny takes Sarah upstairs for a sleep and Ricardo beckons me into the kitchen. He grabs my waist and kisses me. "How did it go babe? I think about you all morning."

"It was fine. It's all done."

"So not so complicated then?"

I shrug. "It's all about using the exact right words. So that it can't be challenged in court."

"But who could challenge?"

"Nick."

"Ah yes."

"And if he does, social services would have to get involved and decide. But the truth is that if Jenny did die Nick probably wouldn't even find out."

Ricardo kisses me again, then separates. "Good. One thing done. Now, Florent phone me."

"Florent?"

"He wants to come down again for the weekend."

I grimace. "I don't think there's room do you?"

"The sofa?" Ricardo suggests.

"Yeah, but what's the point?"

Ricardo shrugs. "We could go away," he says with a wink.

"I don't think we can afford it. That weekend in Nice cost hundreds in the end."

Ricardo nods and sighs. "Yes. The money is not so good huh? I looked this morning and until the flat sells..."

"I'm looking for translation work babe. Honestly. I look every day. But there hasn't been anything worth doing."

"I know. I think maybe I should look for work too."

"Can you? Here? I mean, as a doctor?"

Ricardo shrugs. "I don't know," he says. "I need to look it up. Can you help me look on the internet? I don't know who... you know... controls doctors here."

"Sure."

"So what about Florent?" Ricardo asks. "I tell him 'no?'"

At that instant Jenny bursts into the kitchen and Ricardo and I separate. "Don't mind me," she says. "I just forgot to take my pill."

We stand and watch her fill a glass and swallow the capsule. "And tell who 'no?'" she asks. "What are you two plotting?"

"Nothing," I say.

Jenny shrugs and crosses to the door then pauses. "Oh, by the way," she says. "Florent left me a message. He's coming down at the weekend so if you two want to fuck off somewhere exotic again."

I raise an eyebrow at Ricardo. Jenny sees this and looks at me inquisitively.

"Actually we were just saying that money's a bit tight," I say. "So maybe not the best time for galavanting off to exotic destinations."

"Yeah," Jenny says. "I need to get Mum's place on the market. Sorry about that."

"That's not what I meant."

"But I still do. I can't face going up there to be honest."

"No. I'm sure."

"That's something you could do, if you fancied a little trip," she says. "Go and work out what needs doing. Take some nice photos. Get some estate agents' phone numbers for me. Maybe see Susan and check she's still OK about us staying here... Anyway, something to think about. See you later."

Once she has returned upstairs Ricardo looks at me and shrugs. "What do you think?"

"It's a bit boring up there," I say. "But, well, you've never seen Surrey. And I suppose we could take in Hampton Court or something?"

"Hampton Court?"

"It's a big stately home. A palace actually."

Ricardo nips to the lounge and returns with the laptop.

"Show me," he says.

I google Hampton Court Palace and the instant the first image appears on the screen Ricardo says, "Oh *yes* babe. I want."

***

Though we do drive up to Surrey on Friday evening, we never do get to Hampton Court Palace, and though this is through no fault of our own, we don't get to see Susan either.

In fact other than hoovering up the layer of dust and listing furniture for a future house clearance we don't do anything much that was on our list.

What we *do* do is fuck. Having an entire two-storey house to ourselves with absent neighbours feels like being in an adventure park. So we fuck on the sofa and we fuck on the dining table. We snog in the kitchen and fuck again in the shower. We order pizzas and sleep in Jenny's old room and then in the morning we make love all over again.

On Sunday afternoon I'm packing when Ricardo comes into the bedroom and says, "You know, we haven't use the other bedroom yet."

I pull a face. "It's her Mum's room," I say. "I don't really fancy it to be honest."

Ricardo nods. "Shame," he says, brandishing a condom at me. "We only have one left."

I stare at it and grin. "There's a shed in the garden," I say coyly.

We both glance out at the frosty garden and say, simultaneously, "Too cold."

"Toilet room?" Ricardo says.

"Too small babe. But we haven't tried it on the stairs before."

Ricardo grins lopsidedly. He looks dirty. "Stairs could be good," he says. And though they represent a significant technical challenge in terms of fucking they do turn out to be particularly good for oral sex.

By the time we get back on Sunday I'm feeling incredibly relaxed – something to do with simply spending a few days in a different set of rooms. And of course, something to do with finally feeling sexually sated.

Ricardo drops our weekend bag in the hall and I jingle the car keys at Jenny. "Where's Wonder Boy? I think I need to take him straight away don't I?"

"He's already gone," Jenny says. "They phoned and changed his shifts so he had to go back at lunchtime. He managed to get a train from that tiny station down the way."

"I didn't even know you could," I say.

"Well no. There are only a few trains a day, but it worked out fine."

"You look well," I say, noticing an unusual flush to her cheeks.

"So do you," she says. "How was the house?"

"Fine. Dusty. We cleaned it."

"And Susan? Did you get to see her?"

"Away I'm afraid."

"At her sister's I expect," Jenny says. "So what else did you get up to?"

I glance at Ricardo who is sipping a glass of water and restrain a smirk. "Nothing much to be honest. We just slobbed around."

Jenny looks from one to the other and nods knowingly. "I can imagine," she says. "Did you take photos?"

Ricardo splutters and spits out a mouthful of water. "Photos?" he asks.

"Shit!" I mutter. "We forgot to take the photos." I look at Ricardo's expression and then laugh. "Of the *house*, silly."

"Ah!" he says. "We can always go back huh? I quite like Surrey."

I roll my eyes. "We listed all the furniture," I tell Jenny. "So you can decide what to keep and what to clear."

"Well, that's something."

"And you need a hall carpet."

"God yeah. I had forgotten."

"And what about you? What did you get up to?"

Jenny shakes her head. "Not much to be honest."

"You look funny," I say. "Did you have an argument with Florent or something?"

"No," she says, glancing at Sarah. "I'll, um, tell you about it later."

At nine Jenny takes Sarah upstairs to bed and Ricardo asks, "Did something happen with Florent? I didn't understand."

"I don't know," I say. "I thought maybe they argued, but she seems OK about it if they did."

As so often, Jenny falls asleep with Sarah, and so we are left wondering. And the next morning something else happens and the question of what happened with Florent is pushed from my mind entirely.

The Big Picture

I'm alone in the house when the post arrives.

This is actually quite unusual. In fact, I think that it is probably the first time that Ricardo, Sarah and Jenny have gone out and left me indoors.

I have purportedly stayed behind in order to scour the web for work but so far have found nothing.

Subconsciously I hear the crunch of feet on the gravel outside, followed by the clack of the letterbox. Subconsciously again, I note the sound of a heavier than usual package flopping onto the doormat. But it's not until I have finished reading the onscreen proposal that it all registers.

I straighten my hunched position and frown, and almost as if I'm realising that there may be a burglar in the house, I turn slowly and look across the room.

It's just an envelope. It's perhaps a bigger envelope than usual, but that's it. There is no particular reason to think that this is an important envelope. But maybe we do have senses that, as a race, we haven't yet acknowledged, because I don't jump up to rip it open. I sit and stare at it for a moment. I frown. I take a deep breath. And then, finally, with a powerful sensation of impending... *something*, I cross the room and stare down at it.

I can see, even before I pick it up, that it has been franked by the Colombian postal service. I reach down and grasp the package. It's addressed to Ricardo. Our first batch of redirected mail then. Nothing particularly menacing about that, surely?

I pour myself a coffee and return to the lounge. I sit and finger the package for a moment, and then, deciding that I'm being ridiculous, I rip it open.

It's only once I have done this that I realise that it was, of course, addressed to Ricardo, not me.

But it's too late, so I tip the contents out onto my lap and leaf through the selection of envelopes within.

Most of these I can identify without opening them. There's a mobile bill for me. There's a letter from Maria – I recognise her handwriting from the notes she used to leave when she had cleaned.

There's a bill from Ricardo's old mobile company, and two others from the new one. There are two bank statements. And there is one other hand addressed envelope. Stationary: pink. Postmark: Bogotá.

I sigh and put it to one side. I open my own mobile bill – it contains no surprises. And then I sit and look at the other letters.

I spread them out like Tarot cards. They hold aspects of our lives, the predictable and the unpredictable. My eye is drawn to the pink envelope again and again. I even pick it up and sniff it: paper. Glue. I hold it to the light but it's opaque.

Out of the corner of my eye, I see Ricardo crossing the beach with Sarah on his shoulders. I see Jenny beside him talking animatedly and holding her wig on with one hand. So I slip Ricardo's post back in the brown envelope and position myself casually on the sofa for their arrival.

"We've got post!" I say enthusiastically once Jenny has closed the window behind them.

"You opened it!" Ricardo protests, when I hand him the envelope.

"Only mine," I say, waving my phone bill.

Ricardo squeezes the package so that it yawns open and peers inside. "After coffee," he says.

I jump up, saying, "I'll get it. You look at your post."

When I return, Ricardo waves three sheets of paper at me. "The old people still bill me," he says. "And the new."

"You'll have to phone them."

"Yeah. They're bastards in Colombia, the mobile companies," he says.

"Mobile companies are bastards *everywhere*," Jenny says.

"Anything else?" I ask in a voice I calculate to be casual but interested. I think that I may have got this wrong though, because Jenny frowns at me and stands. "Come on Miss," she says, picking Sarah up. "You come help Mummy with lunch."

Ricardo pats the letter from Maria. "Maria's pregnant again," he says.

"Again!"

"I know. I send her some condom maybe," he says with a smile.

"And?"

"And."

"What else?"

"That's it babe," he says.

"But there's another one isn't there?" I say. "A coloured envelope. Pink."

Ricardo peers back into the envelope which now contains all the other opened letters. "Oh yes," he says.

I fix a neutral smile. I'm smiling at Ricardo, but a beast is edging into my field of vision. Because I don't believe that *Oh yes,* for one second.

Ricardo opens the pink envelope and shakes the folded sheet of paper open. As he does this a photo falls to the table. It falls face down, but the tiniest glimpse catches my eye – I snatch it and flip it over.

A huge lump forms in my throat and tears spring to my eyes instantly.

"Chupy?" Ricardo says looking worried.

I point the photo at him.

"Paloma!" he says.

I place it on the table and stare at it. "God, she's so skinny."

I reach for the letter, but he moves it out of my reach. "It's in Spanish babe," he says.

"Well what does it say?"

He sits and frowns at the letter as if he's having trouble deciphering the words. And then he smiles. And then he laughs.

"What's so funny?"

"She's OK," he says. "They went to the house and found her on the doormat."

"Who?"

"Federico."

"So that's from Federico?"

"Yes! Hey, is good news, huh? Paloma. She's OK," Ricardo says with what seems like genuine relief.

I spin the photo toward him. "That's not OK babe," I point out. "The only time I ever saw a skinnier cat was on the streets of Athens."

She looks starved and dirty and sad.

"But it's when she found her," Ricardo says.

"She?"

"Paloma. It's when Federico found her. And now he gave her to a friend in Bogotá."

"He *gave* her to a friend?!"

"Yes. He has a dog. You know that. So he give her to a girl who likes cats. In Bogotá. She will send another photo soon."

I stare at him, my brain temporarily paralysed by some unformed thought.

And then I look down at the photo again and my eyes water with fresh tears. Because whatever else might be going on here – and I suspect that there is plenty – Paloma *has* undoubtedly been found. And if another photo is coming then she *is* being looked after by someone.

"Now, I'm starving," Ricardo says, folding the letter and slipping it back into the pink envelope.

He stands and starts to leave with it still in his hand but then he pauses and puts it back on the table in front of me.

Just before he heads through to the kitchen, he kisses me tenderly on the head and glances at the envelope and then back at me. He looks as happy as I feel.

I watch him go and then I look at the photo again, taking in every familiar aspect – the colour of her eyes, the blob on her nose, her white booty paws... And then I take in everything that has changed – the ripped ear, the mangy fur... I try to calculate how much weight she has lost and I wonder what adventures she has had to live through to survive.

And then I stare at the pink envelope again, sitting on the table, like a Tarot card – the lightning tower perhaps. It crosses my mind that Ricardo left it there on purpose as some kind of challenge. It says, *believe me.* Or *don't.*

Because of course, even if it is in Spanish I could still get the gist. Even if it is badly written, I could still see if macho Federico really has taken to using pink stationary.

I sit and stare at that envelope and think about Tarot cards again and my life with Ricardo flashes before my eyes. It's the life we have had and the life yet to come. It's working and shagging and living somewhere new. It's possibly even parenting Sarah together. And the strangest thing happens: I decide not to read the letter.

It's as if I'm sitting looking at my life with Ricardo and there, at the edge of my vision, I can sense the beast lurking. I can see the vaguest shadow of stirring, as-yet-unknown, danger.

And I have a choice: to look or not to look.

If I turn to see what is there, then I have to turn away from everything else.

And that thought feels like a new found wisdom. The wisdom to know that you can't see everything at once. Sometimes the picture is so big that you have to choose which bit you want to see.

For the first time in my life, I sense a problem, and I decide not to look.

I clap my hands and stand.

"Hey Jenny!" I shout out. "Ricardo's cousin has only gone and found Paloma. She's OK! Isn't that amazing?"

Dead Or Alive Or...

I dream the strangest dreams that night – dreams of lawyers with luscious lips stroking cats at funerals. But despite my macabre night, I wake up feeling energetic and excited. Rather inappropriately, considering Jenny's long face, both Ricardo, Sarah and I are full of beans.

Jenny clearly still has the will playing on her mind and because the disconnect between her and the rest of us is so great, we offer to take Sarah out.

I drive into Eastbourne and park up not far from the sea-front so that we can take our ritual stroll around the pier.

"I love this pier," Ricardo says, raising a hand and looking out at the horizon like a mariner. "You can see France."

"Can you?" I ask, copying his pose.

"No. I ask the question. You can see France?"

"Oh, *can you* see France? Not from here I don't think. It's too far. Further along the coast at Dover I think you can."

"The weather is better than I think," Ricardo says. "I expect England to be more raining."

"Eastbourne gets more sunshine than anywhere else in Britain," I say. "But it's been a good winter too. Global warming maybe."

"I think I like global warming," Ricardo says.

"Well yes..." I say. "I'm sure if everyone in the developed world liked the cold better we'd take global warming a bit more seriously."

"Hey!" Ricardo says, looking down at Sarah who is tugging as hard as she can to the right. "What's over there?"

"Ah!" I say. "Blue dinosaurs."

"Blue dinosaurs?"

"You'll see."

She leads us to the machine and we each have an attempt at fishing one of the soft toys from the machine. And we all fail.

"Wait," Ricardo says, fishing in his pocket. "One more try."

"It's impossible," I tell him.

"It doesn't work," Sarah says, repeating my own mantra. "There's no point."

But this time Ricardo snags a dinosaur by the tail.

"Wow!" I laugh.

"Wow," Sarah repeats.

"Look how faded it is," I say as Ricardo pulls the toy from the drawer. The underside is a deep royal-blue, but where the daylight has fallen upon it, it's a vague turquoise colour. "I think you're the first person ever to catch one of those."

Ricardo laughs and wobbles his head in a cocky manner. "We Colombians – we know how to deal with dinosaur," he says.

Reluctant to return home on such a stunning day, I drive a little further along the coast to the Wishing Well, an amazing seafront cafeteria that hasn't changed since World War Two. Looking around, I would guess that none of the clients have changed since then either.

The place gives Ricardo the giggles. "Everyone so old," he says, looking wide-eyed around the restaurant. "It's like a old-person's home."

"I know," I say. "Isn't it fab?"

We eat fish and chips and wash the food down with good strong cups of tea poured from a vast chrome teapot. No poncey individual sachets here.

And then, when Sarah gets too fidgety and starts pouring sugar all over the table, we tear ourselves from the view and return to the car.

Back in Pevensey Bay, Jenny too is enjoying the sunshine. She has found a deckchair and is sitting heavily wrapped in blankets in a square of sunshine. At the sound of our voices, she opens one eye and squints at us. "Isn't this weather amazing?"

"It is."

"January!" she says. "Imagine. Did you have fun? Oh, you got one!" she laughs as Sarah pushes the fluffy dinosaur into her field of vision.

"I called him Doris," Sarah says. "Ricardo catched him."

"Doris the dinosaur. That's a good name. But is she a girl or a boy?"

"He's a boy, silly."

"Fair enough," Jenny says.

"We went to the Wishing Well for lunch," I tell her. "It's fabulous."

"Damn, I wanted to go there too."

"I know. But I'll take you another time. Anyway, it still hasn't changed. It's exactly like it was when I was a kid. Do *you* need anything?"

"No," Jenny says. "Or maybe just my sunglasses. They're in the kitchen I think."

"Don't move. I'll get them," I say. "And then I'm going to make a curry for tonight if that's OK."

"Lovely."

"Do you need anything to eat?"

"No," Jenny says. "I had some toast. I feel a bit weird today to be honest."

"Weird?"

"Yeah. Dizzy. And tired. But just sitting here is lovely."

We head through to the kitchen and I send Sarah back with the sunglasses. And then the three of us cook a curry. Ricardo and Sarah wash and slice vegetables and I grind spices and put it all together. Ricardo and I have a brief conversation in French about Jenny, and I explain that I think that the will is simply playing on her mind.

Once dinner is simmering we head through to the lounge and Ricardo opens the laptop.

I turn to Sarah. "So what are we going to do with you until teatime?" I ask.

She looks regretfully out at Jenny and I follow her gaze and see that, to follow the sun, Jenny has moved her deckchair to the far end of the garden. She is entirely enveloped in blankets with just one hand and the bit of face spared by her sunglasses showing - turned towards the sun lizard-like.

"Mummy's having a snooze," I say. "So it's just you and me. What do you want to do? Drawing? Reading?"

"Can we play a game?"

"A game? Sure. What sort of game?"

"A funny game," Sarah says.

"A funny game," I repeat, thoughtfully. I wiggle a finger at her. "What about the tickly finger game?"

Sarah looks unimpressed so I try again. "Then how about the deep sea diver game?"

Sarah looks intrigued by this one, so I laugh and lay her down on the sofa before picking her up by her ankles. She immediately starts to shriek and Ricardo catches my eye, winks, and vanishes upstairs with the computer.

"OK. Now. Listen," I tell her. "*Listen!* Because there's a little song."

"Under the water,
under the sea,
catching fishes for my tea.
Dead or alive or a tickle?"

317

Sarah fails to respond. She seems quite happy hanging upside down.

"You have to choose," I explain. "Say 'dead' and I drop you on the sofa. Say 'alive' and I put you down. Say 'tickle' and you get a tickle."

Sarah thinks for a moment and then says, "Alive!"

When I flip her over and put her on her feet though, she looks thoroughly disappointed.

"It's better if you say 'tickle,'" I say. "Or 'dead' even. Alive is the boring option."

"Again!" she says.

I lift her onto the sofa and reach for her ankles but am interrupted by Jenny's mobile. "Hang on," I tell her, crossing the room. The screen is showing, *Incoming Call: Florence* so I hit the answer button.

"Hi there Florent," I say. "It's Mark. Do you want to speak to Jenny?"

"Yeah. If I can," he says.

I glance outside. "She's all wrapped up, snoozing in the sun," I tell him. "She looks like some film star on a cruise."

"I bet," he says. "Especially with the Monroe hair."

"Yes. Especially with the hair. Hang on, I'll hand you over."

I give Sarah the phone. "Here, take this to Mummy," I tell her, "but be careful not to hit any of the buttons, OK?"

I slide the window back and watch her run across the pebbles, the phone raised high above her head for some reason.

"Mum, tephelone," she says. "Muum! Tephelone."

I watch her shake her mother's elbow, but Jenny doesn't wake, her hand simply drapes to the floor. And then Sarah turns back to face me, gives an amazingly adult shrug, and runs back inside. "She's asleep," she says breathlessly.

I take the phone. "She's a gonner Florent," I say. "I'll get her to call you back when she wakes up, OK?"

"Sure. No hurry," he says. "But I do need to talk to her."

"Right," I say, looking out at Jenny and realising that she hasn't visibly moved for some time. "OK. Laters."

I end the call and put the phone down on the arm of the sofa before carrying Sarah upstairs to Ricardo. "Can you look after Sarah for a second?" I ask him.

"Um?" he says distractedly looking up from the computer screen. "Sure Chupy. What's up?"

"I don't know yet..." I say, plopping Sarah on the bed, and closing the bedroom door behind me.

I run downstairs and open the window a little wider. And then I take a deep breath and cross the pebbles to Jenny's side.

I crouch down and peer in at her face. She looks incredibly pale. I can see myself reflected in her sunglasses. I look down at her chest, but beneath all the blankets, I can't detect any sign of movement. I touch the back of her draped hand gently with my own – it is icy cold.

"Jenny?" I say sharply, but she doesn't stir.

I glance back at the house and see Ricardo standing in the front bedroom. I can see that he has understood what is happening because he turns Sarah to face the other way. With a nod of my head I beckon him to join me.

Within seconds he is by my side. He tests Jenny's hand for a pulse and wrinkles his nose and then reaches out and senses her cheek with the back of his hand. "Cold," he says.

I'm not sure if he means 'out cold,' or 'freezing cold,' or 'stone cold.' I cover my mouth with one hand and hold my breath.

Ricardo crouches down in front of her to remove her sunglasses and then takes her head between both hands and lifts her eyelids open with his thumbs.

Jenny snorts loudly and her entire body jerks in an enormous spasm. I jump, and Ricardo falls backwards onto his arse.

"What the fuck?" Jenny says looking shocked.

Ricardo and I look at her and then glance at each other and then I snort and break into embarrassed laughter.

"Fuck!" Jenny says, looking horrified. "You thought I was dead. Didn't you? You thought I was dead!"

"We... we couldn't wake you," I say.

"I was *asleep,*" she says, looking completely outraged. "I was dreaming. I dreamt you were calling me actually. Jesus!"

She stands and her blankets fall to the ground as she storms towards the house. But just as she reaches the threshold she turns back. "God!" she says. "Honestly."

"Jenny!" I protest. "You were out cold."

"No," she says. "Fuck you! Fuck you *both!*"

Nosolagnia

It takes a couple of hours before Jenny calms down enough to come and sit in the same room as me. Even then, she looks profoundly annoyed. 'I can't believe you guys,' she says as she slumps on the sofa.

"I'm sorry," I say again. "Anyway, what's the score with Florent? I meant to ask you when we got back, but I forgot."

Jenny sighs deeply.

"That bad huh?"

She glances around the room.

"She's upstairs with Ricardo," I say. "He has found some kids' games on the internet. So?"

"Well he's not gay, for one."

"Ricardo?"

"Florent."

I laugh. "I was never that convinced that he *was*. That was more *your* theory."

"Well he *isn't*. He tried it on when you were up at Mum's. God, I have to stop calling it that. In *Camberley*."

"Florent tried it on?"

"Yeah."

"What do..."

"Don't make me go into details Mark."

"OK. But you're sure?"

"Yep."

"Is that why he left early?"

"No. No, he really did have to leave. But I was quite relieved really. Things were a bit sticky by then."

"Sticky?"

Jenny rolls her eyes. "Not that kind of sticky. Awkward."

"So did you... you know... at all?"

"No," Jenny says, frowning.

"OK... why not?"

"Well..."

I shrug. "Well..."

"Well, it's a bit pervy isn't it."

I pull a face. "Is it? Why?"

"Well it's like... necrophilia. Not necrophilia. But I'm sure it's a something philia."

"What is? You're not actually dead are you? Oh my God. You're a ghost!"

Jenny rolls her eyes. "You two wouldn't be surprised if I was."

"Anyway... so... explain the philia business?"

"Well he's a nurse, isn't he?"

"Yeah... and?"

"A cancer nurse. So if he's getting off on women with cancer... that's a bit pervy."

I wrinkle my nose. "I don't think Florent likes you *because* you have cancer Jenny. I think he just likes you."

"Mark. Get real," Jenny says. "I'm ten years older than him, I have no hair left and I've lost so much weight that my tits are sagging like... like something really really saggy."

"Nice simile," I say. "I like it."

"Thanks. But you get my point."

I nod and shrug at the same time.

"What?" Jenny asks.

"Well. That's just silly, isn't it."

"Why is it *silly*?"

"Well you just have a body image problem. Because you have cancer. That seems logical enough. I mean, it's understandable. But..."

"You think?"

"Well yeah. But that's not what other people see when they look at you. They see someone who is witty and rude and funny and vivacious."

Jenny grimaces.

"Well, until you pull *that* face they do," I say.

"Well, I still think it's dodgy," she says.

"I think you need to work on that. Because if I got a chance for a bit of slap and tickle with angel-face I wouldn't hesitate for an instant."

"You wouldn't?"

"Well no. Not if I was *single*. And not if I hadn't had a shag since... when *did* you last have a shag?"

"Don't ask," Jenny says. "I'm not sure I remember. I'm not sure I want to."

"Was it that stockbroker guy?"

"Mark," Jenny laughs. "I said don't ask."

"Well anyway. That's what I think. Go for it. Do him."

Jenny nods and sighs and then shakes her head.

"What now?" I ask.

"I just still can't believe that you thought I was dead," she says.

Jenny: Wanting and Waiting

Of course, I wasn't really that shocked that they took me for dead. Most of my reaction was theatre. It quickly struck me as funny, and watching them trying to squirm out of it seemed even funnier.

The truth is that we were all waiting for it to happen, because you can't wait for something not-to-happen.

People get confused between wanting and waiting. But to wait for something to happen doesn't mean that you want it – not at all. In fact, waiting for something you *really* don't want is a pretty good definition of *dread*. I had a friend who moved to California many years ago. In the early days, before we forgot to keep bothering, he used to write me these brilliant long letters. And I remember that he said that everyone out there was 'waiting for the Big One.' The earthquake to end all earthquakes. And I didn't understand then how anyone could be 'waiting' for something so terrible. But I understood it now.

Even when we weren't waiting for me to die, we were waiting for signposts along the way. We were waiting for the next brain scan after the chemo ended, and then when it came back OK we were waiting for the next one, and the next one. And when those were both OK as well, we switched to waiting for the first scan that *wasn't* OK.

And that process never ends. Because there's always another scan. And eventually, the mind assumes, there *will* be one that isn't OK. Especially in a case like mine. Especially when the therapy has 'failed.' Twice.

So that's how we lived. Through the hottest January on record and the wettest February and on into the first gorgeous days of spring in March.

Mark continued to fill the lounge wall with his seascapes, and after a while we all admitted that they looked pretty good. He started to freelance again too – our financial situation made it necessary really. He would vanish into the bedroom with his laptop at nine in the morning and only reappear at five. He was incredibly disciplined about it. And then in April Ricardo found work too – two part time jobs, one in an STD clinic and one at the Beach Tavern filling in for the owner's wife who was away on maternity leave. Both jobs were beneath him really, but he never complained, or not to me anyway.

I finally sold Mum's house in June. It went almost the second I put it on the market. One of those instances where you wish you had asked for more. But I was glad, because from that point on, I could pay rent to Susan. I knew it made more sense to buy somewhere else, but I couldn't look that far ahead. None of us dared make any changes because we were all just living in stasis. We were all still waiting for the Big One.

One day at the beginning of August I woke up to the sounds of children screaming on the beach. I looked outside, and it was a glorious summer morning – the beach was already crowded. You could smell in the air how wonderfully hot it was going to be.

I looked out to the sea and saw with surprise, Mark and Ricardo and Sarah. They were laughing and splashing around. They were attempting to teach Sarah to swim. And I suddenly wanted to join them – I suddenly desperately wanted to feel the cold seawater envelope my own body. I suddenly wanted to join in the fun instead of just looking on.

I put my wig on and sat for ten minutes trying to tuck my own hair – which had slowly been growing back – beneath the edges. And then I realised that I either had to cut my own, greying hair, or give up on the wig.

And that was what did it. That was my moment. Because the wig had been my cancer bravado. And it no longer fitted me. I threw the wig into the wastepaper bin, but then fished it back out and hung it on the dresser. Perhaps the cancer would "wake up" and I would need it again. Or perhaps that initial treatment, which had so nearly killed me, had killed *it* – only time would tell. In that case, I would be glad to have kept the wig as a souvenir. An "amusing" souvenir of all of this – the first time I had imagined such a future.

"Enough!" I said out loud.

I dug around for my bathing costume and then put it on. I resisted the desire to check in the mirror if it looked OK. I simply put it on and ran downstairs to join them.

Because you just can't live that way. Because we will all pop our clogs at some point but it doesn't stop us from living. Because the fact that life isn't eternal isn't a reason to *stop* living, it's a reason to get on with it while you can.

I told Mark and Ricardo that I wanted them out later that morning. I told them that I wanted them to go and get a life. I told them that I wanted my own life back too.

They protested. We argued.

I promised that I would call them if I needed them and I said I would keep them updated on the scans and blood tests.

And eventually, after a respectable fight, they gave in. I think they were relieved. I think that they too had worried that this stasis would never end. That their lives would go on like this forever.

When they did move, I was relieved that they didn't go too far though. Actually relieved doesn't really cover it.

They rented a basement flat in Brighton with a lovely little garden at the rear.

During the days, Mark and I repainted it from top to bottom. Sarah had started school by then, and Ricardo had gone back to Colombia purportedly to get the rest of their stuff back.

I was surprised, actually, when he returned. Probably because he had let me down I always expected the worst of poor Ricardo. But return he did, not only with all their stuff but with Mark's cat as well.

Mark wept and wept until we were all at it. Even the cat looked a bit watery eyed, but that was probably just from the journey.

When I got back from their housewarming, my own house felt suddenly empty with only Sarah and me, so I took a deep breath and I phoned Florent, determined that, this time, no matter what his motivations, I was going to get a shag.

It was a surprisingly hard call to make because it felt like a vote of confidence. It felt like a vote in the future.

THE END

Post Script: The Pink Letter

Hola, Ricardo mi amor.

I'm not sure if you will get this letter but Juan seems to think you have redirected your post so I suppose it's worth a try. I tried to phone but the numbers don't work again. What is it with you and phones?

Anyway, I left Carlos. I thought you should know that.

He broke my nose, but I knew there would be a price to pay. I'm glad it's just my nose to be honest – I never liked it that much anyway. I'm having it remodelled and re-set at the same time. I chose a new one from a catalogue. I will have a Juliette Binoche nose soon. She's a French actress you know.

So I came up to visit again but the house was all closed up. I thought you had just gone out, but your cat (Palmira?) came out from under the decking and I could see by the state she was in that you had been gone a long time. How could you be so mean to a cat baby? She was starving the poor thing.

Anyway, Palmira kept standing on my feet so in the end I put her in my bag and took her back to Santa Marta with me. She didn't complain at all. I don't think she was enjoying living wild so much. Or perhaps she remembered me.

I stopped at Santa Marta for two nights until I could get another flight back to Bogotá and then I went to my sister' Sofia's place. Her dog had just died which was lucky. Not lucky for Sofia of course, but lucky for Palmira because Tajo hated cats and he would have driven her crazy.

I phoned your nephew Juan to see if he knew where you were and he told me the strangest story babe: he said that the guy who the beach house belongs to – your cousin Federico I think he said – got it into his head that you are a maricon and kicked you out.

I told Juan that I know for a fact that you're as heterosexual as the next guy, and he said that he knew it too. But we both agreed that it was probably better to let Federico carry on thinking that you're a faggot than for him to realise that you have been boning his cousin's wife. Well, second cousin's wife. Soon-to-be ex wife.

Anyway, I hope you don't mind chiquito. I hope we did good.

If you want me to fix it then let me know, because I can, you know, vouch for you! But knowing Carlos' temper, it's probably safer this way.

Anyway, such an incredible story huh? How could he think such a thing? And you of all people!

Anyway, here's a photo of Palmira. I hope it is her and I haven't just taken a random cat from the beach. She's still a bit skinny but I'm giving her good food and cream and she's looking better day by day. If you want her back then you'll have to come and see me. I'm at my sister's place. The address is above.

But then I guess you don't want her back otherwise you wouldn't have left her.

And I guess you don't want to see me either otherwise you would have been in touch.

Oh well. Goodbye beautiful. I hope you are happy wherever you are.

Lots of love.

Cristina and Palmira. Your spurned girls.

PS. I just wanted to say thanks. You're a bit of an asshole, but you made me realise that Carlos is even worse. I know I can do better now. So yes, thanks for that.

Epilogue

I pull my collar up against the wind, whistling across Brighton beach. "Are you sure you're warm enough?" I ask her.

"Yeah, sure," Sarah says. "This is warm."

"Warm?"

"You should try Edinburgh," she says.

"Will you stay there? I mean once you've finished your course?"

Sarah shrugs. "I don't know really..." she says. "Can we head back up – these pebbles are a nightmare in heels."

"Sure," I say, taking her arm and turning back towards the promenade.

"As for Edinburgh, I don't know. I kind of like it," she says. "But, well, you know... change is good too. I'd like to spend some time overseas like you did."

"And Josh?"

"Oh he's total," Sarah says. "I mean good. He's, you know, good with whatever."

"I'm a gay man sweetie," I say. "We're hip. We say total."

"Sure," Sarah laughs. She sounds like she doesn't believe me and she's right.

Though I'm aware of the way everything is *total* these days I actually think it sounds naff. *Naff.* Now there's a word you don't hear anymore. "I suppose as a musician, he can work anywhere too," I say.

"Well that's the theory," Sarah says. "Most of the time he works nowhere."

"But you love him."

"But I love him," Sarah laughs.

"And you?" I ask.

"Me?"

"Yeah. Surely *you* can't work anywhere?"

"Oh, well, law is different all over," she says. "And loads of countries use the Napoleonic code, which is, you know, different. So if I could spend some time in France it would total my CV."

"Sure," I say. "Well France is great."

"Yeah, I know you love it. I think that you banging on about it is probably the reason it appeals."

"I do not bang on about France."

"You so do."

"Well, I still think there might be other reasons. It could be because you were born there. And *conceived* there."

Sarah pulls a face. No one wants to imagine being conceived. No one want's to picture their parents having sex.

"I'm so proud of you, you know," I tell her.

She wrinkles her nose at me. "Thanks," she says. "But I haven't passed my finals yet."

"But you will."

"Eventually," she says.

"First time around."

"I'm nervous this time actually."

"You *always* say that, but you *always* do just fine."

"I guess. Is that the place?" she asks, nodding in the direction of *Piscari* – the latest incarnation of a seafood restaurant I have been coming to for years.

"It is," I say. "Do you remember it? It used to be called Alfresco."

"Sure," she says. "We always end up here." "I don't *mind*," she adds when I pull a face.

"But change is good," I say.

"Yeah," she laughs. "But so is familiarity."

As we climb the steps I can't resist stealing glances at her.

She's taller than me now and carries herself with rigidly elegant poise. When you have known someone since birth it's a constant surprise to see they have become an adult. It's an incredible privilege too, perhaps one of life's greatest honours.

She's healthy and pretty and clever. I kind of worry that she doesn't have enough fun sometimes. I hope that she goes to crazy parties. I hope she gets plenty of sex. I hope that she smokes the occasional joint when I'm not looking.

But I'm sure she does. I'm sure this serious demeanour is simply one facet of her personality – the one she shows to adopted family.

I open the door to the restaurant and Josh, alone in a window seat, smiles at her and I can see the love in his eyes.

And that, so far, strikes me as Sarah's most spectacular success. A fully formed, totally functional relationship at twenty-one. Who would have thought such a thing possible?

"Here she is," he says, leaning across the table to peck her on the lips. "My birthday girl."

He shakes my hand and I grin broadly.

Josh and Sarah will marry soon, I'm sure of it. And Josh is the perfect son-in-law.

He is big and broad and solid and sporty. He's a brilliant and creative guitarist. He's at ease with himself and everyone he meets – always relaxed, always smiling. And he's big enough, on a dark night, in the wrong part of town, to scare most of your average vermin away. If your daughter was off travelling with anyone, you would want it to be with Josh.

"It's freezing out there," Josh says.

"Sarah's been trying to convince me that I'm a soft southerner," I say.

"Yeah!" Sarah protests. "It was way colder than this in Edinburgh."

Josh shrugs. "Just differing degrees of freezing if you ask me," he says.

"Wimp," Sarah tells him.

He grins at me and shrugs.

I hang my coat over the back of the chair and sit. "So where are the others?" I ask.

Sarah nods behind me so I turn and see Ricardo and Jenny bustling through the door.

"Shit, are we late?" Jenny asks looking around for a clock. "Parking was a nightmare."

"Not at all," I say. "We just arrived."

"Just you then?" she asks.

"Just us," I say. "Sorry."

I look at Ricardo and he almost invisibly raises an eyebrow. He's telling me something about having had to manage Jenny's flustered mood all morning. I blink slowly back at him to say, *"Message received. Well done."*

"So how are we sitting? Boy-girl or..." Jenny asks.

"Absolutely not," I say. "I want this one next to me. I've hardly seen you this week, have I?"

Ricardo pulls a face. "Latin-flu jabs all week," he says.

"There's a new one every year," I comment. "And it's always going to kill us all. And it never does."

Ricardo pushes behind Sarah and kisses her on the head as he passes, then sits between us and squeezes my leg beneath the table. The squeeze tells me to shut up. Ricardo thinks that Latin-flu is a big deal and he doesn't like anyone undermining the vaccination program.

He catches my eye and looks down at his pocket where I see a glimpse of wrapping paper protruding, the real reason he and Jenny are late.

Jenny pulls off her coat and then looks around the table taking us in one by one. And then she claps her hands and she, Josh and Sarah all start to talk at once.

I sit and watch them chattering.

Jenny says, "Did you know, we actually forgot your birthday one year?"

"*Yes,*" Sarah says with a sigh. "It was when I was five. You tell me every year."

And then Jenny starts talking about the jewellery class she's been taking, and then Josh and Sarah about an upcoming trip to Paris, a town about which Jenny has many and varied strongly-held views it would seem.

Ricardo and I sit and listen and soak up our extended family like the elixir it is.

I watch Ricardo grinning as he turns to listen to one person and then another and a little wave of love rises in me. He has gone completely grey now but I think he looks even better for it.

I look at Sarah catching hunky Josh's eye at every available opportunity, and at Jenny glowing with her own brand of tough, unexpected resilience.

And my vision clouds over with tears because, though this is Sarah's birthday meal, it feels like my own because I honestly never expected this much joy to be mine. I think about Sarah surviving the punches of an alcoholic father, falling in the sea, her mother's illness... and there she is, glowing like a jewel. I never believed that such good outcomes could come from such mediocre beginnings.

"So is he coming or not Mum?" Sarah is asking as I tune back into the conversation.

"No I told you darling. Twice. They're in Gran Canaria."

"Not Tom. Flo."

"Well of *course* he is," Jenny says.

"Then he's late," Sarah says.

"Florent is *always* late darling. And he always arrives in the end. He'll be here."

"God, he *is* always late," Sarah says. "He was even late when Mum organised..."

In the midst of the hubbub Jenny looks at me across the table. She stares right into my eyes and I see that they are watering like my own.

"You OK?" she mouths silently.

And I blink slowly to say 'yes' and a tear trickles down my cheek.

Jenny winks and says, very quietly, "Difficulty at the beginning?"

I frown, struggling to remember. "Leads to *success?*" I croak.

"Supreme success," Jenny says. "Difficulty at the beginning leads to *supreme* success."

At that moment, Ricardo slides his arm around my waist. And in that instant, around this table, there's more joy and more love, and more unexpected happiness than I think I can bear.

It feels so good it hurts.

The Case Of The Missing Boyfriend

A Novel
by Nick Alexander

C.C. is nearly forty and other than her name (which she hates so much she can't bring herself to use it) everything about her life appears to be wonderful: she has a high powered job in advertising, a great flat in Primrose Hill, and a wild bunch of friends to spend her weekends with. A n d yet she feels like the Titanic – slowly, inexorably, and against all expectation, sinking.

For despite her indisputable success, C.C. would rather be shovelling shit on a farm than selling it to the masses – would rather be snuggling on the sofa with The Missing Boyfriend than playing star fag-hag in London's latest coke-spots.

But opportunities to find The Missing Boyfriend are rarer than an original metaphor, and CC's body-clock is ticking so loudly that at times she can barely hear her mother wittering on about her own Moroccan boyfriend.

Could her best friend be right? Could her past really be preventing her from moving on? And if she unlocks that particular box, will the horrors within simply drift away and leave her free? Or will they sink her?

If she can shake off the past and learn to trust again, will she stop attracting freaks and find The Missing Boyfriend? Or will she just end up tethered and gagged at the bottom of the stairs?

Also Available From BIGfib Books

50 Reasons to Say "Goodbye"

A Novel
By Nick Alexander

Mark is looking for love in all the wrong places.
He always ignores the warning signs, preferring to dream, time and again, that he has finally met the perfect lover until, one day...

Through fifty different adventures, Nick Alexander takes us on a tour of modern gay society: bars, night-clubs, blind dates, Internet dating... It's all here.
Funny and moving by turn, *50 Reasons to Say "Goodbye"*, is ultimately a series of candidly vivid snapshots and a poignant exploration of that long winding road; the universal search for love.

"Modern gay literature at its finest and most original."
– Axm Magazine, December 2004

"A witty, polished collection of vignettes... Get this snappy little number."
– Tim Teeman, The Times

"Nick Alexander invests Mark's story with such warmth... A wonderful read – honest, moving, witty and really rather wise." – Paul Burston, Time Out

ISBN: 2-9524-8990-4

BIGfib Books.

www.BIGfib.com

Sottopassaggio

A Novel
By Nick Alexander

I don't know how I ended up in Brighton. I'm in a permanent state of surprise about it. Of course I know the events that took place, I remember the accident or rather I remember the last time Steve ever looked into my eyes before the grinding screeching wiped it all out. It all seems so unexpected, so far from how things were supposed to be...

Following the loss of his partner, Mark, the hero from the bestselling *50 Reasons to Say "Goodbye"*, tries to pick up the pieces and build a new life for himself in gay friendly Brighton.

Haunted by the death of his lover and a fading sense of self, Mark struggles to put the past behind him, exploring Brighton's high and low-life, falling in love with charming, but unavailable Tom, and hooking up with Jenny, a long lost girlfriend from a time when such a thing seemed possible. But Jenny has her own problems, and as all around are inexorably sucked into the violence of her life, destiny intervenes, weaving the past to the present, and the present to the future in ways no one could have imagined.

"Alexander has a beautifully turned ear for a witty phrase... I think we can all recognise the lives that live within these pages, and we share their triumphs and tragedies, hopes and lost dreams." - Joe Galliano, Gay Times

ISBN: 2-9524-8991-2

BIGfib Books.

www.BIGfib.com

Good Thing Bad Thing

A Novel
By Nick Alexander

On holiday with new boyfriend Tom, Mark - the hero from the best-selling novels, 50 Reasons to Say Goodbye and Sottopassaggio - heads off to rural Italy for a spot of camping.

When the ruggedly seductive Dante invites them onto his farmland the lovers think they have struck lucky, but there is more to Dante than meets the eye - much more.

Thoroughly bewitched, Tom, all innocence, appears blind to Dante's dark side... Racked with suspicion, it is Mark who notices as their holiday starts to spin slowly but very surely out of control - and it is Mark, alone, who can maybe save the day...

Good Thing, Bad Thing is a story of choices; an exploration of the relationship between understanding and forgiveness, and an investigation of the fact that life is rarely quite as bad - or as good - as it seems. Above all *Good Thing, Bad Thing* is another cracking adventure for gay everyman Mark.

"Spooky, and emotionally turbulent - yet profoundly comedic, this third novel in a captivating trilogy is a roller-coaster literary treasure all on its own. But do yourself a favour, and treat yourself to its two prequels as soon as you can..." - Richard Labonte, Book Marks

ISBN: 2-9524-8992-0

BIGfib Books

www.BIGfib.com

Also Available From BIGfib Books

Better Than Easy

A Novel
By Nick Alexander

Better Than Easy - the fourth volume in the bestselling 50 Reasons series - finds Mark about to embark on the project of a lifetime, the purchase of a hilltop gite in a remote French village with partner Tom.

But with shady dealings making the purchase unexpectedly complex, Mark finds himself with time on his hands - time to consider not only if this is the right project but whether Tom is the right man.

A chance meeting with a seductive Latino promises nirvana yet threatens to destroy every other relationship Mark holds dear, and as he navigates a seemingly endless ocean of untruths, Mark is forced to question whether any worthwhile destination remains.

Better Than Easy combines a tense tale of betrayal and a warming exploration of the mix of courage and naivety required if we are to choose love and happiness - if we are to continue to believe against seemingly impossible odds.

"Better Than Easy is my favourite of Alexander's novels so far. It's sweet, sexy, funny and tender... I'm not ashamed to say that I laughed and cried." – Paul Burston, Time Out London.

ISBN: 2-9524-8997-1

BIGfib Books

www.BIGfib.com

Also Available From BIGfib Books

13:55 Eastern Standard Time

A Novel
By Nick Alexander

Alice looks at the phone and then glances at the alarm clock. 13:55 pm EST makes - she counts on her fingers - about 6pm in Berlin. He'll be on his way home. Alice settles into the armchair and dials the number...

If Alice hadn't bumped into Will then she would probably never have phoned that afternoon. And if Alice hadn't called then Michael, poor Michael, might still be alive today...

"Both short story collection and novel, 13:55 Eastern Standard Time finds Nick Alexander at his best. Sometimes disturbing, sometimes funny, these are stories of lives that cross and collide in life-ending drama, or simply run peacefully alongside for a few hours - lives filled with characters who are attracted and repelled, hopeless and yet inspired.
Narrated in Alexander's trademark tense prose, these interwoven stories explore the ripples emanating from our every act, ripples that alter distant destinies, and occasionally bounce back, catching us from behind to haunt or inspire.
13:55 Eastern Standard Time repeats the success of Alexander's first novel, 50 Reasons to Say Goodbye because again, as with life itself, the whole is mysteriously greater than the sum of the parts."

"...the overall effect is dazzling. Nick Alexander has reinvented Gay fiction... '13:55 Eastern Standard Time' is a novel, a collection of short stories, and a whole lot more besides." – David Llewellyn, Time Out, June '07

ISBN: 2-9524899-6-3

BIGfib Books

www.BIGfib.com

Lightning Source UK Ltd.
Milton Keynes UK
UKOW051150241011

180844UK00001B/147/P